Brushfire Plague: Retribution

by

R.P. Ruggiero

Post-apocalyptic Fiction & Survival Nonfiction

www.PrepperPress.com

Brushfire Plague: Retribution

ISBN 978-1-939473-43-1

Printed in the United States of America.

Prepper Press Trade Paperback Edition: August 2016

Prepper Press is a division of Kennebec Publishing, LLC

I dedicate this book to my two sons, Justus and Zaden. As you become young men who I am very proud of, I hope you never have to face a world as horrific as the one depicted in Brushfire Plague.

Acknowledgements:

Writing the *Brushfire Plague* trilogy has been an astounding adventure. I've grown as a person, learned valuable new information and insights, and met some incredible people along the way. I want to thank each and every reader for your support, your comments, and—yes, your gentle nudges—as it took much longer than expected to complete the book you now hold in your hands! I appreciate your patience.

The image of the "self-made man" is a false one. No significant piece of work is produced without many contributors along the way. I wish to thank all those writers of apocalyptic fiction who came before me as you spurred me from a young age to think about what might come next in the event of The End of The World As We Know It! Especially, I want to lift up the works of Octavia Butler, Pat Frank and Larry Niven and Jerry Pournelle—who crafted the stories that had the deepest impact.

Dear readers, if you are not familiar with these gifted novelists, please remedy that soon. Once again, I want to thank the staff at Prepper Press for their continued professional support and guidance from when we started four years ago as the trilogy unfolded.

Finally, I thank my dear wife of twenty-three years. Honey, you were with me from the days of being a nervous teenager on our first date to your years of encouragement to write, and then helping build my confidence to finally put words on paper for the world to read. Truly, *Brushfire Plague* would not exist without you and my only hope is that I did you proud.

About the Author:

R.P. Ruggiero lives in Colorado with his wife and two sons. He spends as much time as he can in the outdoors and strives to live by Robert Heinlein's credo that, "Specialization is for insects." When he is not outdoors, writing, or learning a new skill, he works coordinating people to achieve their common goals. He brings his two decades of experience in group dynamics--particularly when people are under stress--to good use in writing *The Brushfire Plague* series.

Contact the author at rpruggiero@gmail.com with your comments about the novels, visit **www.brushfireplague.com**, "like" the Brushfire Plague Facebook page, or follow him on Twitter @rpruggiero.

CHAPTER ONE

Dranko lay before Cooper prostrate. His breath was raspy, labored. Each breath he took made Cooper wince. The last time he had sat with someone who was in unconscious agony was with his wife, Elena. Her torment finally ended when she succumbed to the ravages of the Brushfire Plague.

This time, multiple bullet wounds threatened his dear friend. Cooper knew that internal bleeding was the likely cause of Dranko's desperate breathing. As before, he was overcome by the fury at his impotence to aid another. His mind drifted to the horrid scene when the machinegun zeroed in on Dranko. He'd watched in shock as multiple rounds from the heavy caliber weapon shredded his friend.

Cooper shifted his position in the wooden chair where he'd been sitting for hours. The chair creaked, as if flexing its own sore muscles, too. His gaze fell upon Dranko's pallid face, shiny from sweat. He was running a low-grade fever. If it spiked to signal rampant infection, Cooper knew that would spell the end for Dranko. His fists tightened involuntarily and his jaw clenched so hard that his teeth ground against one another.

What will I do if I lose him? The thought made his eyes mist over. He was acutely aware that if it weren't for Dranko, he and Jake would most likely be dead. That had been proven to him many times over. Dranko had been much more than a good friend during the havoc wrought by the Brushfire Plague. He had been a protector and Cooper's rock. Cooper knew just how valuable his survivalist-minded friend was—for equipment *and* knowledge.

While part of him fought the notion, he had to contemplate what they would do if Dranko didn't make it. He started with no good ideas and the more he thought about it, the bigger the gaps loomed in just what they'd lose. The best he could manage was knowing that they would continue on as best they could without him. But, he knew their odds of survival would go down considerably. Exhaling in frustration, he rose to leave the room. He took a step toward the door when a dry croak stopped him dead in his tracks. He spun around and vaulted back to Dranko's side.

"What'd you say?" he asked frantically, clasping his friend's clammy hand in his own.

Dranko's eyes fluttered, but did not open. "Stop."

His heart leapt at hearing him speak. "Stop what?"

He coughed, and then caught his breath. "Fretting."

Hard laughter brought tears of joy. "Hell, Dranko, you look even uglier than normal. How can I not worry?"

The left corner of his mouth upturned at an attempted smile before coughing replaced it with a painful grimace. "Don't... make... me...

1

laugh."

Cooper turned serious. "Alright. You are one tough SOB, brother."

He nodded faintly. "Damn. Straight. Jake?"

Cooper grasped Dranko's hand firmly at the mention of his son's name. "He's fine. You made it possible. You saved him."

This time, a half-smile stayed put. "Good." Dranko fell silent as his body shuddered under erratic breathing.

"How do you feel?" Cooper asked.

"Bad... as... your... jokes sound," he returned.

Cooper fought the urge to respond and let it lie instead. A few moments of silence passed between them. Dranko's eyes had never opened, but Cooper felt elated that his friend had regained consciousness.

"You need anything?"

At that, his eyes fluttered open. "Need... drugs... fever... gonna... get... me." Dranko's eyes filled with desperate truth and his words were laced with finality. His arm fell limp to the side of the bed. His eyes drifted slowly shut.

Cooper rocked back and collapsed into his chair. "I'm on it," he whispered

Dranko did not respond. His breath had settled into an uneasy rhythm and Cooper guessed he'd fallen asleep. He hoped that it was no worse. His hand went to Dranko's forehead. *Does it feel warmer than it did an hour ago?* Cooper couldn't know for sure. His friend's words haunted him. While Dranko was the world's worst cynic, he was not prone to exaggerate when it came to something like this. His uncanny words struck Cooper as being true. He shuddered to think, *deadly accurate.*

*
*   *

Cooper deposited himself in the kitchen. Weak, lukewarm tea fashioned from stale leaves and odd weeds Dranko had foraged upon their arrival in Estacada, passed his lips as he sipped. He was lost in thought, mapping out a plan to get the antibiotics that Dranko needed.

A loud yawn broke his concentration. Turning, he saw Calvin's gaping maw as he opened his arms wide and stretched fully into the yawn. He wore red-checkered pajama bottoms and a Portland Trailblazers t-shirt.

"Morning," Cooper said.

"Good morning," Calvin said sleepily. "Any more of that?" he asked, pointing at Cooper's cup.

"Definitely. I made a full pot, but I won't vouch for its worth," Cooper said pointing to the teapot on the counter, which he had swaddled in a blanket to keep it warm for the others. As he did so, he marveled at the ease in which he was learning new habits in the post-Brushfire Plague world: this was to conserve energy.

"Funny, is it not?"

"What?"

"Remember how we would fire up the stove to heat enough water for just one cup or those one-cup coffeemakers?" Calvin's teeth gleamed in a grin.

"And?"

"The collapse of civilization has ended selfish individualism," he said with a coy smile.

"How so?"

"Simple. We can no longer afford to burn propane or wood so frivolously!" Calvin chuckled at his comment.

Cooper smiled in return. "I hadn't thought of that. But, it makes sense. Hell, we did a lot of stupid, wasteful, things, didn't we?"

"You mean like how little most of us knew each other? How we took too much for granted? How we wasted our time and money? Shall I go on?"

"Nah, I think I get the point," Cooper said, shaking his head. Calvin, having poured himself a cup of the hybrid tea, sat down across from him. He rubbed hard across his eyebrows, still waking up.

He scowled as he took a sip, and through wrinkled lips he muttered, "I cannot lie, I miss Stumptown. Best coffee in Portland."

"I need your help." Cooper's serious tone made Calvin sit up a little straighter.

"Of course."

"Dranko roused himself for a moment earlier."

Calvin beamed. "That is great!"

Cooper nodded. "It is. But, he told me that he needs antibiotics. Said the fever is going to get him if he doesn't."

Calvin's eyebrows furrowed. "How does he know that? He is not a doctor."

"I know. But, if you'd been there, you'd believe it. He just *knows*." He let Calvin sit with it for a moment and took another drink of the tea.

"Alright. No use in taking a chance on it."

"That's what I figure, too."

"Have you looked through all his supplies? I am sure he had some on hand."

Cooper shook his head. "'Fraid not. I've looked through *everything* and I can't find any."

Calvin frowned in disbelief. "Really?"

"Really. I found an ammo box marked 'Anti-Bs' but it was empty. I don't know what happened to them. Bottom line, we gotta get some more."

"What about the doctor?"

"He gave him what he could right after the surgery."

Calvin shook his head, and frustration crept into his voice. "So, what's the plan?"

"I figure we need to ask the Doc where we might find some. We could also check the logical places in town. They might not have been looted because Hodges seized control so fast."

"Where do you want to start?"

"The local Walgreens. With Hodges gone, I expect the local control could evaporate very quickly."

Calvin nodded gravely. "Suit up?"

"Yes," Cooper said with resignation. He had no desire to wade back into the potential of violence and bloodshed.

*

* *

Cooper knocked lightly on the Airstream's door, where Angela and Julianne were sleeping. He turned the doorknob slowly and cracked the door open.

"You guys up?" he asked softly.

Julianne's dark mane shifted as she turned to face him. She rubbed her eyes. "I am now."

Angela's eyes flickered open and they immediately locked onto his. "Yup."

"You need us?" Julianne asked.

Cooper nodded his head toward Angela. "Just her. Calvin and I are going into town to find some antibiotics for Dranko."

Disappointment clouded Julianne's face. "Okay. I guess I'll sleep a bit more." She rolled back over and pulled the pillow up to cover her head. *She's been wounded, but not enough to cloud her sleep,* he mused.

Angela sat up halfway in bed. "Alright, just give me five minutes and I'll be ready." She sounded cheery through the tiredness.

"Great, thanks," Cooper said, as he pulled his head out of the room and closed the door behind him.

He went back to his room so that he could gather his weapons and other gear. He tried to be as quiet as possible, but Jake awoke nonetheless.

"Arrr...," he muttered as he stretched himself awake. "Where are you going?"

"Into town. We need to find some antibiotics for Dranko."

"You want me to come?"

Uncertainty tore at Cooper. He didn't want to put his son in harm's way, but he also never wanted to leave him out of his sight again. He quickly

4

found a balancing point. "Yes, I do. I'll need someone to watch the car as we scout out the Walgreens."

Jake nodded and yawned again. "Sure thing." He rose out of bed, and began dressing.

Cooper finished before he did and left the room, rifle in hand and pistol on his hip. "See you in a few."

As always, the weight of the pistol on his hip and the heaviness of the rifle in his hand comforted him, especially at a moment like this. He found Calvin waiting in the living room, ready to go. He checked on Dranko once more, but saw that he was still sleeping. When Angela and Jake filed into the room, he turned to Angela. "Can you tell Julianne to get up and keep an eye on Dranko? I forgot."

"Sure thing," she said before retreating back the way she had come.

They waited a few minutes for her return. "Princess will be out in a few. What's our game plan?"

"It's simple, really. We will need to get into town and assess the situation. Let's hope we can barter for the antibiotics, but we need to be ready for action. I have no idea what's happened since word got out that Hodges is down. We could be walking into descending chaos or it might still be relatively well ordered. Any questions?"

*
* *

The group of four rolled along the country road toward town in Dranko's Jeep. Cooper felt odd behind the wheel, missing his friend Dranko by his side. Angela and Jake kept up a soft banter in the backseat as they drove, talking about their favorite foods that they missed. Cooper opted for silence as he gripped the steering wheel. He could smell fires burning and was surprised that he still noticed them, given the constant backdrop they had become. His mind was playing with different scenarios.

"When we get into town, if I say 'heavy,' it means bring your rifle with you. If I say 'light,' it means pistols only."

"Why would we *not* bring our rifles?" Calvin asked.

"It depends on the profile we want. If Hodges' men are still keeping order, getting out with rifles might draw too much attention than they are worth."

"What's the signal if a situation turns bad and we are about to start shooting?" Angela asked.

The question gave Cooper a moment's pause. "If you hear me say the word 'badly.' Or, if you all see something and say 'badly,' it means we are going to go hot."

"And, what if we should just draw weapons, but not open fire?"

Cooper turned to look at Calvin, who had asked the question. "Just say 'poorly.' Like, we can say our friend needs the antibiotics 'badly' or that our friend is doing 'poorly.'"

Angela and Jake both laughed.

"What?"

"We ain't from West Virginia," Angela began.

"Or, the 1800s!" Jake added.

"...So saying 'poorly' will seem odd," Angela finished.

Cooper smiled. "Okay, good point. Let's go with 'afraid,' like 'I'm afraid for him.'"

"So, it is 'badly' to start shooting and 'afraid' for draw weapons?" Calvin clarified.

"Yes—make sense?"

Everyone nodded at Cooper.

"I hope we can remember this under stress," Angela remarked skeptically.

The squeal of tires taking a turn too quickly caught Cooper's ear. *Good thing I drive with the window half down.*

"Afraid we have heavy company," he shouted out, louder than he'd wanted to. The others grabbed their rifles. Through his rearview mirror, Cooper spotted a pick-up truck with armed men in the back. He rounded another turn and they dropped from view. "Pick-up, full." Instead of trying to handle his rifle while driving, he drew his pistol and laid it in his lap for easy access and then put both hands back on the steering wheel. He felt the familiar rush of adrenaline as it poured into his bloodstream. His vision grew sharper and his hearing more acute. Bile crept into his throat as his body readied itself for action.

"Everyone, take three deep breaths. It will help calm you down," he ordered. Then he followed his own dictates. He welcomed how it made everything appear calmer. "If they try to pull alongside or pass us, I'm going to slam on the brakes to throw off their aim if they plan on firing on us. If they open fire from distance, I will be doing zig and zag," he alerted the others.

The road opened up onto a straight path and he saw the pick-up gaining on them quickly. In his rearview mirror, he saw Angela and Jake turn around and face their weapons rearward. As they turned, the strain on their faces was revealed in deep lines and furrowed brows.

Tense seconds passed as the pick-up closed the gap. Cooper kept expecting to hear the "pop-pop" of rifle fire at any second. The pick-up moved into a passing position, drifting to his left. When they were about ten yards off his bumper, he jammed his brakes down, tires squealed, and they shot past them. In a blur, he saw four men in the bed brandishing their weapons and yelling and laughing as they passed.

6

"Estacada is ours!" a weathered, gray-haired man shouted at them.

Cooper sighed with relief when no shots were fired. They rounded the next bend in the road and watched the pick-up truck disappear up ahead. That corner also revealed several columns of black smoke racing skyward. Estacada was burning. *I guess that burning smell wasn't just the normal cooking or heating fire*, Cooper thought. Inwardly, he chastised himself for *not* noticing the distinctive smell of burning buildings. He resolved to raise his situational awareness. He knew that failing to be alert and noticing the small things could get him—and others—killed.

*
*　　*

"What do you think we will find?" Calvin asked him.

"We have to hope it's just a few scattered buildings throwing up all that smoke," Cooper answered with a frown.

"Then we have to hope that the drugstore is alright, too," Calvin continued.

Cooper nodded and stroked his chin in response. Like he always did, he fiddled with his firearms to burn the stress. He only had one hand free, so he was limited to moving it from his hand to the seat and back again. Calvin watched in silence.

A corner of Cooper's mouth downturned. "Humph."

"What?"

"I couldn't get through my ritual of messing around with my guns before Dranko would fire some witty remark at me." Cooper felt Calvin studying him, understanding his pensiveness. Cooper continued, "It's a funny way to miss someone, isn't it?"

No one answered the rhetorical question.

"You know what's funny that I miss about mom?" Jake piped up from the backseat. He rarely spoke about Elena, so his comment took Cooper off guard and demanded his full attention.

"I dunno."

"The way she would *always* lose her cell phone. At the *worst* possible times!" Cooper chuckled at the memory. It was one of his own pet peeves with his late wife. Invariably, this would happen just as they were leaving for something that they were already running late for. Though frustrating at the time, Cooper would do anything now for the opportunity to see her scramble in a mad flurry searching everywhere for her phone.

"Yeah, she did do that," he said, his smile already starting to fade as he thought about his dead wife.

"What I wouldn't give to watch her running around the house, looking for it, right now," Jake said. His words raced toward melancholy.

7

Cooper reached back and squeezed his son's knee. "I know, son."

Angela beamed a smile and tried to change the subject. "You know what I *don't* miss about cell phones?"

"What?" Calvin asked.

"How you'd be on a date with a guy and he'd do nothing but keep looking at it throughout!"

Grinning, the three males looked at each other awkwardly for a moment, but Calvin spoke first. "I think I can honestly say that not one of us knows what you are talking about!" That brought laughter into the Jeep.

"You know what I mean!" Angela exclaimed.

"Wait, I'm still trying to figure this out. A guy. Out on a date. With you. Looking at his phone and not you?" Cooper delivered the words in perfect deadpan.

"Are you trying to make fun of me or is that compliment?" Angela looked at him with a furrowed brow.

Cooper smiled back. "Whichever you prefer."

She thumped his shoulder playfully and then sat back into her seat and returned the smile.

Cooper had to stifle a laugh when she winked at him playfully. Jake folded his arms and sat back as well. He squinted intently at his father through the mirror.

Damn, I shouldn't have said that with him around. He's too sensitive. So much for harmless flirting!

"You know what *I* don't miss about cell phones?" Calvin intoned. "We actually pay attention to each other now. Before, people were forgetting *how* to talk to one another!"

"Amen, brother," Angela remarked. "It *was* more than just the dates! My niece, who was like fifteen, *broke up* with a boyfriend over text!"

"Really?" Calvin asked in disbelief.

"Oh yeah," she nodded emphatically. "Now that I think about it, I think they got *together* over text."

Calvin shook his head. "Well, I welcome the fact that we now *have* to talk to one another."

"Alright, let's get ready," Cooper said, ending the chitchat as he pointed into the distance with his free hand.

They were approaching the outskirts of town. The others directed their view forward and what they saw caused a collective inhale and gasps. At some point, someone in town thought it was a good idea to form a roadblock and signage with dead bodies. It looked like a family—an adult man, woman, and two young girls. The bodies were spread across the road leading into town in zigzag pattern, forcing any decent person to slow down and maneuver around the bodies. However, the smallest girl had tire marks crossing over her body.

"That was either done on purpose or the driver was blind," Cooper commented at the macabre scene.

Two wooden-staked signs rose from the dead adults' abdomens. Cooper scowled and his stomach tightened further.

Angela's hand flew to her mouth and she pulled Jake's face to her chest to shield his view. "I think I'm going to be sick," she lamented.

The signs were handwritten in blood, presumably from the dead. Cooper read them in sequence. The first gave an explanation for the grisly scene:

Cross Bobby Red
You end up dead!

The second sign proclaimed Bobby's ascendance to power:

I'm in charge now!
See my men at the Flea Market. NOW!

"Looks like Mr. Red might be the new Hodges," Calvin remarked.

"I'm not so sure about that," Cooper replied. "If it was true, he'd have armed men out here wouldn't he?"

Calvin nodded, but then Angela spoke up. "Or, it could be true and he just doesn't have the manpower yet to staff up roadblocks."

"That could be," Cooper said.

"In any event, we will know in a few minutes. Everyone needs to stay sharp," Calvin said, ending the conversation.

As Cooper carefully steered the Jeep between the bodies, he could not keep his eyes off of the children. They looked to be about eight and ten years old. Both girls were in pajamas, which meant they must have been rounded up while sleeping and then executed. Neat entry holes in the middle of each forehead at least told him it had been a fast and painless execution. The dirty cheeks, riven with tearstains, told him that they had been terrified. He shook his head slowly as they passed. He gritted his teeth when it struck him. *Two weeks ago, I would have tried shielding Jake from seeing this carnage. Now, the thought never crossed my mind.* Like a tongue searching constantly for a recently lost tooth, his mind played with the notion of how this new post-Brushfire Plague world was changing him… and his son.

He focused his thoughts on the task in front of them to distract himself away from the worrying that he could do nothing about right now.

"Alright, everyone remember the drill? Let's do this right!"

CHAPTER TWO

As the Jeep rounded the last corner, they were given a wide-open view of Estacada, and the chaos became immediately apparent. Two hundred yards ahead, a pick-up truck was burning ferociously. Heavy black smoke failed to conceal the dark outline of a body's charred remains slumped over the steering wheel. Beyond that, another vehicle—a four-door sedan—lay smoldering with wisps of gray smoke drifting skyward. Shielded by the buildings in Estacada's small downtown, other columns of smoke rose up from at least three locations. Cooper could not tell if they were coming from vehicles or buildings. Based on the size, he guessed cars or extinguishing building fires.

As they approached the clutch of buildings that made up Estacada's downtown, they could see the few people on the street running in between buildings in furious sprints. Each carried a pistol or a rifle, out and at the ready.

"Are we going to the flea market to check in with Bobby Red?" Angela asked.

"I would not advise it. No one is in control here," Calvin answered.

Cooper nodded and steered the Jeep toward the local drugstore. "We are going in hot and heavy," he informed them, his face grim and tight.

"I guess we didn't need those code words after all," Angela remarked.

The others responded by raising their weapons to ready status. Cooper drove cautiously, deliberately rounding each corner—listening intently. The tires crunched glass in several places. He started when he heard a woman's shrill scream—or perhaps a child's—from far away and to his left. Not for the first time since the beginning of this deadly outbreak, the stench of burned flesh hit his nose. *Welcome back, old friend,* he thought dourly. He jumped when a quick staccato of three rounds being fired from the next block over went off, *pop-pop-pop.* Then, silence. He could hear Calvin's accelerated breathing next to him.

"Breathe deep, everyone," he reminded.

As he rounded the next corner, he drew a deep inhale in shock.

"Stop!" a man closest to the Jeep shouted. Four men barred the road. Cooper's mind spun, cataloguing the threat. *Two AR-15s. A shotgun. One AK. All pointed directly at us. Point blank range.* Cooper stopped the Jeep with a quick jam of his foot onto the brakes.

"Hands up, you sonofabitch!" the lead man screamed. He looked to be in his early thirties, with a black knit cap covering his head, and his face alight in the redness that only stress or anger can bring. Cooper knew that at this range, there was no way to get out of the situation without one or more of them being killed. He knew they had to comply.

10

He raised his hands slowly from the steering wheel. From the corner of his eye, he saw Calvin put the rifle on his lap and raise his hands up. He assumed Angela was doing the same.

The man took a step closer, the barrel of his rifle not more than two feet from Cooper's head.

"You with Red?" The man artfully asked the question so that Cooper could not guess the correct—and safest—answer. Of course, in his case, with his inability to lie, he had no choice.

"No, we are not," he replied. The almost imperceptible dip of the barrel told him it was the right answer.

"That means you get to live another few minutes at least, friend!" The man's expanding smile also told Cooper that he shared the relief.

The man holding the shotgun, who was standing just behind the lead man, cocked his head and stared intently at Cooper for a few seconds. Then, his eyes flashed.

"Oh, damn! You are that guy, right?"

Confused, Cooper squinted his eyes to narrow slits in return.

The other man bobbed his head up and down quickly. "Yeah, the plague guy! What's your name? I can't remember it for the life of me!"

"Cooper," he replied flatly.

Now, both men were smiling widely at him. They fully lowered their long guns and the man closest to him extended his hand. "Yeah, we've heard of you. Pleased to meet you, Cooper. I'm Jared." Cooper took his hand in a firm grip and shook it. He did the same with the man with the shotgun.

"The name's Jimmy. You're like a hero," he said while pumping Cooper's hand.

Cooper tipped his head down. "No, I'm not. I just did what anyone man would do."

Jimmy shook his head. "Yeah, if they were Superman!" He laughed at his own joke, but the others only smiled.

Jared broke the awkward moment. "What are you doing here? You know you just stepped into the middle of World War Three, right?"

Cooper shook his head and noticed the other two men had taken up defensive positions around the Jeep and were facing out from it. "No, I didn't." His words trailed off as he became distracted by what he was seeing.

Calvin leaned across him. "Can you tell us what is going on?"

"Since the word got out that Hodges was dead, everyone and their brother is declaring themselves Estacada's new leader," Jared filled them in.

"So, who are you with?" Cooper asked.

"We're with the Giles Miller crew. We want to establish a city council and a real mayor. Y'know, with elections. Democracy," Jared answered.

11

"Yeah, America," Jimmy finished.

Cooper nodded. "That sounds good to me."

Jimmy beamed again. "You should join us! Your name carries weight in this town. And, hell, we all know you can carry yourself in a fight. Everyone 'round here has heard about what you did to Hodges and his crew."

Cooper was about to tell him that wasn't going to happen, but then his father's voice was in his ear once more. *When you are going to tell someone 'no,' timing is everything.*

"That's an interesting idea. I'd like to find out more, but right now we need some antibiotics for our friend. He's gonna die without them and he saved my son's life. So, I've got to find them first. You guys have any?"

"You might find some in the drugstore, but it was pretty tore through," Jared offered.

Jimmy nudged him in the back with the butt of the shotgun. "Or, you could join with us and get some! I know we have a good stash on hand. The vet joined us straight off."

Cooper pretended to consider the offer. "I think we'll try the drugstore first. We'd all need to talk it over before deciding to join up. How can I find you to get word to you all?"

Jimmy's face fell. "Well, don't wait to too long. We might have this thing won pretty damn soon. We already control the eastern side of town. Just approach slowly." Jimmy paused in thought. "It's better to declare for the winning side sooner rather than later, you know!" Jimmy's enthusiasm was contagious and he winked at Cooper as he finished talking.

Jared took his hand again. "Good luck, Cooper. We gotta move out, anyway. Keep your head up—there's a sniper from Red's group that we're after. He shoots damn near anyone he can get a bead on."

Reflexively, Cooper scanned the windows and building tops above him. "Alright. Good luck to you, too."

Jared leaned in and whispered, "I hope you'll join us. Despite what Jimmy says, we need every gun we can get. Red is bad, bad news for this town."

The men's eyes met. Jared's were burning with intensity. Cooper was solemn while he nodded. "Gotcha."

With that, the men continued moving past the Jeep while Cooper slowly drove away.

"Sounds like a good old civil war going on," Angela intoned from the backseat.

"Sure does," Calvin agreed. "I wonder in how many thousands of other towns and hamlets this very situation is playing itself out right now, not to mention the cities."

"Yeah, we'll talk about it later. Let's focus on finding us the drugs we need for Dranko," Cooper replied. He wanted everyone to remain clear on the task at hand.

One more rounded corner brought them to the drugstore, or what was left of it. Cooper's heart fell and he stopped the Jeep a dozen yards from the entrance.

Glass littered the street in front of the store, twinkling in the morning sun. What had been large plate glass windows were now gaping holes in the store's façade. No longer did the windows display their latest sales and enticing products. Those days were long gone. A variety of ripped or broken items were strewn about the sidewalk and onto the street. *Things discarded in a hurry.* Cooper surveyed the mishmash of society's fall. Clothes. Broken bottles. Smashed bits of plastic. Wrappers from candy greedily consumed on site. His feet crunching down on all of it. *Civilizations sure are messy when they are falling apart at the seams,* Cooper pondered.

"You ready?" Calvin's strong voice shook him out of his reverie. Calvin ducked his head into the window's opening, scanning the inside of the drugstore. He motioned Cooper forward with a swing of his rifle barrel.

Cooper darted past the Jeep toward the entryway. One side of the double doors remained in place, while the other had been torn off its hinges. Cooper knelt behind the intact door panel, taking what cover was available. *This thin wood might stop a pistol round if I'm lucky, but a rifle would tear right through it.* He looked inside carefully, taking time for his eyes to adjust to the darkness. He did not see anyone else inside, but took another minute to look into the most likely places someone might hide. Satisfied, he waved Calvin in. He wasted no time in stepping through the window opening and moving among the aisles. Cooper then moved in as well.

"You know what we're looking for... anything that's a possible antibiotic," Cooper called to Calvin.

The store had been trashed. The floor only revealed itself in scattered patches, most of it being covered by other debris. Most pronounced was the disturbing smell of decaying flesh; *a dead body.* Cooper smelled it before he could find it. He wrinkled his nose.

"There's a body somewhere in here," he called out.

"Yes, tell me something I do not know," Calvin replied, a macabre chuckle underscoring his words.

After a few minutes of making their way through the store, Cooper reached the body first. It was a woman slumped over the pharmacy counter. A blue flannel shirt and green jeans covered her, which almost caused Cooper to walk right past the body. Then he saw the blood stains on the jeans in between her legs and covering the left leg down to the knee.

"You see this?" Cooper indicated the area to Calvin as he reached him.

Calvin twisted his face into a grimace. "Damn."

"Hard to tell if she was raped and came here for help and bled out. Or, if she was attacked here and the scumbag pulled her pants back up to try and hide the crime," Cooper ruminated.

Calvin stepped up to the woman and tried pulling back her hair to get a look at her face. Most of the hair stuck in the dried blood and resisted his effort.

"Looks like door number two. She has been shot in the head, so the crime happened here."

"Fuck!" Cooper's guttural yell reverberated back from the store's walls. It failed to release all of his anger, but it helped a little. "Don't we have enough misery without this kind of bullshit?"

Calvin nodded gravely. He went back to scouring the place for antibiotics, which helped Cooper refocus on their search. Ten minutes later, it was apparent they were coming up empty. Their consolation prize was two packages of Maxi-pads that made excellent bandages. Many people had overlooked them as helpful items beyond their intended uses. Cooper had found them covered in torn bags and lying in the remnants of a broken bottle of apple juice.

When they left the store, Angela and Jake were looking alertly about them, standing guard.

"Any luck?" Jake asked first.

"Nope," Cooper answered flatly.

"What was your prehistoric yell about? You nearly gave us both a heart attack," Angela asked lightly.

"We found a body. A woman. Dead and more than that," Cooper answered, trying to use a code for Jake's benefit. Angela's face fell and she nodded glumly.

"You mean she got fucked first?" Jake asked. His voice was devoid of emotion and his words made Cooper flinch.

He was on his son in a second and grabbed him by the chin. "You do NOT talk like that. Ever. You hear me?"

Jake recoiled in fear and nodded rapidly until Cooper released him. The two continued to stare at one another and Cooper was startled to realize it felt like he was staring down another man on the precipice of a bar fight. For a moment, he was not staring into the eyes of his young son.

Calvin stepped between them, kneeled, and put a hand on Jake's shoulder. "Yes, son, she was raped. Then they killed her. But, it is not something you should ever speak of like that. Understand?" He looked at Jake intently.

Jake shrugged Calvin's hand off his shoulder and jumped back into the Jeep, slamming the door.

"We should get out of town and regroup and figure out what to do next," Cooper said as he felt exhaustion slowly begin to blanket his body.

"We don't have time for that, Cooper. Or, should I say, Dranko doesn't have time. He's needs those antibiotics now." Angela's tone was desperate.

Calvin clapped Cooper on the shoulder. "We can jump over to Carver

14

and see if we can barter for what we need."

Cooper's face wrinkled in disdain. "Those bastards? Don't you remember they were putting people into slavery over there?"

Calvin's smile faded from his face, and was replaced by a clenched jaw and fiery eyes. "Do *not* get self-righteous on *that* issue, my friend. It is not something that will leave a good taste in *my* mouth—but what other option do we have?"

Cooper noticed that Calvin had taken, perhaps unconsciously, a half step in his direction as his voice level spiked. He started to match the aggressive stance and step closer as well, but fought the instinct. Instead, he turned away, at ninety degrees, and considered their options.

"I think you're right, Calvin. We either try Carver or throw ourselves into the civil war erupting right here. "

"Neither is a good option, but Carver is the best for us, while Dranko is down, at least," Calvin added.

"Yeah, it's bad news, but short-term bad news. Joining a faction is news we don't even know—could be good or very, very bad," Angela finished.

They piled into the Jeep without another word.

*
* *

The journey to Carver gave Cooper another thing to worry about. *Gas.* He knew very soon they would lose the ability to freely use their vehicles as they had been by siphoning and burning through stored supplies. The realization hit him as they tried three stranded vehicles before they got to one that hadn't already been drained. *Without a resumption of fuel deliveries, we probably have two, maybe three, weeks before the siphoning opportunities give out.*

"What do you think happens when the gas runs out?" Cooper said aloud without realizing it.

"We all get screwed," Jake offered defiantly from the back seat. Cooper chose to ignore him.

"Everything gets harder, that's for sure," Angela said.

"I see two big things. Everything becomes local. And, those with access to fuel will wield enormous power." Calvin's words landed like two boulders slamming into the Jeep. Silence prevailed for long seconds. The hum of tires churning pavement filled the cabin. "Think about it. If you have fuel, you can move your men around in any way you see fit while the other guy is what—stuck with the speed of Nike? Mobility is an enormous advantage in battle," Calvin continued.

"And, think about what you could promise your followers—if you have gas and no one else does," Angela added.

"Heat and light, most importantly," Calvin responded.

15

"The keystones to any civilization," Cooper finished as his stomach knotted, realizing that much worse days lay ahead.

*

* *

The rest of the journey was uneventful and tension filled the Jeep as they approached the outskirts of Carver. Cooper found himself hoping the same trade-based ruler was in charge of the town because he knew it would facilitate the transaction, but then immediately reprimanded himself for the thought, given how repugnant the regime had been.

Calvin exhaled loudly. "Wow, look at that!" He pointed toward a billboard advertising the town's only diner.

Cooper couldn't believe what he saw. Blocking out some innocuous beer ad, in blood-red block letters, a slogan screamed out:

Unite, Cooperites!

He involuntarily stopped the Jeep and they all stared at the graffiti. A jumble of thoughts tore through Cooper's mind. *Who are the Cooperites? Is this some local thing or is it bigger than that? How could a group form, using my name, that I had no idea about?* An odd feeling that was sandwiched squarely between pride and disbelief crept into his gut. His left hand rubbed his temples furiously and he shook his head from side to side in a futile attempt to make sense of it all.

"You're famous, dad," Jake deadpanned. *At least he's holding onto a sense of humor, amidst the darkness.* "Oprah should be calling any minute. That is, if the phones worked anymore." Jake's tone had turned acerbic on a dime.

"I guess I spoke too soon," Cooper said in response.

Jake looked confused. "What?"

"Never mind, just thinking out loud," Cooper said with a wry smile.

"You have any idea what this is all about?" Calvin asked.

Cooper shook his head. "Nope. Your guess is as good as mine."

"It does make me think we need to have Angela do our negotiations with the men at the roadblock," Calvin continued.

"Why?"

"Well, with this graffiti, you might have a greater exposure in this town—you might be recognized. Which could lead to them kidnapping you and delivering you to the governor," he said.

"And, what about you?" Cooper asked.

"In case you have not noticed lately, the end of the world has not changed one fundamental truth—I'm still black." Calvin emphasized the point by cocking his head and raising his eyebrows.

"And, some might react to you based on your skin color up here." Cooper concluded Calvin's point for him.

"Exactly. In times like these, we need every advantage to get what we need. I can accompany Angela and play the bodyguard role. People rarely object, and mostly expect folks like me to be in a supporting role. You know, like in *Driving Miss Daisy*, but with guns" he said with a wink. "You stay in the car, we put Jake up front, too, so they see we have at least four guns to respond to any nonsense they might be thinking about," Calvin finished.

Cooper nodded and resumed driving the last stretch of road before they would undoubtedly run into the roadblock up ahead.

*

* *

They rounded the bend and spotted the roadblock a few hundred yards up ahead. Cooper stopped the Jeep. Angela and Calvin wasted no time in piling out. Calvin fell into step behind Angela. Cooper was aghast at the other, more subtle changes he saw in the man.

Calvin normally held good, erect posture in every situation. Now, his shoulders slouched. Gone, too, was his normal self-confident stride. Instead, his gait was shortened and uneven—which had the effect of presenting as a man unsure of himself. In an instant, Calvin had transformed himself into a non-threatening, subservient man. Cooper was so shocked by the change he had to will himself to continue focusing on what was happening before him.

The men at the roadblock moved their weapons to the ready position, but did not aim at them. Two large vehicles made up the roadblock. A blue Cadillac Escalade with all of its tires shot up formed the left side, while a cement truck made up the right. It appeared they could pull the cement truck back if they wanted to allow anyone to pass. Holes had been cut into the Escalade's roof, and sheets of metal were fastened to the side that faced them. *Probably to make it all bulletproof.* One man had a scoped hunting rifle, while the other had a military-style rifle. Cooper only spotted one man on the cement truck, but there was another portal cut into the large cylinder and he guessed another man—probably in a sniper role—was hidden out of view within it. Mesh covered the hole, making it impossible to see in, but no doubt someone could see out. *I'll have to remember that trick,* he thought.

From this distance, all he could do was watch while Angela dickered with the man leading the roadblock. Cooper took to flicking the safety on and off and replacing the magazines in and out of the rifle, as he always did when nervous and without something else to do. He stopped and sat up straight in the seat as the duo re-approached the Jeep. Angela's face worried him.

"They said 'no'," Cooper guessed, hoping to soften the blow for her.

Angela, frowned, shaking her head, "Nah. We got not one—but two full courses of antibiotics."

"So, what's the problem?" Cooper asked, puzzled.

"They didn't want silver," she paused for a moment. "Or any of our trade goods, either."

Now it was Cooper's turn to frown. "What'd they want?"

Her eyes met his squarely, "Your rifle."

"My FAL!" Cooper yelled loud enough for the other men to hear and they looked up quizzically.

Calvin motioned with his hands for Cooper to calm down. "We tried everything, but their only need was for a hard-hitting weapon capable of semi-automatic fire."

Cooper shook his head in disbelief. "You've GOT to be kidding me!"

"Yes, we are, actually," Angela said as she and Calvin descended into gut-wrenching laughter. Jake's was a little delayed, but even louder when he realized the joke. As it registered, Cooper could only smile and shake his head.

"I TOLD you it'd work," Angela gloated to Calvin. She danced around in a full circle, celebrating.

"So, what'd they *really* want in exchange?" Cooper asked, smiling.

Calvin took a step closer to the driver-side window before answering. "Well, the truth is funnier than our joke."

"Meaning…?" Cooper said, a little exasperated.

Calvin gave a look to Angela, who then answered. "They only want your autograph." The way she looked at him belied any notion that they were joking once again.

"Meaning…" Cooper tone grew more acerbic as his eyebrows shot up.

Calvin's face grew sober. "Remember that sign we saw—the Cooperite one?"

He nodded vigorously. "Yeah?"

"Well, they are big fans of yours," Calvin continued.

Cooper's mind immediately turned to whether his friends had violated their basic operational security protocols. "How'd they know I was even here?"

Angela picked up his concern and irritation inflamed her voice. "C'mon Cooper, we aren't morons."

"We brought up the sign we saw and they started going on and on about what a great service Cooper had done for the country and how much they hated the authorities for attacking you," Calvin said, jumping in.

With hands on her hips, Angela finished. "So, we thought telling them you were with us would be to our advantage."

Cooper held up his hands, palms up. "Okay, good. You *knew* I had to ask, right?"

Angela's glare softened, but she yielded nothing more.

"So, what's next?" Cooper asked.

Calvin shifted his weight. "They are going to bring up the antibiotics. They also sent for Chester McKenna. He's the guy running the show here. He wants to meet you."

Cooper shrugged. "Alright."

"We should move the Jeep up to the roadblock," Angela said. As they moved to get back into the vehicle, Angela grabbed his arm. He turned to her, surprised.

"What's up?"

"You need to be careful here, you know that right?"

Cooper's brows furrowed. "No. What are you talking about?"

"You are a political figure now. What you do and say matters. And, you remember this town was running slavery—including sex slavery—when we drove through here last." Her eyes burned along with the words.

Cooper's mind flashed. "Yeah, I got it. Get the antibiotics, but don't become a prop in this guys' rule here, right?"

A smile brightened her face and she swatted his backside. "That's it, rookie! I'm so *proud* of you."

Impulsively, his hand returned the playful pat. "Thanks coach, keep me in the game, I *can* play!"

She pantomimed smitten eyelashes fluttering at him. "Oh, I *bet* you can."

He gave her a good-natured groan as he climbed back into the Jeep.

*

*   *

They only waited a few minutes at the roadblock before Charles McKenna made an appearance. It was enough time for Cooper to shake the hands of the men stationed there. It felt awkward to Cooper to receive such adulation from anyone—particularly complete strangers. He remembered his father was just as uncomfortable with it, and he recalled those words of advice: *The handshakes and kind words are about the other person's need to express it, not you. So, I just accept it all as best I can. It's really just about being polite. To reject it is the rude thing to do.* Cooper struggled to remember this as the men heaped praise upon him. He kept a close eye on Jake as the various men came up to him. Jake's face was impassive. Cooper could tell he was paying attention, but trying hard not to appear to be doing so.

An open top Wrangler raced up to the roadblock and two men jumped out. Cooper correctly guessed that the heavy-set man with a shiny bald dome was McKenna. The man was a walking advertisement for the energy and enthusiasm one would expect when entering a used car lot. *A very used car lot,* he thought.

"Damn fine to meet you, Mr. Adams. Charles McKenna is my name and delivering Carver through this mess is my game!" The man laughed heartily at his own attempt at levity and failed to notice—or didn't care—that it only generated weak smiles in those around him.

Cooper extended his hand. McKenna responded with one of those bone-crushing handshake attempts that some men felt obligated to do. The other man angled to take a snapshot of the greeting with a camera—a traditional 35mm film camera. Cooper frowned and immediately held up his other hand to shield his face. Angela's advice had proved even more prescient than he would have guessed.

"No photos, please," he said. Noting the anger flashing onto McKenna's face, he quickly added, "Not trying to be unfriendly here, but it's a security issue when the president himself is calling for your head." He offered the best smile he could along with the sincerest statement that might mollify McKenna.

McKenna clapped him on the back. "Of course, no problem. Completely understand, friend!" He knotted his thumbs under his belt before continuing, "Those antibiotics you need will be up here in just a few minutes."

"We greatly appreciate the help," Cooper answered.

"As you might have heard, we have officially declared Carver a Cooperite town and I'm a damn sight proud of it, too!"

"I'm afraid I don't know what you are talking about," Cooper responded.

McKenna cocked his head to the side. "Not a complete surprise. It's still a little on the new side, but spreading fast through good old-fashioned word of mouth, Ham radio, and what's left of the internet."

"What is *it*?"

McKenna clapped his shoulder. "Of course! Sorry, partner. Communities, and some prominent individuals, are coming out in support of what you provided us. We've looked at the information and have concluded that you *are* telling the truth! So, we are publicly declaring our support for you. Hell, we gotta do something to send a message to the president and the world, for that matter!"

Cooper shook his head in wonderment. "Really?"

"Yes, sir."

Cooper found the nearest vehicle so he could lean back against it for support. His mind reeled. "It's gonna take me a minute, here. I never thought something like this could happen."

McKenna harrumphed. "Hell, son. I never thought I'd wake up one morning to find out that this much death and destruction was *intentionally done to us!"*

Cooper smiled. "True enough. So, what's all this mean? I mean, aren't you worried about the president or Governor Gibbs punishing you for this?"

The portly man shrugged. "A little. But, that is basically the point of the movement. If enough of us come out publicly—the president or the governor can't come after us all, can he? The old safety in numbers thing!"

Cooper nodded as his smile grew. His father lived that truth and Cooper had absorbed it by osmosis. "But, why haven't I heard a thing about this?"

"Well, like I said. It's very new. Spreading like wildfire, but new. Most importantly, though, the remnants of the media are doing their damnedest to keep the lid on the whole thing. But, they won't be able to do that forever."

"And, what's your all's goal?"

"To convince everyone that you presented the TRUTH to America. I bet you and I agree that this is the first step in rebuilding America?" McKenna's eyes blazed.

Cooper nodded. "Of course."

The two sat in silence for a few seconds, and Cooper recognized the respectful pause that McKenna was offering before he began firing questions at Cooper.

"Can I ask *you* a question, friend?"

"Sure."

"Is there any more to the story than what you released? I just gotta know!"

Cooper shook his head. "No, not really. I am working on some more digging, but I don't want to say anything until it's all complete." Inside, his gut tightened as he thought about what he *had* learned about profit and the plague.

McKenna bit his lower lip as he nodded in understanding. "And any chance I could get a statement from you thanking Carver for coming out as a Cooperite community?"

Cooper saw the clear implication—a quote from him about Carver would also benefit its current leadership—namely McKenna. Cooper was no politician and this was yet one more moment in his life when a white lie would be vastly simpler to offer than the truth.

He leaned forward so that he was at eye level with McKenna. "I'm guessing one of the things you respect about me is how I always tell the truth, right?" McKenna nodded vigorously. "And, sometimes the truth isn't any fun. But, Charles, I cannot give you the quote that you ask for."

"Why not?" McKenna asked, his face flashing pink.

"When we drove through here on our way up the hill, we saw evidence of your community practicing some new form of slavery. I cannot lend my name to such a thing."

McKenna's face now turned crimson, but he offered a broad grin. "What? Slavery? No, no, no. You got us all wrong, friend. It's more like indentured servants paying off their debts. Just like the old days of America."

Cooper's eyes narrowed. "And the women?"

Somehow, McKenna's face turned an even deeper shade of red. "I'm not proud of that. But, in these trying times, certain concessions have to be made."

Cooper decided not to ask for more clarity about what *that* meant. "While that may be, I cannot do anything that will indicate my support for these kinds of things. I do appreciate the support and your aid, though."

He watched as a bevy of emotion swept through McKenna. He imagined the internal war the man was going through. He was clearly enraged, but was reluctant to vent it at Cooper. *He must be weighing the political risks of the options open to him.* Finally, he was resolved, and his face drained of color.

"I guess we'll have to do what makes America great—agree to disagree."

Cooper extended his hand. "I appreciate it, Charles.

He took Cooper's hand reluctantly. "Yeah, I just hope you'll think it over," he said, mustering a smile.

Cooper, knowing his mind would not change, smiled in return and changed the subject. "What news do you have from the other Cooperite towns?" The word, "Cooperite" felt odd as it rolled off his tongue.

McKenna stepped back and rubbed his chin in contemplation. "Well, it's becoming more difficult. Every day, the internet is becoming more temperamental or just plain unusable. Thank God a couple of our residents were avid Ham radio operators, so they have the knowledge and the gear to keep us plugged in."

"Yet one more example of fifty year-old technology trumping the latest whiz bang stuff," Cooper said, trying to lighten the mood.

McKenna nodded. "You heard about Hawaii, right?" Cooper nodded gravely.

"Pakistan?" Cooper shook his head in surprise. "From what we heard, India dropped a couple nukes on 'em. Some say that Pakistan hit back with a few going India's way, but I wouldn't bet my house on it. Too many conflicting reports on that part."

It was Cooper's turn to step back. "Oh my lord," he said as he scratched the stubble on his chin.

"Yeah, the reports aren't good. Millions more dead." McKenna paused for a moment before proceeding. "The rest of the country is a mess, but I'm guessing you know that, right?"

"Yeah. Has there been any recent news the last twenty-four to forty-eight hours?"

McKenna's eyes looked upward, as he recalled information. "Let's see. The mayor of San Francisco was literally strung up and hung by a mob after a food riot. From what I can tell, the Chinese are here, for real. There was a confirmed report of Chinese troops and a National Guard unit up near Seattle that mixed it up. Several dead on both sides. Ain't no police, that's just plain hogwash." Cooper's stomach tightened at the news as his mind wrestled with the implications. "The governor in Washington is kicking some ass, though. Just ordered all National Guard *and* civilians to engage the Chinese soldiers! He signed an executive order declaring hostilities against the Chinese military units and authorized deadly force against them in all situations. Who would have thunk it? A *governor* essentially declaring war on another country!"

Cooper exhaled loudly, lips fluttering. "Whew, that is big news."

"The president is going nutso over it. Prattling on about the fed's authority and all that drivel."

"What about our state and California?" Cooper asked.

"Same old. Still 'investigating' the assertions of the military presence. Still welcoming the humanitarian aid." His eyes lit up. "Oh, damn. I can't believe I forgot this! Yesterday, a freighter arrived in San Francisco from China. The longshoremen—well, those still alive and working—refused to unload the ship! It led to a big standoff and the governor sent the National Guard in. They just massacred the damn guys. Like twenty dead and twice that wounded. The survivors claim they saw heavy weapons on that freighter—tanks and armored vehicles. Supposed to be a video on YouTube, but I ain't seen it... the internet being what it is."

Cooper shook his head, absorbing it all. Another man walked up, handed a bag to McKenna, and left without acknowledging Cooper. McKenna gave the bag to Cooper. "Well, some good news. Here are the antibiotics. I hope they help your friend. I do need to warn you, though. The bottles say they are for fish, but they will work on people just fine."

"What?"

McKenna smiled. "Yeah, I thought it was pretty weird, too, when our pharmacist told me about it. But, many of the antibiotics for fish are the *exact* same as they are for people." He paused for a moment, but continued when he saw Cooper's continued skepticism. "Trust me, I've seen them work fine on a couple people since this all started.

"How will we know the correct dosage?"

"Our guy put instructions in the bag."

Cooper tentatively took the bag. "Thank you. I do need to warn you... Governor Gibbs might be sending men out after me."

McKenna shook his head, "Doesn't surprise me. Well, if they come through Carver, we'll give them a damn good welcome." The smile that was draped across McKenna's face gave Cooper a chill.

"I appreciate it. I'm gonna get this back to Dranko as soon as I can."

The men shook hands again. Cooper clambered back into the Jeep, contemplating something his father had once said: *"When making alliances, you're a damn fool if you expect purity."* He wondered what his father would have said about Carver.

He filled the others in on what McKenna had told him as he drove back toward Dranko. They were halfway back when it happened.

CHAPTER THREE

The Jeep rounded a bend in the road and Cooper noticed a blur of motion from the right.

Thump! There was another blur off to his right and Jake shrieked from the backseat.

Cooper's mind spun. *Did I just hit someone?* His foot shot at the brake. Tires screeched.

"You *hit* him! You *hit* him," Jake yelled.

Cooper looked at Calvin. He was looking right back at Cooper, his mouth agape.

I just hit someone. The Jeep lurched to a stop and Cooper stumbled from the vehicle. A clump of clothes lay off to the side of the road a few hundred feet back. Cooper's legs started running before he could recall telling them to do so. It started as a slow run, as if waking from a dream. Gradually, it gathered into a full sprint as Cooper's mind came online to join his body. He could hear Calvin trailing behind him.

When he reached the figure, he knelt down beside it. "Are you okay?"

A pained groan replied.

From the clothes and the tenor of the groan, Cooper guessed the face down person was a man. He was barely moving. Ragged and worn clothing bundled him from head to toe. His boots were worn, already a few holes in the soles. The stench of sweat and urine assaulted Cooper.

"Can I roll you over?" Cooper asked as he put a hand on the man's shoulder.

The man moaned an indeterminate reply.

Calvin arrived, breathing hard.

"Help me roll him. Support his lower spine," Cooper ordered. Calvin moved into position. "On three. One, two…"

They rolled the man over and his forehead was bloodied and his left arm was bent awkwardly, indicating a painful break.

"Are you conscious?" Calvin asked.

"Yes," the man muttered, his eyes still closed.

"Why'd you just step in front of me?" Cooper pleaded.

The man took a pained breath before responding. "Just look." His right arm pulled back the grimy trench coat he was wearing. Then he pulled up two other layers of clothing.

Seeing the man's stomach, Cooper recoiled. Ribs stood out in stark relief, even through the filth that covered the man. *Like something from Auschwitz.*

"He is starving to death," Calvin muttered in shock.

"What happened?" Cooper asked reflexively.

25

"Just kill me," the man drew a ragged breath. "Please."

Cooper drew back. "What?"

The man's eyes opened. They were intense and pleading. His right hand found Cooper's shirt collar and he pulled him down, with surprising strength.

"Please!"

"No. Wait. What *happened* to you?"

"I ain't eaten since," the man hissed at him, desperate.

"Since when?" Cooper asked.

The man released his grip as his sudden burst of strength faded.

"Since it started." His words hit Cooper like a sledgehammer, leaving him speechless for a moment. Next to him, Calvin gasped.

"Since it started," Calvin repeated.

The man dipped his head and groaned in agony.

"Plea...," he began, and then inhaled deeply, reacting to the pain.

"How's that possible?" Cooper asked.

The man's eyes shut again and he labored out a response between pained breaths. "No food in my house... paycheck to paycheck y'know... family all in Iowa... no friends here... just moved... you get... dirty... no one wants to help ya... not one man alone... too dang'rous..."

Cooper gripped his chin in sympathy and disbelief. He took a minute to absorb everything. The man just kept talking.

"Please... too far gone... just kill me... please... that's why... I jumped out... finish it... please." Midway through his pleas, the man's eyes opened again. He had deep green eyes that were wet with emotion and encircled in grime. Cooper's head spun and the bottom of his stomach fell out as it hit him this man was asking him to kill him. He took a deep breath to try and clear his mind.

"You gonna do it?"

Jake's voice made Cooper spin around, his hand involuntarily reaching for his pistol, and his heart racing.

"*Don't* sneak up on me like that, son!" Cooper nearly shouted.

Jake shrugged. "Just walked up. You gonna do it or not?"

Cooper looked at his son through narrowing eyes. *Indifference.* That was what shocked him. There was such flatness in his son's words as he contemplated a man's death. His boy was devoid of emotion.

"Just give me a minute, will you?" Cooper said, standing up. "I just need a minute to think it through." He turned to pace in a circle. His steps were heavy and his eyes downcast as he looked at the pebbles and rocks amid the asphalt. He ran a hand through his hair as his mind tried to catch up to events.

He didn't really hear the first pop, as it took a second to register. Then, another "pop, pop!" He whirled around to see Jake standing over the man.

Calvin rushed toward him and forced the arm that held the pistol to point toward the sky. Smoke curled lazily upward from the muzzle. Cooper's eyes were riveted to his son's face. His expression matched his words from just moments before. It was slack and there was not a trace of emotion clouding it. Cooper staggered toward his son and his gaze drifted to the man. Blood was pooling from the back of his head, from where Jake's rounds had struck home. His face was a mash of torn flesh and bone. Unrecognizable.

He reached Jake and fell to his knees. "Why'd you do that?" he shouted as his hands grabbed his son by the arms.

Jake's eyes met his. They were cold, resolute. "It's what he wanted. Dranko needs us back there with those antibiotics. The faster the better. So, I did it." He shrugged his shoulders as he finished speaking.

Cooper's mind reeled. The cold logic was irrefutable. His insides turned to ice as it dawned on him that his son was conforming to the needs of this violent new world faster than he was.

"Where'd your heart go?" he blurted, knowing it was the wrong thing to say as soon as the words tumbled from his lips.

Jake looked at him curiously. "Heart? The man was half-dead. In pain. He *wanted* to die. It was the humane thing to do!" He stopped talking, but the look he gave Cooper indicted him. The unsaid words could well have been: *where is your heart to leave a man so?*

Cooper's hands dropped from Jake's arms. He covered his face with them for a moment and then ran them hard over his forehead and finally through his hair. His fingers gripped his face and skull hard, as if he squeezed hard enough, it would ward off all that was happening around him. When he looked at his son, all he saw was indifference. *Cold. Hard. Resolute. Indifference. At killing a wounded man,* Cooper's mind screamed at him. Cooper held the gaze for a moment. It seared into his brain. It was a look he'd never forget.

Cooper stumbled to his feet and shuffled back to the Jeep. Calvin had already drifted off toward it. Cooper could tell Calvin was just as shocked by the horrifying events that had just occurred. Cooper heard Jake's footfalls behind him and the soft brush of metal against leather as he holstered his pistol. Within a few seconds, Jake passed him. His confident stride outdistanced Cooper and Calvin's plodding, unsure steps. He never looked back before he stepped past Angela and climbed into the Jeep.

*
* *

The Jeep was engulfed in silence as they drove back to the cabin. The only interruption was the metallic "click... click... click" as Jake reloaded rounds into his pistol's magazine. *Replacing those that had so recently been fired into a man's skull, by* my *son,* Cooper's thought bitterly.

Was Jake right? Was granting the man's wish the right thing to do? Has the world changed so fast that I haven't kept up and Jake has? Or has my son become an unfeeling killer? The thoughts roiled in his mind. No matter the answer, Cooper could not escape the shocking fact that his son had just killed a man and showed not a shred of emotion. *That* worried him more than anything else. Driving, he tried to catch a glance of Jake in the rearview mirror, but only saw a few furtive looks. Jake's face had been mimicked a millions times over by bored boys on a country drive. He looked vacantly out the window as the outside sped by.

"Holy shit!" Angela screamed so loud it pierced Cooper's right eardrum.

Cooper hit the brakes even before he could refocus from the rearview mirror to the road. Time slowed. The screech of tires shredding rubber met his ears first. Up ahead, he saw the road blocked by a couple of pick-up trucks, and pinprick flashes of light were flashing from all around them. From his right, Calvin's hoisted rifle began firing out through the windshield. Inside the vehicle, it sounded like a cannon and Cooper was deafened.

He jerked the steering wheel hard to the right, sliding the Jeep to land ninety degrees to the road. Pockmarks tore across the Jeep's body and windows, showering them in glass. Jake yelped from the rear seat. Cooper's eyes flashed alarm.

Cooper wasted no time before he began barking orders. "Get out! Get out! Get out!" he yelled. His right hand pushed Calvin out toward the door that was now facing away from the blockade. He ducked, trying to get what scant protection from rifle fire the sheet metal doors would offer—which he knew was very, very little. Calvin jerked the door handle and fell out of the car onto the ground in his haste. Jake slithered on the Jeep's floor and out the rear passenger door. Angela was right behind him. Cooper followed quickly behind Calvin, but not fast enough to escape a bullet from grazing his right thigh. He felt no pain and only noticed the sensation of flesh being torn. He dragged his rifle behind him by the sling. Cooper ducked behind the engine block and motioned Calvin and Jake to lie prone behind the wheels. He knew these were the only parts of a modern car that would stop bullets.

Cooper shot his head up to get a two second read on the situation. He figured there were four to six men manning the roadblock. Before he could get any farther, Jake was at his side.

"I'm going to flank them—cover me!" Jake yelled and then, madly, kept moving past his father. Cooper grabbed out, trying to catch him, but he was a second too late and had to watch in anguish as his son disappeared into the brush alongside the road. Angela, who had been trailing Jake, kept doing so and ran after him. His mouth flew open in shock and he popped up again, taking care to appear two feet to his left from where he had popped up last time. He shot wildly in the direction of the blocking pick-up trucks, a fool's prayer in trying to help his son. He could hear the first few bullets ripping past where he had just been, to his right. They sounded like an angry crossbred monster between a bee and a buzz saw. When the bolt rocked back and locked—meaning his magazine had run dry—he dropped behind the vehicle and looked frantically to his right. There was no sign of Jake or Angela from the Jeep... across the open ground... nor down the embankment that sloped sharply downward. *That's a good thing, Cooper.* He had to convince himself of this as his heart crept into his throat. However, not knowing where his son was now, he quickly decided not to follow after him. The risk of them accidentally shooting each other was too high.

The firing from the blockade had slowed and Cooper knew *that* was a bad thing. *With Angela and Jake flanking to the right, we need their undivided attention on us.* His head jerked back to look at Calvin as his hands rammed a fresh magazine home, and then he yanked the bolt back and released it to chamber another round.

"Can you hear me?" Cooper yelled. Calvin nodded. "Lay down fire. Just enough to keep their attention. Move along the vehicle, coming up in a different spot each time!"

Calvin nodded again.

Cooper waited until a volley of Calvin's bullets had been fired and then sprang into action. He threw himself underneath the Jeep and crawled forward, praying that the shadow cast by the Jeep would keep him out of his enemies' view. He caught one last muzzle flash as he got into position. He focused his sights there, hoping the person on the other end would make the foolish mistake of appearing in the same place again.

The seconds crawled by. Sweat was beading up on Cooper's forehead. His stomach churned in worry about Jake and he gritted his teeth in helplessness. He managed to keep his breathing steady—ready to shoot—only through sheer will. Calvin had moved hard to the right and was firing from in front of the Jeep, using the angle to protect himself. Five brisk shots rang out, just as the first salvo of return fire began.

Cooper saw his opponent's rifle barrel first as it rose above the bed liner, and then began coming downward as the man's head appeared to aim it.

Cooper didn't have to wait. He knew that his rifle would tear through both walls of the truck bed without being slowed down too much. Sheet metal was no match for .308—or lesser calibers, for that matter. He aimed carefully, using the rifle barrel to judge the man's center of mass. He breathed, released half of it, held it and then squeezed the trigger smoothly. The FAL thundered and as soon as the barrel returned back to the aiming point, he fired another quick shot. As he swiftly scurried backward, he caught a glimpse of the barrel pitching forward into the truck's bed. *Got him! But, how many are left?* He wished, futilely, that he could know.

He scraped his knees and bashed his head on the Jeep's underbelly in his haste to retreat so that he could find another firing position. His mind spun. *I don't have time to try to pick them off one by one. Jake will be upon them soon.* He cursed himself for not immediately following after his son. He waved his hand to catch Calvin's attention, who was bent down, reloading.

"Aimed fire now!" he screamed at him.

He steadied himself and popped back up, bracing the FAL on the Jeep's hood. Now he planned to stay exposed and prayed that he could hit the opponents before they could get him. This risky approach was the only one he could think of that might save his son. He breathed deeply and kept the trigger halfway depressed. Movement near the front of the rightmost pick-up truck caught his eye. He let half his breath out and held it. The man stupidly brought his head up first, too slowly. This gave Cooper a second to sight in. His eyes registered the University of Oregon emerald green ball cap and used the black Oregon "O" as his target. A second later, the man's head had been blown apart by a round from Cooper's rifle. He wasted no time watching the body slump down toward the ground; he was already scanning the rest of the blockade. *Maybe we get one or two more and we can break their morale so they will flee.*

Calvin began firing furiously into or through the cab of the first pick-up truck. Cooper could not see what he was shooting at, so he held his fire. As quickly as he'd started, Calvin stopped. The crisp smell of gunpowder and cordite gripped Cooper's nostrils. A few seconds passed and he heard a battle cry from the opposing roadblock.

Suddenly, four shapes appeared, rifles firing. Cooper pivoted his rifle to a man with a scoped rifle—what his brain subconsciously identified as the worst threat. He fired a quick shot, hoping to rattle the other man's aim. He got lucky and the man's shoulder jerked back from the impact of being hit. As suddenly as he'd appeared, he disappeared once again behind the truck. Cooper heard bullets ripping into the Jeep and through the air all around him. He felt lucky the other men were showing rookie mistakes and were "spraying and praying," rather than lying down aimed rifle fire. He made no such mistake.

Despite the hail of gunfire all around him, he rotated his sights to the next target. He took a second to sight in. This man held what looked like an AK-47 rifle and had exposed his chest by standing upright behind the hood of the second pick-up truck. Cooper put his sights square in the man's chest and fired once, waited for the rifle to return to center, and fired again. That man collapsed forward, sprawling across the hood of the truck.

Just then, rapid firing from the trees off the side off the road and behind the roadblock erupted. Cooper's adrenaline ratcheted up another notch: *Jake and Angela!* He searched frantically for the next target, but the remaining men had dropped out of view. The men were yelling, but Cooper had a hard time figuring out what they were saying amid the gunfire coming from Jake. He heard jumbled words, broken up by the shots, and it took a moment to piece them together. "We surrender!"

A smile crept upon Cooper's face. He rounded the front of the Jeep and sprinted toward the blockade. Calvin was already several steps ahead of him. The distance closed rapidly. He noticed that the shooting had stopped and he shouted as he ran.

"Stand up. Hands up!"

As Calvin arrived at the blockade, the men were slowly standing up with their hands in the air. Cooper followed close behind.

There were three men still unharmed and one wounded—the one Cooper had hit in the shoulder. They were dressed in the typical garb of men who lived in the area—jeans, Carhartt's, and flannel.

"Whatcha gonna do with us now?" one of the men asked. Just then, Angela and Jake emerged from the brush alongside the road. The same man whined loudly. "Oh, geez, it was a girl and a damned kid that got us?"

Jake beamed and Cooper could not repress a smile.

Angela shifted her weight and poked the offending man with the muzzle of her rifle. "Girl? It's 'woman' to you, buddy!"

The man's face migrated from surprise to indignation to fear. "Yes, ma'am." He ended with downcast eyes.

"Yup, a kid. But, he ain't damned," Cooper responded.

"So, what are we going to do with them?" Calvin asked, keeping his rifle trained on the men.

"We are going to disarm you, down to the folding knives you have in your pockets and the toothpicks in your teeth. Then, we are going to let you pile into this pick-up, here," Cooper said, pointing to the most damaged of the two. "Then, you're going to drive away."

The man wearing Carhartt clothing from head to toe responded. "Thank you, sir, that's really…"

Jake interrupted him. "No, we're not."

Then, everything happened in slow motion. Cooper saw the man get shot and it took him a second to realize it was Jake doing the shooting. The man was hit by a half dozen .22 rounds in quick succession. The other men began diving to the ground and reaching for their weapons. Reflexively, Cooper's rifle went back to his shoulder and he shot the wounded man who was grabbing for his scoped hunting rifle. He heard Angela's rifle fire twice in a row at a man who was sprawled on the ground but had a pistol in hand, turning to face them. Calvin and Jake shot the final man at the same time. He was squatted in a crouch and reaching for an AR-15 on the ground. Then, just as suddenly, silence. The smell of spent gunpowder, mixed with the coppery smell of blood and the stench of discharged bowels reached him quickly as the seconds passed.

Cooper stood in shock, surveying the death and ruin in front of them. The quiet moans of a few who were dying haunted an already gruesome scene. He pulled his pistol and went to the first man who was moaning. Dispassionately, he dispatched him with a shot to the head. The sharp report of another pistol to his left told him Calvin had done the same. Slowly, his eyes turned toward Jake.

He was still stunned that his son had executed someone twice within the past hour! His mind was a blur. "Why'd you do that?" he asked, exhaustion and disbelief robbing his voice of any power.

Jake looked up to meet his eyes slowly. "They were bad men, dad. Letting them go would have just have exposed others to their evil." Once more, his son's cold, calculated words rocked him to his core. It struck him as even worse that he found difficulty in arguing with the logic.

"We'll talk about this later," was all that he could manage.

"I think I should take Jake in this pick-up here, and you and Calvin can drive that Cherokee over there," Angela offered, motioning to a vehicle that had been parked behind the roadblock that he hadn't even seen yet. "The Jeep was shot up way too badly. Luckily, we are not too far from getting back to Dranko's place."

Cooper nodded numbly and began shuffling back to the Jeep to retrieve their belongings. He was halfway there before he thought to tell them to grab the weapons from the dead. But, he didn't even bother. He staggered into the Jeep, gathered their gear in a fog, and stumbled back to the Cherokee.

He was about to open the driver's side door, but a strong hand stopped the door from opening. "Other side, friend. You are too far out of it. You do not even have the keys," Calvin said, jiggling them in front of his eyes. "I will drive," his deep voice boomed. Cooper complied without a word, and dumped the gear into the back seat. Then, absentmindedly, he clambered into the passenger seat. As they drove away, he stared out the window.

After a few minutes, Cooper finally came out of his mental fog.

"What's happening to my son?" he asked Calvin.

Calvin scratched his chin with his free hand. "That is a good question. I think it is too much of a pressure cooker."

"Ya think," Cooper answered, his voice sharp.

Calvin returned a stern look. "Let me finish. That part *is* obvious. What I mean is, you need to get him around some other kids. Or, at least *play* with the boy. That is a way to relieve some of the pressure and remind him how to be a kid."

Cooper's eyes widened and he rubbed his temples. "Oh my Lord! You are exactly right, Calvin. Why didn't I think about this?"

Calvin chuckled. "Cooper, you have been a little preoccupied."

He smiled briefly, before his face turned serious once more. "Do you think it's too late?"

Their eyes met his and his words broke Cooper's heart. "I think it would help him, Cooper, for sure. But," he turned his head to look out at the road once again, "...there is no going back to before."

Cooper looked out the window once more. An expression his father had said over and over again came to him. *Some bottles, once opened, can't ever be closed again.* It was such an odd expression that it had stuck with him. He felt his stomach drop as the hope of hanging onto at least some part of his son's childhood began to fade away.

Time to get back in the game. When the Cherokee stopped, he clutched the bag of antibiotics to his chest tightly and raced inside.

*
*   *

Julianne was sitting next to Dranko, who was propped up and sipping tea from the cup she was holding up to his lips.

"You're up!" Cooper shouted in glee, sounding like a five year-old at Christmas.

Julianne beamed a smile back at him as she turned. The corners of Dranko's mouth upturned, but that was all that he could muster.

"I have them," Cooper exclaimed. "The antibiotics," he said holding up the bag like a trophy.

He vaulted into a chair on the other side of where Dranko lay. He pulled a sheet of paper out of the bag and began reading the instructions.

"These are fish antibiotics, but the guy said they'd work. You ever hear of that?" He was talking excitedly—the combination of seeing his friend conscious and the antibiotics gave him renewed hope.

Dranko's head dipped in a shallow nod. "Yes," he croaked.

Cooper looked at him. "It's good to hear you talk, brother. These are going to get you over the hump." Dranko's eyes met his in recognition.

"This is the first that he has spoken," Julianne remarked.

Cooper turned to look at Julianne. "Yeah, well, he *always* saves his yapping for me!" Somehow, Dranko managed to poke him in the leg with his thumb and Cooper yelped in surprise. Julianne giggled at it all.

Cooper had finished the short instructions. "You gotta take two of these caplets every four hours. Amoxicillin. Can you swallow?"

Dranko declined his head shallowly and then raised it slowly. Cooper reached his hand and tipped the pills into his friend's mouth. Julianne held the cup up and Dranko dipped his head back and raggedly swallowed them with some effort. His face was twisted in discomfort by the time he finished.

"Okay, you done good. Now, you should rest up." Cooper finished and patted his friend's shoulder. He and Julianne helped recline Dranko once again and they left the room in silence.

"So, how was it?" she asked. Her eyes pulled him in, as was becoming the norm.

He looked around, trying to see if they had privacy, before speaking. Seeing this, she grabbed him by the hand and pulled him into the bathroom. He braced himself against the sink and began relaying what had happened with the starving man and the firefight on the road. As he talked, he was only dimly aware of Julianne's words of sympathy and how her hands migrated from holding his, to caressing his arm or cheek. The words kept tumbling from him; words laced with doubt, worry, and fear. Julianne continued drawing closer to him and he welcomed every bit of it. When he had finished talking about how his son had executed the prisoner in cold blood tears stained his face.

"Oh, you dear sweet man," she said as her nimble fingers wiped the tears from his cheek. Cooper purposely avoided her eyes, but welcomed the comfort of her touch. As he finished the story and his attention returned to the here and now, he slowly became aware that Julianne was close up against him. His legs had been pushed out as she had embraced him and now straddled his legs. Her stomach pressed against his groin, given their height difference. Her breasts brushed against his chest. When he opened his eyes, hers were just inches away, looking at him intently. They were moist with empathy. Their eyes locked. He saw softness, sympathy, and desire mixed into an irresistible potion. He wanted to be swallowed by those deep pools. They looked at one another for a very long time, each savoring the moment, until they were both smiling. After what seemed like forever, her eyes dropped. He felt a tug on his shirt as her fingers danced across his belly. His pent up desire—born from intense stress without release—of the past several weeks, spiked. He desperately wanted to distract himself from all that had just transpired with Jake.

When her fingers found and then undid the first button on his pants, he could sit still no longer. His fingers found her chin and he pulled her lips to his. They kissed greedily, hungrily. His body screamed, wanting to be inside of her, but he willed himself against it. He took a deep breath and forced himself to slow down. As they kissed and their hands clutched at each other's body in desperation, the pace grew frantic. Her touch was deft. She knew when to touch softly and when to grab him hard and wild. Elena came crashing into his thoughts at one point, but rank desire pushed this away. Julianne moaned when his mouth found her neck and she purred when he turned her around so that his lips could graze across the back of her neck. He kissed her there while his hand pressed firmly against her

34

stomach and then drifted down. He pushed her hair up so that he could kiss her neck and earlobes more easily.

"I want you… now," Julianne breathed back at him.

He was beyond thinking and his instincts took over in wild abandon. He hoisted her easily onto the sink's edge and she wiggled out of her pants as he tugged on them. She clumsily and feverishly undid her shirt's buttons. The rest became a blur. His hands and mouth danced across her body. Her hands alternated between clutching his back and holding the back of his head, guiding him where she wanted his lips to linger. He had no idea how long the foreplay lasted, but when he was inside of her, the pleasure overwhelmed him and he was lost. Lost in the lust and desire that can consume a man. As they fell into a steady, desperate rhythm together, he lost track of time. Somehow, through luck or by design, their bodies tensed, convulsed, and released within seconds of each other.

He collapsed against her, sweat on sweat. Her fingers wandered over his body, tracing different areas. As conscious thought returned to Cooper, and he had a realization that both thrilled him and terrified him: *that was the best sex that I have ever had.* "Deal with that later," he whispered to himself, without realizing it.

Julianne pulled her head back to look at him. "What'd you say?"

"Nothing," Cooper demurred.

She ignored his evasion and beamed a smile at him instead. "Pretty good, eh?"

He allowed himself to smile back. "Yeah, I was pretty pent up."

"I could tell and I don't think you're done yet," she laughed quietly. Her fingers continued their dancing and he was surprised as she guided him into her again. *I'm in trouble,* Cooper thought as they went at each other once more.

*

*   *

"What now?" Julianne asked as she was dressing after they had finished the second time.

Cooper grinned. "Hell if I know. This is a crazy thing at a crazy time in a crazy world." His face had turned grim by the time he'd finished.

"You mean you still hate me for what I did." Her look pierced him more than her words.

He grabbed her hand and looked right back at her. "You know I don't hate you. But, it's hard to explain."

"Can you try?" Her eyes were expectant.

He looked around the room, his brain searching for answers. "I'm not sure I can look past what you did."

35

Her eyes fell. "That's what I thought."

Cooper grunted and his fingers gently pulled her chin up so he could look at her again. "But, I'm drawn to you like nothing before in my life. None of this even makes sense to me, so how can I explain it to you?"

She pulled his hand away, squinted at him, and nodded. Emotion clouded her eyes as she faked a cavalier response. "Okay, well you call me, big boy. If you want to, someday, that is. I'd give you my number if my cellphone worked, but I guess you know how to find me." She gave him an impetuous kiss on the lips and then strode from the room. Cooper was left shaking his head and smiling. He straightened his clothes and then left the bathroom.

CHAPTER FOUR

He checked on Dranko, who was still sleeping, and then found himself on the porch. Calvin and Jake were working in the garden area. Angela passed him, heading out to the Airstream trailer that housed the women, and gave him a warm smile. The high-pitched whine of a motorcycle engine made him find his rifle quickly. He watched the others take up fighting positions spread out across the property. It was definitely coming up the long driveway toward the cabin. Cooper went into a crouching position and sighted in on the approach to the cabin.

Thankfully, he recognized the motorcycle as his own and quickly identified the rider as Freddie. He relaxed and shouldered the rifle. Gravel spun as Freddie braked the bike hard in front of the cabin and leapt off. He was out of breath from excitement. The others were jogging up.

"We... gotta... get out... of here," he gasped.

"What? Why?" Cooper's adrenaline spiked and his mind was already realizing what abandoning this place would mean.

"Soldiers. In town. Asking about you. Trying to find out where you are," Freddie continued.

"How many?"

"Too many. At least twenty or so." Freddie's breath calmed as he relaxed.

Angela yelped, her hand covering her mouth in surprise. Calvin whistled and Jake was silent. The others were now huddled around him.

Cooper rubbed his head. "Damn. Where can we go?"

"The Stotts have a place. A hunting cabin. I heard them talk about it," Calvin finished.

"Do you know where it is?" Cooper asked.

Calvin nodded. "He once showed it to me on a map. He was telling me about their bug out location. I think he was partly joking, but I think he wanted me to know where it was in case something happened to him."

Cooper's mind clicked into action. "Alright, Angela, can you get Dranko ready to move? Calvin, Freddie, and Jake, you all are on supply detail. Plan on a two-week stay. We'll be moving on after that. Julianne, I want you to get as much information onto paper as you can about the Brushfire Plague. I'll be standing guard out here, but can answer any questions that come up, too. We move out in thirty minutes."

Everyone ran off to get to his or her assigned tasks. The next thirty minutes were a flurry of activity. Cooper was answering questions constantly, mostly about what to bring and what to leave behind. He prioritized food, water, medical supplies, and weapons. He knew once Dranko was healthy, they'd be on the move again. This was why he made sure they brought every scrap of light and portable food. The newly liberated pick-up truck was where they laid Dranko out on a mattress from the cabin. Angela would ride in the back with him, to keep him as immobile as possible. Freddie was driving the truck and Julianne piled into the cab with him, adroitly avoiding eye contact with Cooper. He was driving the Cherokee and Calvin drove the other truck. Jake rode with Calvin, which stung Cooper. *Maybe the boy just needs some space right now,* he told himself. Calvin led the short convoy down the driveway thirty-seven minutes after Freddie had arrived with the news. The pick-up holding Dranko was in the middle, and Cooper brought up the rear.

After a few minutes of driving, Cooper was happy that he had been left alone in the Cherokee. His thoughts were able to wander without interruption. He hoped that Dranko came out on the other side of this hasty journey no worse for wear. He hoped the antibiotics would work and get him back on his feet quickly.

But, mostly his thoughts were consumed with what was happening with Jake. Part of him believed that any kid growing up in this new world had to be hard to survive. Part of him wondered what surviving really meant if you became an emotionless, heartless person. Something deep within him knew that he had to fight to hold onto his—and Jake's—humanity. Otherwise, what was the point of it all? But, was it a hopeless task? While they drove for almost an hour, he was unable to answer any of his questions. They headed east and farther up the mountain.

When they arrived, the cabin was *truly* a cabin. It was about a twelve-by-twelve foot room. Four cots were braced against the walls. There was a sleeping loft that could hold two more people, tightly. The furnishings were threadbare, but reflected its use as a hunter's base. Faint aromas of stale beer, wool blankets, and gun oil permeated the place.

"Ladies and gentlemen, welcome to the Hotel de Luxor," Freddie deadpanned as soon as they had all piled in. He received only groans and a few playful shoves in response.

"Okay, let's stack what we can of the supplies in here. Leave the rest in the Cherokee. And, let's get Dranko in here before we do anything else."

"It's a good thing we brought the mattress with us from Dranko's place," Angela added.

Cooper nodded. "That was a good idea. How did he fare in the trip?"

"It wasn't ideal, but he's fine," she replied.

Cooper nodded and turned toward his son. "Jake, can you go down to where this driveway meets the road and try to cover our tracks up here? Smooth the gravel, get some branches onto the driveway, and things like that?"

Wordless, Jake nodded and began walking back the way they had come. His gait was listless and his head downturned. *I've got work to do on him.*

*
* *

Two hours later, they had the small place organized as best they could and had eaten a makeshift lunch of peanut butter on very stale pita bread slices. Cooper didn't know if they should pick off the moldy parts or not, but decided to be safe and did so. He was leaning against the Cherokee collecting his thoughts, when Calvin walked up.

"Julianne is getting the ham radio rigged up," he said.

"Good, we could use some updated news."

"What are you thinking about, Cooper?"

"That I have to deal with the governor and how I'm going to do it," Cooper replied, his face tight.

"What do you mean?"

"I mean I'm not going to be running my whole life. I can't live like a rabbit with a fox on its tail."

"You know killing Governor Gibbs will not stop that."

"Now, what the hell do *you* mean?" Cooper asked, his eyes intense.

Calvin's sinister grin made a chill run down his spine. "Killing a man only makes his friends and allies come after you instead."

"And?" Cooper asked impatiently.

"I am talking about humiliation. Disgrace. A destroyed man has no friends or allies... only rats jumping off his ship."

Cooper had never seen the look that was upon Calvin's face. It was a potent mix of glee and malice. Cooper realized his arms had broken out in goosebumps. "So, you are saying I need to expose the governor for his misdeeds and *then* kill him?"

Calvin nodded with satisfaction. "That's right, boss."

Cooper rubbed his chin. "That's a very interesting idea. How can I do that with the internet fading every day? And, hell, I put *everything* out there on the Plague and not everyone believed *that!*"

Calvin looked back at him thoughtfully. "Agreed. I never said it would be easy. However, you have a budding movement of 'Cooperites.' You can use that. Second, you will have to think old school news distribut—"

Cooper jumped up and interrupted him. "I get it. Flyers. Word of mouth. Paul Revere with a twist of modern."

Calvin's white teeth gleamed against his dark face in a wide smile. "You have it, my friend."

"If I can get him on video admitting to the Chinese connection or the profits they all made..."

Now, it was Calvin's turn to interject. "Or, can you get one of the ac-

39

complices to do so? Are any of them in Oregon? Getting to them will be a hell of a lot easier than getting to the governor."

Cooper threw his hands up and his face was flush in excitement. "Yes! That's it. I could get one of them confessing on video *and* use *that* to lure the governor out where I can get my hands around his scrawny neck!"

Several seconds passed as both men thought about the ideas that had been sparked. Cooper looked back at Calvin. "Where'd you learn how to think like an evil bastard?"

Calvin's laughter boomed deeply before the grin left his face. "Watching the life my brother led. Talking to him about how he survived on the streets. He paid for those kind of lessons in his blood." By the time he had finished, his face and voice was clouded with pain and anger. His eyes had welled up and he averted his gaze from Cooper.

Cooper put his hand on his shoulder. "I'm sorry, Calvin. I shouldn't have asked."

Calvin's jaw tightened. "It is fine, Cooper. How could you have known? I will be alright."

Cooper clapped his shoulder. "Thanks for the good advice. I gotta see if any of Gibbs' cronies live around here. Julianne will know."

*
* *

He found Julianne huddled in a corner of the room, opposite from where Dranko lay sleeping. She was fiddling with some connections on the ham radio that they had brought with them. He pulled a folding chair over and sat down next to her. He was close enough to smell her and his mind wanted to wander, but he deliberately shook his head to stop it from doing so.

"Can I interrupt for a sec?"

She turned to him, her hand pushing her hair behind an ear. "Of course." Her smile was captivating.

"Do any of the accomplices in the conspiracy live in the area?"

Her eyes cocked upward as she thought for a moment. "Yes. Can I ask why?"

He jostled her knee. "In a second, antsy one! Are any of *them* close to the governor?"

Julianne giggled. "Cooper, you really *don't* know how the world works, do you? These people? They are *all* connected!"

Cooper exhaled loudly in frustration. "Yes, okay. But, are any of them closer than the others?"

"Relax, honey. I just wanted to play with you for a minute." Her hand fell upon his knee and gave it a tight squeeze. "Jonathan Goodwin lives up

40

in Camas. He and Governor Gibbs were roommates in college. They are pretty tight. He's made a fortune off software contracts with the State of Oregon."

Thinking, Cooper nodded. "Camas, Washington, huh?"

Julianne laughed again at his inane comment. "Yeah, there isn't a Camas, Oregon last time I checked!" He playfully pushed her hand away and stood up to go, but her hand caught his and pulled him back down. "Bring me up to speed on what you're thinking. I can probably help you make a better plan." Her eyes were bright and piercing.

He reseated himself, cupped her chin, and whispered in her left ear. "You know you have *the* most beautiful eyes I've ever seen?" Her fingers splayed across his arm in response. "Alright, let's get down to business," Cooper said and he began to explain what he and Calvin had thought of so far.

Fifteen minutes later, he had a plan that he was confident would rain revenge down upon the governor *and* free him once and for all from being chased around like a dog.

*

* *

After that, they gathered the others together so that Julianne could share what she had heard over the ham radio. They sat, or stood, around the small table in the cabin, while Julianne filled them in. Cooper noted how Angela stood opposite Julianne and he could feel the whisper of tension in the air between them.

"Well, the biggest news is probably that the reports of disease from things like cholera and dysentery are spiking up all over the place," she said, the worry lines creased on her face.

"Why's that?" Jake asked.

"The water systems failed in too many places. People can't wash. Human waste piles up. Disease spreads," she answered.

"How many dead?" Calvin's question boomed across the room.

She shook her head. "I don't know. I don't think anyone knows. But, the reports out of many places sound pretty bad." She paused for a moment before continuing. "The violence is also spiking as people are running out of food and even water is becoming hard to come by in some places. Government is really starting to collapse all over the place." She suddenly stopped and slapped her own forehead in disbelief. "Oh damn!"

Cooper looked at her. "Oh damn, what?"

"I can't believe I didn't start with this. Basically, the old Confederate states announced their secession from the United States!"

The room exploded in exclamations and shouts and questions. Once again, Calvin's voice resounded through the noise. "Quiet!" Like an ocean tide, the noise ebbed from the room. "Tell us more," Calvin instructed.

"I don't know a lot more, except that most of the old states that belonged to the Confederacy have announced their independence from the United States. They are calling themselves the 'Confederated American States.' Texas remains independent, though. You might recognize their flag." She said the last sentence with sarcasm dripping from it.

"Damn traitors," Angela spat. "Things get tough and they bail. So much for 'big and bad' Texas."

Dranko looked at her blazing eyes and proceeded anyway. "I think, given the circumstances, they have a right to get the hell off a sinking ship."

"We are better off without them, if you ask me," Calvin added.

Cooper could see that Angela was about to fire back with a stiff retort so he held up his hand and changed the topic. "And, what's the latest with the Chinese?"

Her face darkened. "In one word? Escalation. I heard scattered reports of clashes in Washington State mostly, but at least one in Oregon. And, in California, what happened to the dockworkers has sparked fights and more clashes there, too." She rubbed her hands together while she talked.

Cooper nodded. "Any more details?"

She cocked her head to one side. "Well, in Washington, it's involved both National Guard troops *and* civilians taking them on. But, in Oregon and California, it's been only civilians fighting back." Cooper could feel the tension in the room rise. Julianne looked around to see if anyone else had questions, but there were none. She continued. "The other news internationally is pretty bad. The world is generally still furious with the U.S. for starting the Brushfire Plague. More acrimony and threats coming from many quarters." Her eyes welled up. Cooper guessed she was experiencing that now familiar feeling of guilt at what she had participated in. He felt the now familiar surge of anger laced with sympathy in his heart. It was an odd mix of emotion that he suspected he'd never get used to.

Angela muttered something under her breath, while her eyes burned toward Julianne. Cooper caught Angela's gaze and saw a chilling rage. "What else?" Cooper asked, hoping to break the tension.

Julianne paused for a moment and then her face brightened. "Well, this Cooperite thing seems to be spreading. Lots of chatter on the radio about the plague and amidst all that is a bevy of voices—who are now self-identifying as 'Cooperites'—speaking out in support of the information you put out there. Calls for the president to come clean, or resign, those kind of things."

"I guess you might be our next president," Freddie deadpanned.

The room exhaled the tension in a short burst of chuckles and laughter.

Cooper waved his hand and added to the levity. "Only if you are my

Comic in Chief." He let the room embrace the humor before he turned serious once more. "Any sense of the Cooperites' level of organization?" The word still felt funny crossing his lips.

"Well, it's most heavy in the Northwest. But, that could be based on who I can pick up on the reception as anything else. But, I did pick up the same kind of chatter from several other parts of the country. Hell, I even got something in Spanish. Not sure what they were talking about, but I heard 'Coopertistas' several times and the tone seemed excited and positive toward it," Julianne finished and sipped water from her cup.

"Anyone have any other questions?" Cooper asked.

"Just one," Freddie said, his face taught with tension.

"And?"

"Well, this has been killing me," he wrung his hands together in a show of consternation.

"Spit it out," Julianne said in frustration at the delay.

"How *are* the Kardashians doing?"

The room exploded once again. Calvin slapped him on the shoulder as he guffawed. Cooper shook his head in amusement. When it had subsided, Cooper led them in a brief discussion about needed tasks and dividing up the responsibilities to cover the next few days.

*

*   *

Cooper slept deeply that night. He had a confused tumble of dreams visit him, but none forced him awake. In the morning he could only recall scattered images. He had been with Julianne on a forest floor. Dappled light from between the thick canopy shined off of sweat-soaked bodies. Somehow, they had lain together on a lush mattress, surrounded by wildflowers and sapling trees. After that, he was suddenly alone, lying on a hammock, and Elena approached. She stood over him, looking at him for what seemed like an eternity. She never said a word, but her eyes pierced him like a sunbeam through the gray Oregon sky. Guilt-ridden, he had started to speak shakily to her, but she was suddenly gone. The last dream he remembered was a terror-stricken sequence of being back in the Lincoln street home. Inside with Jake, bullets were ripping through the house and bombs were exploding outside. Amid bullets whizzing by his head and splintered wood raining down upon him, he was in perpetual motion trying to cover Jake's body with his own, but Jake kept dodging the cover. Jake's body was repeatedly hit by bullets and wood fragments. Jake didn't die in the dream, but instead was constantly screaming out in pain. His heart was lodged in his throat as he watched his son's body exposed again and again to the deadly fury that raged around them.

He sat on the edge of the cot, awake before anyone else, rubbing his forehead as he reviewed the confused tumult slideshow of dream fragments from the night before. He checked his watch; it was shortly after six. That meant Angela was on guard duty. He stood up, stretched, and ventured outside.

*

* *

Angela was crouching, rifle in hand, leaning against the cabin's wall. She rose up slowly as he closed the door behind him.

He spoke quietly. "Good morning."

She nodded at him with a half-smile and motioned for him to follow as she began walking away from the cabin. "Mornin'."

He fell in step next to her. "How was your shift?" he asked.

"Boring, with a capital B. How'd you sleep?"

"Really good. Best I have in a while."

Her face tightened and accusatory eyes beset him. "I bet."

He looked at her quizzically. "What's that supposed to mean?"

She gave him a look of disbelief. "C'mon Cooper. You know it's a small house we were in yesterday. A *very* small house."

The bottom fell out of his stomach and a reply got stuck in his throat. They walked in silence for several steps. She stopped, took his arm, and pulled him so he had to look at her directly.

"You know she's bad news."

"It's complicated," he offered, weakly.

An exasperated look of disbelief consumed her as she shook her head at him. "Well, Cooper. Say what you want. But, despite how good it might feel to be *with* her, how can you forget that she *killed* your wife?" She spat the last words from her mouth like they were poison. Her eyes implored him.

Her words pierced him and the world fell away from him. His body nearly shook as he contemplated the conflict she was forcing him to confront. His hands found her arms and he gripped her violently. "I don't know." Her face turned to one of disdain and she worked to free herself from his grasp. He held on. "Please," he pleaded.

"Please, what?" She looked at him incredulously.

"Give me time," he begged.

Fury gripped her now. "Time for what? So, you can screw her again?"

"That's *not* what I meant."

"So what *do* you mean?"

"Angela, just give me time to figure it out."

She had succeeded in shaking free from his clutch. "Figure what out?"

He looked to the ground. "To figure out what the hell I'm doing."

44

She exhaled deeply, and her eyes softened. "I can't promise you that."

He nodded. "I understand."

"I hope you figure it out, Cooper. I really do. If not for your sake, then for your son's. She isn't what *either* of you need." The pain in her words hit him hard in his chest. She turned away from him and took several steps before turning back toward him. "Can I ask you one question?"

"Sure."

"Why do so many really good men do so many stupid ass things?"

She didn't wait for an answer, but turned and strode away, leaving him wordless and ashamed.

*
* *

Later that morning, he was sitting vigil with Dranko, when his friend awoke. His eyelids were heavy and his face was drawn, but the fever was ebbing like a low tide.

"How are you, brother?"

"Other than feeling like a sick skunk crawled up inside me and died... two weeks ago... I'm doing quite chipper." The corners of his mouth upturned as he spoke.

Cooper smiled at him. "Well, if anyone can wrestle a skunk on their insides and squirt that carcass out of him on the flipside, it's you."

Dranko's mouth formed a proper smile at that.

"You're on the mend, aren't you?"

"Despite your clumsy and misguided efforts, I think that's right," Dranko answered.

"It's good to see that spunky spirit of yours coming back."

"Well, I thought about dying. I really did. But, then I thought what a god-awful mess of this world you'd make without me around, so I fought through."

Cooper laughed and smiled at his dear friend. "Glad you did, my friend. Glad you did."

Dranko started to offer another retort, but his words caught in a dry throat. "So, what's the news?" he croaked.

Cooper filled him in, answered his questions, and briefed him on his plan to go after the governor. Dranko's ears perked up on the last part and he made Cooper promise that he'd wait for him to heal before moving forward on that plan. Cooper made that promise easily. *As if I'd want to do something that risky without his best combat hand ready to go.*

"I think you need to make another public statement before you move the plan, though," Dranko said when he had finished.

"What do you mean?"

"I mean, get it out on the ham radio that you are going to issue a statement on such and such a day and time. Let that spread through the airwaves. Gather your audience. Then, bring them up to speed on what you know now."

"Why?"

"Well, two things." He paused to drink some more water. "First, you don't want your next communication to be after the plan is in motion. Talking to people again will build more trust and get your supporters fired up. Probably gain more people on your side."

Cooper nodded. "Okay. Makes sense. What's number two?"

"You should slant your statement to indicate you are launching a propaganda war. Get the governor to use his time thinking about how to counter you on that. It just might confuse them and take their focus on what you *really* intend to do."

Cooper rubbed his chin, thinking. "I actually have a better idea."

"What's that?"

"I think I'll use it to foreshadow a direct attack on him. That will do more to divert them from what I really want to do."

Dranko smiled. "Alright now, that's my boy. Very good idea. Just one thing."

"Yeah?"

"Given my current infirm condition, you aren't going to go around and brag about you having a better idea than me, right?"

"No. I don't need this one to brag about."

Dranko looked confused. "What do you mean?" The words had barely left his lips when he realized he'd walked into a trap.

"Our history book together is littered with a litany of times I had a better idea than you did!"

"What?" Dranko rasped loudly.

"I'll go and write you up the list. Should have it to you in a couple years, it is so long," Cooper said as he stood up and walked away.

"I thought you never lied, Cooper... Cooper," Dranko playfully and loudly called after him.

*

* *

That afternoon, he was on guard duty with Jake. They alternated between walking the perimeter, surveying the drive that led from the road to the cabin, and standing around. There was always a *lot* of standing around when it came to guard duty.

Two hours into the monotonous shift, Cooper decided to dive into the topic that had been plaguing him since the other day.

"Son, how are you feeling about what you did?"

Jake looked up at him vacantly. "What do you mean?"

His son's words sent a shock of adrenaline through him like a rocket. Cooper became acutely aware of everything around him, much like how his senses activated during combat. A light breeze rustled the trees above them. The flutter of three dragonflies called to him from near his feet. The smell of pine was thick in the air and his nostrils drank it in. His skin chilled and goosebumps sprang up across his arms.

Jake must have caught his agitated look because he continued. "Oh, you mean the shootings, right? I thought we already talked about that?"

Cooper lost a brief battle to keep the irritation out of his voice. "But, how do you feel *now* about what you did?"

"No different," Jake said, shrugging his shoulders.

Cooper grabbed him and shook him by the shoulders. "What the hell do you mean? Do you have no heart, boy? What is wrong with you?" His words were nearly suppressed by the rage that was coursing through his body like lava down a mountainside.

Jake's eyes flew wide open. They stood, staring at one another, their eyes locked. Cooper felt as if Jake was looking right through him. Then, Jake began shaking violently. Cooper grew scared as he tried to hold him tight but the shaking continued. *Is he going to have a seizure?* Panic gripped him. He slapped Jake hard across the face, out of desperation. This made Jake refocus on Cooper's face. Their eyes caught once more, then Jake's fell as tears tumbled down his cheeks.

Words fled his mouth in between deep sobbing, as Cooper hugged him tight. "What do you want from me... the blood, the blood... I can't get it off... I smell it... I taste it... I had no choice... did I... did I...did I... I hate this world... and what I've done." His tears quickly soaked Cooper's shirt and his heart ached for his son. Jake fell silent and then his breathing slowed. Calm returned almost as fast as the chaos had arrived.

He pulled his son back so that he could look him in the eye. "That's good, son. You gotta talk about what's going on inside, okay?"

Jake nodded. "I guess so. But, there's things I have do in this world to survive."

Cooper patted his back while he nodded. "That's true. But, killing should never become easy. It should truly be a means to survive, used when absolutely necessary." He stopped himself, realizing the enormity of what he was telling an eleven-year-old. He breathed deep before proceeding. "I don't know, either, son. I just don't want this world to take away your heart... your soul."

Jake looked up at him again with plaintive eyes. "But, I don't *want* to feel... anything."

Cooper's heart fell. *What could he say to that?* His mind spun, searching for

47

the right words. He exhaled loudly, buying himself time. Finally, something sparked inside him. He collected his thoughts before continuing. "That's a choice you'll have to make, son. At some point in his life, every man must make that choice. You're just being forced to make it earlier."

Jake looked at him, confused. "What do you mean, choice?"

"To keep feeling things when you've been hurt real bad or to let hate or anger or indifference take away the pain. It's really the choice between staying alive inside, or letting yourself die in there." He poked his finger against Jake's chest to emphasize the point.

Jake looked down and a long silence hung in the air between them. Finally, he looked back at his father. Cooper saw icy cold confusion. "I don't know if I can do that."

"Can you try?"

Jake shrugged his shoulders and his response was unconvincing. "Sure."

Cooper released his grip in defeat. He knew this was the best he was going to get. "Alright, son. I will just check in with you from time to time."

Jake nodded and they resumed their patrolling in silence. Cooper replayed the conversation in his mind as they walked. He was at a loss about what else to say to his son; suffering through traumatic events at a rapidity that made his head spin. He wanted to keep him shielded or at least whole. But, it slowly dawned on him that the events were reshaping Jake in ways he could not predict, nor control. Watching him vacillate between cold indifference, and dark depression, and deep sadness gnawed at Cooper's heart like a ravenous rat.

By the end of their guard shift, Cooper had resigned himself to picking up the pieces and the wreckage that this new world had given them as best as he could. He felt a bitterness toward a fate that revolted him, but that he was powerless to control, and the bitterness filled his mouth so fully that he had to spit several times. He kicked himself at his stupidity for not seeing all of this sooner. When he set his rifle down inside the small cabin, he had a firm resolve never to touch Julianne again. *I was a damn fool before. She's cost my family too much. I must not let myself go there ever, ever again.*

CHAPTER FIVE

The days blurred into themselves. He adroitly avoided Julianne and Angela. Of course, it was impossible to entirely evade them in such a small cabin, but he was able to prevent himself from being alone with either of them for more than a few moments. Neither woman pressed the issue with him, although Julianne tried flirtation and covert touches a few times before finally giving up.

Dranko continued healing as the antibiotics did their work. Soon, he was up walking and talking, albeit slowly. Angela marveled at his quick healing. They found a mostly intact game of Monopoly and played it to death. Most games included multiple rounds of gut-wrenching laughter. Tension enabled the laughter to vastly outweigh the actual humor involved.

Going to bed one night, it struck Cooper that they'd been experiencing the most normalcy they'd had since the plague's outbreak. Earlier that day, he and Jake had rolled around the floor in a fit of laughter and Cooper marveled at seeing his son be a child once more. Lying in bed, he smiled to himself at the pleasant memory.

Cooper enjoyed these days. They spent one day hiking a few miles away from the hunting cabin and taking the time to practice shooting. Cooper wished he had more time, but by the day's end, Freddie, Calvin, and Jake were all better shots than when they had started. He left Julianne at the cabin to watch over Dranko while they hiked.

On another day, they successfully hunted some small game and one unfortunate doe. Cooper knew he'd never forget the triumphant look on Jake's face when he came back with two squirrels dangling from a string. He proudly showed his father how he had shot both in the head and, therefore, not wasting any meat. One shot, he exclaimed to his father, had been from twenty-five yards away! They spent the next day smoking and drying the meat, following Dranko's careful instruction.

The days continued, as they ate through their rations. Cooper grew apprehensive as the rations dwindled. He knew food would not be easy to come by back out in the world. But he managed to push the fears aside and focus instead on their exit plan. One day, he was doing just this when Julianne yelled out in excitement for him to join her.

"Get over here, Cooper!"

He rose from his seat. "Yeah, I'm coming," he lazily replied.

"Hurry!"

When he got to where she was, next to the ham radio, she turned up the volume on the tiny speaker as she yanked the headphone cord out of its jack so he could hear too.

"...eclaration proclaims the town of Lincoln City as a free truth zone

49

and officially proclaims itself a Cooperite town. Furthermore, the city council has passed a resolution calling upon the Federal Government to admit the truth of what happened with the Brushfire Plague."

"Do you believe this?" he whispered to her in the brief pause.

"I do. I heard last night that Arcada, California and Camas, Washington did much of the same thing."

The radio beckoned for their attention once more. "We have an unconfirmed report that there was a major clash between federal troops and Cooperites outside of Denver."

They looked at one another with confused expressions.

After a brief pause, another person broadcast on the same frequency. "That story is true. I'm in Arvada, Colorado, and my cousin was one of those wounded during the fighting."

The back and forth included more details about Denver and soon faded to a discussion about what foodstuffs they each had on hand and how they were going about procuring more food. Cooper's mind was spinning as he clumsily sat back in the chair and looked up at Julianne.

"I guess this is good, people declaring themselves to be Cooperite towns."

She nodded enthusiastically. "I know! I heard something like that about Boulder, Colorado a few hours ago. But, I didn't think it was true. Now I do!"

"Well, it's a damn fine thing," Cooper responded.

"It's even better than that," Dranko called to them from across the room.

"What's that?" Cooper asked.

"Didn't you hear yourself? You said Camas, didn't you?"

The light went off in Cooper's head. "Oh, yes. Yes I did!"

"Your fiendish plan just got a helping hand, didn't it?"

The trio exchanged smiles and Julianne spoke first. "It sure did!"

"I just have one more question for you," Dranko said.

"What's that?"

"Do I get a t-shirt?"

Cooper looked at him, puzzled. "A t-shirt?"

"You know? 'My friend got elected president of the Altered States of America and all I got was this lousy t-shirt'?" Devilish delight glinted in Dranko's eyes.

"Oh, that? Sure. I'll give you your t-shirt as long as you jam it up the proper place!"

"Ouch! That's your gratitude to this wounded man over here who saved your bacon not even two weeks ago?"

Cooper began walking toward where Dranko lay. "I'm sorry. You're right. I'll come give you a big hug instead."

"Oh, no you won't! Nurse! Nurse," he shouted as he threw a pillow at Cooper. Cooper knocked it aside, laughing. Instead of delivering a crushing hug to his healing friend, Cooper patted him on the shoulder and turned serious.

"How are you feeling, brother?"

"Pretty good. I should be ready to move in another few days. Everything is feeling real good. Just sore."

"Alright, I'm gonna get us ready to move out the day after tomorrow. I really want to make our move on Camas."

"Me too. You know what keeps me going some days?"

"My good looks?"

Julianne laughed from across the room.

Cooper shook his head. "No. Sorry to ruin your self-image." He clenched his fists and his voice turned cold. "Nah, it's the thought of watching that man beg for mercy and knowing he won't find an ounce of it."

Dranko's face tightened and he nodded to his friend. "For Elena," he said as he grabbed Cooper's hand.

"And a billion other souls," Cooper answered.

Out of the corner of his eye, he saw Julianne slip from her seat and leave the cabin. The door made a hollow sound as it shut behind her.

*
* *

The relatively quiet and happy interlude was interrupted again a few days later when Freddie and Calvin returned from a scouting run down to Estacada. Cooper was fashioning what passed for dinner when they drove up the driveway. As they piled out of the Cherokee, he could tell that the news was not good. He wiped his hands clean on a hand towel and brushed it across his mouth and left the cabin to meet them out front.

His raised eyebrows asked for the report.

Calvin's eyes were downcast and he shook his head from side to side. "It was a mess down there, Cooper. A god-awful mess. I have..." the words caught in his throat and his hand went to his mouth to cover it.

Freddie picked up where Calvin left off, red and swollen eyes from crying meeting up with Cooper's. "Estacada is just *gone* man. Gone!" Freddie virtually shrieked. The others had gathered round.

Cooper put his hand on his shoulder. "Slow down. Just walk us through it. What's going on down there?"

Calvin took a deep breath and then continued. "Where do I start?" He paused for a moment, collecting his thoughts. "First, you have bodies all over the place..."

"Kids, too," Freddie said, disgusted.

Calvin looked at him for a moment before starting again. "Second, the place has been looted to the bone. Third, half or more of the little downtown has been burned to the ground."

Cooper and the others took a moment to let the news sink in.

"There is one bit of good news," Calvin offered.

"What's that?" Dranko asked.

"The fighting seems to be over. The fires are all burned out. No one was around the town at all, really, except for a few desolate souls wandering around aimlessly. I think the Civil War ended in a stalemate."

"The fighting for control could have moved onto a street by street or even house by house battle," Dranko offered.

"Ever the optimist, this one," Cooper maligned, pointing a hooked thumb in Dranko's direction. Dranko simply grunted in response.

Calvin shrugged. "Sure, I guess so. It just did not have that *feel* to it."

"What do you think, Freddie?" Angela posed the question to him.

He shrugged nonchalantly. "I dunno. I mostly agree with Calvin... I think it's over. But, I don't know much." Freddie fell to one knee, eliciting puzzled looks from the others. Angela's face contorted with confusion when he grabbed her hand and broke out into song. "But, I know how to love you!"

Angela threw his hand down in mock disgust. Laughter besieged the others. Freddie fell over onto the ground, his sides rocking. Cooper laughed, then waited patiently for the others to regain their composure. Freddie was the last to quiet down and then he stood back up, dusting the dirt from his knees and butt.

"Damn, I needed that," he said, wiping the happy tears from his cheeks.

"I guess you did," Cooper responded. "Anything else you all saw down there?"

"Oh yeah, we forgot the posters," Freddie exclaimed.

Cooper's ears perked up. "Posters?"

Calvin's face became serious. "Yes. Posters of you. All over town, or what's left standing in it."

Cooper nodded, not that surprised.

"Tell him the funny part, Calvin. Tell him," Freddie said excitedly.

Calvin shot Freddie an annoyed look. "I think he is talking about the contact information."

Calvin began fishing in his pocket. "It is not a phone number. It is a radio frequency." The flyer emerged from his pocket and he handed it to Cooper. "Freddie just thought it was the funniest thing in the world." Calvin winked at Freddie as he finished.

"Damn, this one has a photo on it," Cooper howled, holding it up for others to see.

"What? They used your DMV photo," Angela said after looking at it.

"Looks like it," he responded. "Good thing my hair has grown out and I have more stubble than before." His hand rubbed the thin beard that had sprung up recently.

"Well, that's a new twist... and significant," Dranko said, after reading the flyer in detail.

"What?" Calvin asked.

"The reward isn't stated in U.S. dollars. It says you get two *pounds* of gold if you turn this flea-bitten ragdoll of a man in to the proper authorities."

Freddie whistled. *"Two pounds?"*

"I know. I would have put him at two *pinches* of gold dust. Maximum," Dranko said playfully.

"Oh, I would have done two *ounces*. I mean, you have seen him in his jeans, right?" Julianne tried to join in, but the air left the room at her attempted joke. Cooper winced. *Does everyone know what happened between us?* He instantly knew the answer: *most likely.*

Cooper coughed to clear his throat—and the room—of its heaviness. "Dranko, tell us what it means."

"It means the State of Oregon thought it better to offer a reward in gold than in U.S. dollars. That says a lot about the likely very short-lived future of the almighty dollar."

Nods followed his words around the room.

"I think we move out tomorrow," Cooper declared after a few moments of silence.

"Why?" Angela asked.

"I don't like the vacuum of power down in Estacada. Someone is going to fill it. Or something called chaos will. Either way, that's not a good thing. Better we move before that happens. Even without that, Dranko is ready to move and I need to settle things with this governor."

The others indicated that they understood. Cooper's stomach tightened when he thought about moving into an unknown area where they lacked a friendly face. And, one where they would be thrust into a dangerous mission once more. He was able to bend the tension to burning rage as he thought about bringing the governor some small measure of justice.

They spent an hour discussing the details of packing up and getting to Camas. There was a spirited, but very brief, debate about heading back to Dranko's cabin to get more supplies.

"The supplies won't be there, or they'll be poisoned or bugged or wrecked if they are," Dranko declared. "And, they will probably be watching the place. It's crazy."

"That's exactly it. It's so crazy that they will never think we'd do it. It's worth a look to see what they left behind," Freddie said.

"That only works in the movies, son," Dranko replied and that ended the conversation. Freddie's regular smile disappeared into a frown, but he nodded at Dranko after a moment.

After the meeting, Dranko pulled Cooper aside. "I think we can do some good on the ham before we head out."

Cooper just grinned at him. "Can I tell you my idea before you go?"

Dranko smirked. "Sure, boss."

"I think we use the frequency on the flyer to announce a meeting of Cooperites at the wrecked marketplace for tomorrow afternoon. You know, we can be blasting it on other frequencies and make sure we do enough there so that they get it. That will give them something else to think about as we scoot out of town in the morning."

Dranko nodded. "I like it. *And*, it will work well with *my* idea." His grin had turned impish.

"And, what is *that*, oh wise one?"

"Just before we leave here, we call into that ham radio frequency and shout out all about how I just saw you heading up the road that just happens to lead up to my old cabin."

Cooper scratched his head. "I think it's too obvious. Give me a second." He held up a finger to keep Dranko at bay as he thought. Suddenly, he snapped his fingers. "I got it!"

"What?"

"Same idea, with a tweak. You call in and you say you saw the black guy who hangs out with Cooper and a Cherokee full of guys heading up *that* road. I think that sells better."

Dranko's grin widened. "I like it. Worst case, it gives them one thing to think about as we are getting out of town."

"True," Cooper said as his face slowly fell. "But, we should be ready to shoot our way out, in any case."

Dranko nodded grimly.

*

* *

Dull, gray light greeted them the next day. The mornings were becoming warmer as spring settled in. The brisk scent of pine was stiff upon the gentle breeze. It didn't take them long to load up the vehicles with their possessions.

Julianne came up to Cooper and Dranko. "I think I have the solution to what you both were talking about last night." Her eyes sparkled.

Dranko shook his head in confusion. "What are you talking about?"

Cooper put his hand on his friend's chest to stop the exchange. "I think she's talking about where we can set up camp in Camas—since we don't know anyone there."

Julianne nodded and Cooper motioned with his hand for her to continue.

"I was thinking about it last night. You said we needed a place that was only temporary but where we wouldn't be bothered, right?" She paused while she waited for them to agree.

"Okay. I think we should check out the marina." She stopped again as they both screwed up in their faces. She held up a finger. "Here's my thinking. Anyone who was living on a boat would probably either have set sail for somewhere else or moved into some regular housing that has... umm... become available. I lived on a boat while in school in the Bay Area and they are not good long-term, especially now."

Cooper scratched his chin. "Hmmm, that's interesting. Makes sense. What about people moving in and out to fish? I think there will be a lot more of that right now."

Dranko spoke first. "That's a good point. But, usually the permanently moored boats are in a different part of the marina than the rest. I think with that, and a permanent watch set up, it wouldn't be easy for someone to get at us without us seeing it coming."

Cooper smiled at Julianne. "Alright, we'll check it out first when we get into Camas. Seems better than the other options we had thought of. Neighborhoods will be hard to get into in our short timeframe. Industrial parks and businesses are too likely to have to deal with would-be looters or scavengers. Thanks for the good idea, Julianne."

She grinned at him and went back to getting her gear into the vehicles.

*
* *

Thankfully, Dranko had paper maps of both Oregon and Washington. More importantly, he had maps of the Portland, Oregon and Vancouver, Washington metro areas—which on the Washington side included Camas. When asked by Cooper about it, his response was priceless.

"Yes, the whole world *used* to use GPS on their cellphones to get around. That is precisely why paper maps went into my preparations. I knew the grid wouldn't always remain up and that a map is invaluable for a million reasons."

Cooper replied. "I'd never thought of that, but I see your point. In the GPS-less world, the man with a map would be king."

Dranko simply nodded in response, but his broad smile belied his pride.

The drivers of the three vehicles clustered around the hood of the Cherokee as Dranko reviewed the route with everyone. He laid out primary, secondary, and tertiary routes for the trip. Cooper would lead, but Calvin and Angela were taking copious notes, in case they all were separated. They reviewed rally points and timelines and protocols to deal with stoppages or ambushes along the way. In the middle of the tense exchange of information, Freddie broke in.

"I guess Sunday drives are a bit more complicated than a picnic basket and a tank of gas these days, eh?" That elicited a round of smiles from everyone, but no more.

While Dranko sent out the planned messages over the ham radio, the others heeded nature's call one last time. When he had finished, Dranko called for everyone to help him load the equipment, but the smile on his face was as wide as the Rio Grande.

"Boy, that was fun!"

Cooper thumped him on the shoulder. "Yeah, brother. I can see that! Do I have to start calling you Agent 007 now?"

Dranko gave him the middle finger and a steely-eyed look in response.

The trio of vehicles left a cloud of dust swirling around the cabin as they drove away.

*
* *

Cooper's stomach was tight as they hit the roadway. He dreaded the possibility of confronting the governor's men who were undoubtedly looking for them. He feared that they would be outnumbered and outgunned if they had to fight them. His knuckles were white as he navigated the vehicle over the twisty roads heading west.

"You alright?" Julianne asked, leaning in from the backseat and motioning at his hands. In the close proximity, he caught her scent, and while he knew she could not be perfumed, her sweet smell lit his senses up nonetheless.

He nodded. "I'm okay. I'll just feel a lot better when we have Estacada firmly in our rearview mirror."

Her hand found his shoulder lightly. "Well, you are better than me. I want to be on the other side of the Columbia like nobody's business." She let out a soft chuckle.

Cooper grunted his agreement. "Yeah, I'm probably worried about..."

He was cut off by Calvin's voice, a few octaves higher than normal. "Cooper, we need cover now. I hear a chopper coming in from behind us!"

Cooper's heart jumped into his throat, as he scanned the road up ahead. Julianne jumped back into her seat while letting out a yelp. Seeing nothing that offered any protection, Cooper jammed the accelerator, hoping they could find something quick.

Dranko jabbed the mic on the radio. "Do you have eyes on the chopper?"

Calvin must have given the radio to Freddie, as it was his voice that responded. "No. But, it sounds like it's getting closer." Everyone in Cooper's vehicle could hear the near panic in Freddie's voice.

They rounded another bend in the road and Cooper spotted what they needed—a dirt driveway that led into the trees on their right—not more than fifty yards up the road. He slowed just enough to take a hard right, tires squealing on the asphalt and then sliding a bit in the gravel as he sped up the driveway. The other two vehicles made the maneuver successfully as well. The groups spilled from their vehicles and then gathered near the last one, Calvin's truck, to get off the road.

As soon as his feet hit the ground, Cooper had heard the "whoop-whoop" of a helicopter's rotors splitting the mountain air.

"Did they see you?" Cooper asked Calvin as soon as he saw him.

He shook his head. "I don't think so. I had Freddie looking backward—in the direction we heard them—and he never saw them." Freddie nodded emphatically.

"We should be shielded from view and be alright then," Cooper said, exhaling.

Dranko rubbed the stubble on his chin. "Not unless they have FLIR."

Everyone exchanged confused looks at that. Dranko grinned.

"It's equipment that can be used to see heat signatures—from people..."

"And vehicles, I bet, right?" Cooper finished.

Dranko nodded glumly.

They all looked skyward, into the tree cover above them, as the helicopter suddenly got louder—probably from cresting a ridge near them.

"We'll know soon enough if they have it," Dranko said, shouting a bit to be heard.

They all sat in stupefied silence, necks craned, as the noise grew louder and louder. Jake suddenly pointed just south of where they stood and Cooper's fists clenched—if Jake could see the chopper, it was possible they could see their parked vehicles—with or without FLIR. Their heads followed the arc of the helicopter as it flew almost directly over them. Sure enough, they could see bits and pieces of the helicopter between breaks in the trees as it roared overhead. Then, the din began to recede.

Dranko came up next to Cooper and spoke loudly into his ear. "If it turns around, it means they've seen us." He nodded at his friend, who was stating the obvious, and let it go—he was in no mood to joke.

As the noise from the helicopter slowly receded into the distance, the group exhaled loudly almost on cue.

"That was close," Angela intoned to a lot of nodding heads.

"Luck is on our side. Let's saddle up and get moving," Freddie said.

Cooper shook his head. "Not so fast. We nearly got caught with our pants down. We need a contingency plan if we see that chopper again."

"What do you suggest?"

"First things first. Did anyone get a good look at it?"

"I think it was an old Huey transport chopper, probably National Guard," Dranko replied.

"Did anyone see any machineguns or rockets on it?"

The others shook their heads before Dranko spoke again. "I'm not sure we can count that as definitive, though—the trees are pretty dense here."

Cooper rubbed his head. "I'm not sure we have a lot to plan with here. I think our Alpha plan will be to run into the trees, if we can. And, plan Beta is to shoot it out with them if we don't."

"What about a plan Charlie?" Angela asked.

"Sure. Shoot," he responded.

"If we can't get into cover, we use some bait to get them on the ground."

Cooper's face grew quizzical. "And?"

"We swap Julianne into my vehicle. If we can't get into cover, we pull over, put up our hood and do the damsels in distress thing."

"And, what about the other two?"

"They speed around the next bend to get out of sight. These roads are very curvy—so unless we get caught flat-footed out in the open, it should work. And, once that chopper is on the ground—you come back into the picture and we light the bastards up." The look on her face was triumphant.

Cooper smiled involuntarily—hers was so contagious. "It's risky, but probably better than just a full-on shoot-out, like plan Beta."

Dranko coughed to get their attention. "I like it, too. But, one change. A chopper is at its most vulnerable as it is coming into land. You two would be better off opening fire when it's about ten or twenty yards off the ground. The pilot will be focused on landing and whoever is inside can't fully deploy to fight like they can once they are on the ground."

The others nodded. "Now, can we go?" Freddie whined like a five-year-old deliberately, offering some comic relief before they loaded back into the vehicles and headed out.

Cooper slapped himself in the leg. "I can't believe I forgot this!"

"What?" Dranko asked.

Cooper keyed the mic on the radio. "Everyone, listen up. Make sure to drive with the windows down and keep an ear out for our little friend upstairs." Dranko gave him a knowing look of approval.

"Roger that," Angela replied.

"On it," Calvin came over the radio right after.

They backed out back onto the roadway and resumed their journey.

They made good time heading west on the patchwork of back roads that Dranko had mapped out. They had figured the main roads would be far too risky of a route given the arrival of the governor's men. Cooper was just beginning to think they might make it out of the area when he saw it, just after they had rounded a bend in the road. His stomach fell as his foot jammed the brakes.

"Damn it!"

Up ahead were three pick-ups. They were blocking the middle of the road, and the front truck had its hood up while a bevy of men were working on it. About a half dozen men were lazily scattered around the trucks in a loose guarding formation. Most of them wore camouflage of various patterns, while a few wore hunting garb. All were armed with a hodgepodge of military-style and hunting rifles. At least one man held a shotgun instead. Those men quickly fell into a skirmish line as soon as Cooper's screeching tires reached their ears. Only about thirty yards separated the two parties.

Cooper just looked at Dranko with exasperation. "You take the wheel. A shootout leaves half of us dead. I'm gonna go and talk to them. They shoot me, run like hell."

Dranko began to argue, but Cooper's look stopped him in his tracks. "Good luck," was all he said instead.

Cooper nearly ripped the door of its hinges as he flung it open and bounded out. He dropped his pistol onto the seat before walking briskly toward the other men and slowly putting his hands into the air.

He closed the gap quickly. A middle-aged man, gray hair at the temples, walked toward him, emerging from between the trucks. He was wiping grease from his hands with a dingy rag. *This must be a good sign,* Cooper allowed himself to hope.

"How goes it, friend?" the man called to him when they were about twenty yards apart.

"Going well. Making good time on this road today. We just want passage by."

They kept walking toward one another. "You can rest your hands at your side. But, no sudden movements," the man responded. Cooper let his hands fall, slowly.

"Thank you," Cooper said as the two men stopped near one another. The other man gave his hands one last rub with the rag and extended it to Cooper. He took the man's hand and they exchanged a firm shake. His eyes were gray, like steel. His face was weathered—undoubtedly a man who had made his living outside in the elements. He was decked out in camouflage from head to toe, but Cooper noticed that he had not rank, unit, or name attached to his clothing. More telling—there was no evidence—no discoloration or leftover stitching—to indicate it had ever been there. *Civilian*, Cooper thought to himself.

"No problem. You were asking about passing on by?"

"That's right."

"Well, that depends."

"On?"

"Can you help us fix a diesel engine?"

Cooper's grin grew wider than the Columbia Gorge. "Yeah, most likely. I did some of that over in Iraq."

The man looked pleasantly surprised, "Well, can you have a look for us?"

Cooper smiled at the man. "Sure can, but I'd like to move our vehicles to the other side of yours."

The man grinned back at him. "Is that so in case we were to put a bullet in your head after you finish working, your boys can take off for safety to wherever you are headed?"

"Something like that," Cooper fired back at him.

The man waved his approval. "Sure thing. My name's Red. Nice to meet you."

"CJ is what I go by," Cooper responded and the men shook hands once again.

As Cooper waved Dranko and the others forward, Red motioned for his men to move aside and allow their vehicles to pass by. Red began walking back to the broken down truck, while Cooper came alongside Dranko as he drove up and filled him in on what was happening.

"I'll come and help you and have the rest use the time to eat some food and keep us squared away on that," Dranko said after hearing the news. Cooper nodded his approval.

"Have them keep someone on guard and keep our people away from small talk," Cooper paused. He lowered his voice to a whisper, "I don't want someone giving away who I am or where we are going by mistake."

Now it was Dranko's turn to nod. He put the Cherokee back into gear and led the other vehicles about fifty yards past the convoy. Cooper followed in Red's footsteps and soon clambered up the side of the truck to look into the engine's compartment. Red filled him in on the problem and Cooper set to work on it.

He and Dranko worked on the engine for almost forty-five minutes. Both men were grease and sweat stained from their efforts. Dranko was tightening the last bolt back to the proper torque when the men heard a bone-chilling cry.

"You'll never guess who the hell is working on our truck!" One of Red's men was sprinting back toward the convoy. *Apparently my small talk prohibi-*

tion failed. Dranko and Cooper's eyes met and they exchanged a knowing look of *oh, damn.* Cooper figured the best course of action was to continue working, so he did. Out of the corner of his eye, he watched Red walk out from the truck toward the shouting man. The other man was excited as he talked to Red.

Cooper made an exaggerated display of wiping his hands with a red shop rag. "All done here. Fire it up," he called to a man standing next to the driver's side door of the truck.

"Just a minute," Red called from where he was standing. "There is something we need to talk about."

Cooper's stomach lurched as he hopped down from the truck's engine compartment. He forced a smile onto this face, while his mind played out different reactions to the various scenarios that could unfold.

"What's up?"

Red's face was flat when he responded. "It seems you have been hiding something from us. Something pretty damn important, too."

Cooper met the other man's eyes. "You could say that."

"Don't you think you should have been up front with us?" Red shot back.

"I don't see how relevant it was to fixing your diesel truck here," he responded evenly.

That's when a smile splayed across Red's face and the tension fled the moment liked a spooked rabbit. "I wouldn't have had someone as brave as Cooper Adams getting his damn hands dirty on my truck!" Red culminated the remarks by slapping him on the back. Cooper exhaled and a reluctant and sheepish grin emerged in relief.

"So, you're on our side in this whole thing?" Dranko asked.

Red nodded vigorously. "Hell, yeah. That's actually where we are going."

Cooper rubbed his chin. "What do you mean?"

"First, what the government had done in covering up this whole thing didn't sit well with a lot of us." Red paused and waved his arm to indicate the men all around them. "A lot of us knew the government was up to no good before this damn thing even started. The news we heard from you just showed how deep the corruption had run. Honestly, even deeper than I could ever have imagined!" He nearly shouted the last part and his hands jerked as he pointed emphatically at the ground.

"So, where are you headed, then?" Cooper brought him back to task.

"Yeah, sorry. I can get fired up. Anyway, we are heading down to Salem. A variety of groups are gathering down that way."

"Cooperites?" Dranko asked.

"Them too from what I've heard. But, I was talking about the groups that we belong to." Red said nothing more to identify them, and Cooper thought it was wisest to leave it be. "We need to hold those bastards accountable. The damn plague and now the Godforsaken Chinese? Enough is enough." Red planted his feet squarely and crossed his arms in defiance.

Cooper nodded. "That makes sense. Glad you are on the right side of this. We can use the support."

"You need anything?"

Cooper thought for a moment. "We are mostly good. We just need more firepower."

Red's face lit up. "What are you planning?"

"Hey, not to be a jerk here, but I think it's best for both of us if you don't know. You know, operational security."

Red's eyebrows shrugged. "Yeah, you are probably right. The good news is that what you need is what we have."

Dranko's face brightened. "Really? What do you have?"

"Well, these trucks weren't ours before all this started. But, several of these guys were in the Guard—and members of ours. When stuff began to get off kilter, they brought some goodies to the right side of the fight," Red explained. "So, the real question is: what do you need?"

Dranko's response was matter of fact. "Small arms firepower, explosives, and a good sniper rifle. In that order."

Red shrugged. "You satisfied with two out of three?"

Cooper laughed. "Probably! What's the two?"

"We could give you a SAW and a half-dozen claymore mines. But a sniper rifle is a no go."

"A squad automatic weapon would really make a difference and some claymores could definitely come in handy," Cooper replied, trying hard not to sound *too* excited. He extended his hand. "Thank you so much, Red."

Red took his hand and shook it firmly, meeting his eyes squarely. "No, thank *you*, Cooper. What you did was good for this country and took some big time balls to do it. We owe you." By the end, he had turned somber.

Cooper felt his face redden a bit. "I just did what anyone would do. The people deserve to know the truth."

Red chuckled loudly. "Most men would have sold their story to CNN for a million bucks or blown their own damn brains out. Mr. Adams, take some pride in what you've done."

"Well, thank you. You are very kind."

Dranko broke in, "I don't want to be rude, but we should get rolling."

Red nodded. He barked some orders to a few men standing by the rear truck. Within minutes, Dranko was cradling what appeared to be a brand new light machinegun.

"There's three thousand rounds for it," Red said, indicating several metal ammo boxes. "Belted." He pointed to another wooden crate. "And there are eight claymores. All I can spare."

The men shook hands one more time. "Thanks for everything, Red."

"No, thank you for standing up for what is right and also for fixing that engine of ours. I gave Dranko our ham radio sign and we have a plan to check in once per day. If you need anything, you just holler, okay?"

"Yes, I will do that. But, you might end up being damn sorry for extending the offer!"

Red joined the laugh. "I just might. But, you let me be the judge of that!"

Cooper stopped himself. "Hell, I can't believe I almost forgot. Have you seen a chopper today? We had one overfly us earlier."

He nodded gravely. "Yeah, it flew right over us about twenty minutes before you all showed up. We were ready to light that bad boy up—but it just cruised right over us. Didn't even give us a second look."

"We think they are looking for us. You might have just confirmed that," Dranko added.

"In that case, if we see it again, we will do our best to bring that bastard down," he responded.

"Thank you, Red."

With that, the men separated. It took Dranko and Cooper a few minutes to explain the new hardware to the group when they returned. As soon as they had answered everyone's questions, they got back into their vehicles and drove away.

CHAPTER SIX

As they drove, Dranko cradled and explored the machinegun the way a mother does with a newborn baby.

"You gonna name it?" Cooper asked him in jest.

"I was thinking of naming it Pima, in honor of my best friend."

Cooper played along, out of boredom more than anything else. "Pima? That's a unique name. What's it mean?"

"It's an acronym. Pain. In. My. Ass. PIMA."

He grimaced to mimic pain. "Ouch. That hurts."

"Sometimes, the truth hurts, brother. I don't make the rules, I just have to live by them." He flashed him a wry grin as he talked.

"I'm glad you finally figured that out. It will save us a lot of time from arguing and such when I tell you how damn ugly you are." Cooper chuckled in response to his own mocked pain.

"You know how big a deal this is, right?"

"It means we can kill people a lot faster, right?" The two men jerked their heads to look back when Jake joined the conversation. His emotionless tone simultaneously grated on Cooper's nerves *and* made his heart fall. He realized he hadn't gotten through to his son as successfully as he'd thought. *So much for our heart-to-heart,* Cooper thought mournfully.

"Well, that wasn't what *I* was thinking," Dranko replied.

"But, it's true, isn't it? That's what matters now in this world. That we can kill people better and faster than they can kill us." Jake's tone was planted firmly between sarcasm and deadening depression.

Cooper failed to contain his indignation and replied through clenched teeth. "Yes, son. The better we can defend ourselves, the better off we are. But, it also matters how we treat people and one another. It matters that we keep being brave enough to love in the midst of all this chaos. It matters that we hold onto our humanity, despite all the violence."

"Was it holding onto our humanity when we burned those bodies? Or, when we let those refugees wander the streets without offering shelter? Is that what you mean?" By the time he had finished, angry tears were running down his face and his voice was cracking with emotion.

That display made Cooper's anger fade away and instead he was crippled by his son's emotional swing and did not know what to do. He looked to Dranko for guidance, and Dranko only shrugged. The tires hummed on the asphalt and they drove in silence for several minutes.

Finally, Cooper broke the painful silence. "Jake, I know all of this is hard to deal with, but we have to at least do our best to hold onto the best parts of the old world, while we struggle to survive in the new. Does that make any kind of sense?"

From the backseat, Jake looked up at Cooper. He could feel the heaviness behind his son's gaze. It was reinforced when his son spoke. "Yeah, I guess." With that, he dropped his eyes once more.

Cooper was not convinced that his son agreed with him or even understood what he meant, but he resigned himself to let it lie for now. It was the best he could do in the moment.

The trees swept by them as they drove. He welcomed the smell of pine and evergreen trees that penetrated the Cherokee. As Dranko worked some lubricant into the machinegun, he noted the synthetic smell of it. Mostly, he was thankful they carried some serious firepower with them now. Next to him on the seat lay the belt of ammunition, which held hundreds of rounds. Without thinking, his hand drifted over and patted the coil of ammunition. As he did so, he realized that it offered strange comfort. Dranko chuckled when he saw the display of affection.

"I'd have done the same thing if I wasn't holding this beast, I have to…"

Cooper held up his hand suddenly, asking for silence. The two men heard it at the same time.

"Shit," Dranko shouted.

"Chopper!" Cooper called out.

Cooper scanned the road; a bend lay up just ahead, but there was nowhere to get their vehicles under cover. *Plan C it is.*

Dranko was already keying the mic on the walkie-talkies. "Everyone ready for Plan Charlie?"

"Affirmative," Julianne's voice came back.

"Roger, on it," Freddie responded from the vehicle he shared with Calvin.

Cooper gunned the accelerator. In the rearview mirror, he saw Angela pulling their vehicle to the side of the road while Calvin gunned his engine as well. The bend was about two hundred yards farther up the road. He noted that Angela was positioning the vehicle much closer to the bend, so just one hundred yards separated them. The roar from the helicopter's rotors was growing quickly. Dranko had hung his head outside the Cherokee and was scanning the sky.

"Go, go, go!" he shouted.

Cooper threw the Cherokee into a tight turn so that it faced back the way they had just come, but tucking themselves tightly into the side of the road and the cover offered by the trees. As soon as they had stopped, Dranko was shouting orders.

"Jake, grab me that rope back there," he barked, while pointing at a container in the cargo area.

"What are you going to do?" Cooper asked.

"You are going to tie me to the top of the Cherokee. It's the only effec-

65

tive way for me to use the machinegun when we attack."

Cooper looked at him with frustration. "Dranko, you are losing it. Didn't you see? Angela is only a hundred yards down the road. We need to get into the trees and engage from there."

"But, Calvin and Freddie..."

"They can lay down fire on the chopper. You and I can do effective aimed fire from here. If we can't, we ain't worth a damn."

Dranko nodded. "Grab that," he said to Jake, pointing at two of the metal boxes holding the belted ammo for the SAW.

Cooper grabbed his gear and jumped out of the Cherokee. "Grab your gear and follow me. Quickly!" Cooper called out to Calvin and Freddie, who had just pulled their truck in behind the Cherokee.

The group hustled themselves through the trees so that they could see Angela and Julianne. Cooper was pleased to see them playing the part well. The hood was up and Angela was underneath, pretending to fix something. Julianne was pacing around the vehicle with the walkie-talkie in hand. She appeared to be switching the channels and testing each one out. He noticed she had tied up her shirt, revealing some of her midriff, and adding more to her already striking figure. He saw that as she walked, she exaggerated the swing of her hips as well.

Just then, the helicopter swept over the tree line from behind them. Julianne waved excitedly to them and then kept working the walkie-talkie. Angela peered out from beneath the hood and waved them down. The helicopter began hovering behind them. Cooper saw the gunmen in the doorway, with rifles pointing down. He thanked God that he saw no machineguns mounted on either doorway.

He heard Dranko scramble to set up *his* machinegun into a position where he could retain cover, but angle the gun for effective fire onto the chopper. Jake was next to him and Dranko was showing him how to reload and feed the belted ammunition into the SAW. Cooper found himself a good tree to brace himself against.

"I've got the guy on the left," he informed the others. "Calvin and Freddie, your job is to lay as much firepower down on the chopper as possible. Keep their heads down. Keep the pilot dancing the lead and copper jig, alright?" The other men smirked at the strange reference, but nodded their understanding.

Julianne appeared to now be talking to the chopper via the walkie-talkie. *Damn, that was smart... and lucky,* Cooper thought.

The helicopter was carefully descending to land on the road. Julianne walked back toward the front of the truck. *Likely where they have their weapons stashed.* Sure enough, he noted how Angela's right hand was moving back into the engine compartment.

Cooper focused his sights on the man on the left side, who was hanging halfway out of the side gunner's door. The man was more relaxed than he should have been. His rifle was lazily trained on the women below. He wasn't really looking around, but instead focused on what was directly in front of them. His rifle was not even tucked tightly into his shoulder. Still lower, the helicopter came.

"Wait for my shot, then let them have it," Cooper commanded.

Cooper took a deep breath and released half of it. His sights were squarely on the man's chest. He slowly squeezed the trigger until the gun erupted, surprising him slightly in the way it should have when you were practicing good trigger control. He quickly recovered from the recoil, sighted in again on the man's chest, and then fired.

Cooper started when the buzz saw that was the machinegun to his right opened fire. It had a surreal sound and one he had not heard in a long time. He quickly surveyed the scene. The man he had fired upon had fallen from the chopper and now dangled from it, with the retaining harness holding him up. Sparks were alighting all across the plexi-glass window and the body of the chopper itself. Dranko had shredded the right side and he saw that man fall to the ground—the restraining harness was either unused or shot to pieces by the machinegun.

The chopper then bounced again off the ground, came up a few feet, and then settled onto the ground, with the rotors still whirling. A man exited from each side, firing rapidly as they did so. Their fully automatic fire did what it was supposed to as rounds peppered the windshield and into the engine compartment and forced Angela and Julianne to dive for cover on the opposite side of their vehicle. Cooper lost sight of the two men as they found cover on the opposite corner. They fired another burst of gunfire, shattering the remaining windows, before stopping to presumably reload.

Cooper was struck with an idea. "Stop firing, stop firing," he ordered the others. They complied after a moment's delay.

The pilot emerged with his hands up, staggering. He had clearly been hit and the man quickly collapsed to the ground.

"Throw your weapons down and we'll let you live," Cooper shouted to the men remaining behind the vehicle.

"How can we trust you?" one of them yelled back.

"You don't have much choice and if you delay, your pilot buddy is going to bleed out!"

Seconds passed as the two men likely discussed what to do.

"Okay, we're coming out, so don't shoot."

Their M4 rifles were placed on top of the roof and they saw raised hands. Cooper relaxed, but then was taken by surprise as the two men broke into a dead run down the hill and away from them.

"Let him go," he shouted before anyone did anything different.

Angela rushed to the side of the downed pilot and began attending to them. Dranko kept an eye on the retreating soldiers.

Cooper tossed his keys to Freddie. "Bring up the vehicles, will ya?" His words were directed at Calvin and Freddie. Turning to Jake, he continued. "You go with them, too."

Jake did not wait for an answer, but stepped out onto the shoulder of the road, his rifle pointed in the chopper's direction. Dranko fell in step to his right, the machinegun at the ready position. It was only now that Cooper smelled the acridness of the gunfire. The two men walked toward the truck.

"Everything alright?" he called to Julianne.

She held up her left arm. "I got dinged by some fragment of a ricochet, but I'll be alright. There was only a small amount of blood coming from just above her elbow."

"Let's go," Cooper said as he began jogging toward them. Dranko fell in line slightly behind, with his still-healing wounds and the machinegun's heavy weight slowing him down.

When they arrived, Angela was just sitting back on her haunches and shaking her head. "He's gone," she said. Given the noise, Cooper read her lips more than heard her.

Cooper and Dranko moved quickly past her to check on the other bodies lying around the helicopter. All were dead or near death. The overpowering noise was driving Cooper mad.

"You know how to turn one of these off?" he yelled into Dranko's ear.

Dranko just shook his head and shrugged his shoulders. Cooper walked over to the cockpit and peered inside, trying to make rhyme or reason out of the controls. He saw the switch but did not know if just shutting that off would work. While he stood there, he was surprised when a black hand reached in and worked a few different controls, causing the blades to slow down and the noise to diminish. He turned to see a smiling Calvin.

"You know how these work?"

Calvin nodded. "Yes."

"I didn't know!"

"Well, you never asked, did you?"

"Can you fly this?" Calvin just nodded convincingly. "When did you learn to fly helicopters?"

"It was a hobby of mine."

Cooper's jaw dropped in surprise. "I never would have guessed."

"I know it is shocking, but some black men have expensive hobbies, too," Calvin said seriously.

Cooper got red under the collar. "It's not that. I'm just surprised when *anyone* flies choppers as a hobby."

"But, you *are* a bit more surprised because I am black, right?"

Cooper thought for a moment. "Yeah, probably."

"Thanks for being honest. That is all I ask for. And, I hope, next time you will not be as surprised if you meet another brother who can fly."

Cooper nodded, understanding his point. "Can you see if this thing can still fly?"

Calvin nodded and began to walk around the chopper, checking for damage from the small arms fire.

Cooper walked back toward where the others were huddled, debriefing the firefight.

"…and then I got them on the horn and it was easy to talk them into helping us," Julianne finished.

The others were talking faster than normal, adrenaline still running the show.

"That was damn smart, Julianne," Cooper said. She smiled back at the compliment. "You all did a great job."

"What's next, boss?" Freddie asked.

"Well, Calvin is checking to see if the chopper is still operational. If it is, I think we might just have to launch Cooper Airways for the remainder of our journey."

Dranko reacted first. "What about our vehicles? We just leave them all behind?"

"I know it's hard, brother, but we could avoid all the potential problems and danger by just flying *over* all of it! And, what I've seen is that vehicles are pretty easy to come by these days. It's the *fuel* that is getting tricky."

Dranko nodded reluctantly. "But, we'd have to leave some of our supplies behind."

Cooper nodded. "I agree. But, I think we can carry enough of what we need. And, I think we can count on our supporters to provide us whatever else we might need. Oh, and don't you think having a chopper on the other side could be a huge asset?"

"Alright, you convinced me. I'll start prioritizing our supplies," Dranko said as he walked over to the Cherokee.

A few minutes later, Calvin walked up. "She will fly. Enough fuel to get us to Camas, but that is about all."

Cooper slapped him on the shoulder. "Ha! You can read my mind!"

Calvin looked at him flatly. "I do not think it took a rocket scientist on that one, my friend."

As Cooper continued to punch him on the back, he mustered a weak grin for Cooper's benefit. Cooper clapped his hands together. "Okay, let's load it up! See Dranko for what needs to go on board and let's get it done. Freddie, post up around that bend to keep an eye out. Julianne, can you do the same back that way? The rest of us will get it done."

Within twenty minutes, they were loaded up and sitting in the heavily loaded helicopter. Calvin sat behind the plexi-glass window, pockmarked by bullets, and worked the controls slowly and deliberately. Dranko was in the co-pilot seat, maps in hand.

Cooper watched Jake's excitement build as the helicopter slowly lifted off the ground. He broke into a giddy laugh when they started to move forward with growing speed. Cooper put his arm around his son, pulled him in close, and yelled into his ear so he could hear him. "Pretty awesome, huh?"

Jake nodded emphatically and gave him a big thumbs-up sign.

Cooper tussled his hair and smiled back. He reveled in his son being a boy, even if for a brief moment. Cooper recalled what his father used to say. *"Son, everything is short-lived in this life. Remember that the good stuff won't last forever. Cherish it. Remember that the bad stuff won't, either. Get through it."*

"I wonder if he meant stuff like the plague," Cooper muttered to himself at a level that was inaudible above the chopper's noise.

He pulled Jake in tight and reveled in the moment.

*
* *

As they gained altitude, Cooper's heart sank. Fires burned in every direction, stretching out to the horizon. These were not tranquil cook fires, although those also existed. What everyone noticed were the larger fires that decorated the landscape, each one telling some tale of a home or city block that had come to destruction through one means or another. What disturbed Cooper the most was seeing ones out in the country—a farm or an isolated homestead.

He leaned in to shout into Dranko's ear. "I would have thought the country would have been safer, away from the towns."

Dranko shook his head. "Nope. Wherever there are resources to be had, there will be someone trying to come and take them."

"But, I thought you survivalists were all about having your bunker on some farm out in the middle of nowhere."

Dranko looked at him reproachfully. "First of all, *none* of these are in the middle of nowhere. Second, most of us knew that farms would actually make a lucrative target and would be very tough to defend by yourself, and they'd get hit by people looking for food and such."

Cooper nodded. "I know *that*. I'd just thought they'd be a little safer than the cities."

Dranko shrugged. The two men went back to surveying the landscape beneath them. Everyone on board was bundling up as best they could, the chill air growing colder as the wind whipped through the helicopter.

As they came abreast of Portland, the devastation grew wider. They could see entire sections of the city were no more; they had been burned to the ground. They used Mount Tabor as a reference point and found that their neighborhood looked intact. It was too far away to tell if individual houses still stood, but they could see that the neighborhood itself remained.

Cooper leaned in. "Calvin, you think we should drop down onto our old hood and see how they are doing?"

Calvin looked back and flashed a smile, but then refocused on keeping the helicopter airborne.

"Dad, look!" Jake shouted at him, pointing toward the Willamette River.

Cooper almost did a double take, not believing his eyes. Large sections of the Hawthorne and Burnside bridges had fallen into the river. Seeing the river without two of its iconic bridges was so off putting; it was like looking at Mount Rushmore with one of the president's faces removed. Cooper thumped Calvin on the shoulder and pointed it out. In both cases, it was the middle section that had collapsed into the water below. Cooper guessed that explosives had done the work, given the neatness of the collapse and the placement.

"Who'd want to blow up the bridges?" Julianne asked him.

He shrugged his shoulders, also wondering the same question. He leaned in to yell into her ear over the din of the chopper's engine and wind noise. "Someone who doesn't like cars?"

Her face lit up with a broad smile and she punched him in the shoulder playfully. *Damn, she's beautiful as hell when she's smiling.* Cooper scrunched his face up and turned away to keep his mind from wandering down that alley.

Dranko leaned in. "Someone who wants to restrict people's movement. I'm guessing it's the military. Remember Major Cummings?" The others nodded.

"Probably him doing this to better protect downtown from people moving in from the east," Dranko finished. Soon, the wide expanse of the Columbia River loomed beneath them. Cooper had never seen it from this height, which made its size even more impressive. *I guess the rivers will always still roll, no matter what happens to us,* he ruminated. He couldn't help himself from pointing the obvious river out to Jake as they flew over it. He even shouted, "Look!" He knew it was completely unnecessary, but it was done before he had time to think about it.

Soon, Calvin set the helicopter down into the parking lot of a warehouse that lay between Camas and Vancouver. This confused Cooper. "What are we doing here?" he asked Calvin before the engine died.

Calvin held up a finger, signaling for Cooper to wait. He did so, very impatiently, as the noise died down enough to talk without yelling.

Dranko spoke first. "Calvin just saved our bacon."

"Whaddya mean?"

Calvin took a half step forward. "It is simple, really. There is no way we can land this helicopter and not attract a ton of attention."

71

"I'm kicking myself for not having thought of it! So, the plan is to hot-wire a cargo van here, load our supplies into that, and then drive down and find us a boat," Dranko said.

"What about the chopper?"

"We will camouflage it the best we can. It *is* almost out of fuel anyway," Calvin responded.

Cooper nodded as he clapped Calvin on the back. "Okay, good catch! And, good plan, let's get to work."

It did not take them long to find a large cargo truck with about a quarter tank of gas, and they had it running within minutes. Fortunately for them, the warehouse was for plumbing parts and so it had not yet attracted any attention.

Cooper directed Freddie, Angela, and Julianne to make a run through the warehouse for salvageable supplies. Meanwhile, Dranko and Calvin siphoned what fuel they could from the smattering of vehicles in the parking lot. He and the rest stayed guard. It started to drizzle and Cooper cinched up his coat to ward off the rain and the chill.

Twenty minutes later, the trio emerged from the warehouse with smiling faces.

"What did you get?"

Angela was beaming. "A lot, actually! We found three pretty good sized first aid kits, we emptied a vending machine full of snacks, and we found two handguns in people's desks." As she talked, she pointed out the wares that they had found and which had been loaded into backpacks.

"Great work! Jake's gonna love those M&M's!"

"Well, it was a great idea to scout the place for supplies, I'm not sure I would have thought to do so in a plumbing warehouse," Angela said.

Cooper nodded. "While it's true it's not a grocery distribution center, any place where people congregate is going to have useful supplies." Cooper inspected the two handguns. One was a semi-automatic and the other was a revolver. Both had only the ammunition they contained and no extra, but both were in excellent condition.

"That makes sense," Angela replied.

Calvin and Dranko approached. "Truck's gassed up. Almost full now."

"You mean like you are after a dinner of chili?"

The group groaned at Cooper's remark. Dranko seized on the momentary advantage. "See Cooper, you *are* losing it!" Cooper grinned, hung his head in mock hangdog fashion, and walked away from the group. Various playful catcalls followed him.

They had soon transferred the supplies from the helicopter to the cargo truck and covered the helicopter in some canvas sheets they had found inside. Standing back from it, Calvin unleashed his deep, bass-filled laugh. "Not very camouflaged is it?"

Cooper struck him on the back and joined in the laugh. "No, not very. But, at least it will be protected from the elements."

He turned to face him. "That is why I like you, Cooper. You always look on the bright side."

"Let's go," Cooper shouted to the group. Within minutes, they had piled into the cargo truck and were rumbling toward the marina.

"Even with the lousy food, horrible service, and those luggage fees, I have to say that I prefer flying," Freddie deadpanned after they hit one of many bumps as the truck lumbered down the highway. The others laughed and Jake flashed him a thumbs up.

*
* *

It was a short drive to the marina. Cooper left the driving and navigating to Calvin and Dranko. He was in the truck's cargo area with the others, huddled amidst their supplies and equipment. They stabilized themselves as best they could, but the lurches and bumps made it like trying to surf during a storm. By the time they stopped, several passengers had bumps and bruises to show for their efforts.

When they arrived at their destination, the cargo door came screeching open to reveal a smiling Calvin. "Good news! This place looks empty. We have not seen any evidence of movement or habitation," he said, offering a hand to Julianne as she exited.

"That's great," Angela said.

Cooper jumped down from the truck and lifted Jake to the ground. He turned to survey the Camas marina, which overlooked the Columbia River. Calvin handed him a pair of binoculars.

"Thanks," he muttered before taking them. He first scanned the area without their assistance. About half the slips were empty. The other half were mostly occupied with small, metal fishing boats and skiffs. He quickly noted several houseboats clustered to one side of the marina, which looked to be promising and just as they had predicted. None looked occupied. One houseboat was scarred by fire, with the heaviest damage near the engine. *Probably an engine fire caused by someone without a clue about what they were doing.* He brought the binoculars up and gave the marina a closer inspection. From what he could see, everything looked to be in order. He handed them back to Calvin.

"I think we found ourselves the perfect place to use temporarily," he announced to no one in particular.

"Shall we go and scout it out?" Calvin asked.

Cooper nodded and reached into the cargo area to grab his rifle. His other gear was already on. "Calvin and Angela, come with me. Dranko,

73

Freddie, and Julianne, keep an eye out up here. Okay?"

They had not taken five steps before a shotgun blast sent them clattering to the ground and coming up with their guns pointing toward the loud report, to their right and slightly behind them. Standing about thirty yards in that direction was an old man with a white beard, clad in dark blue overalls. The shotgun was cradled in his right arm and smoke from its barrel curled upward. *He must have fired that into the air,* Cooper thought.

"Whatcha all doin' here?" the man called to them, his voice thick with age and tobacco use.

Cooper slowly rose to his feet, keeping his hands away from his rifle, and letting the sling do its job. The others followed suit.

"Good afternoon, sir. We are just looking for a place to hole up for a few days," Cooper raised his voice enough for the man to hear him.

"And, do any of you folks own any of these boats here?"

"No, sir. But, we were hoping to use them. We can pay rent, if needed."

The man scratched his chin. "It's a good thing you didn't try and bullshit me. I got all the records up here 'n this office."

"Yes, sir. Wouldn't dream of trying to pull one over on you."

"Why don't you come on up here and we can talk this over, civ'lized like," he said as he lowered the shotgun and turned to walk back up to the office.

Cooper turned to the others, shrugged, and gave them a quizzical look. He secured his rifle onto his shoulder and began climbing the steps up to the office. When he reached it, the door was open and the man had sat himself down behind a large gray metal desk that was covered with papers and notebooks.

The old man stood up and extended his hand. "I'm Monty McCain. Pleased to meet you."

Cooper took his hand in a firm grip. "Cooper. Cooper Adams, likewise."

The man's eyes widened and Cooper immediately regretted using his real name. He had done it without thinking, the man's folksiness having lulled his wariness. The man fell back into the chair, which rolled backward a few feet before clattering into the wall behind him.

"Cooper? Cooper Adams? From Portland?"

Cooper's hand slowly drifted to his holstered pistol. "Ah, yes sir."

"Did you give another old coot a .45 pistol down there?" He paused, recollecting, "A few weeks back?"

Cooper cocked an eyebrow and smiled, his hand relaxed. "Yes, I did."

The old man clapped his hands together. "Well, ain't that some damnation!"

"You mind filling me in?"

74

He shook his head, rose back to his feet, and took Cooper's hand in both of his. "That man is my brother. He was through here not three days ago. He told me the story."

"Really?"

The old man nodded furiously, his white hair bobbing up and down. "Indeed, I am serious. Seems like you been the only decent fella he's found since this whole thing started."

"Well, your brother is a good man, Mr. McCain." Cooper's mind drifted back to when the outbreak began, and he'd met the old homeless man handing out bottled water and life wisdom.

Monty released Cooper's hand and waved his own about. "Please. Call me Monty. And, thank you for what you done for my brother."

"Where was your brother heading?"

Monty harrumphed loudly at that. "Who knows? He's been wanderin' for years now. It was just a damn fine thing to see him after all this damned mess."

Cooper rubbed his chin thoughtfully. "I would have liked to see him again. To thank him, really. He was a decent man even in the middle of this insanity."

Monty nodded with wistful eyes. "That he is. He was always the better of us." His gaze drifted out onto the river and Cooper allowed the man the time. After a few seconds, his eyes returned to the room and he looked again at Cooper. "So, what can I do for you all?"

"We just need to occupy one or two houseboats for a few days. We promise to leave things as good as we found them."

"Sure, that's not a problem. Let me just look around here for some keys," Monty said and he began rummaging through a desk drawer.

"I gotta ask you, sir. What are you doing *here*? It seems like everyone has abandoned this marina."

Monty looked up, with a twinkle in his eye. "Son, when you get as old as me you will understand. If I weren't comin' down here every day, doin' my job like I used ta, what would happen to an old timer like me? I'd shrivel up and die. That's the thing." With that, he returned to looking for the keys. Cooper nodded to himself, understanding exactly what the man meant, old age not required.

"Ah, here we go!" Like a man holding up a championship trophy, he held up a bright blue keychain with a floater on it. "I thought they had left me that key at some point!" Monty stood up once again and handed the key to Cooper. "It's the largest one down there. Let me know if it don't fit you all. Use it as long as you like. Just give me the key when you're done."

Cooper shook his hand. "Thank you. We appreciate it."

"Not a problem. I'm here every day from dawn till dusk. Usually fiddling my day away in this office. You let me know if you need anything."

"Sure thing, Monty. Thank you."

Cooper turned and left the office, marveling at how he could have been renting a patio boat on a summer's day, as normal as it all had seemed. He was left shaking his head at the odds that Monty was the old homeless man's brother from Portland. *My father always told me someone was looking out for me upstairs. Maybe he was right?*

*
* *

The houseboat that Monty had turned over to them fit them all just fine. It took them a bit of time to figure out all of the proper places to stash their supplies and equipment. Jake enjoyed discovering all of the boat's cubbyholes.

When they had finished, Cooper called them together on the foredeck. "Alright, I think we have a couple major next steps to get done. First, we need to make contact with the Cooperite organization here in Camas. Second, we need to secure some working vehicles and fuel for them as well," Cooper began.

Julianne raised a finger. "I can begin broadcasting over the short wave. It should be easy to make a connection point." Cooper dipped his head to acknowledge her.

"If Calvin and Freddie are in, I can get us a couple vehicles, no problem," Dranko added.

Cooper clapped his hands. "Perfect. Let's get to it."

The group moved to disperse, and as they did, Angela grabbed his arm. "Can I get a minute?"

He nodded. "Sure. Let's take a walk." He picked up his rifle before stepping onto the pier.

They walked together in silence to get some distance from everyone else. The sun was low on the horizon; it was about an hour before sunset. The sky was clear now, and the lazy, orange light made everything glow.

As they walked, Angela did not break stride when she caught his eye for a moment. "Can you tell me what's going on?" Her voice was heavy, emotion hiding underneath the surface.

Cooper paused before responding. He had expected this conversation and had played it out in his head several times. But, now that it was upon him, he still felt unprepared. "I don't know," was all that he could muster.

She exhaled in exasperation. She grabbed his hands, turned him toward her, and locked eyes. "Cooper, you gotta figure it out. I thought we had something going between us. The start of something. But, I'm not just gonna sit around waiting for you, either."

Cooper looked at her, silent, as tears welled up. Like blurred vision be-

76

ing slowly brought into focus, he watched her emotion turned toward anger. She looked away, shook her head once, and her voice grew sharp. "I don't get it. I mean I get how she's a beautiful woman and is probably a damn good lay. But, you aren't some nineteen-year-old kid." She paused and then looked right through him. "And, in *this* world, with *Jake* to think about, you need more than a pretty face and a piece of fine ass to be at your side, Cooper!"

The truth of her words stung. His eyes narrowed and he gripped her fingers tight in his hands. "Don't you think I *know* that? You don't think I'm very aware that this *thing* with her makes absolutely *zero* sense?" He paused, out of breath.

Her eyebrows raised up. "And?"

"And, I'm not the kind of guy to feed you some bullshit. I can't deny my feelings for her either. And, until I figure that out, I'm not gonna tell you things that aren't true. That would be wrong and dishonest. You get that?"

"Yeah, I get that." Angela's voice was heavy with disappointment. She looked at the ground for several seconds, dropped his hands, and then her eyes met his once more. He saw steady resolve in them. "I wish you the best, I really do. But, I need you to understand that I'm not waiting around for you either. You let me know when you figure it out. But, I'm not sitting still any longer. You get *that?*" Her words were serious, unthreatening, but steady.

He nodded. "Yeah, I get it. And, I have no right to anything else."

She held his gaze for one second longer, turned on her heels and strode back toward the boat. He watched her go, deep in thought. *The heart wants what the heart wants,* kept playing over and over in his head. As she stepped back onto the boat, he turned, spotted a bench and went over and sat on it. He leaned his rifle against it and ruminated. His thoughts ran the same circles that they had before. He knew he'd find no clarity, but kept thinking the situation over anyway. He had lost all track of time.

"You want some company?" Calvin asked, startling him out of his deliberations.

Cooper looked up. "Sure," he said as he patted the bench next to him.

Calvin sat, leaning his rifle against his side of the bench. "You figured it out yet?"

"What's that?"

Calvin let out a deep laugh. "Cooper, there are not any secrets in a group this small. You should know *that!*"

Cooper chuckled, mostly to himself. "Yeah. I should."

Calvin cocked his head to the side and put a hand on his shoulder. "You, sir, are grappling with one of man's oldest questions."

Cooper looked back at him. "What's that?"

"Fire and earth. Practicality versus passion. Should versus want." Calvin paused for a moment and his smile grew impish. "In short, do you want a woman who is going to make your bed or one that will mess *up* your bed?"

Cooper nodded slowly. "I guess that sums it up." He dropped his gaze to the ground. "And, what would you do?"

Calvin squeezed Cooper's shoulder and laughed heartily. "That does not matter. It is your life and not mine. I am just here to listen to a friend. "

Cooper looked back up at Calvin and nodded once again. "I'm not sure I want to really talk about it," he said.

"And, that is okay, too," Calvin responded.

The two men sat in silence as the minutes ticked by. They watched the sun set as the orange globe turned red and added a crimson glow all around them. When the sun began to wink out on the horizon, Cooper turned to Calvin. "You ever had a situation that you were sure was going to burn you, but that part of you was alright with getting burned?"

Calvin nodded. "Yes, I have. But, you know what I would say now?"

"What?"

"I would ask myself why that is." He paused for a moment, debating whether to proceed and then did. "Also, I would be more careful about getting burned when the world all around me is already on fire and my son was smoldering."

The truth of his words burned and Cooper held Calvin's eyes. "But…"

Calvin waved him off. "Now is not the time to argue, Cooper. Just think. At the end of the day, only you know what you can live with." He squeezed his shoulder one more time, stood up, grabbed his rifle, and walked away from him. "I got first watch," he called over his shoulder.

Cooper leaned back on the bench, splayed his feet out, and let out a loud breath. His mind was reeling, which he hoped was a good thing. He watched the light fade and darkness crawl across the river until it enveloped him. He noted, with some pride, that they had kept light discipline on the houseboat. He knew lights had to be on inside, but he could not see anything from where he sat. The boat was nothing more than a dark silhouette on the water. Calvin walked up the pier to stand guard over the only approach to the houseboat. *Absent a frogman approach out of the water, we should be alright,* Cooper chuckled to himself.

"And, if the Navy SEALS are coming after us, we are in trouble, anyway," he muttered out loud. He heard footsteps approaching from the boat.

"You out here somewhere, Cooper?" Dranko called out.

"I'm over here." He heard Dranko pause for a moment before reorienting himself and striding over to him.

"You want some company?"

"Not really."

"Good. Neither do I. I just wanted a place to drink this." He held out a bottle of whiskey and jiggled its contents. He had two small cups in his

78

other hand. Cooper smiled at him and reached out for one. Dranko passed him a cup and filled it. He sat down on the bench and did the same for himself. He held his glass aloft. "To women!"

Cooper shot him a chagrined smile and muttered. "To women." He took a swig and welcomed the warm burn as it made its way down his throat and settled in his belly. They sat in silence, drinking. Cooper could almost imagine that they were in one of their backyards before all this.

As they were midway through round three, Dranko piped up. He gestured wildly with his drink. "You know what the prudent and prepared thing to do is, right?"

Cooper was a little lightheaded and laughed. "No, but I bet you are going to tell me."

He pointed at him with his glass. "That I am, brother. That I am. It's simple really. It's all about persavat... I mean, preservation of resources."

Cooper smiled to himself. "In English, please?"

Dranko thumped his shoulder. "Patience, my good man. Patience. Julianne is the wise choice."

Cooper looked at him with his mouth agape. "What?"

Dranko laughed at his expression. "You heard me. Did I stutter? No, I did not. Julianne is the prudent choice."

Cooper was still flabbergasted. "Really?"

Dranko was emphatic. "Yes, really. It's really very simple. You want to hear it?"

"Yes!"

Dranko stood up, adding drama to his pronouncement. "That way, Angela will end up with me. And then her skills stay in our group. And Julianne is so damned pretty we can trade her off at some really important moment and for some critical resources!" He fell out laughing when he finished.

Cooper feigned indignation. "Oh my lord, you are drunk!"

Dranko looked hurt. "Maybe, just a little."

"Three drinks?"

"It's been a awhile. And, I'm weak."

Cooper shook his head. "You had me going there. I thought you were being serious."

Dranko's eyes caught his in the near darkness, burning intently. "I was serious... about the first part." His voice was laden with an odd brew of pain and defiance. Then, Dranko walked off toward the houseboat, not saying another word. Cooper watched him go before leaning back.

"Oh, shit. This is *really* complicated," he said to himself. He was thankful he had a few drinks in him to dull his thinking. It was then that he noticed that Dranko had left the bottle behind. He fished it out from the corner of the bench, put it to his lips, and took a long pull. *I'm not going to think about this until tomorrow.* It wasn't until a few hours—and an empty bottle—later that he staggered back to the boat and found a spare place to lay down. Even in his stupor, he knew he'd be feeling it in the morning.

CHAPTER SEVEN

When he awoke the next morning, his mouth was sandpaper and his head was consumed by a dull ache. *I wonder why, of all possible nights, last night was the one I decided to tie one on?*

"Women," he muttered out loud. He rubbed his fingers hard against his temples to assuage the pain.

The others were already awake and the distant din of rattling metal and glass told him that breakfast was being prepared. *What I wouldn't give for a plate of eggs, pancakes, and bacon right now.* His mouth salivated at the thought. *No doubt, it's some mash of beans or rice.* He rose from the small bed and made his way toward the commotion. When he saw his FAL leaned up against the wall, he was grateful that he'd kept track of his firearm, even when drunk.

He exchanged paltry greetings with Freddie and Julianne and made his way straight to the pitcher filled with water. He drained two glasses in rapid succession, nearly inhaling the water. He wiped his sleeve across his mouth when he had finished. "Ahhh…"

Freddie chuckled at the display. "Rough night at the office?"

Cooper flashed him a crooked smile. "You might say that. Where's Dranko?"

Freddie rose, shoving a last mouthful of food into his mouth. "He just left. Calvin, too. I'm joining them at the top of the pier. You need something?"

He shook his head, "No. Just curious. Good luck out there and keep your eyes and ears open. Stay sharp."

Freddie nodded sincerely and then was out the door.

"How are you feeling, there, slugger?" It was Julianne, seated diagonally from where Cooper stood. He couldn't tell if the lilt in her voice was genuine affection and concern or if it was intended to be subtly seductive.

He turned to her, having poured himself a cup of what passed for a cup of coffee these days. "I'm alright."

"When I heard you come in, I almost came over to see if I could make you feel a little better." Her smile was dripping with charm.

Cooper could not help but crack the beginning of a grin. "And?"

"Oh, I just waited until you'd fallen asleep to do what I was thinking about." Julianne's eyes dropped to his pants as she finished. He frantically looked down and his free hand went to zip up an imaginary open fly. Julianne burst out laughing. "Oh, Cooper, you are so easy sometimes!"

He took a moment to recover, then looked up sheepishly. "You got me. That was good."

She stood up and crossed over to the water pitcher. As she brushed past him, her hand slipped under his shirt and her fingers snaked across his abdomen. "I'm *always* good," she breathed into his ear. Cooper was left astonished and briefly aroused as she stepped away to fill a glass of water. She drank it slowly as he watched in silence. When she'd finished, she turned to face him. Her demeanor and tone instantly transformed. "So, I made contact last night. We have a meet set up in a few hours, eleven a.m." The transition was jarring. It was as if they could have been standing in some corporate boardroom.

"Sounds good. Where? And, what's the set up?"

"I kept us in the driver's seat. We call them thirty minutes before the meet to tell *them* the location. I'm thinking the warehouse we were just at?" She looked at him for an answer and he nodded before she continued. "As to set-up, I told them just two people on each side. What I like about the warehouse is we can sweep it beforehand and keep an eye on the only road in, so you'll have backup."

Cooper furrowed his brow. "This seems like a lot of precaution for people who are supposed to be on our side. Are you worried about something?"

She laughed out loud. "I guess you're right! Maybe Dranko has rubbed off on me too much. But, I was also thinking better safe than sorry, right? What if someone was listening in? It's not like we have an encrypted line."

He nodded. "Yeah, that makes sense. Thanks… you did a good job."

She gave him a look with a twinkle in her eye and he wagged his finger at her to stop the commentary he'd opened himself up to. They both chuckled at the unsaid joke.

"I'm gonna go wake up Jake," Cooper said to cover his hasty retreat.

*
* *

Two hours later, he was assembled with Dranko, Angela, Julianne, Calvin, and Freddie. The vehicle team had come back with an extended cab pick-up, a midsized SUV, and an off-road motorcycle. Cooper briefed them on the time, location, and set-up for the meeting with the Cooperites in town.

"I think I should be your second in the meeting," Julianne said as soon as he had finished. Though she sat directly across from him, Cooper could feel the chill coming from Angela.

"Why?" he asked.

"It's obvious. I know the most about the guy we want to find and kidnap. I can convince them why we need to go after him, etcetera."

"But, if this goes south, you are the least helpful in an up close and personal firefight," Dranko cautioned.

"If this goes bad, I honestly don't think anything we do will matter, despite our best precautions. They could come in with thirty or forty guys."

"I think she's right," Angela said, stepping into the argument.

Cooper was surprised and impressed by her objectivity. "So do I," Cooper said. "Julianne is with me at the meet. I think everyone else is in the vehicles basically parked at the entrance to the warehouse."

"We're gonna need to tell the Cooperites that's what we're doing, right?" Julianne asked.

"Sure."

"Shouldn't we keep one ace in the hole? Like a sniper concealed somewhere? Or one or two people inside the warehouse?" Dranko asked.

Cooper nodded. "I like Angela on a bolt-action, concealed where she can keep watch on the entrance as well as where Julianne and I will be meeting with their guys. You good with that?" Their eyes met and she nodded. "Alright, Julianne, let's give these guys a ten minute head start and then radio in to the Cooperites the meet up location."

The others nodded and walked away to finalize their preparations.

*
* *

Cooper and Julianne stood outside in the cool air. He was in constant motion, burning off energy. He cinched up his coat's collar against the chill. His hand slid, unnecessarily, to the pistol on his hip to ensure it was still there. He stamped his feet to ward off the cold that was seeping in from the cement, through his boot, and into his feet. The FAL was slung across his back. He knew having it in the ready position would be too aggressive, but he didn't want to be without it—in case something went wrong with this meet up.

Julianne watched him fidget and her smile betrayed the humor she saw in it. "Like a cat on a hot tin roof," she said, her eyes lighting up in delight.

He grunted. "I *wish* it was hot out here. And, I wish they'd show up." He glanced at his watch. "Now they are fifteen minutes late. I don't like it."

She shrugged. "They'll be here. I trusted that voice on the other end."

He gave her an upturned eyebrow to show his skepticism. Just then, he heard the hum of tires on the road, approaching. He shot a furtive look toward where Angela was hidden, glad that he could not see her. Dranko had done an admirable job camouflaging her. He looked back to the road as a red Ford Bronco, followed by a gray Chevy Tahoe, pulled into the lot, stopping where the others were parked. He saw them exchange words from between open windows. Dranko pointed in their direction. A few moments later, two men got out of the front vehicle and began walking toward where Cooper and Julianne stood. They both had rifles in hand, but quickly slung them over their shoulders.

"See, I told you," Julianne said, poking him in the side.

"Good to see," Cooper agreed. *For now.*

The two men walked at a brisk pace and closed the gap between them quickly. As they approached, Cooper took stock of what he could see. The man on the left was dressed in red flannel and dun colored work pants. Wavy gray hair said he was in his late-forties or fifties. He had a friendly, round face, and was smiling broadly. The other man was in camouflage from head-to-toe and looked much younger. A full beard, once likely trimmed and hip, was now bushier and more haphazard. His head was shaved. He wore an angular, hard face, but was smiling just like his companion. Both men had pistols on their hips. The rifles slung across their backs were military-style weapons—an AR15 and an AK-47. *Well, maybe this group is well-armed, which would be very helpful.*

Once they were within shouting distance, the younger man waved and called out. "How do you do?"

Cooper raised his hand to greet them and elevated his voice. "Good. Well, good considering that one billion are dead."

The man on the left guffawed loudly, but the other man did not. Cooper saw them give him a final look over, and smiled inside as they lingered much longer on Julianne's shapely figure than they had on him. She had somehow managed to be dressed in clothing that was both functional and that played up her features well—wool yoga pants, snug wool sweater with an open down vest, and boots.

The younger man extended his hand. "Cooper Adams?"

Cooper took it and grasped it firmly. "'Fraid so."

"Jeff Daniels is the name. It's quite an honor, sir, to make your acquaintance." He turned to his companion. "May I present, Mr. Lewis Jenkins."

Cooper shook his hand as well. Both men had firm grips. Jeff's hand was a bit clammy, the type of sweat that normally comes from nerves.

He motioned to Julianne. "This is Julianne. She knows a lot about the people involved in the Brushfire Plague."

She eagerly shook his hand, but Jeff raised it to his mouth and kissed it. Cooper looked on in surprise. Jeff's strange speech pattern—and now this—marked him as an odd one.

He must have noticed Cooper's reaction. "You may note that I'm most peculiar in some fashions. I humbly ask for your patience and good graces." He dipped into a slight bow.

Lewis let out a loud laugh. "Yeah, Jeff's on the eccentric side, but he's smart as all get out and like old Clint Eastwood in 'Heartbreak Ridge,' he can put a round through a flea's ass at three hundred yards."

Jeff turned pink and smiled with embarrassment. "My compatriot is too

84

kind, I assure you."

Cooper looked amused. "Are you British? You talk a bit like that but you don't have an accent."

Jeff shook his head. "No, sir. But, my father was from England and I got my Master's degree in Victorian Lit. I do believe some of it rubbed off."

"And, where'd you learn to shoot?" Julianne asked.

"That? I've had the pleasure of participating in the sport of elk hunting with my father in eastern Oregon since I was a young lad. Out there, you cannot flatten your prey without being able to make the long shot." They nodded at him. "It is a full pleasure to meet you, Mr. Adams. I do believe you are the most courageous chap in America," Jeff said, sincerity and emotion shining through.

Cooper smiled politely. "I did what anyone else would do. But, I appreciate your kind words. And, I'm glad you have a group that possibly can help us."

Jeff became animated and rubbed his hands together. "There was not another thing to do, I'm afraid. With the government putting out so much drivel and rubbish, when it was so plain that you had put out such proven truth, I *had* to do something."

Lewis nodded. "Me too. It was such bullshit." He spat onto the ground.

Jeff pulled an old-fashioned looking silver case from his pocket and filched a cigarette from it. "You mind?"

Cooper and Julianne looked at each other, grinned with amusement, and shook their heads to Jeff. He proceeded to light it with a bronze Zippo that was adorned with the Union Jack. He inhaled deeply before blowing the smoke away from them.

"How many men do you have?"

Jeff looked at Lewis, who responded. "Forty-two are in our group."

Cooper's eyes widened. "Really? Wow. Are they all armed?"

He nodded. "Yes. They all got something. But, I'd say we really have a dozen men who are armed like us. Most of the others have hunting rifles and such. But, about fifteen of 'em are just armed with hand-me-down antique shotguns or a handgun they just picked up. Things of that nature."

"That's pretty impressive," Julianne said.

"So, how might it be that we can assist you?" Jeff asked, puffing on the cigarette as one might expect an English gentleman to do.

"One of the financiers of the Brushfire conspiracy lives here in Camas. We want to get our hands on him," Cooper said.

"Why?" Jeff asked. "Justice?"

"We want to use him to get to the governor. They are close," Julianne said.

The other men nodded excitedly. Lewis spoke first. "We've been waiting for something like this. How can we help?"

"First, if you could help us put the guy—his name is Jonathan Good-win—under surveillance…"

Lewis interrupted him. "Jonathan Goodwin? The computer guy?"

Cooper drew back in surprise. "Yeah, why?"

"That's unreal. I went to high school with him!"

"Really?" Cooper said out of shock.

He nodded emphatically. "Yes! Really!"

"This would seem to be a serendipitous circumstance," Jeff added.

Lewis held his hands up. "Oh, it's even better than that. I can probably get *him* to come out into the open, which would be damn good because he lives up in a compound."

"How so?"

Lewis's face clouded over. "Let's just say he owes me one," he said with a pained expression. Cooper decided not to ask more about it.

"What do you think are the next steps?"

"Let me contact him. Set up a meeting. Then, we make our plan."

Jeff clapped his hands together. "Most excellent!"

"I gotta ask. Is he a friend of yours? You know, this could get ugly," Cooper asked.

He shook his head. "I wouldn't say that. We just went to high school together. And, I lost my wife to this thing and one of my boys. If he was a part of it, there ain't no love lost, to say the least."

"Alright then. You'll contact us on the shortwave once you've made contact with him?" Julianne asked.

"Yes, ma'am. Please listen in at the top of each hour."

They shook hands and then Jeff held up a wagging finger. "Next time, Mr. Adams, I hope you won't feel the need to put a sniper in the grasses."

Cooper squinted at him, surprised again. "How'd you…"

"I have developed very keen and astute powers of observation, my good man," he responded cheerily. "Have a charming remainder to your day, good sir."

With that, the two men pivoted on their feet and marched back toward their vehicles. Cooper and Julianne looked at each other in silence, but both marveling at their good fortune.

"I can't wait to tell Dranko about this. If this doesn't make him an op-timist, nothing will," he said to her, chuckling.

"Darling, I wouldn't be optimistic about *him* turning optimistic."

*

* *

Cooper waved everyone over to gather at the vehicles, and when they had reassembled, he filled them in on the conversation. They shared in the surprise that Jeff had spotted Angela hidden a hundred yards away. And they laughed together as Cooper mimicked Jeff's strange manner of speaking.

"So, we wait," Angela asked.

Cooper nodded. "Yeah, I think we get back to the marina and get ourselves organized there."

They clambered back into their vehicles. The return trip to the marina was uneventful, except they saw—for the first time—refugees on foot. The bedraggled group was using a bike trailer as a handcart and a haphazard assortment of backpacks to carry their belongings. Their pace was sullen and Cooper's gut turned over.

"The gas is finally starting to run out," Angela commented.

Cooper had barely yanked the emergency brake into position when he saw Monty running out toward them in the parking lot. He ran like an old man, tottering a bit from side to side due to stiff hips and joints. Cooper hustled out of the car and strode toward him, partly to get whatever news it was faster and partly to save the old man the effort.

"We got trouble," he panted, nearly doubling over from the short sprint.

Cooper grabbed one arm, lifting him up to face him. "What is it?"

"Ch...olera. Or, maybe it's that disease that starts with a 'd' and gives everyone the shits? I don't know."

"Dysentery?"

He nodded. "Yeah, that one."

"What have you heard?" Cooper demanded, frustrated with the lack of detail.

Monty looked up at him, concern blazoned across his face. "I think it's broken out here, in town. Sewer's been down almost since day one."

Cooper looked at the hand he'd used to shake Jeff's hand and tried to remember if he'd brought it to his face. He couldn't recall. Out of the corner of his eye, he saw Julianne doing the same thing to the hand that Jeff had kissed.

Dranko stepped in closer. "What, specifically, have you heard?"

Monty nodded, waved his hand for a second, as he was still catching his breath. "One of my old customers stopped by here on their way out of town. Over two dozen people have come down with the shits in the last two days. Every single one of them from the west side of town."

"Yeah, that sounds like it's pathogen-based, spread by contact," Dranko shared with the group.

Cooper raised his voice. "Well, that just seals our original plan. We won't stay here long. We do what we came for and then get the hell out." Cooper paused for a second, turning to Monty. "No, offense."

He flashed him a chagrined smile. "None taken."

"So, we minimize contact with people from town. And, we get extra vigilant on policing our waste. Sound good?"

The others agreed. They spoke a few more minutes together making assignments for the rest of the day. Cooper was overcome with a wave of tiredness and begged off any immediate assignments. He made his way to the boat and invited Jake to take a quick nap with him. He was pleasantly surprised when the boy agreed. Cooper quickly fell asleep, welcoming the heat and comfort of his son snuggled up against his chest.

He dreamt of Elena. They were at a wedding. He thought it was theirs, but he could not be sure. He was pursuing her, and was losing her on the sprawling wedding grounds. She was always out of reach, teasing him. She reached out a hand from her smiling, adorable, beautiful face, but then it receded into the darkness and was lost amongst the crowd. As the dream progressed, Cooper became frantic. He tried sprinting after her. He tried cutting off her route of retreat. He tried shoving the others out of the way. All to no avail. He had given up and collapsed into a white wooden folding chair in exhaustion. Just then, he felt *her* hand on his chin and she lifted it up. He was able to gaze into those delicious eyes once more and he leaned in for a...

"Wake up. Get up!" Jake was screaming into his face and shaking his body. Cooper was disoriented until he heard a succession of gunshots ring out that were loud and close by. This brought everything into sharp relief immediately.

He shoved Jake onto the floor of the boat. "Stay down," he barked as he peeked a look out of the window to see what was going on. He saw nothing so he whirled to the other side of the boat, and from there he saw two boats rigged up with sheet metal and plywood armor. His mind was still spinning, but he made a guess that what he was looking at was some version of river pirates. His mind clicked. *The light machinegun!*

He quickly located the storage bin they had put it in and yanked open the cover. In a flash, the weapon was in his right hand and a box of ammo in his left. He kneeled to the ground, pulled the cover open, and jammed a belt of ammunition into it before slamming the cover down. He pulled the bolt and chambered a round. He quickly threw a few more belts around his neck and then ran outside. He figured the boat would shield him from their view and he'd be able to catch them by surprise.

He crept carefully toward the boat's bow, shielding himself from the pirate boats. If it had been him, he would have pulled the boats in close enough to disembark. Accurately shooting from a boat in the waves was nearly impossible. And, they were bobbing in the waves that they had created.

The two boats had aligned their bows to face the marina. Men were behind the makeshift gun shields that they had built onto the boats, complete with gun slits to fire out of. There was no cover for Cooper on the pier, so he slid down next to a mooring pole since it was all that was available. The pirates were completely focused on what was in front of them and weren't looking to their left or right. *Just like a quarterback who stares down one receiver.*

He saw a bullhorn pop over the lip of one of the gun shields. It squelched loudly before it carried a plaintive voice over the water.

"We just want your medicine. We have sick people we need to take care of, please help us and we'll be on our way!"

Cooper wished he could see the face behind the bullhorn. His gut warred with his brain. It was telling him that that the tone didn't match the words. He couldn't escape the notion that the plaintive tone behind the words felt forced to him. *But, maybe it was just the stress of dire need?* He shook his head, steadfast, and decided to trust his gut.

He steadied the machinegun on its bipod and aligned the sights on the closest boat. A part of him felt elation at how easy and complete this surprise attack was going to be. Another part of him felt horror at the death and destruction that was about to happen. At about fifty yards, he knew the machinegun was going to cut a swath of it.

The bullhorn sparked again, "Please, we have *children* that are sick." Now, the men on the river had lost him for good. *You shouldn't have played that obvious card,* he thought to himself.

"We don't have much medicine," a voice—Freddie's—shouted from his left. Cooper glanced in that direction and saw him foolishly walk out from cover, waving his left hand toward them. Cooper couldn't believe what he was seeing. *You fell for that!* His words of warning were caught in his throat and drowned out by a fury of gunfire that erupted from the boats.

In an instant, he spun his head back toward the boats and squeezed the trigger. While the ragtag armor of metal and wood might have stopped a pistol, shotgun blast, or even a round from a hunting rifle, it was no match for a machinegun shooting a flurry of high velocity rounds. Cooper recalled enough of his training to fire short, controlled bursts. His first ripped through the bow of the closest boat. He saw a man topple over and disappear onto the boat's floor. Chunks of metal, wood, and other debris shot skyward as the rounds found their way home. He fired a second burst at the bow to complete the destruction. Now, things slowed down for him and he saw everything more clearly. A man, who was half crouching behind the armor, was hit and stumbled backward. He was wearing a Hawaiian shirt with an olive drab army overcoat. As multiple shots hit him, Cooper saw the common dumbfounded look that often spreads across the faces of dying men. Then, he toppled backward over the boat and fell overboard.

The boat he was firing from threw itself into a hard reverse, water churning madly from its rear as the engine spun the blades furiously. The second boat came into Cooper's view. He heard shots ringing over and around him as the men on the boat panic-fired in his direction. The sheer *amount* of lead a machinegun can throw was terrifying for most men, but especially those who'd never experienced it before.

He jerked as one round clanged loudly off the pole just a foot above his head. He recovered as quickly as he could and pivoted the barrel slightly and fired two bursts into the bow of the second boat. Both bursts went wide right. The shock of adrenaline from the near miss had fouled his aim. In contrast, the men on the boat had steadied themselves from their panic. Their rounds were landing closer. Cooper saw the cement a few feet to his left spark as a bullet hit it. The pole clanged loudly again, but ever closer. He knew he had to move. He quickly cradled the machinegun to his chest and barrel rolled several yards to his left. He hoped the relative darkness would throw their aim off for even the briefest of moments.

He came out of the roll and resumed a prone fighting position, his muzzle facing the boats. One man had been foolish enough to stand up, without cover, as he scanned the ground trying to find Cooper. Cooper aimed and slowly squeezed the trigger for a short burst. His body was racked by a three second burst of gunfire, shaking him like an angry child shakes a ragdoll. Red spray misted into the air and he collapsed in a heap, which silenced the fire coming from that direction. Cooper jumped when a round splintered the wooden pier just two feet to his right. His eyes caught someone shooting at him from the stern, but before he could shoot back, the man dropped down quickly. Cooper presumed someone else had hit him.

Cooper paused. He deliberately didn't shoot at the boats' pilots. He *wanted* them to run. He had no need to kill them all. And the longer a gunfight went on, the longer it was for someone on your side to get hit. Luckily, the wannabe pirates had had enough and both boats sped downriver. Cooper tracked them with the machinegun to make sure they went away, but he refrained from firing.

He gathered himself back up, cradling the machinegun against his shoulder. A triumphant smile crossed his face. Pride mixed with relief. He walked back toward where those on guard duty would have been. His gait was sure. When he rounded the corner, he saw the Angela and Dranko looking down. He followed to where they were looking and saw the dead body on the ground. He collapsed onto one knee. The machinegun slid slowly down out of his arms and came to rest on the ground.

*

* *

Cooper's stomach turned. The left side of Freddie's face was a bloody mash of flesh and bone. His right eye stared vacantly toward the sky. The rest of his body was untouched, pristine. While Cooper had seen the horror of war, seeing Freddie's face like this was deeply unsettling. *He always had a devilish smile on that face. Now his face was an unrecognizable mess.* He grasped Freddie's hand, still warm, and tears gathered in his eyes as he stared at the morbid scene in front of him. Angela and Dranko stirred and he looked up just as they were stepping over Freddie's body. The words he heard next sent a chill down his spine.

"Dad?" Jake's words were vacant and hollow. Shock.

Cooper whirled around and saw Jake's gaping eyes and mouth transfixed on the mess that had been Freddie's face. Dranko, with the head start, reached him first and blocked his eyes with a hand.

"Cover him up," Cooper yelled. He cursed himself for not thinking of it sooner. Angela stepped back and went looking around the immediate area for something to cover Freddie's body with. Cooper scooped Jake up in his arms and hugged him tightly. Jake's heart was pounding. "I'm sorry you had to see that, son," Cooper offered.

Jake was unresponsive. He barely held onto his father in the embrace. Cooper could feel tears drip down his neck. He kept holding Jake as tightly as he could, taking care to keep him turned away from where Freddie lay.

"It's done," Angela intoned a few minutes later, and Cooper carefully spied a look in that direction. She had found a torn white sail and secured it to cover Freddie's body.

Cooper released his grip on Jake, who wiped his eyes with his sleeve and looked intently at his father. "Why? Why him? He was always so funny." Jake's words trailed off at the end.

Cooper shook his head. "I don't know, son. I think he was just unlucky."

"It doesn't make any sense."

He cupped his son's face in his hands. "I know. It doesn't. Sometimes life is like that. Not everything makes sense."

"Just like mom."

Those words hit him like a sledgehammer to the gut and he could barely muster a reply. "Yeah, just like mom." He took his son in his arms again. The tears had stopped flowing and Jake was listless in his embrace. This worried Cooper. He knew withdrawal was his biggest enemy with Jake.

Cooper touched the barrel of the boy's rifle and made knowing eye contact with Dranko. "I'm glad you came prepared, Jake. Can you join Dranko in keeping a look out for the bad men who attacked us? Make sure they don't come back."

Jake nodded and walked toward the end of the marina with Dranko. Cooper was doing the only thing he really knew how to do when people were flirting with panic or emotional crisis: keep them busy.

Calvin had joined Angela and Julianne as they clustered around Freddie's body. Monty stood off at a respectful distance, a ball cap clutched in his hand.

"What the hell happened?" Cooper asked.

"It all happened pretty fast. They approached slowly; we barely had heard them when they gunned their motors and were upon us. They shouted at us to drop our weapons, so it turned into a gunfight pretty darn fast," Angela said, never raising her gaze from the sail covering Freddie's body.

Cooper rubbed his hand through his hair, kneading his scalp. "Did you see him get hit?"

Angela and Julianne shook their heads.

"I was up top, watching the parking lot and the road in," Calvin answered.

"It's a damn shame, but I don't think we could have done anything different. River pirates," he muttered in disbelief. "For the love of God. This *was* the United States of America just like a month ago, right?" Cooper kicked the ground in disgust to punctuate his words.

The others nodded in bitter agreement.

"And Freddie was dishing jokes and coffee to customers going to *work*." Angela broke down in tears on the last word. She fell to her knees, sobbing.

Cooper moved toward her and offered comforting hands on her shoulders. He felt her body wracking from the sobs, but eventually her breath slowed and her body calmed.

Julianne looked at her watch. "I'm sorry, I've got to go and get on the ham. It's nearly the top of the hour."

Cooper nodded to her as she moved off. He waved Monty over. "Can you get us a sail needle and some cord so that we might wrap our friend up here?" Cooper asked the old man. Monty nodded and drifted away toward the office and shop area of the marina. "We're gonna have to bury him here in the river, I think," Cooper said to the others.

"Shouldn't we take him back to our old neighborhood and bury him there?" Angela asked, looking up expectantly.

He shook his head. "It's too dangerous."

"Yeah, I guess you are right," she said, her voice clouded in disappointment.

"Freddie had told me he wanted to be buried in the ocean," Calvin said.

Cooper saw something in his eye that told him he was making this up to make Angela feel better.

"I guess this will be a close second," Angela offered, a grin reappearing on her lips.

"Exactly," Calvin answered. Cooper decided to let it go. *It isn't exactly a lie and what's the harm in it?*

Monty returned and the three of them carefully wrapped and sealed Freddie's body in the shroud made of spare sailcloth. Cooper felt like a grave robber as he took everything of value off of his body before they sealed it.

"We can't afford to lose valuable equipment or ammunition right now," he offered in his defense.

When they had finished, they stood up over his body.

"We will gather at sunset and commit his body to the waters," Calvin said. His words and the tenor of voice offered solemn respect.

*

*   *

For the next few hours, Cooper sat with Jake to play gin rummy. This had been Elena's favorite card game and they had often played as a family. He left the other needed tasks to the group. In the wake of Freddie's death, he did not want to leave Jake alone. They played for quite some time in silence. Cooper's attempts at commenting on the game, his desperate attempts at engaging his son, fell flat. Eventually he gave up and they continued the silent routine of playing the hands, keeping score, shuffling the deck, and starting each new game in dull silence.

In the middle of their umpteenth game, Jake finally spoke up. "I guess it's a good thing," he said.

Cooper cocked his head to the side. "What?"

Jake kept his eyes on the cards at hand, "Freddie. He don't have to deal with all this *shit* anymore." He spat the profanity, full of anger and hate.

Cooper discarded the notion of reprimanding his son for swearing, judging it more important to keep the conversation going. "What do you mean?"

His eyes met his father's. "Who wants to live *like* this? He's better off."

His son's flat response and the despair that plagued his words made Cooper's stomach feel empty. He put his cards down on the small table in the boat. "Your mother would want us to, son."

Jake shrugged his shoulders nonchalantly. "But, she isn't here to care, is she?"

Hopelessness overcame him at those words. He sat with it, watching his son closely. Jake looked straight back at him, unyielding. "What about me?" Cooper challenged.

Jake's face turned to confusion. "What?"

Anger crept into his voice. "What about me? I'm still here. I care."

His son looked back at him, a flurry of emotions roiling his face. Despair turned to anger, which ended up in sadness. Jake's eyes clouded over and then tears fell freely. He collapsed and cradled his head in his arms, resting on the table and sobbing. Cooper pivoted out of his seat and nestled himself beside his son, putting his arms around him. As difficult as it was to watch, he knew sorrow was a much better thing to consume Jake than hopelessness or despair.

93

He pulled Jake in tight. "That's it, son. Let it out."

Jake rocketed out of his grasp, glared at him, and cried out like a wounded animal. "I don't *want* to let it out! I have *too much* to let out! It never, ever ends!"

Cooper took his son into an embrace, overcoming his resistance. "I know, son. I know. But, it's all we can do."

"I just want to *not* care anymore. About anyone." His words fell from his lips, desperate.

Cooper pulled Jake's head back a bit so he could look his son in the eye. "If you do that, then you've lost."

He glared back at him. "Huh?"

Heated passion to reach his son overwhelmed Cooper. "Once you stop caring, then the bad guys have won. It's always been true in this world, but it's even truer now; the good people in the world *have* to keep caring. Otherwise, the bad guys win. The bad people who want to reduce this world to a hate filled place with no love or decency left will win. Is that what your mother would have wanted? Is that really what you want?"

Jake fell back into his seat. His hands rubbed his forehead as he considered what his father had said. After a while, he looked up. "No."

"No, what?"

When he saw the look on his son's face, Cooper felt a bit of hope once more.

"No, it's not what mama would have wanted. It's not what I want." Jake paused for a moment. "But, it's hard." At that, he collapsed into his father's arms once more, crying.

Cooper enveloped Jake in his arms and whispered into his ear. "I know. But, you don't have to do it alone." Underneath the embrace, he felt his son nodding his head. "You aren't alone, son, ever."

They held each other as the minutes passed and until his son had calmed down. Jake pulled away, dried his tears, and met his father's gaze once again. "I want to say something at Freddie's funeral. Is that okay?"

"Of course, son. I think he would have wanted that."

When Jake smiled weakly, Cooper felt like he had achieved the greatest victory of his life. He gave his son a one armed embrace, moved across the table, and they resumed playing their game. As they played, they made tentative conversation. Laughter and jokes crept into their game. Eventually, the game felt as if they were playing back in their house on Lincoln Street, before the madness of the Brushfire Plague had descended upon the world. Occasionally, Cooper felt Elena's absence acutely, but he kept those feelings to himself and, thankfully, Jake never appeared to notice.

This continued for almost another hour before Julianne opened the door, poked her head in and called to Cooper. "I have news."

He nodded to her and gathered himself from the table. "Give me a minute?"

Jake nodded amicably. "Sure."

He followed Julianne out the door and joined her on the pier. "What's the news?"

"Good news, we just made contact. They have a meeting set. Tomorrow morning."

"Where at?"

"Lewis's house. I have the directions. They want us to arrive tonight, after dark, just in case Jonathan suspects anything and puts the place under surveillance."

Cooper nodded. "That makes sense. We'll head out around ten."

"I'll let them know. Lewis will meet us back at the warehouse. We'll put our people into his work van and he will bring us to his house, under cover of darkness."

"I guess they thought of everything, eh?"

"Well, this last part was my idea. We can't leave anything to chance. Getting our hands on Jonathan is too important."

Cooper nodded and smiled at her. "Damn smart thinking."

She returned the smile. "Beauty and brains—I told you I'm the full package." She winked at him before turning on her heels and sauntering off. He shook his head in amusement as he watched her walk away. Then, he went back into the boat and resumed playing cards with Jake.

*

* *

The sun was low on the horizon as they gathered around Freddie's covered body. During the day, someone—Cooper guessed Monty—had attached various weights to the funeral shroud. They took turns talking, remembering Freddie, and sharing their favorite stories about him. So many of the stories were about a joke Freddie had made at an important moment. The group laughed at many of the stories and cried at others. However, it was at the end, when Jake stepped forward to speak that everyone was reduced to tears.

"I want to thank Freddie. I will miss you. You made me laugh *after* the plague. And...," Jake paused, looking up at his father, "and, that was very hard to do. I'm going to try to hold onto that. To hold onto you *that way*," Jake's voice cracked at the end and then he began sobbing. Cooper pulled his son toward him and kept his hands on his shoulders, offering comfort. After that, no one else spoke for several long minutes and each was alone in their thoughts and sadness.

Then, Calvin stepped forward. "With these words, we commit you to your grave. May God and the angels welcome you into Heaven, brother.

Rest in peace." Calvin stooped to grab a corner of the shroud and the others all followed his lead. They aligned themselves with the pier.

"On three," Cooper said. "One... two... three."

They cast Freddie, in his canvas shroud, into the waters of the Columbia River. They watched him drift downriver, slowly fading into the waters, until they could no longer see the white canvas. Eventually, the group fell into paired embraces and exchanged words in soft murmurs.

Cooper broke the mood when it seemed right. "Let's gather for dinner in twenty minutes. We need to review our plans for tonight and tomorrow."

*

* *

The group was spread out across the houseboat, eating another meagerly prepared repast. Cooper pushed a spoonful of cooked beans into his mouth. This was following a bite of rice he had shoveled in a few seconds before. Eating had become a process that put calories into his body, but rarely involved the pleasure it once had. He worked his jaw, mashing the food in his mouth, and swallowed it as soon as he could. Once again, as he looked around, he worried that the despair over Freddie's death might infect the group when they could ill afford it to. He decided to see if he could lighten the mood, using the popular topic of food.

"Outside of how to stay alive, I think about food more than anything else," he said to no one in particular.

Angela's spoon clattered against her plate. "Oh my word, me too!" Her face was alight in excitement. "What I wouldn't give for a cheeseburger!"

"Mmmmm... with bacon on it," Jake chimed in, as he rubbed his belly in dramatic fashion.

Dranko waved his hand. "Can we just torture ourselves? When I hear about your missing food, it just makes my stomach turn worse." His smile took the edge off of his words.

Angela waved her spoon in agreement. "Sure thing, sour belly boy!"

Their lively reaction told Cooper that they *wanted* to be distracted from their thoughts. Cooper had eaten his last bite and stepped forward. "We should plan for tonight, anyway. Julianne, why don't you bring everyone up to speed?"

"Lewis has a meeting set for tomorrow, with Jonathan, at his house. Tonight, we are going to meet Lewis back at the warehouse, get into his work van and get into his house that way. This might be a little overly paranoid..."

"Or, just good preparation," Dranko interrupted.

"Or, just good preparation," Cooper repeated, with a nod to Dranko. "But, it should keep the element of surprise no matter what Jonathan is doing."

"Are we all going?" Angela asked.

Cooper nodded. "I think so. I think we are all in. I had considered having one or two people post up nearby in the neighborhood, in case things go bad. But, I don't think we can spare anyone now." He paused in a moment of awkward silence at the mention of Freddie's recent departure. "Plus, if the Cooperites are on a double cross, we are all dead, anyway."

"I agree. But, once we are there, we ought to ask Lewis if any of the houses across the street from his are vacant. If they are, it'd be smart to put someone over there. Would be a further element of surprise for the potential fireworks tomorrow," Dranko finished, looking expectantly at Cooper.

"Good idea. We could put Jake there, too, as that should be safer." Cooper caught his son's eye as Jake gave him a slight knowing nod that struck Cooper as far too mature for his age. "We'll leave here at nine. Bring your weapons and ammo, knowing that if this goes south, it's all going to be *very* up close and personal."

"That means you leaving the FAL behind," Angela mentioned impishly.

"Probably," Cooper said and then went into a mock sobbing routine. The others chuckled at his antics.

"I am not sure you've been without it since this whole thing began," Calvin commented.

Cooper shrugged. "Hey, I'm not gonna lie. I love the thing. But, I know how to adapt and use what tools I need for the job. We got a shotgun I can use?" he asked, turning his attention to Dranko.

Dranko nodded, rising from his seat. "Yeah, I think so. But let me go check."

"I'll help you," Angela offered as she stood up. Cooper watched the two of them exit the boat together. He didn't know what to think of it.

*

* *

The cargo van bumbled down the road. Cooper was driving with Julianne and Jake at his side. Calvin, Dranko, and Angela were in the cargo area. Cooper drove as carefully as he could, trying to avoid any potholes that would toss his friends around like a ping-pong ball. He was wearing the bulletproof vest that Dranko had given him in what seemed like a lifetime ago. Indeed, they'd had an extra shotgun for Cooper to use, a solid home defense model. His trusty Smith and Wesson pistol was holstered at his side. He had extra magazines for that on his belt. Completing his "loaded for bear" outfitting was a bandoleer of shotgun shells strung across his chest.

"Do you really need to wear *that?*" Julianne asked. "Couldn't you have put that in back with the other extra gear?"

Cooper grinned. "I'm gonna let Jake take the first stab at answering."

"I think you're crazy, too," he responded, deadpan.

Julianne burst out laughing. Cooper shook his head and feigned disgust by blowing out loudly and letting his lips flap.

"Very disappointing, you two," he said, sounding exhausted. He let the silence linger for a few moments.

Exasperated, Jake exclaimed. "So, what's the reason?"

"What if we got attacked while driving? Would I really want my ammo in the back?"

"Man, you *are* paranoid," Julianne said, laughing.

"Nah, that's Dranko."

"I'm not so sure anymore. I think he's rubbing off on you."

"Why couldn't you just have them on the seat next to you?" Jake asked.

"Well, that's a very *easy* question to answer," Cooper began. He cocked an eyebrow in gallant, dramatic fashion. "If I did that, I wouldn't get to look so manly and dashing."

Jake groaned. "Jeez, dad."

Julianne reached across and rubbed his shoulders. "You *always* look dashing to me, *daahhhlinnng.*"

Cooper nodded seriously to her. "I'll take that as a heartfelt compliment, that I will!"

Jake's laughter stopped abruptly and he turned his attention intently out the window. Cooper knew that Jake was not comfortable seeing them flirt. He exchanged a look with Julianne and she nodded quietly. The cab fell into awkward silence as they drove on down the road. Cooper did not want to let it linger.

"I hope Lewis is on time," he said.

"Me, too," Julianne returned.

No response from Jake.

"Jake, did you bring your twenty-two?" Cooper asked him directly.

"Yup, but it's in the back. Guess I'm not smart like you," he said, disgruntled.

Cooper reached across to tussle his hair. "Well, it's never too late to learn!"

Jake simply grunted and continued staring out the window. Cooper decided to give up. They'd be at the rendezvous in less than ten minutes. His mind was beginning to rehearse how the scenario would unfold tomorrow.

Let tomorrow take care of itself. His father's words rolled through his mind. But, these words he found impossible to accommodate.

CHAPTER EIGHT

They pulled into the warehouse parking lot. A white van with red lettering advertising "Joe's Electric" was already parked there. Lewis stood next to it, sucking on a cigarette and exhaling smoke like a locomotive climbing a steep hill. He waved to them with his free hand as they drove up next to him. The cigarette had been smoked to a nub and he dropped it to the ground before stubbing it out with his boot.

Cooper exited the cargo van and shook his hand. "You still got those?"

He grimaced. "A few. Looks like the apocalypse is gonna make me do something I've failed at for a good long while," he paused, "quit."

Cooper grinned at him. "I guess there are a few good things to emerge from this mess, huh?"

"It ain't a good thing for me," Lewis said, chagrined.

"So, the game plan is that we load into your van and you get us into your garage so no one sees us coming in?"

He nodded. "That's right. Should be simple."

"You worried about anyone specifically on your street keeping an eye on you?"

"No," he said, shaking his head. "But, with the meeting set up, I'd hate to mess it up if Jonathan was keeping an eye out on me."

"Makes sense. I wanted to ask you if there is a vacant house across the street from yours?"

Lewis looked puzzled. "Sure, the one across and to the right of mine is. That family got the hell out of dodge when this all first started. Ain't seen or heard from them since. Why?"

"We were thinking that we move Angela and my son over there, in the early morning before light. Angela could provide aimed fire from there if we get into a firefight in the street."

He nodded and smiled in Jake's direction. "Is he going to be our grenade thrower?"

Cooper chuckled. "No, I just think with all the action inside your house, it will be safer for him there."

"Why didn't you leave him back at the boat?"

"We didn't have someone to leave behind with him. Besides, we were attacked by river bandits so it isn't any safer there."

His face knotted up. "Everyone alright?"

"No. We lost Freddie," Cooper said, casting his eyes to the ground.

"Sorry to hear about that. I can't even count how many friends I've lost to *violence* since this thing started, not to talk about the damned plague itself."

"Thanks, Lewis. He was a good man. The funniest one I've known. He kept our spirits up a lot during all this craziness."

"I hear you," he responded and then paused to let silence hang in the air for a moment. "You guys ready to saddle up?"

Lewis cranked open the van's rear access doors and they all climbed in. He had removed most of the gear from the van and added milk crates as makeshift seats. Still, it was crowded. Knees and elbows knocked against one another as the van drove. Whenever Lewis hit a pothole, the jumbled mass of passengers moaned and exclaimed loudly. They had put Dranko in the passenger seat because they felt anyone else would have aroused more suspicion.

Thankfully, the trip was short and everyone was happy when the van came to a stop for the last time inside his garage.

"Give me a minute," Lewis said as he exited. A few seconds later, the garage grew dark as he pulled the door shut. A bit of light shined in as he opened the back doors and then put his flashlight on to guide them out of the van and into his house.

Calvin made a display of extending is arms and legs wide in dramatic fashion. "Freedom!" His mouth was wide open in a full throttled scream, but only a whisper emerged. The others smiled or chuckled quietly.

Angela coming out next nudged him. "Keep it moving," she said in a similarly hushed tone.

Lewis kept his light on the path that led to the door into his home. "Through the door, take the first right and those stairs will take you into my basement. I want to keep you guys out of sight."

Cooper followed his directions and found his way down into the basement. A kerosene lamp burned from a table in the middle of the room. This first room was a large rumpus room common to so many homes built in the 1950s and 1960s. The lamp put off its distinctive smell, but it wasn't enough to overcome the musty odor that plagued most basements. A fireplace commanded the center of the room on the north side. A blank TV stared down from the west wall and couches flanked the room's south and east walls, facing the TV. On their opposite side, a hallway led to other rooms deeper into the basement. Jake wasted no time in flinging himself onto one of the couches and stretching his arms and legs wide. The others clustered around the entrance.

Lewis pushed his way through them, faced them, and spread his arms. "Welcome to my humble abode. We'll keep you guys here 'til morning. Bathroom is first door on the right. Bucket has water in it to flush, but let it mellow if it's yellow," he chuckled at his own joke. "The swimming pool out back is where to get more water when you need it. There are two bedrooms past that. I'll let you guys fight it out on who gets the beds and who gets the couches."

"Very good. When do we plan for tomorrow?" Dranko asked.

Lewis nodded. "Let me get some food down to you. The others should be here in about an hour. We're gonna make it look like an all-night poker game and they'll end up crashing here, in case anyone is keeping an eye on this place. So, we'll plan this out when they get here and you all have a full stomach."

"Sounds like a plan, thanks," Cooper said.

Lewis passed through the group and headed back upstairs. They quickly sorted out who would be the lucky ones sleeping on beds. Cooper and Jake got a small room that looked more like a closet than a bedroom, but it had a twin bed in it.

Cooper was suddenly and overwhelmingly consumed by the need to sleep. He told the others to wake him when he was needed. Jake declined his invitation to nap with him, but Cooper collapsed in the worn out bed anyway and was asleep within minutes.

*
*   *

Dranko nudged him awake with his boot. "Time to get up, Sleeping Beauty."

Cooper pushed his foot away with his hand. "Ah, shut it," he shouted, using an awful fake British accent.

"Now, be nice, I saved you a sandwich," Dranko said, thrusting a plate out to him.

Cooper sat up and took the plate. "What's the meat?"

"Venison. A welcome change."

"And, how the hell does he have bread?"

"He had some hard wheat stored, ground it up, and his daughter makes some mean bread. It's the best sandwich I've had in a very long time. She made some kind of honey-based dressing that is really damn good."

"When are we meeting?"

"In about ten minutes."

"Anything exciting happen?"

"Nope. Just some card games and chatter."

"Alright, thanks. I'll be out soon."

Dranko turned to leave and Cooper took a big bite of the sandwich. As the texture of the meat and bread—things he hadn't tasted for a while—hit his tongue, saliva flooded his mouth. The dressing was indeed both sweet and spicy and he relished it. He had a hard time *not* smacking his lips as he devoured it. Only when it was all done did he grab his water bottle to drink—he'd simply wanted to keep the delightful taste in his mouth as long as possible.

He clambered to his feet and went into the main room, just as the others

101

were assembling. Lewis and Jeff were there, as were two other men who he hadn't met. They exchanged introductions before gathering around a card table. Cleverly, Lewis had drawn up two maps by hand, showing the basement and the main floor of his home.

On paper, the plan was simple. Men would be positioned hidden in the kitchen and the back bedrooms on the main floor. Once Jonathan arrived, they would converge on him and take him down.

"What if he has men who come in first and search the house before he comes in?" Calvin asked. It was an obvious question that no one had considered.

Jeff clapped his hand against his forehead. "I can't believe I was so dense," he exclaimed.

"Good point, Calvin. Question is, can we do anything about it?" Dranko asked.

They were silent as they thought.

"I think we put three people across the street in the abandoned house. If he does that and gets spooked, we can at least try to prevent his getaway," Cooper finally said after sorting it out in his head.

The other nodded reluctantly. "I think it's the best we can do," Jeff responded.

"Dranko, Calvin, and Angela can be the team across the street, with Jake in a safe spot over there, if that's alright with you guys," Cooper offered.

Jeff shrugged. "Fine by me. They should move across the street around four in the morning. The meet up is at eight."

"Alright, sounds like we have a plan and just time to kill in the meantime," Cooper said, closing out the discussion.

Lewis gathered his maps, collapsed the card table down, and carried everything back upstairs. Jeff and the other two men followed him to begin simulating the faux poker game in case Jonathan had men watching the home in advance of the meeting.

Cooper and the others spent the next few hours in nervous small talk, fidgeting by cleaning their weapons and reviewing the overall plan and each person's assigned role multiple times. Cooper patiently answered questions and did his best to assuage the fears that always bubbled up in advance of a violent confrontation. As usual, he used the excuse of cleaning, lubricating, and checking his weapons as his favorite tactic to pass the time before what lay ahead. He kept an eye on Jake, who mostly sat in a corner reading some comic books that Lewis had given him.

He encouraged the others to get what sleep they could and ushered Jake into his room with him. "You take the bed," he said to his son.

Jake gave him a wounded look and hesitated before speaking. "Can you sleep next to me like you used to?"

A warm smile came to Cooper's face. "Sure thing, son. Happy to."

They curled up together. Jake pulled in close to his father and Cooper wrapped him tightly in his embrace. He seemed to shrink under his arms and it was as if his son was four years old again. Cooper welcomed the feeling. Soon, Jake's breath grew labored and deep as he fell into slumber. Jake's peaceful breathing lulled Cooper into a hazy state and within minutes, he was asleep.

*

* *

In what seemed like only minutes later, Dranko jostled Cooper awake. His eyes opened reluctantly.

"I thought you'd want to see Jake off," he said. Jake was already standing next to Dranko, clothed and armed.

"How'd you wake up without waking me up?"

"My ninja skills, dad," Jake responded, a playful smile on his lips.

Cooper sat up on the bed and took him into his arms. "You be good now, you hear?" He felt Jake's head nodding against him. "You do *whatever* Angela or Dranko tell you to do, without a moment's hesitation. They are going to keep you safe."

Jake drew back as his father's instructions continued. He nodded. "I will, don't worry."

Cooper's eyes narrowed. "And, you keep your rifle ready to go. God forbid you gotta shoot, don't hesitate for a second."

His son nodded gravely. "I will." Cooper saw his grip grow tighter on his rifle as he spoke.

Cooper stood up and tussled his son's hair. "Alright. Be safe and I will see you in a few hours."

He took Dranko's hand in a firm grip and grasped above his elbow with the other. "You keep a good watch on my boy, alright?"

"Of course," his friend said. There was no mistaking Dranko's commitment.

Angela and Calvin were standing near the stairs, waiting for them. Julianne lay sleeping on one of the couches, her back toward them.

Cooper took Angela in a soft embrace and whispered in her ear. "You take care of yourself and Jake, will ya?"

"That's the plan," she whispered back. "*You* be safe, too," she said, shooting a deliberate glance in Julianne's direction.

A flash of crimson raced across his face. "I will," he said in a hushed tone. He pivoted to face Calvin and took his hand. "Good luck."

Calvin nodded. "We will keep a good eye on Jake."

"Thank you," he responded.

The four of them then ascended the stairs. Melancholy overwhelmed

Cooper as he watched them go. *I know they are just going across the street,* he thought. But, he knew, too, that the potential for a violent episode in a few hours could make that short distance an insurmountable chasm. He returned to his room and dozed off just as quickly as his head hit the bed.

He was awoken by a feeling of someone watching him and jerked awake, his hand reaching for his pistol that he had laid on the floor next to the bed. A feminine hand belayed him.

"Easy, Cooper. It's just me," Julianne whispered. She was sitting on the edge of the bed. He went to sit up but she put her hand on his chest and gently pushed him back down. "Stay there. Just be comfortable," she said.

He reluctantly followed her instructions. "Whatever you say," he mustered. She must have lit a candle when she'd come in because one burned on the nightstand. She turned to face him. The soft lighting made her even more alluring.

"Have you made a decision?"

"I guess you get right to it, don't you?" he said, chuckling.

Her face remained intense. "I'm serious."

He paused for a moment as the grin faded. "I don't know what to tell you."

She turned away from him. "You are infuriating, you know that?"

"Yeah, I guess I do."

She pivoted back to face him and her hand fell onto his stomach. "Tell me you don't want me and I'll walk out right now."

The effect of her hand on him was electric. "Do I want you? Of course. What man wouldn't? But what does that mean?"

Now, she leaned in. "It means you should know your damned decision by now!"

He sat up, pushing her away to do so. He looked right at her, his face inches from hers. Somehow, her scent was still as it was on the first day he'd met her, and he drank it in despite himself.

"Do I want you? Yes," he exclaimed. "And, if this is all you want," he said, grabbing her hand and putting it on his groin. "You can have it. But, I can't decide the rest of my life right now. I mean…," he stammered and then stopped.

"What?" she pleaded, grabbing his hand with her free hand.

"Me… or you… or my son could be dead in a couple hours," his voice cracked when he mentioned Jake. "So, what do you expect from me?"

"I'm sorry," she said, looking down. She paused, thinking, and then turned back to him. Her deep, dark eyes had softened and she moved her hand to his chin. "Just what we can. Right now. We can leave the rest for later."

He devoured her full lower lip into his mouth. Her hand moved underneath his shirt and she greedily kissed him back. Once again, they fell into a passionate embrace. He hadn't thought it was possible, but this time was even better than the first had been. The release she provided sucked the energy from Cooper and they fell asleep together afterward and remained so until the alarm on his watch woke them both.

*
* *

As soon as the beeping on his wrist woke him, adrenaline coursed into his veins. *A pavlovian response to the apocalypse,* he joked to himself. He gently moved Julianne off him and got out of bed, stretching. Her eyes fluttered open gently. Her hand grabbed his thigh, dangerously so.

"Was that alright?" She nearly purred, flashing him that seductive smile she had.

He smiled back at her. "Yeah, you could say that. Isn't it always obvious on our end?"

She laughed at that. "True. But still sometimes are better than others, no?"

"Nothing better, I can tell you that. And you?"

"No complaints," she said, a wry grin accompanying her words.

He grabbed the pillow and mocked suffocating her. Muffled laughter escaped through the pillow and she made a display of frantically freeing herself. He let her go easily.

"You're welcome to get back on Tindr if you want," he said.

"If only the internet was still working," she replied, unfazed.

"Ah, you are impossible," he said, turning away as he holstered his pistol belt over his pants.

She pulled him back closer to the bed and caught his eye. "Seriously, Cooper. It was astounding. I might just fall for you." She turned away at that. It didn't go unnoticed by Cooper, the slight catch in her voice.

He steadied his voice. "We need to get moving."

At that, she stood up and gave him a peck on the cheek. They got ready without another word between them, the awkwardness stultifying any conversation. They trod up the stairs, weapons in hand.

Lewis was waiting for them, sitting in a La-Z-Boy chair. He raised his hand to halt them.

"You'll need to belly crawl from there, around the counter, and into the kitchen. I didn't want to pull the drapes because I don't want to do anything to spook Jonathan if they have eyes on us," he said.

They complied with his instructions, and after a few moments were sitting on the kitchen floor, leaning against the fridge and oven respectively.

"Now, we just wait. I'll give you any worthwhile updates as they happen."

Cooper pulled his walkie-talkie from his chest strap. "You guys all set?" There was a moment's delay before it squelched back at him. "All set."

He looked at his watch. Only thirty minutes remained until Jonathan was expected to arrive. Cooper had to fight against the giddiness when he thought about the possibility, through Jonathan, of getting his hands on the governor. Then, he had to push against the rank fear of something happening to Jake, him, or any member of their group. These emotions warred within him as the minutes ticked away.

*

* *

"Five minute warning," Lewis called from the other room. It was a needless reminder, as Cooper had been compulsively checking his watch every few minutes. He knew Dranko would be doing the same across the street and decided not to send them a cue over the walkie-talkie.

Cooper checked the shotgun's chamber one more time, ensuring that the comfort of a 12-gauge shell loaded in 00 Buck was where it was supposed to be. Someone being hit with it would experience the same force as if being hit by a blast from a submachine gun. In the confines of a home, or within fifteen or so yards, Cooper believed it was the best weapon to have at hand.

"He's early," Lewis called from the next room. "Black SUV. That's not his normal car."

"Two men getting out, look like bodyguards," chirped Dranko from the walkie-talkie.

"Any sign of Jonathan?" Cooper barked so both Dranko and Lewis could hear him.

"No," they echoed in unison.

"We take 'em down either way. Do *not* let that SUV get away," he directed at Dranko, hissing the words.

"Angela is already sighted in on the driver," he replied.

"No! He probably has bulletproof glass on it. Get the tires first," Cooper fired back.

"Roger that," Dranko returned. Even over the walkie-talkie's scratchy static, he could hear his friend's feeling of chagrin.

Cooper scooted along the kitchen floor so he could safely look out at the men approaching the front door. He thought it strange that they still wore suits, weeks into society's downfall. *For some, I guess old habits just die hard.* They each carried a submachine gun and cast wary glances around them as they approached. Each also had the telltale earpiece firmly planted for communications.

They suddenly stopped, and before Cooper could process what he was

106

seeing, the gentleman closest to the house leveled his gun at the bay window and emptied a magazine, sweeping from left to right. Glass shattered and sprayed. Lewis cried out from the living room and Cooper scrambled to his feet. The other guard spun around and fired haphazardly into the house where the others were positioned, but Cooper could not see the effects. He heard the sharp report of shots being fired *from* the house across the street as well.

Cooper was on his feet, just as the man outside was slamming a fresh magazine into his weapon. He stood amid a shining sea of spent brass at his feet. In an instant, he lined up the shotgun's ghost ring sight and pulled the trigger. The blast caught the man squarely in his midsection. He abruptly sat down, the submachine gun clattering to the ground at his feet. His wrinkled and worn dress shirt slowly turned red as blood spewed forth. Cooper racked the slide and felt the gratification of a fresh shell slamming home. He heard the loud "pop...pop" of a handgun firing from behind him and the second guard flinched twice as Julianne's rounds hit him in the shoulder and then the back. The guard was spinning around when Cooper fired again and his face disappeared under nine balls of steel hitting it. His body slumped to the ground.

"Help Lewis!" he shouted to Julianne as he rocketed toward the front door. The SUV was gone.

Jeff and one of the other men got to the door a second before Cooper and he yanked it open. Cooper ran through without a thought. Tires were squealing and he heard metal grinding on pavement as the SUV raced down the street away from them. He heard gunfire continue from the house across the street and he saw the glints of bullets striking the SUV. The glass was surely bulletproof as rounds glanced off of them.

Cooper leveled the shotgun on the right rear tire and rushed a shot off as the SUV was quickly getting out of range. "Get Lewis's van!" he screamed in Jeff's direction as he ran down the street after the SUV.

He racked another shell home, firmly planted his feet, sighted once again on the tire, breathed, and fired. He heard the gratifying sound of air exploding out of the tire and the rubber quickly peeling away from the rim as the SUV sped down the street. When a big piece of rubber careened off, the SUV jerked to the left before the driver righted it. Soon, the SUV made a sharp right turn and then disappeared from view.

"Where's my van?" he screamed at no one in particular. Reflexively, he fed new shells into the shotgun to top off the tube-fed magazine.

The seconds ticking by seemed like hours to him, although in reality, Jeff had Lewis's van backed out and on the street in less than a minute. Cooper jumped into the passenger seat. Calvin and Angela had managed to get onto the street just as the van backed out of the garage. Angela jerked open the side door and they piled in. Cooper guessed that Dranko's lingering injuries had prevented him from joining what must have been a pell mell escape from the second floor of the house so quickly.

"Go, go!" he yelled at Jeff. He swung his head around to the back. Calvin and Angela were sprawled across the van's cargo area, trying to right themselves, but they were spun out again as Jeff jammed the accelerator.

"Is Jake okay?" Cooper asked.

Angela nodded. "Yes, we had him on the opposite side of the house. It woulda taken a missile to hurt him."

"We got both tires facing us," Calvin reported, while slamming a fresh magazine into his rifle.

"And I got the right rear one," Cooper added.

"I'm just guessing which way they went," Jeff bawled. The panic on his face matched the stress in his voice.

"They'll take the fastest route out of here," Cooper offered.

"I'll do my best, but I've only been over here a couple times," Jeff returned.

"Roll your windows down," Angela yelled. "That SUV running on three rims is gonna make quite the racket."

He cranked the window down as fast as he could. "You're a genius," he yelped as giddy laughter consumed him. The others looked at him with a worried expression. "No, I'm not losing my mind," he screamed at them.

Cooper stuck his head out the window to listen better. Sure enough, he could hear the grind of metal on asphalt. "To the right!" Jeff took the first right he could. Then it occurred to Cooper that the SUV was probably leaving rubber or grind marks on the pavement. He scanned the road in front of them. "There, see it! Follow those marks!" Cooper yelled, pointing to the marks that he'd seen in the road. In an instant, the trail was very clear. Every few yards, they found a patch of fresh, black rubber or a gouge in the asphalt.

A few sharp turns later, they spotted the black SUV up ahead. It was fishtailing madly as the driver struggled to keep up a breakneck speed and control the vehicle. Most of the tires from the three shot up wheels had abandoned their cause, but a few shreds clung to life. The distance closed rapidly, as the van they were in had much better control.

"Here we go!" Cooper shouted to alert Angela and Calvin. "Hold onto me," he hollered at Calvin. He quickly scooted along the van's floor as it was careening around another corner. Calvin's arms locked around Cooper as he sat on the edge of the van's window and hung his body outside.

Wind whipped past him as they chased the SUV. They emerged onto another short straightaway and Cooper aimed the shotgun. The right rear window opened and a pistol emerged, pointing in his direction. They needed Jonathan alive, so he declined the urge to take out the threat to his own survival. Instead, he aimed at the SUV's remaining good tire. Once again, time slowed down.

He saw fire spit from the muzzle of the pistol aimed at him. He heard the whine as the bullet zipped by his left ear, barely missing him. The shotgun roared as he fired at the tire, but a last second bump in the road caused the volley to fall short. The bump made his body slam against the van and the side mirror gouged his arm. He steadied himself, racking the slide on the shotgun to chamber a new shell.

He looked forward and saw the pistol firing at him. The SUV was approaching another turn up ahead. Just then, the engine in the van sputtered and died.

Cooper barely heard Jeff scream. "Bollocks, we're out of petrol!"

Fear gripped Cooper. He knew Jonathan would get away if he missed the next shot. Underneath him, he felt the van already beginning to slow.

"Steady me," he bellowed at Calvin. Calvin grabbed him even tighter than before.

Cooper lined up the sights on the tire, let out half his breath, and squeezed the trigger. He watched in horror as he saw the shotgun pellets pockmark the pavement a foot in front of the tire only for the tire to race harmlessly over the pockmarks a split second later.

The SUV glided into a right turn. Cooper's hands feverishly worked the slide again, knowing he had no time for another shot. His stomach dropped and his eyes flew open in shock. His mind raced to deal with the consequences of his failure. Hope drained away from every pore in his body.

He heard a deafening explosion from inside the van and moved his head inside to see what had happened. As he did, he saw the SUV's tire explode, causing it to flip onto its side and slam to a stop against a light pole. Inside the van, Angela squatted with her knees wide, the scoped rifle pointing forward, and smoke curling upwards from its muzzle. Elation leapt into Cooper as quickly as despair had arrived. Jeff rapidly brought the van to a stop. Cooper jumped back into the van, only to yank the door open and leap back out.

His left ear was ringing loudly from the gunshot and his right was afflicted with what sounded like a murmur, but he could still hear enough to function. He raced toward the overturned SUV. The engine was still running. The two wheels dangling in the air turned; one was still driven by the running engine while the other spun wildly on its axis.

He was ten yards away when the passenger side door began to open very slowly as the person inside fought gravity to open it. "Come out with your hands up!" Cooper shouted. His shotgun was at the ready. He felt that Calvin was to his left, just a pace behind him and spread out several yards.

The passenger flung the door upwards and it stayed open. Bare hands were raised above the SUV's frame and turned in all directions. "I don't have anything in my hands, but I cannot climb out if I can't use them," a reedy voice called out from inside the van.

"Alright, use your hands to get out, but move them slowly," Cooper called.

Gradually, the figure emerged as he crawled out from the wrecked SUV. *Jonathan.* He wore an expensive, dark suit. It was crumpled and one sleeve had been torn halfway off at the shoulder. An emerald dress shirt had come loose at the waist and hung flapping in the faint breeze. A gash of red was across the left side of his forehead. He raised his hands as he sat on the edge of the SUV, just behind the front wheel.

"Can someone help me down?" he called out. His voice was nasally and thin. It hit Cooper like nails on a chalkboard.

Cooper turned to Calvin. "Cover me?"

Calvin looked blankly at him, pointed toward his ears, and shrugged his shoulders while shaking his head. *Of course, he still can't hear because he was inside the van when Angela fired.* Cooper nodded and pointed at Calvin, and then turned to aim his shotgun at Jonathan. He looked back at Calvin who nodded back at him.

Cooper walked toward Jonathan, slinging the shotgun over his shoulder. He made sure his Smith and Wesson pistol was still firmly in his holster as well. "Don't try no bullshit," Cooper ordered.

He shook his head. "I wouldn't dare." His voice was shaky and full of fear; Cooper had no choice but to believe him.

Cooper held up his arms. "Whenever you're ready?"

Jonathan looked aghast. "What? You want me to jump down?"

His face filled with disgust. "Ah, yeah. You aren't Rapunzel. You jump, I'll make sure you don't smash your face on the ground."

The man took a moment to digest his situation before his body tensed up and he leapt from the SUV. Cooper, just as promised, grabbed him by the armpits as he landed, took a few steps backward to help absorb the blow, and was able to keep Jonathan on his feet as they came to a stop. Cooper quickly moved away and got his hand back on the grip of the holstered pistol. He could see Calvin out of the corner of his eye and noticed that he had his rifle pointed squarely at Jonathan's midsection.

"Anyone else in the SUV?" he asked.

"The driver. Dead though," Jonathan answered. Cooper drew his pistol and then motioned for Calvin to search the SUV. Jonathan pointed at the pistol. "Is that really necessary?"

Cooper grunted. "For now."

"Are you going to tell me what this is all about?"

"You'll find out soon enough. All you need to know is that if you cooperate, you will get out of this alive."

Calvin emerged from the SUV. He nodded to confirm what Cooper had said. Cooper spied a German submachine gun slung across his chest and an extra pistol stuffed into his belt.

"Let's siphon the fuel," he said to Calvin. "Alright, let's go. Into the van," Cooper commanded.

As he turned, he saw them. On all sides, in front of about half the houses, mostly men—but some women—were clustered outside their homes. All had weapons of one kind or another brandished. *How the hell did I not notice* this? The people were clearly uneasy about what they had just witnessed and Cooper knew the spectacle made his group appear to be the aggressors.

"And, let's get it done quickly," he added under his breath. He walked a little faster and prodded Jonathan forward. Angela was inside the van, pistol drawn and trained on Jonathan. Cooper got him into the back with Angela and stood guard as Calvin went to work. He anxiously kept his eye on the people. Most soon drifted back into their homes, uninterested, but a stalwart few kept watching them. The tension rose as a boy came out from inside one home and handed his father a shotgun. Cooper called out to those that remained, "We mean no one here harm, but this man we apprehended is a bad man."

The handful of people looked impassively at them and no one responded.

Calvin was soon dumping fuel into the van's carburetor and then the fuel tank. As soon as Calvin was finished, he got into the front seat and then Cooper jumped into the cargo area of the van.

He called out to Jeff. "Let's get moving!"

The ride back to Lewis's house was longer, but much less frantic. When they arrived, the bodies had been moved to the front yard of the empty house across the street. Not unexpectedly, they had been stripped of their weapons and ammunition. Julianne was outside Lewis's house and smiled at their return.

Cooper ushered Jonathan out of the back of the van at gunpoint. When Julianne saw him, her face turned ashen. Then, a second later it flushed crimson. She charged right at him with clenched fists. "You scheming bastard," she screamed, spittle shooting from her mouth onto his face. "How could you?" Her fists battered against his chest and he struggled in his bonds to avoid them.

Jonathan barely defended himself before collapsing onto his knees and raising his hands up in a futile effort to block Julianne's strikes. "Stop her, please," he whined.

Cooper moved, but slowly, to pull Julianne back. He didn't mind Jonathan taking a beating. "C'mon, we need him alive," Cooper reminded her after she had kicked his knee and Jonathan howled.

She allowed herself to be pulled backward.

"Alright, lemme go."

Cooper complied. But she still glared at Jonathan and hurled a litany of abuse at him that would have made a drunken sailor proud.

"How's Lewis?" Cooper asked after he'd grown weary of the display.

That broke whatever spell had consumed her and she looked up at him as if seeing him for the first time today. "Oh. He's gonna be alright. Dranko worked on him."

Cooper motioned Jonathan to move inside the house and he wearily complied, moaning loudly. Lewis was in his La-Z-Boy, bandaged across his midsection. Dranko was putting the finishing touches on the bandage and looked up when Cooper and the rest strolled in. Jake sat on the couch across the room, nonplussed.

"So, you got him," Dranko asked.

"Sure did. Angela made the shot that saved our day," Cooper answered.

Dranko turned toward her smiling broadly. "Not surprised at all. I knew you had it in you."

She beamed back at him. "I'll admit it was a surprise and it felt good. Damn, good."

It took Cooper a moment. *Something is off here.* His mind struggled to find it. *Oh my Lord, he is* flirting *with her!* His mouth fell open when he realized that she was flirting right back. He quickly closed it and scratched his head to conceal his realization from the others.

He cleared his throat. "I think we need to move as quickly as we can back to the wharf. If this guy has anyone who still cares about his carcass, they'll come looking for him."

"You have no idea," Jonathan said, his words oozing with self-satisfaction. "And you," he said pointing at Lewis, "how could you do this to me? We were friends!"

Lewis sat up in his chair. "Don't lecture me. I know what you've *done.*"

"Can he move?" Cooper asked, indicating Lewis with his head.

Lewis croaked. "No need. Me getting shot will give me a good cover story. Some goons came and grabbed Jonathan. I tried to help my old friend and got shot."

"You can also give them bad information that might throw them off our track," Calvin suggested.

"Damn fine idea," Cooper responded. "I must be losing a step!"

Dranko shook his head in mock sadness. "Brother, I don't know how to tell you this, but you never *had* a step." The others chuckled.

"Well, that might be true, but you never even had a crawl," Cooper retorted. His joke fell flat and most in the room gave charitable groans.

"Exhibit A," Dranko crowed proudly.

"Why don't we get going?" Angela asked.

"We'll come join you as soon as things are clear here. By early afternoon at the latest, I'll send someone." Cooper nodded and shook his hand before

112

turning to leave.

Within minutes, they were loaded into Lewis's van with all their gear and headed back toward the wharf. Lewis, his men, and his wife stayed behind, but Jeff came with them. If the van was crowded before, now it was jammed tight.

*

*   *

They arrived at the marina without incident and pulled Jonathan out of the back of the van. His voice was shaky as he asked them what they were going to do with him.

Cooper grabbed him by the throat. "I bet you wish you knew, but we know what you've done, how many you helped kill."

"What are you talking about?"

Cooper used his free hand to strike him across the face and he brought his face to within inches of his own. "Don't you *dare* play dumb with me. The Brushfire Plague and all that blood are on *your* hands."

Jonathan's eyes bulged and his legs buckled. Cooper kept him standing with a firmer grasp on his throat. His face went ashen. "I...I...," he choked.

Cooper released his grasp. "What?"

He gulped air. "You have it wrong... I... didn't know how... bad... it'd be."

Hearing his denial made unfettered rage boil up within Cooper. He could feel his face flush red. His hands balled into fists. His lips curled into a disgusted smile. "You better come up with something better than that."

Jonathan began stuttering again, but Cooper punched him in the mouth. He staggered backward and Dranko had to catch him to prevent him from hitting the concrete. Blood trickled from his busted lower lip. Dranko pinned his arms behind him and began force-marching him toward the marina. Jonathan's legs flailed about and Calvin stepped in to help the effort of moving him to the houseboat. Once Jonathan could see where they were taking him, he began blubbering.

"*What* are you going to do with me?" he wailed.

Dranko rapped him on the head from behind and he winced at the blow. "Shut it."

They manhandled him into the houseboat's rear bunk. They tied his hands and legs up tight, and thrust him onto the bed. Cooper rifled through the boat until he found a dirty rag that would work as a blindfold. When he returned to Jonathan, the man's eyes were wide with fear.

"You better think long and hard about what you can do to atone for your sins if you wanna save your skin."

113

Jonathan's eyes grew wider and he dropped a shade closer to ghost white. "Who *are* you?"

Cooper chuckled and grinned. "Who am I? Oh, I'm nobody. I'm just a man who lost his wife to what *you've* done. I'm just a man who's watched childhood being snatched from his son. I'm Cooper Adams, you sonofabitch!"

His eyes fluttered and appeared to lose focus and for a moment Cooper thought he was going to faint. Instead, he tried crawling into a fetal position and began sobbing uncontrollably. Cooper dropped the rag across his eyes and tied the blindfold.

"You better think about how to make it all right," Cooper hissed at him. He thrust Jonathan away and turned to leave in haste.

"I'll keep first watch on him," Angela offered as he passed by.

Cooper stepped out onto the marina and drank in the fresh air. The others, except for Angela, filtered out from the houseboat and gathered around him. He gave himself a few moments to collect himself.

"I hate liars," he vented.

"The worst," Calvin agreed.

Dranko waited a few seconds before speaking. "So, what's the plan, boss?"

"We let him stew on his own juices for a good long while. Let his imagination work its magic on him," Cooper said.

Calvin stepped forward. "Can I make a suggestion?" Cooper waved him on. "I will take over from Angela in about an hour. When I am watching him, I will chat him up and feign sympathy. I can tell him his only hope is to come clean. That you detest liars and if he has any hope, it is to confess everything."

"Classic good cop, bad cop," Julianne intoned.

Calvin nodded. "Exactly."

Jake, who had been standing just outside the circle of adults, now stepped into it. He cleared his throat. "Before you go in, let me go in and fall upon him. I can pound on him and scream at him asking him why he killed my mom. You can then come in and pull me off. That should soften him up good."

The group looked at him in disbelief. The words, falling from the mouth of a boy whose voice hadn't yet switched to manhood, made them even more sinister. Cooper winced at seeing his boy think and talk in such a way. But, no one could argue with the wisdom of his suggestion.

Dranko responded first. "I think it's a good idea."

"Alright, let us meet back here in an hour then."

Cooper nodded wearily and staggered away from the group. He went to the marina's edge and looked out over the rushing river. His thoughts roiled over his son and he squatted down as he rubbed his chin. From somewhere, he recalled something his father had said to him when he was going to prison: *kids adapt to what they face every day*. His father had offered those words to comfort Cooper as he'd wondered how he would go on living with his father shuttered in a prison for a crime he did not commit. Now, Cooper found that they plagued him.

"I wish it wasn't true, Dad. But it is," he muttered to himself. He buried his face in his hands. After a few moments, he looked up again at the river. He heard the soft caw of a crow that had alighted upon a tree about twenty yards downstream. He locked eyes with the crow. Unlike crows that normally cast their gaze about in different directions constantly, this crow just stared at him, holding his gaze. It reminded him of the crow that had visited during Elena's makeshift funeral in his yard. His gut told him that it was the *same* crow. He shook his head at the absurd notion. "It can't be."

The crow dipped its beak in what looked like a nod and then took to flight, gliding low over the water before turning midflight and buzzing just inches over Cooper's head. He turned to watch it as it disappeared into the trees upstream. By the time it was gone, a wry smile had found Coopers' lips. He stayed where he was, looking out over the water. He felt calmer now. As he pondered his next steps, he found his strength again. *I'll wade through this with Jake. He'll be alright.* "I can do this," he whispered to himself as he stood up again.

"What can you do?" a deep voice startled him from behind. *Calvin.* Before he could turn, a firm grip was upon his shoulder.

"Survive," Cooper said to him as he stepped next to him.

Calvin's baritone chortle sounded. "Yes, you can, friend!"

"Thanks."

"You alright?"

Cooper nodded. "Yeah. Hearing Jake think and talk like that just threw me for a loop is all."

Calvin's eyes were sympathetic. "I think we were all surprised." He paused, surveying Cooper before continuing. "But it is a good sign."

"How so?" Cooper asked curiously.

He drew a deep breath. "Honestly?"

"Yeah."

"It gives him the best chance of surviving in this new world. He is smart. He is learning what he has to do."

"But he's only a boy."

Calvin moved his hand from his shoulder to his forearm and faced Cooper. "No. He is not a boy anymore. In fact, he *cannot* be a boy anymore. Not if you want him to live."

Cooper looked to the ground and he exhaled. "Yeah, I think you're right. But, it's so wrong."

Calvin smiled back at him. "Well, if it makes you feel better, a hundred or so years ago, a boy about his age would have been considered a man."

"Really?"

"Yes. Adolescence is a twentieth century invention."

Cooper thought for a moment. "Hmmm, that's interesting. Not sure it makes me feel better, but it's interesting."

Calvin laughed. "I understand."

"Can I ask you a question?"

"Sure."

Cooper smiled. "I notice you speak pretty formally. You know, you never use contractions, ever. Why is that?" Calvin laughed heartily, his body shaking. "What's so funny?"

Calvin collected himself. "Just an inside joke with myself."

"So you gonna answer my question?"

"You know how we were just talking about survival?" Cooper nodded, noting how Calvin's voice had turned serious. "Well, do you have any idea what it can take for a black man to survive?"

"Probably not."

Calvin looked down and shifted his feet. His eyes grew wistful. "Well, when I was growing up, my father and mother taught me a lot of things I would need to know to survive." He paused, now looking out across the river.

"Go on, please," Cooper said.

"One of those lessons was the need to talk formally, if I wanted to be accepted." Cooper stayed serious for a breath, but a smile crept onto his face. "What?" Calvin asked.

"I just think you overdid the advice, friend. You sound like Spock most of the time when you're talking!" He laughed and Calvin looked at him for a moment, stung by his comment. Slowly, he began to smile and then that turned into laughter.

As their laughter subsided, Calvin spoke up. "How 'bout this? Let's go 'n see how the others are doin'?"

Cooper laughed again, and made an exaggerated "okay" sign with his fingers. "Well, young chap, a splendid job. A splendid job indeed!"

Calvin looked at him seriously. "That, my friend, is the worst English accent ever."

He shrugged his shoulders. "Yeah, I know."

Calvin clapped him on the shoulder. "Alright, let us go and see the others."

The two men were smiling as they walked back together.

CHAPTER NINE

Cooper chose to be at the far end of the marina when it was time for Jake, and then Calvin, to visit Jonathan. He trusted Calvin to make sure that no harm came to Jake, but he had no desire to see the prelude, nor the aftermath. He wished Elena was still alive at a time like this. There was nothing he wouldn't do to be able to talk to her again. Hell, he even wished Freddie was still alive so that he could crack one of his jokes and break the tension. Instead, he stood alone, ostensibly on guard duty. Despite the recent attack by river pirates, his gut told him that they'd have no disturbances for a while. Nonetheless, the loaded FAL rifle was slung on his shoulder and his pistol was on his hip. The rifle's weight was heavy on his shoulder. *Price you pay for the power of .308.* He patted the weapon's stock. *Don't worry; I still love you, even if you are a heavy bastard.*

"Penny for your thoughts," Angela said, walking up.

"Just keeping my mind off what's going on across the way," he replied.

She came up to him, slinging her rifle. "It's going to be alright."

"I think so, but I just want this whole thing to be over."

She shifted on her feet. "Meaning?"

"That we get that bastard Gibbs disgraced and then put him in the ground." Cooper could not help the venom that flew out with his words.

Angela reached out, grasping his forearm, and looked up at him. He felt tenderness wash over him. "Relax, Cooper, it's all going to come together."

He held her gaze. "Yeah, I think you're right." She broke his gaze, looked down, and laughed lightly. "What?" he asked, smiling.

She looked at him again; her eyes alight and her hand moving slowly down his arm toward his hand. "They just never talked about it in those end of the world movies?"

Something inside him stirred and his voice dipped an octave. "Talked about what?"

"Oh, you know," she returned coyly.

His smile grew wider. "You mean that the apocalypse makes it nearly impossible for two people who like each other to be alone?"

Her hand found his and their fingers intertwined. "Yeah, something like that." He noticed how her voice had suddenly lowered and become husky.

His hand found the small of her back and pulled her up against him. "Is this what you want?" he breathed into her ear.

"Yes," she whispered back, her hands pushing him even harder against her.

His mind spun. He heard one of his father's favorite lines tear through his head. *The trick in life, son, is to stay off the paths paved with stupid stones.* But, neither the line, nor the advice stuck right then.

She nestled her head against his chest and he gently pulled her head back so he could look her in the eyes once again.

"What about Dranko?" he asked with concern.

She shook her head, confused. "I don't know. Nothing's happened yet." Her eyes fell to the ground. He left her there, to sort it out, as the long seconds passed. Pressed together, he felt a willing body, but he knew her mind was struggling. Her indecision was on the verge of causing his foolish desire to wane, but then she sparked out of her trance. Her hand moved between them and he felt her finger slide inside his pants as she grabbed his belt tightly. Her other hand found its way under his shirt and danced on the small of his back.

Their eyes locked again and he saw lust consuming hers. Her voice was urgent, almost desperate. "*This* is what I want right now," she said pulling him up against her. "One chance to show you how you are making the wrong choice with *her.*" She jerked her head in the general direction of the houseboat, where the others were clustered.

Her passion and frantic words overwhelmed him; he grabbed her head, jerked it back toward him, and his lips fell upon hers. At that, any doubt or confusion fled from Cooper. He took a look past her, spotted the nearest boat with a cover, grabbed her hand and led her toward it. She stumbled at first, so great was his pace and her surprise, but she caught up. They were at the boat in a handful of seconds.

They shed their weapons onto one set of cushions in the cruiser, while their bodies collapsed into the one opposite. The two were feverish in their kissing at first. But, by the time that their hands were clumsily trying to undo buckles, buttons, and zippers, their pace had slowed and they easily found a shared rhythm. They took each step slowly, but passionately. Cooper was reminded of some of his first experiences with a woman... how nervousness slowed everything down, but anticipation eventually overcame it. However, now it wasn't nervousness, but experience that guided their slow evolution. By the time her soft, supple body lay naked beneath his, he was consumed once more by lust. They slowed and found a rhythm as if they'd been lovers for years. They both lost track of time, but in the middle of it, Cooper thought, irrationally, *damn those river pirates if they show up now!* They reached the point of climax at almost the same moment and collapsed together. They lay together for a few minutes, in satisfied silence.

"I think they might have heard you," he said, playfully.

She nudged him in the belly. "Who cares if they did? Everyone knew what happened with you and Julianne." Bitterness clung to her name as she said it.

"That was amazing," he said, his hand grazing her belly, causing new goosebumps to arise across her midsection.

"It was a'right," she replied, grinning widely. Their eyes held for a moment, before he saw sadness cloud over hers. "I guess we'll find out if it was amazing enough, eh?" At that, she slid out from him and quickly began dressing.

"What?" he asked, confused. He reached out to grab a hand. "Come here." She shook him off and continued pulling on her pants.

"It's nothing," she said, avoiding eye contact with him. He began to stand up, but she held up her hand and spoke vehemently. "Don't. Just *stay there.*" He reluctantly complied and watched her dress. When she was grabbing her rifle to leave, he tried one last time.

"Can we talk? I have no idea what I did."

Finally, she looked at him, stepped in and kissed him gently on the lips. "It's okay. This was very nice. It's all about seeing just *what* you are going to do. I'll just wait and see and I sure as hell don't want to stick around for all the hem and hawing and hand wringing." She turned on her heel, slung her rifle onto her shoulder, and walked quickly away from the boat and back up toward the parking lot above the marina. Cooper was left to his own confusion, but her words hit home. He took his time gathering himself before he dressed and resumed walking the marina on guard duty.

*
*　*

A half hour later, as he trudged back and forth along the riverfront, Jake came into view, walking toward him. His pace was brisk and his face carried a satisfied grin.

"Dad, you shoulda seen it! I got him good. He was panicked and frightened. Of me! Can you believe it?" His words shot from his mouth like a machinegun.

Cooper tried to match his son's enthusiasm, but failed. His words came out worn, tired. "Sure son. Glad it went well."

Jake noticed his father's flagging words, but was undeterred. "It felt *good!* To finally *do* something that matters."

Cooper nodded at his son. "What's going on now?"

"Calvin thinks he's ready, told me to come get you. Julianne has a video camera, too! She found one that still has battery power." Jake's excitement made him jump and thrust both hands into the sky, fists balled.

Cooper clapped him on the back. "Let's go then."

As they walked back to the houseboat, he was consumed by mixed emotions. He welcomed seeing Jake so animated, especially when compared to the doldrums that had become commonplace. But, he worried that it was based on violence and inflicting pain on another. Calvin's words came back to him. Was he right? Did his son have to become this to survive in the new, post-Brushfire Plague world? Cooper's determination to help Jake

119

hold onto his childhood clashed with the new reality all around them. By the time they reached the houseboat's mooring, clarity still eluded him. He grunted and pushed his thoughts aside. *You got a job to do.* He shrugged his shoulders and cracked his neck to set his body physically for what was to come.

Julianne was waiting for them, a video camera in her left hand and a notepad in her right. She beamed when she saw them. "You ready to go? I have all the questions we need to ask him," she said when he'd walked up to her.

"Yeah," Cooper said wearily. "Let's get this done."

She grasped his arm. "What's wrong? We are on the verge of our plan coming together."

He caught her eyes. "I'm good." He shot a quick side-glance to indicate Jake. "I'm just not excited about how we got here."

Understanding flashed across her face. "Oh, I see." Her excitement waned from her face and her body as she slumped. "Well, let's get it done." She handed him the notepad that had a series of questions laid out in neat handwriting.

"I put them in order as best I could, but you might have to jump around," she said.

"Yeah, I see," he replied as he surveyed them.

"The most important thing is for his confession to seem genuine, so ask whatever you think makes sense to achieve that."

"Alright. Just give me a minute here," he said. Cooper studied the questions. "Do you have a pen?"

She fished one out of her coat pocket. "Sure, right here," she said as she handed it to him. He jotted down a few notes and added a few questions of his own. After reviewing the notepad for a few minutes more, he took a step toward the door to the houseboat.

"Let's go," he said turning to Jake. "You stay outside."

Jake's mouth fell open as his smile faded. "Really?"

"Yeah, really. It might get ugly in there and you don't have to see it."

His lips curled down. "C'mon! I helped. I wanna watch it!"

Cooper shook his head flatly. "No. But, we'll show you the video later."

Jake kicked the ground and his eyes burned fury toward his father. "It's not fair!"

"You're probably right," Cooper said as he opened the door and stepped into the houseboat. Julianne was close on his heels. He heard Jake stomp the ground outside before the door closed behind her.

To his surprise, Jeff Daniels was sitting on the rearmost bench in the boat. His feet were kicked up and he was reading a paperback. Cooper could not see the title. When he saw Cooper come in, he sat up, dropped his feet to the floor, and smiled. "Cheers! How are you, Cooper?"

120

"I'm good. Good to see you. Things alright up at Lewis's?"

He nodded. "They were when I left. He was giving it a few more hours to be safe."

Cooper turned his attention to his right. Calvin stood, solemn as a statue, with his rifle at the ready. He dipped his head slightly to acknowledge Cooper and he responded in kind. Jonathan was sitting at the table, eyes downcast, with a few red splotches on his face. *Jake must have hit hard.* Cooper slid onto the bench seating opposite of Jonathan.

"You ready?" Cooper asked.

He looked up with sullen, bloodshot eyes. "Yeah."

Cooper removed the Smith and Wesson pistol from its holster and put it on the table. He kept his hand on it as his finger plied it from muzzle to trigger to grip and back again. Jonathan's eyes were transfixed by it. Cooper leaned forward for effect. His eyes turned to narrow slits and he lowered his voice to just above a whisper. "I'm only going to say this once. This pistol holds fifteen rounds. You get one chance. You play games. You lie. You will go into the river and we'll see if you can swim with fifteen rounds of lead added to your body weight. Got it?"

His lower lip quivered before he answered. "Yeah, I got it."

Cooper softened his demeanor and spoke normally. "You *can* get out of this alive. You do what we need and you live."

"How can I believe you?"

Cooper laughed. "Jonathan, ask anyone around here. I *never* lie. Ever." The man looked incredulous. Cooper shrugged his shoulders. "Believe it or not. But, even when this all hit and my son, who I know you've now met…"

The shock of surprise burst across Jonathan's face. "That was your son?"

Cooper nodded. "As I was saying, when all this hit and my son asked me if his mother was going to die, I told him the truth. Of course, like any father who wants to comfort his son, I *wanted* to lie." Cooper turned his face away and looked out the window before continuing. "I desperately wanted to lie. Even then, I couldn't." His throat caught on the last few words. He turned back toward Jonathan, "So, if I couldn't lie at a moment like that, I think you can trust I'm not lying now." Jonathan nodded, still wearing a doubtful expression, but also visibly impacted by Cooper's powerful words. "And, if that doesn't convince you. You know Julianne's role in all this, right?"

"I do."

"And, you'll admit she's still alive."

He grinned, awkwardly. "Of course."

"So you can stay alive, too. You do what we need. You fulfill your *use* to us, you go free at the end of all of it." Jonathan fidgeted with his tied up hands. Cooper put his pistol back into its holster. "Untie him." Calvin stepped in, pocketknife in hand, and sliced the bounds that held Jonathan's hands. He then stepped back, his rifle trained on Jonathan.

"Thank you," he said, rubbing his hands and wrists. "So, what do I have to do?"

"Two things. First, we are going to interview you, on video, about your role and the governor's role in unleashing Brushfire Plague. Then, you are going to help us get in front of the governor."

Jonathan gulped. He breathed deeply, but his voice was frantic when he spoke. "I'll be hunted if I admit everything on video. I'll be *ruined!*" By the time he was finished, panic gripped him.

"Yes, you might be hunted. Just like I am now. Yes, you might be ruined, but how many lives have *you* ruined?" Cooper paused to let his words sink in. "But, guess what?"

"What?"

"You'll have a fighting chance to survive. Which is more than my wife had." Bitterness clouded the final words.

Jonathan's gaze fell to the table. His hands fidgeted as he pondered. Eventually, he looked up. "Okay. I'll do it. But, I don't know how I can get you in front of the governor without you being killed."

Cooper laughed. "You wanna know something else?" Jonathan looked at him expectantly. "Men on death row are the most creative people on earth at figuring out how to save their own lives." Cooper let out a laugh when he'd finished. Jonathan turned a paler shade, but nodded. "Let's start, Julianne."

She started by filming Jeff and then Calvin as witnesses to the interview before turning the camera to Cooper. "Can you state your name for the record?"

He looked squarely in the camera. His voice was steadfast and clear. "I am Cooper Adams. Formerly living on Lincoln Street in Portland, Oregon."

"Is there anything you want to say before this interview begins?"

"Yes. Since I released the unaltered truth about the origin of the Brushfire Plague, I've been called a liar and a traitor. Our so-called president has made me public enemy number one. Our own governor in Oregon, Governor Gibbs... one of the men with untold blood on his hands... has put a bounty on *my* head." Cooper's voice was gathering momentum; gaining strength. On the other side of the camera, he saw goosebumps spread out across Julianne's arms. "These men, if you can call them that, are the *true* liars and traitors to our country. On the other hand, I've never lied a single time as a man. I didn't even lie when my young son asked me if his mother was dying. I told him the truth, despite every part of me wanting to shield him—even if just for a moment—from *that* ugly truth." He let emotion have free reign over him as he spoke. The tough side of him wanted to hide his pain from the world, but he knew the effect it would have to show the world his agony.

"For the liars and anyone who they have confused, I'm about to interview a man who will tell you how the Brushfire Plague started and the governor's role in all of it. I've only asked him to tell the truth and only the truth. I believe America is owed that." He turned away from the camera and toward Jonathan. Julianne's camera followed suit.

He quickly moved through getting Jonathan's name, where he lived, the kind of work he had done, and how he had known the governor pre-Brushfire Plague. Then he went to the key questions at hand.

"What was your role in the Brushfire Plague?" Cooper asked.

Jonathan visibly swallowed. "Well, it is complicated." Cooper greeted that with silence and a steely glare. Jonathan fidgeted and shifted his weight, wringing his hands. "We thought the world needed a reprieve from spewing so much CO2 into the atmosphere," he began.

Cooper's fist slammed into the table and thundered, "The truth. Now!"

Jonathan gulped out loud and licked this lips. He held up his hands. "Okay!" His voice shook in fear. "A group of us—"

Cooper interrupted him. "Did this group include Governor Briggs?" He nodded. "Say yes or no," Cooper prodded.

"Yes! It included the governor."

"Who else?"

Jonathan then rattled off a series of names. Cooper recognized some of them. Those he did were corporate titans with direct business interests in China. He assumed the others were similar.

"And?"

Jonathan's face contorted in fear, like a murderer about to confess. "We had watched the long-term economic and political trends on China's ascension to world dominance. For example, we had watched their GDP grow from—"

Cooper stopped him with a glare. "Get to it."

He shook his head as if to collect his thoughts. "In short, we knew they would soon dominate the world's economy and were a rising military force on the world stage. So, we decided to help them... errr... speed up the process."

"By bringing America to its knees?"

"It wasn't just America."

"Meaning?"

"We knew the plague would significantly weaken not just America, but China's other chief rivals on the world stage."

Cooper's stomach somersaulted. Even though he already knew the story, hearing it told by Jonathan roused another round of repugnance.

"So, what did you do?"

"We worked with a team of scientists." Jonathan paused, looking like a deer caught on high beams.

"To do what?"

Jonathan's gaze fell to the floor. "To carefully design an infectious agent that would accomplish our ends."

"To kill half the world's population!"

Jonathan looked up, his eyes indignant. "No! We modeled the effects of the agent to affect approximately twenty percent of the world's population."

Cooper bit off each word as he said them. "You mean kill."

Fear clouded Jonathan's eyes once again. "Yes, kill."

Cooper clenched his fists, willing himself not to leap across the table and throttle the man. He had to forcibly remind himself of the value of this video. He exhaled deeply. "Tell us how you did it."

His mind wandered as Jonathan recounted how they had done what they did. He already knew from Julianne and didn't want to focus on hearing how this horror was released upon the planet and just how they had killed his wife. When Jonathan had finished describing their plan and delivery of the Brushfire Plague on an unsuspecting world, he continued.

"Now, tell us why you and this group of yours wanted to accelerate China's rise to power."

"Our group had an aligned set of economic and political interests—"

"Speak plainly man," Cooper screamed at him, punching the table again.

"We knew there would be a lot of profits to be made," Jonathan choked out the words and he was shaking.

Cooper's voice turned cold. "So you killed over a billion people to make money?"

"Well, it was more to it than that."

"Answer the question," he returned flatly.

Like a drowning man frantically looking for a life preserver, his eyes darted about the room. He found none. "Yes. That was the primary motivator."

The world fell away from Cooper. He was dumbstruck into silence, swept up in an avalanche of pain at reliving once more the terrible misguided beliefs that led to his wife's death and all of the death and destruction that had ravaged the world in its wake. He was filled with revulsion toward Julianne and Jonathan. In Julianne's case, it was tempered by other emotions, but such was not the case with Jonathan. Cooper knew killing had happened before in history so a man could make a buck, *but to kill well over a billion people for money?* He lifted a cup to his lips and spat the bile collecting in his mouth into it.

Absentmindedly, he asked some follow-up questions to get Jonathan to provide more details on the profits they had planned on and how they had helped prepare China to minimize the effects on their own population.

After the interview was over, Julianne asked a question before turning off the camera. "Have you been threatened to do this interview?" Cooper and Jonathan looked at her with surprise. "Please, answer the question."

"Yes, I was threatened."

"With what?"

"With death."

"Say more."

"Mr. Adams told me that I would die if I did not do this interview or if I lied at all during it."

"Do you believe him?"

"Yes."

"So, have you lied?"

"No," he answered, incredulous.

"So, do you think Mr. Adams will kill you because of this interview?"

"No, I do not."

Julianne clicked the record button and the red light went dark.

Jonathan breathed a deep sigh of relief. "You want to know something funny?"

"Sure."

His eyes leveled with Cooper's. "I was terrified of doing this. I know what this means for my future. And, I hope you believe me, we had *no* idea it was going to be this bad. But, it felt good to just talk about it and get it off my chest."

The absurdity of this man feeling more at ease after his confession, while Cooper's wife lay dead in the ground, filled Cooper with fury. His fingers balled into fists. "Just remember, relief is something my wife will never get to feel." Cooper spat the words at Jonathan through clenched teeth. He pushed himself out of the seat. "Tie him back up," he hissed at Calvin and stormed out of the houseboat before he did something he'd regret.

He took grim solace in knowing that they now had exactly what they needed to topple that bastard Governor Gibbs—*if* they could get the information out. Jonathan's testimony had been detailed and damning. Most importantly, it was as credible as the honest words of a child.

*

* *

Cooper stood on the dock once again. He began shaking as rage overtook him. He pounded his fists against his chest several times and cursed the empty air around him. He stomped his feet as he paced in a tight circle.

"Easy, brother," Dranko's voice called to him from behind.

"I want to kill that bastard," he fumed, turning to face him.

Dranko put a hand on his shoulder. "I know."

Cooper stared at him for a moment, wordless. His hands grasped his head as he leaned back and let loose a primal scream. Dranko stepped back in surprise. The sound echoed from a few of the larger boats moored nearby. Birds clustered in a tree at the water's edge took flight. When his scream lost steam and faded, only the rush of the river was heard. Like a dog after a fight, he shook his body from head to toe. Calm slowly returned to him. He took a step toward Dranko and exhaled loudly.

"Alright, I'm ready to go," he said.

Dranko extended a fist and Cooper gave it a bump with his own. "I knew you'd recover quickly, brother," Dranko returned.

"Are the boys just going to decide everything?"

Both men turned toward the voice, which belonged to Julianne. Calvin and Jeff were following, a few steps behind her.

"You didn't think *everything* would change after the end of the world now did you?" Cooper shot back, a wry grin punctuating his words.

"And... a man still speaking for a woman," Julianne deadpanned for a round of chuckling.

As the four of them gathered in a circle, suddenly tense, Cooper asked, "Who's got eyes on Jonathan?"

"Angela and Jake are still there," Calvin replied.

Cooper breathed a sigh of relief and then clapped his hands with a loud slap. "So, what are our next steps?"

Dranko answered first. "What's the situation in the wider world? I think that affects our play here." He was looking at Julianne and Jeff.

"The world's been tossed badly, lads. Most other countries have their knickers wound up good and tight over the plague breaking out here," Jeff said, eyebrows cocked. "Domestically, it all just continues unraveling. The military is falling apart with different units siding with the secession states or the feds. Clashes happening now all over the place. There are reports that more Chinese are arriving in California ports and they are no longer disguising themselves—these are straight up military units coming in."

Cooper's jaw tightened at the news. "What about the Cooperites? What's our strength?"

Jeff nodded. "That's some good news. It's spreading like a brushfire!" He did a double take and shook his head. "Sorry, bad analogy."

Cooper ignored him. "What are the numbers?"

"Alas, hard to say exactly. What are you pondering my good man?"

"In a week, could we put a thousand armed men in Salem? With demonstrations throughout Oregon and southwest Washington on the same day?"

Jeff's eyes widened. He lowered them and scratched his head. Suddenly, he raised his head, recognition flashing bright. "Transport will be the biggest challenge, but by George, I think we could!"

"How? The roads are jammed up and everyone *has* to be running out of gas," Dranko asked incredulously.

Jeff answered with the smile one holds when answering a child. "Our supporters are all over the state. They'd get into Salem from all directions. And, we have a *big* group of supporters right in Salem! Hundreds, easy."

"I don't believe it," Dranko said, undeterred.

"Bollocks! You *don't* understand, chap. The entire Cooperite phenomenon is about just how *furious* people are. Mass murder for profit? A cover up? People will *crawl* to Salem to get revenge!" Jeff said, eyes blazing and agitated.

Calvin raised his hands. "Everyone, calm down."

"Why don't we take a step back," Julianne said. "Cooper, why don't you tell us what you are thinking?"

He nodded. "Yeah, right. Good point." He paused and then spoke rapid fire, "First, we get the video out everywhere we can. Second, we are on the ham radio day and night *telling* people about the video. You know, reading the transcript telling them where they can find it on the internet—what's left of it. Then," he paused for breath, "then, we announce a march on Salem to demand answers because we know *they* will say it's all lies. We challenge the governor to debate me on the grounds of the capitol! Everyone who can get to Salem gets to Salem. Everywhere else, they rally in their local towns!" His face was beaming by the time he'd finished.

The others were smiling too, but Dranko looked askance. "Wait a second. Why wouldn't he just kill you?"

"With a thousand armed men on hand," Cooper retorted. "He'd start a revolution."

"Maybe he doesn't care. With the video out, he might have nothing left to lose," Dranko said. "And, what if they have thousands more men with the National Guard? Or hell, this is a big enough deal that the feds might throw people here, too!"

"When the video goes out, I'm not sure they will be able to count on the National Guard. And, hell, the feds are on their back," Cooper scoffed.

"Why would Gibbs show up to a debate?" Calvin's calm, deep voice broke the tension between the two.

"Huh?" Dranko asked.

"Why would he come to a debate *if* the video is already out?"

Cooper stepped back. "Keep going."

"I believe the video is your leverage. Why not hold the video back?"

"And do what?" Julianne asked.

"Do everything that Cooper described. Tell the world what we've learned from Jonathan. Plan the march and demonstrations. We contact the governor and tell *them* that we have a video of it all. Tell him he either shows up for the debate or the video goes out."

"Why would he believe us?" Jeff inquired.

Calvin shook his head. "I am not sure he will. But, I think it is a better plan than if the video is already out because then, the damage is done. That is the thing about leverage, once you use it, it is gone."

"What do you want to achieve?" Jake's voice from outside the circle surprised them all. "You always asked me that when I was figuring something out. What is your number one goal, you'd ask, remember?"

Cooper laughed. "Nothing like a kid to keep us focused, eh?" He scratched his chin for a second and then the words flowed naturally, easily. "I want to kill Governor Gibbs myself."

The others looked on for a moment. Cooper could tell he had surprised them with the cool, casual way he spoke of murder. The ease at which he'd spoken the words surprised him, too.

"Then, we need a plan that puts you in front of Gibbs," Calvin said.

There was silence and thought as minutes drifted by.

"I've got it," Cooper finally said. Everyone turned to him. "We are trying too hard. I tell the governor what I have—the video and Jonathan. And, I tell him I can be bought. Men like that will always believe that greed rules everyone else because it rules *them*. I will tell him I am tired of running. That I want five million in gold and silver and for him to call off his dogs."

The room was silent as his idea sunk in.

"That just might work," Julianne said.

"Jolly good, chap!" Jeff exclaimed.

"Wait. How can you get him alone?" Dranko asked.

"That should be easy. I tell him that if he kills me, the video goes out."

"Why wouldn't he think you'd take the money and *still* release the video?" Dranko pressed.

Cooper shrugged. "I bet it's a risk he will take. What choice does he have? His *whole* life is about being in the public eye. I bet he'll risk it to try and save his reputation."

"Why won't he think you'll just kill him?"

Cooper's grin grew wider as he talked. "Yeah, I thought of that. My father taught me about arrogant men like him. He will easily believe that he's beaten me. That I'm weaker than him. That I've given up. Think about it— his entire life, he's won! Everything has been handed to him. He's *always* come out on top. He'll believe he's won again. After all, I'm just some two-bit traveling salesman." By the time he had finished, the others were nodding with excitement. "And, then, after I put him down like a mongrel dog, we put out the video," Cooper exclaimed.

"Wait, I thought you never lied," Dranko asked, shocked.

Cooper's smile turned sardonic. "I'm not going to. Julianne will handle all the communication with the governor. In fact, back in Estacada, I told the governor's man I was going to kill him. So, my conscience is clear."

The others nodded, wry smiles crept onto their faces and several couldn't help themselves and laughed out loud with malice.

"I can reach out now. And, I can use Jonathan to confirm to the governor that we have him," Julianne said excitedly.

"If you could be so kind, please set the meeting one week out. I still want time to plan the march on Salem," Jeff said, rubbing his hands together.

"Won't that mess up our plan? I thought Cooper was supposed to be tired and broken, not defiant," Julianne asked.

"This isn't just about Cooper anymore, lass. The Cooperites can do this. The governor has no idea we are working together," he said with a fiendish smile.

Cooper smacked his hands together. "I love it! It's the classic pincer move."

"We just have one more problem," Dranko said flatly.

Cooper clapped him on the shoulder. "Shoot, Mister Problem Man!"

"We need gas if we want to move people to Salem."

Jeff scratched his chin for a second before exclaiming, "I know where there is some petrol… there is just a teensy bit of a dilemma with it."

"What's that?"

"Genius Hammond owns an independent gas distributor. He's been selling it out at a handsome profit since this all started."

"His name's really Genius?" Jake asked.

"To be polite, it was a nickname his schoolmates gave him that is, shall we say, ironic," he answered. An embarrassed smile crossed Jake's face.

"So, I have gold, we can buy some. No problem," Dranko said.

Cooper clapped an open hand over his heart and staggered backward. "What's this? Dranko *solving* a problem and not just naming them all?"

Dranko mimicked Cooper's feigned heart attack. "What's this? Cooper being a smart ass?"

"We do have one other problem I wanted to address with you," Jeff said.

"What's that?"

"There is a radio station in Portland that I think we need to take down. It's damaging our cause by besmirching your good name, sir. While it has been a trifling annoyance up until now, I think it will become a bigger problem as we try to organize the march on Salem and it will certainly sow confusion as we try to get the word out with the video."

"Well, that's a different kettle of fish, isn't it?" Dranko commented.

"But an important one. We need to start making these liars pay and shut them down," Cooper replied. "Can you two develop a plan and we'll talk about it tonight? I want to get working with Julianne on contacting the governor."

At that, the party broke into smaller groups to discuss the upcoming activities in excited tones.

*
* *

A half hour later, Julianne and Cooper were huddled around the shortwave that they had set up earlier in a different boat to ensure privacy as they communicated with the governor's men. They had been reviewing what Julianne should say and how best to respond to likely questions or objections that they raised. Once they were alone, Cooper was keenly aware of the heat and tension between the two of them. From the way their eyes would meet, and then withdraw, he was pretty sure that she was feeling it, too. Her irrepressible smiles that would alight on her face as she snuck a glance at him confirmed its truth over time.

But, he kept himself focused on the task at hand. Now that they had a clear path to the governor, the bittersweet taste of revenge that involved killing was upon his tongue. His mind was clear and he was focused and as sharp as a razor. His emotions were so powerful; he had to stop himself from becoming giddy at the prospect of exacting justice upon the unscrupulous governor of his state. He paced within the small confines of the boat as they worked.

When they had finished their preparations, he turned to her and asked. "Anything else?"

Her hand found his arm, her fingers played on it, and the now common electricity between them fired once more. Cooper was ashamed when his arm erupted in goosebumps. Her eyes pondered his deeply as she purred at him. "You know, there's always something else that *should* be happening with the two of us."

He pulled away sharply. "Not today it doesn't. We have…"

He was interrupted when she abruptly grabbed him and pulled her into him, hard. Now, he was acutely aware of every place their bodies met and how she good she felt up against him. Her eyes were full of fire.

"We could be dead tomorrow or the day after that. Why do you deny what's between us?" Her words were passionate.

A curious fury overtook him. It was a devilish mix of anger, lust, and futility at being unable to resist her. Instead of pulling back again, he fell upon her. He kissed her feverishly and deeply. He found her mouth welcoming and greedy in return. His hands were upon her breasts, undoing her shirt buttons in quick order. She returned the passion as her hands found their way under his shirt and she pushed her pelvis even harder up against his

130

groin. Cooper's mouth turned to find her exposed neck as one hand laced its fingers through her hair and pulled her head back sharply. She moaned in response.

Then, something unexpected and unfamiliar snapped inside him. He felt the desperate passion turn to sadness and remorse. He stopped kissing her neck and drew his himself back, first his head and then his body.

"Is this really what you want?"

She looked at him, her face alight. "Yes, Cooper. Yes."

His body went limp and his hands fell to his sides. "I'm sorry, I can't do that... *be* that right now," he said sadly. He breathed in deeply and then his words had turned flat, emotionless. "Call the governor's people and let's get this done."

He turned away from her, straightened his clothing, and stormed off of the boat without looking back. Julianne was left confused and hurt, he was sure, but he knew he had to get away from her, and quickly.

*
* *

Cooper paced the docks, avoiding anyone else. He was weary of the confusion. For someone so accustomed to clarity, the bewilderment as he thought about his conflicting emotions between Angela and Julianne was infuriating. Inevitably, the guilt he felt over his so recently deceased wife, Elena, would occasionally descend upon him and confuse matters even more. As he walked and kept his eyes on the river, his mind drifted to his father once more.

"So, what do you think?" Cooper's father asked him with a droll smile, as Cooper hung up the phone.

"Whatdya mean?" Cooper answered.

His father let loose a belly laugh. "Don't think I can't see, son, you have a decision to make, don't you?"

His face flushed as pink as a watermelon. "How'd you know?"

"I been around awhile, son," he answered.

Silence pressed upon them both for a few seconds before Cooper responded, hanging his face in his hand. "I don't know what to do."

"Let's start with the basics, what are their names?"

Cooper looked up. "Emily and Jeanette."

"And?" his father asked, expectantly.

Cooper didn't look up and began talking in excited tones. "Well, Emily is the most beautiful girl at school and when I see her, my stomach feels all funny, you know, excited. But, Jeanette is someone I can just talk to for hours and she makes me laugh and laugh and laugh!" He continued talking about both of them, switching between the pros and cons of the two girls.

Ten minutes later, he stopped to catch his breath and looked up. His father was sound asleep on the couch. Cooper's face flushed red again, but this time from anger, as he threw his hands up into the air in exasperation. Just then, his father began snoring, as if to extenuate the point. At that, Cooper jumped to his feet and stormed out of the room.

Later, his father tried apologizing to him, but couldn't get through it without laughing at his own folly, which only enraged Cooper more.

As Cooper's mind came back to the present, he was smiling at the memory now. However, it did nothing to answer his current predicament. It had turned out that he has been a victim to his own inexperience and optimism, as he had quickly learned that neither Emily nor Jeanette liked him "in that way."

His aimless walking ended after about twenty minutes and he pledged to stay focused on taking down Governor Gibbs and not let anything else get in his way. He'd recalled other words he'd often heard from his father: *delay is sometimes the best decision.*

*

* *

He was walking toward the main houseboat, when he spotted Julianne waving a piece of paper above her head excitedly. Dranko and Angela were standing next to her.

As he came into earshot, he could make out what she was yelling. "We got it! We got it!" He jogged the rest of the way. She was jumping up and down by the time he arrived next to her. "We got it! An appointment!"

Cooper smiled at her. "Good job. Where and when?"

"We set the when, a week from today. High noon."

"And, where?"

"That's the best part, *we* will tell them where the meeting is, one hour before it happens. That way they can't do any prep work ahead of time, but *we* can."

Angela shrieked in excitement and enveloped Julianne in an embrace. She then realized what she was doing and withdrew awkwardly.

"That's great, Julianne. Really good thinking."

"I know," she exclaimed and did a ballerina twirl around. "I'm a really smart girl," she said, mimicking the demure tone of a child.

Cooper couldn't help but smile at her antics, but he kept it straight. "Well then, we are in a good situation. Now, we just have to see about getting gas and knocking out this radio station."

*

* *

132

Cooper, Jeff, Dranko, Calvin, and Angela were gathered around a picnic table that was up near the parking lot. Cooper had entrusted, after Dranko's insistence, Jake to be in charge of keeping watch over Jonathan. With Julianne within earshot, Cooper was finally convinced that it was a prudent risk to take. Cooper simply had no answer to their shortage of manpower to get everything done that needed doing. While they discussed it, Cooper couldn't help but notice just how badly Jake wanted to take on the task.

"Lads, here is the lay of the land for Genius Hammond's business lot," Jeff said. He proceeded to point out the major features to the others. As he finished, he made his feelings known. "I cannot fathom why we are lolly-gagging so much time on this, because all we have to do is parley with the man and buy the petrol."

Cooper's jaw tightened. "Because if things go like you say, all we've done is wasted time. But, if it doesn't and we have no plan B, we'd end up with wasted lives. Which do you prefer?" He'd made no attempt to hide his irritation, which cut through the room like a lighthouse beam in weak fog.

Jeff put both his hands up, open palmed. "Cooper, my apologies my good man. I had no idea you felt quite so strong on the matter."

Cooper nodded to indicate it was fine. He pointed to the business just above Hammond's on the long drive that sloped down toward the gas lot.

"Here, we get Angela up on top of one of the RVs parked there and she can provide us good viewing and cover fire from there." She nodded. "Plus, I think we have Calvin hike in from farther up the road so that he is on the opposite side of the lot from the main entrance. That way, if things go badly, we've got a way to lay down some cross fire. Any questions?" he asked when he had finished.

CHAPTER TEN

The next day, the group gathered near the cargo van in the crisp morning air.

"Everyone know the plan?" Cooper asked, rubbing his hands together to keep them warm.

"Are we going to have a signal if anyone thinks it's going south?" Dranko queried.

Cooper thought for a moment and then nodded. "Good idea. Just say, 'this isn't what I was expecting' to signal everyone else."

The drive up to Hammond's was uneventful. They passed a few haggard refugees moving their belongings by bicycle or carts. Two other vehicles passed them, bent on errands that Cooper could only guess about. Everyone was armed and made a display of it; Cooper couldn't help but notice that firearms were becoming a common fashion accessory. They dropped Calvin off at the easiest place for him to walk in from the opposite side of the main entrance. Then, as they neared the RV park above Hammond's place, they slowed down enough for Angela to slip out of their vehicle. Cooper watched her slither and zigzag into the lot of RVs.

Then, Cooper turned his attention to his task at hand. When they reached the entrance, there was already a line. Three other vehicles were in front of them, as well as a man on foot carrying a five-gallon jerry can and a pistol on his hip. The man looked worse for wear, with clothes unkempt and scraggly, and oily hair stuck on the sides of his head. Cooper, Dranko, and Jeff spilled out of the van to wait.

The man ahead of them spun on his heel and his hand went to the butt of his pistol. Cooper knew Dranko would have him covered, so he took the other approach, leaning in and raising his hands, palms out. "Easy there, partner, just waiting just like you," he called out to the man.

The man nodded furiously and began cackling. "Just like me? Ha, that's a good one." He paused, mouth open, and scratched his head. "Yep, yep. That's a funny one. No one is like me. Nothing like me." He paused again, looking at Cooper and cackling. But, his hand had fallen away from the pistol and hung limply at his side.

Cooper kept his hands up. "I'm sure that is true. What are you here for?"

The man looked about, agitated, before turning back to face Cooper. "I'm here for gasoline. What else?" He then turned away from them and continued muttering under his breath. "Some people ask the stupidest questions. Don't they?" Then he nodded to himself.

Dranko caught Cooper's eye and rolled his eyes. Cooper cocked an eyebrow and nodded emphatically. By now, the first vehicle was making a U-turn after getting the gas it had bargained for and passed them as it left.

Cooper turned his attention to what lay before him. Genius Hammond had fashioned two firing ports on either side of the entrance. He'd taken what looked to have been iron doors, perhaps from a ship of some kind, and soldered them together. Then, they'd cut firing ports out of them. The simple design allowed a bulletproof firing position that was probably easy enough to move around. On the left, he saw the muzzle of a hefty 12-gauge shotgun pointing out. To the right, he identified the barrel of some version of the German G3 battle rifle. *Smart. He's got the power of 7.62 to punch through most vehicles and a shotgun to clear the space of any pesky soft-skinned people.* Then, there were two men out in front of the gate. The shorter of the two had a clipboard and was the person who dealt with the negotiations. A few paces to his left, a tall man had an AR-15 at the ready, keeping an eye on the people in the vehicles queuing up. Finally, he saw a mid-sized tanker truck backed up against the gate, but shielded well with a curtain of heavy iron. Only a hose and the nozzle snaked their way out through a cut out portion of the cyclone-fenced gate.

"Genius Hammond has this set up pretty well, doesn't he?" Cooper remarked.

"Yeah, buddy," Dranko murmured back.

They watched and listened to the proceedings with the second car in line—a beat up Toyota Corolla with peeling black paint and streaking rust. Cooper noted the passenger door was powder blue, obviously a replacement part from a junkyard. The back and forth was fairly rudimentary bartering, although as expected, the price for gas was very, very steep.

"At least the Corolla doesn't need much," Dranko commented. Cooper nodded.

As the gas hose was being removed from the Corolla's gas tank after the quick filling, he signaled to Dranko that they should get back into their van.

Just then, the man in front of them stepped into Cooper's path. "Do you have a light?" the man asked, fidgeting with a cigarette in his left hand.

"Are you nuts?" Cooper gasped. "Don't you see all this gasoline all around us?"

The man's head cocked to the side. "Nuts? You call me nuts?" His body was shaking in a way that made Cooper take an involuntary step back and put his hand on his holstered pistol. Out of the corner of his eye, he saw the Corolla turning and driving away.

"Just calm down," he said, with one hand up. "It was just an expression, it's all good."

The man bobbed his head from side to side. "No, I'm not letting you get away with it. No one calls me crazy," he shouted and stepped in closer toward Cooper.

The man with the clipboard stepped toward them. His sidekick followed closely behind. "What's the problem with your little group here?"

What happened next was a blur. The man pushed Cooper with one hand and yanked his pistol and brandished it overhead with the other. Cooper called out, "He's not with us," in mild panic as he realized the implication of that *particular* misunderstanding.

A deafening "boom" rang out and Cooper watched the crazed man in front of him collapse, a red blossom appearing in his chest. Cooper quickly realized that the barricaded guard had already been tracking him in his sights and the shot into his back had been swift.

Almost simultaneously, he heard other shots ring out from where Angela and Calvin must have been positioned themselves, and the rapid "clang, clang" as rounds impacted the iron shields from the opposite sides. He could only hope that some of those rounds were hitting their intended targets as well. The other man dropped the clipboard and pages fluttered on its way to the ground. To his right, the bodyguard's rifle came up all too quickly, the muzzle swinging toward Dranko.

Reflectively, Cooper had his pistol out and, without aiming, point shot at the man standing a few yards in front of him. The first bullet smacked him on the right side of his pelvis and the second hit him just above the bellybutton. He fell backward, arms flailing outward, and his pistol fell to the ground. Cooper spun toward the other threat, just as he heard the sound of a rifle firing from behind him. Sure enough, Jeff had fired through the van's windshield and plowed three rounds into the bodyguard before he could bring his rifle to bear on Dranko.

The immediate threats neutralized, both Cooper and Dranko swung to fire on the iron-door barricades. However, they saw no gun muzzles pointed out at them. Cautiously, they moved closer in, guns at the ready. When the were close enough to peer through, they saw bodies on the ground, blood pooling onto the dirt next to them. *Angela and Calvin came through,* he thought quickly.

"Let's get the gas quickly and get the hell out of here," Cooper barked at Dranko. "They'll either regroup quickly or have reinforcements on the way."

Already, Jeff had pulled the van up closer to the gate. Cooper grabbed his rifle from the van's cab and stood watch while Dranko and Jeff worked to fill the van and then the five-gallon gas cans they had brought with them. He heard a few more sporadic shots from Angela and Calvin, but could not see what or whom they were firing at. He guessed it was Genius Hammond's other workers who were scattered about the yard. From his vantage point, he saw the trailer that looked like the offices for the lot. He fired two rounds through the door as a warning to anyone inside who was thinking about coming out, but he saw no movement inside, nor did the blinds flutter about.

The minutes dragged on as they worked to get all the gas that they could carry. There were two more shots fired from his crew, again at people that Cooper could not see. He kept moving his rifle from left to right and back again, sweeping everything that he could see in the lot. It was a menagerie of vehicles, equipment, and cylinders used for storing propane and gasoline. But, he did not see anyone trying to move or return fire. After what seemed like an eternity, he felt the welcome tap on his shoulder from Dranko, telling him it was time to go. On the way back to the van, they stopped to gather the weapons and ammunition from the three men lying in the dirt. Cooper still curled his lips in disgust when he did this, as it always made him feel like a grave robber.

Dranko saw his expression. "Brother, you gotta get used to the new world!"

He snorted in reply. "Some things I don't want to get used to, brother."

The exit was uneventful, as was the reunion with Angela and Calvin. When Calvin piled into the van and they sped away, he called out from the rear.

"Why was that so easy? Hammond was sitting on a goldmine to have it so easily overrun." Cooper could hear the excitement of adrenaline livening Calvin's speech.

"I told you chaps he was never the quickest bat on the pitch," Jeff chimed up first.

Dranko didn't smile or chuckle like those around him and he replied seriously. "It's more than that. It's all evolving. What security measures he had set up was good enough, until it wasn't. Next time, he'll have more elaborate security measures, I promise you that."

"You mean it's like an arms race," Angela said.

"Yes, just like that. As people experience—and live—or hear about different situations, they'll respond. Everything that is happening now is so damn outside almost every Americans' experience. Everyone is learning on the fly."

Calvin grunted. "That makes perfect sense."

"It's a lesson we need to all take to heart. If we can anticipate what might be thrown at us, we can avoid learning the hard way," Cooper added. The van fell silent as they contemplated the events.

Cooper welcomed the silence. He breathed deeply, but then coughed as he inhaled the fumes from the gasoline. He was glad the operation had gone so smoothly and he knew that they had been damn lucky. *Thank you Mr. Hammond for not putting anyone on over watch!* His mind was already turning to the raid on the radio station as the excited post-action talk built up into a robust chatter in the van.

They made it back to the marina safely and, as he was wont to do after combat, Cooper found a bunk in the houseboat. Shedding gear in seconds, he collapsed into the bunk and was asleep within minutes.

An hour later, he awoke. He heard the buzz of Calvin and Jake talking at the other end of the boat. He massaged his sleepy facial muscles with his hands as he stood up and took the few steps needed to reach them. "Whatcha talking about?" he asked.

"Ah, Jake here was telling me about the time you almost fell into the outhouse at Opal Creek park," Calvin responded with a smile that revealed unfettered joy.

Cooper chuckled and reached over to tussle Jake's hair. "Yeah, that's a funny story."

"And Calvin was telling me about the restaurants in Portland he'd be going to if things were back to normal," Jake chimed in while pushing his father's hand off his head.

"What was your favorite?"

"My answer to that question always makes the 'keep Portland weird' crowd very upset. My favorite spot was Ruth and Chris' steakhouse," Calvin responded.

Cooper cocked his head in surprise. "That is a head scratcher, with all of our good independent restaurants." Anticipating the same question being directed at him, Cooper patted his stomach for dramatic effect. "Mine was, without question, Clay's Smokehouse on Division." His mouth watered as he remembered their delectable food.

Calvin nodded. "They did have some good eating there, I will not argue with that. But, for me a well-cooked prime rib or T-bone was always the answer to any question."

Not to be left out, Jake squirmed excitedly in his seat. "I miss Burger-ville!"

Cooper nodded morosely. "Yeah, it's gonna be awhile before we can get one of their in-season shakes, that's for sure." Jake made a deliberate sad face and folded his arms. "Do you know where Jeff is? We need to gather everyone to talk about this radio station," Cooper said, turning to Calvin.

"He is guarding Jonathan, last time I checked."

"Alright, let's plan on meeting in fifteen minutes at one of the tables near the river. I'll round everyone up," Cooper said.

Calvin nodded to him as he exited the door.

A short time later, they were clustered around the table, the faint roar of the passing river behind them in the background. They had left one of Jeff's men to guard Jonathan so that they could meet.

"I know we talked about attacking the station to shut it down, but I think we should consider occupying it and then broadcasting *before* we wreck the place," Julianne said before anyone else could speak.

Cooper cocked his head and scratched the back of his neck. "That's an interesting idea. What do you all think?"

Dranko shuffled his feet before responding. "It increases the risk and I don't see it as worth it. We're going to create the big bang with the governor's stuff. So, it's risk we don't need right now." He looked Cooper directly in the eye with an exasperated look on his face.

"Listen mates, we need every bit of propaganda we can get to win the blokes over to our side," Jeff said, gesticulating emphatically with his hands.

Dranko shook his head furiously. "Look, every minute we stick around there, we increase our odds of reinforcements arriving."

Jeff was undeterred. "From who? The police? They are barely out and about anymore."

Cooper watched Dranko's face turn red after hearing Jeff's mocking tone. "Police. Private security. The military. When's the last time you were in Portland? Do you have any idea what the situation on the ground is there?" Now, it was Dranko's turn to fire a scathing tone across the room.

Cooper's father's voice called out to him. *The worst thing for a united group of people is personal attacks. By innuendo or direct, it tears people—and then the organization—apart.*

Cooper held up his hands. "Hold up, everyone. Let's keep this focused on the facts, as we know them. No reason this needs to become personal." He shifted his feet to a wider stance and continued with a firm voice. "More than that, I won't allow it."

Jeff took a deep breath before answering. "I haven't been there since this all started, but we have people there. The police and military presence has virtually disappeared. What's left is guarding food and fuel, not radio stations."

"But, what about tipping off the governor's people with a Cooperite attack and then broadcasting on the air? We'd lose that element of surprise." Dranko's face turned to a look of deep satisfaction as the room fell silent.

Cooper looked around while he digested what he'd heard. His palms landed on the table as he leaned forward. "Here is what we are going to do. We will take over the radio station and then broadcast a general anti-government message. We will weave in some key things that promote our cause, but we'll wrap it in the anti-government stuff. This way, we get the best of both worlds—getting more of our message out, but not doing it as Cooperites."

As he talked, smiles spread across people's faces and it was Angela who spoke for the group. "Very smart. I guess that's why you are our fearless leader."

He dipped his head to acknowledge the compliment.

"There's just one problem," Dranko noted, his face serious.

"What's that?"

"We won't be able to fit everyone we need into the transport we have."

Cooper couldn't conceal the frustration and confusion in his voice. "Why the hell not?"

"With that compliment, your inflated head's gonna take up too much room in the van," Dranko deadpanned before letting loose a big grin at the end.

The group fell into deep laughter.

"Oh, he got you on that one," Angela laughed.

At that, Cooper surprised everyone as he vaulted himself across the table and grabbed Dranko by his jacket before he could jump backward. He looked up into the smiling face of his friend. "You might have got me on that one, but just remember I can *always* get you!" That elicited another chorus of laughs as Cooper backed himself off the table and stood back up once again. He straightened his shirt. "Alright, should we talk about our plan of attack?"

Jeff stepped to the table and pulled out a diagram of the building and surrounding block out of his pocket. As he spread it out on the table he said, "We got this from one of our most reliable contacts in Portland. This should be a piece of cake, there isn't much security…"

Dranko waved his hand to interrupt him. "You know you just cursed this mission, right?"

Jeff looked from him to Cooper, confused. "How?"

"You just said 'it should be easy', which means it won't be now."

Dranko's tone had been light, but the laughter that greeted this remark was tight and nervous. Jeff looked around and let the laughter settle before continuing.

Within thirty minutes, they had a plan of attack, and it turned out to be very straightforward.

As Jeff gathered his notes back up, Cooper turned to Julianne. "Can you work up the statement of what we'll read on the radio?"

She nodded. "Sure."

"Who's willing to read it?"

He was greeted with silence.

"You want this to look like an anti-government attack, correct?" Calvin asked.

"Yup."

140

"Then Dranko should do it, because it can't be you and for it to be believable, a white man's voice would be better than a black man or a woman."

"Even I can't argue with that," Dranko said.

"Alright, it's settled then. We leave here in two hours. We'll hole up in a building across from the radio station so we can attack in the morning."

*
* *

Cooper walked along the marina once again, breathing in the fresh river air. He was lost in his thoughts when Jake came up to him. Without a word, he sidled up next to his father, slipped his arm around him, and laid his head gently against his side. Cooper shifted his rifle so he could wrap an arm around his son's shoulder, and pulled him in close. They stood together for a while, Cooper basking in the glow of the father and son bond. He closed his eyes and soaked it all in: the affection he felt from his son, the clean air, and the river's gentle rush. He was so lost in the beauty of the moment; the words his son spoke next cut him like a blade.

"I want to be a part of the attack." Jake untangled himself from the embrace and looked up at him with expectant eyes and a tight jaw line.

"Son, you're only eleven years old!" The blood in Cooper's veins felt electrified.

Jake shook his head slowly. "No, I'm twelve now."

"What?"

"My birthday was last week," Jake said.

Cooper stalled, speechless for a moment. "Wait, what? How'd I miss that?"

"I've been keeping a calendar since this all started," Jake answered.

Cooper pulled him into a rough bear hug. "Oh, I'm so sorry, Jake. I feel horrible."

Jake pulled back from so he could look his father in the eye. "I'm fine. I know things are different now and I'm not sure anyone's keeping track of dates anymore. But, I want to be on the attack."

Cooper shook his head. "Why?"

His son planted his feet wide. "I need to learn how to fight. This is what the world is now."

He grimaced. "But, you're too damn young."

"Yeah, I know. Too young to see my mom die. Too young to see people die all around me. Too young to kill." His words were laced with bitter sarcasm. "Yes, I'm too young, but it is what it is. I want, I *need*, to be a part of this." Cooper surveyed his son closely. What he saw was a man's words and face on a twelve-year-old body. His gut tightened at the sight. Jake

141

seized the silence. "Don't you want me to survive?"

"Of course I do."

"Then, you gotta let me learn how to fight," he said firmly.

Cooper rubbed his forehead, trying to squeeze out the stress. "Okay. We'll put you in a supporting role—"

"But..." Jake started to interrupt him.

He held up a finger to silence the boy. "And, we'll begin some serious training for you for the future. I agree you need to learn, but I'm not going to put you in a stupid place where you'll just get killed," he said before pausing for effect. Then, he leaned in, put his hand on his son's shoulder, and made eye contact at his level, in order to give his words maximum effect. "Being smart is the first rule in fighting *and* survival."

Jake's face turned sulky for a moment, but as he thought, his face brightened. "Great. Thank you!" He vaulted himself back into his father's arms for a brief embrace and then he dashed off, nearly skipping, toward the houseboat.

Cooper gazed after him. *That was too easy.* Again, Jake looked like a young boy dancing home from the playground. It was a surprising contrast from the young man who had just pleaded with him to go into battle. His eyes welled up and his hand slowly descended down the side of his face in disbelief. *My father told me the hardest time of fatherhood was seeing your boy transition to being a man, and the back and forth of it.*

"But, doing so in the midst of a violence filled world is far worse," he said to the river.

The river had no answer other than the soothing sound of the water rushing by.

*
* *

Minutes later, Julianne came running toward him. As soon as she saw him, she shouted his name and gestured wildly for him to join her. Her face was distraught, worried lines etching across it. Fearing the worst, his heart immediately began racing and he sprinted the twenty yards that separated them.

"What's up?" He almost shouted at her.

She bent over, hands on her sides, and caught her breath. He grabbed her and lifted her upright. His face repeated the question to her.

"You gotta hear this," she said, gulping air. "I just heard over the ham radio," she gasped again before continuing. "The president repeated his attacks on you."

Cooper shook his head, confused, "So?"

She waved him off, breathing heavily. "And... and he announced a new

142

effort to capture you. Said a new force has been organized for deployment in the Northwest to launch a manhunt for you." She gathered herself. "He even called you a damned cockroach!"

A chill ran down Cooper's spine. His first thought was of Jake's safety. Then he thought of his friends. "Anything else?" he asked sternly.

She looked up at him, her beautiful eyes shining with concern. "That's pretty much it. Said the force would be arriving any day."

"Did he say what kind of force?"

"No, just that it was a 'highly trained military unit.'" She searched his face to ascertain his thoughts.

He pursed his lips and his jaw tightened. "I'm not so sure we need to be that concerned." She turned to a confused look.

"As I think about it, I bet he's bluffing," he continued.

Her head cocked to the side. "How do you mean?"

"Well, think about it, why would he tell me he's coming for me with a special military unit? Wouldn't he just want to surprise and then capture or kill me?"

The corners of her mouth tipped downward. "Hmmm, I see what you're saying."

"I'm not sure I'm right, but I'm not sure what else I can do prepare if it is true, either," he said, shrugging his shoulders. "What else did you hear? What's the other news?"

Her face darkened, "It's all so bad, Cooper. Disease is spreading like crazy. So many dying or dead," her eyes welled up and drifted into the distance as her voice trailed off. As seconds ticked away, Cooper had to snap his fingers to refocus her. "Across the world, separatist movements are declaring their independence from their national governments. Ireland, the Basque, Chechnya, the Sicilians, the Quebecois, and on and on and on."

"What about here at home?" His voice belied his irritation.

"Riots most everywhere. People are hungry and desperate. Honestly, Portland seems to be doing relatively well, with a mix of government and private forces still managing food distribution at key sites across the city. Those grain ships in port are making a huge difference here. There's a few other cities that seem relatively stable, but most of what you hear is mayhem and chaos across the board."

"And the Chinese?"

"Oh, damn, I can't believe I forgot! There are reports of massive food aid arriving from China into San Diego, Los Angeles, and San Francisco. Mostly rice, of course. California's governor is wetting himself on praising 'our dear friends from the Orient' for their help. There are reports of stuff heading for Portland, but nothing for Washington State," she finished, breathless.

Cooper stepped back, taking a minute to consider the flood of new information. "Any news on this whole 'Cooperite' phenomena?"

She nodded vigorously. "Definitely. A whole bevy of other cities have declared themselves in opposition to the government and in support of the 'truth' and aligning themselves with the Cooperite movement. Baton Rouge, Austin, Atlanta, Dallas, Cleveland, St. Louis, Denver, Tampa, Boston, and Portland, Maine," she paused, thinking. "Hell, I can't remember them all, but I did write a list as I heard them. It's over by the ham radio." As she was talking, Cooper's mind started spinning. Slowly, an idea formed from disparate thoughts until clarity hit him. Suddenly, his face lit up and a devious smile spread across his face. "What?" Julianne shouted at him, a mischievous tone in her voice.

"I don't know why I didn't think of this before!"

"What? For God's sake!"

"It's so damn obvious. We need to contact the *Washington* governor! He's clearly standing up for what is right. They could offer us protection, hell, maybe even sanctuary from the feds."

Her smile widened, for a brief moment, surprised at what he'd said. Then she threw her arms around him and planted a deep, wet kiss on his lips before he could react. At her touch, his body tingled from electricity shooting through him.

She let go of him and rocked back on her heels. "That's very smart, Cooper."

"Yeah, well, if I was a genius, I would have figured this out days ago!"

She smiled at him brightly. "We need to tell the others and figure out how to make it happen." She grabbed his hand and turned to race back to the rest of their group, but paused, and leaned in to whisper in his ear with a husky voice. "And, you gotta know that you being so smart is sexy as all hell."

The recent passionate kiss, the feel of her hand in his, and the sound of her breath in his ear nearly overwhelmed him. It took a major force of will for him to stay focused and begin jogging back to where the others were likely gathered. After a few steps, he deliberately shook his hand loose from hers. He didn't want Jake or Angela to see. The maneuver earned him a quick backward glance of disappointment from her, but she didn't say a word.

*

* *

They were quickly able to gather the others together. Jeffrey's men were on guard duty and watching Jonathan as well. In rapid fire, Julianne filled them all in at what she had told Cooper. When she mentioned the deployment of a new military unit hunting Cooper, he noted the concerned gazes

144

and worried expressions that were shot in his direction. Jake, who was standing next to him, grabbed his hand and looked up at his father with deep, concerned eyes. He gripped his son's hand firmly and did his best to reassure him.

When Julianne finished answering their questions, Cooper rapped his knuckles on the table to get their attention. "I have an idea that quite frankly I'm embarrassed I didn't think of days ago." He paused as the words of his father rang once more in his mind. *When you are dropping a big idea into a room, you want to give it as much dramatic effect as you can so that everyone listens intently. And silence can be a very powerful way to do that.* As he saw the intense focus directed at him, he realized that, once again, his father's advice was full of wisdom and insight. "We are going to contact Washington's governor and ask that he give me sanctuary and protection."

The group was silent for a few seconds, but then he saw clever smiles slowly creep onto people's faces.

"That is a damn fine idea," Calvin said, the first to speak.

Murmurs of agreements came from the rest.

Dranko held up his hand. "Hold on a second. We need to really think this through first."

Cooper shot him a raised eyebrow and wanted his words to match, but instead said. "What's on your mind?"

"First, how do we know we can trust him?"

Cooper's voice flashed irritation. "My God, he's fighting the damned Chinese for one!"

Dranko waved his hand. "Yeah, yeah, I know that. But, what I'm talking about is this: you go under his protection and you give him a huge plum. Hell, the entire world wants you, Cooper. Can we be sure he doesn't use you as a trading chit with the president?"

Cooper shifted his feet; Dranko had his attention now. "Keep going."

"We just have to consider it. If this conspiracy is what we think, we have to consider everything. Does he hand you over if they agree to pull the Chinese out of Washington? Does he trade you for food shipments to his state? Stuff like that."

"What do you think, Jeffrey? You know this state best," Angela said, turning to him.

Jeff cocked his head. "It's a splendidly fair question. Of course, I can't know for sure, but I doubt he'd do something like that."

"Why?" Dranko asked.

"First, there is major support for Cooper in these parts. He'd likely have a rebellion on his hands if he ventured down that path…"

"Hungry people only care about being fed. Everything else is a distant second," Dranko interrupted.

Jeff looked back at him, irritated. "As I was saying, chaps, the second

145

reason is that our governor has a strong streak of liberty in him. So, I don't see him getting on his good knee for the feds."

"It's still a big risk," Dranko said, undeterred.

Cooper thought for a moment before responding. "Jeff, do you have any way to contact the governor through your people?"

Jeff feigned insult. "Are Irishmen always drunk?"

He smiled back at him. "Point taken. Here is what we do. You have your people contact the governor. You tell them you've been contacted over the ham. You tell them I'm seeking sanctuary and that I'm hiding out with a trusted friend in my old neighborhood. You ask them as a sign of good faith that I want him to publicly declare Washington State unwelcome ground for the federal government's posse that's been sent after me. Tell him I want Washington State National Guard troops on the ground in Vancouver. You good with that?" he finished, turning his attention to Dranko.

"Reluctantly, but yes. It helps minimize the risk."

"Jeff?"

"Sounds like a splendid plan to me."

"I can make it a touch better," Angela added.

"After the raid tomorrow, I can go visit our old neighborhood. If I see or hear about new activity there, it would tell us if the governor sold that information out."

Cooper shook his head. "It's pretty risky. They could capture you."

She scoffed. "The whole world is risky these days, Cooper. Haven't you noticed?" The group chuckled at her dig. He squinted, but smiled back at her. "Besides, I can just say that we had gone our separate ways and I was coming home to check on things."

"It *is* a good idea," Dranko intoned, winking at Angela. "It would give us more certainty on whether we can trust him or not."

He waved his hands. "Alright, so be it. How quickly can you get this word to the governor, Jeff?"

"In a jiffy, mate. Within the hour. Our people up north have thrown in with the National Guard on some of their actions. They are tight as bedbugs up there."

"Perfect," Cooper said, satisfied. "Since we are all together, let's review our plans for the radio station attack once more."

To that, the group showered him with a cavalcade of groans, befitting a seasoned squad of war-weary grunts. By the end of the review and a modification of their plan, he was satisfied that Jake had been assigned a low-risk role keeping watch on their escape route as the rest of the group attacked. The rest was out of his control.

*
* *

Once again, they were bounding down the road in the cargo van and some of Jeff's men were on point in a Ford Expedition SUV. Cooper was driving, with Jake in the middle seat, and Dranko in the passenger. The others were riding in the cargo area in back, along with their supplies for the night. Dranko was busy scanning the roadway and its sides with binoculars as they drove. They road in silence for the most part, with the occasional attempts at small talk failing to ignite a conversation. Cooper was lost in his thoughts about the upcoming raid as he reviewed every detail over and over again. Dranko was preoccupied with his observations, while Jake was amped up about his upcoming role in the attack.

As they approached the bridge over I-270 that led into Portland from Washington, the lead vehicle slowed to a stop about two hundred yards from the entrance. They had chosen I-270 because it was wider and easier to survey for potential ambushes from a distance. The bridge over I-5 that went into Portland, while a more direct route, would have made it more difficult to avoid an ambush because it was narrower. The downside of the 270 bridge was that it was much longer, but Jeff remarked, "Man is always being forced to choose their favorite poison to imbibe."

The door creaked when Dranko disembarked and walked forward to join Jeff as the pair looked over the long highway bridge in front of them.

"You alright?" Cooper asked Jake.

He nodded and patted his rifle. "Yeah, I'm good." He looked up and smiled broadly at his father. "Thank you."

"For what?" he answered, with a quizzical look on his face.

"For trusting me. For *listening* to me," Jake said.

Now, it was Cooper's turn to nod. "Sometimes, as a parent, you have to know when to let your kid do what he wants, even if you disagree with it. It's part of growing up." Cooper paused to think for a moment. The truth hit him and stuck partly in his throat as he spoke. "I've realized you have no choice but to grow up."

"Yeah, I know," Jake answered, a morose and knowing look clouding his eyes as he looked off into the distance.

Cooper grabbed his chin and locked eyes with him once more. "But, it doesn't mean that you can't hold on to the better parts of childhood: wonder, curiosity, some innocence, even."

His son nodded once more, but his face was full of doubt.

Dranko was back at the cargo van and yanked the door open. "Looks all clear. But, we're gonna drive it as fast as we can, just to be safe."

When they reached the other side without incident, there was a collective sigh of relief and Cooper reflexively patted Jake's knee. The drive through north Portland was an emotional roller coaster. Some neighbor-

147

hoods looked nearly normal with scattered businesses still in operation. Few vehicles traversed the roads, but pedestrian and bicycle traffic appeared to have replaced it in these areas.

They passed an open coffee shop. The sign, proclaiming the establishment as Rain or Shine Coffee, looked normal except for a few bullet holes. It reminded Cooper of the time before the plague had struck. He saw people outside on the patio sipping coffee and conversing. He even saw laughter and smiles. The only difference was the armed guard out front, toting a carbine. Also, the customers all had some kind of weapon on their hips—from pistols to swords to knives. A large chalkboard on the sidewalk listed drastically inflated coffee prices. Cooper did a double take when he saw that the prices were listed in U.S. dollars *and* silver.

"Can we stop?" Jake asked expectantly.

Cooper looked at Dranko, who shrugged before laughing. "I could probably kill a man for a real cup of coffee right now."

Cooper nodded, so Dranko radioed the SUV ahead of them to pull over. As Cooper pulled the cargo van into the ample street parking, he remarked, "Let's leave our rifles here. Otherwise, we could draw too much attention to ourselves." Dranko nodded and communicated that to the other vehicle as well.

Stepping out, the delicious aroma of strong coffee—that had long been missed—hit Cooper. He closed his eyes and inhaled deeply, reveling in it. He rounded the van and opened the rear door.

"What's going on?" Angela asked with a worried face.

He flashed a wry grin. "Time for a coffee break."

The others slowly flashed recognition as the smell hit them, too. The group merged on the street corner.

"I'll stand guard over the vehicles if someone will get me a cup of joe," one of Jeff's men offered, motioning with his rifle to the sign showing the absurd prices. He was already lighting a cigarette with a Bic lighter.

"I got you," Dranko said and the group began walking the short distance to the coffee shop.

The guard stood up and the other customers warily eyed the large group of armed people who were unknown in the neighborhood.

Cooper held up his hands, open palmed. "We are down from Vancouver and haven't seen coffee in quite a while."

The guard, a man in his twenties with tattoos along the length of his arms, nodded slowly. "Just don't start no trouble. I probably don't have to tell you, but this whole neighborhood loves this place and won't tolerate no BS."

"Understood," Cooper said.

They clustered inside and reviewed the bare menu, also on a chalkboard behind the counter. Dranko burst out laughing.

"What is so funny?" Calvin asked.

"Since common sense could never do it, it took the damned plague to get rid of all those silly Frappuccinos and Macchiatos and double skinny whatevers!"

Angela punched him in the shoulder. "I hate you! Some of us liked those drinks."

He shrugged. "Yeah, there is no accounting for good taste." She playfully punched him again, more lightly this time.

"Can we get a round of coffees for everyone here, plus one?" Dranko ordered.

The woman behind the counter, also heavily adorned with tattoos, a nose ring, and several earrings scribbled on a pad of paper before responding. "You gotta pay up front." She showed Dranko the piece of paper with the amount circled.

Dranko whistled. "Once upon a time, that was the cost of a week's worth of groceries!" Despite the outburst, he dug into his pocket to retrieve some silver coins.

Jake stepped forward. "Wait, do you have any hot chocolate?"

The woman frowned in exaggerated fashion. "I'm sorry, son, we are all out." Jake stepped back, disappointed.

"How are you all still in business, anyway?" Cooper asked.

"One of our owners had a good relationship with the folks over at Stumptown. So their warehouse keeps us supplied… for now, at least! We had solar power on the roof so it wasn't hard to rig it to keep us with some power."

"What about your water?" Dranko asked.

"Well, we had some rain barrels on site and we take water in trade, too. So it's been working out fine so far."

Dranko handed her the money. This is when he noticed a sign where the register used to be that listed barter items accepted by the coffee shop and their equivalent value in U.S. dollars.

He slapped Cooper on the shoulder with one hand and pointed to the sign with the other. "Didn't I tell you that .22 ammo would be an ideal trade item after the apocalypse!"

Cooper looked at him confused. "Actually, you never said anything like that to me."

His face fell for a moment before turning defiant. "Well, I told *someone* that!"

"Must have been one of your crazy survivalist friends," Angela joked.

When the woman finished filling their cups and handed them across the counter, Cooper leaned in. "We're from over in Vancouver. Could you tell us what's been going on in Portland?"

The woman flipped her rag onto her shoulder and put her hands on the counter. "That's a big question. It depends on where you are. Around here, the neighborhood held itself together pretty well. Some parts of town are mostly burned out, maybe with some scattered squatters or hangers on. Other parts are controlled by a local church group or gang. Hell, over on Foster, some union members are running the show using their union hall as a base."

"Which one?"

She shrugged. "I don't know. They wear purple jackets, though."

"What about downtown?" he asked.

"That's really the only place left that is mostly still under the government's control. What's left of the police and the military is down there. Well, and over on the docks, where they protect the grain ships that were in port when all this started."

He nodded to her. "Thank you, that's helpful."

"What are you all in town for?" she asked him with a friendly smile.

Cooper was flummoxed for a moment, as he knew he couldn't tell her the truth of their impending raid and his inability to lie crashed head on in his mind.

"We are meeting some folks later on to trade some things, just south of downtown," Dranko said, coming to his rescue.

With that, they moved back outside and sat down at two adjacent tables.

"Run this over to my mate, will you please?" Jeff said to Jake, who happily scampered off.

There was collective silence as people took their first sip of full strength coffee. Then, there was a simultaneous—and loud—exhale of "oohs" and "ahhs." Everyone was smiling from ear to ear.

"This is *sooooo* good," Angela remarked.

"I can now die happy," Calvin grinned.

"Better than sex," Dranko said.

The group threw him skeptical faces. "Someone needs to teach you how to properly entertain a woman then, chap," Jeff said to an enormous round of laugher. Cooper was glad that Jake was still out of earshot.

Red-faced, Dranko shot back. "It's just an expression, for crying out loud."

Angela rubbed his arm in a comforting gesture. "As the representative of women here, don't worry. I won't put that on Facebook or anything to ruin your reputation with the ladies!" This earned her a lot of laughter.

"I'm sure that has less to do with you being nice and more to do with the lack of reliable internet," Dranko fired back to another round of chuckles.

Drinking their coffee, very slowly, the group descended into pairs and trios of conversation. Cooper sat back, savoring every drop as he drank it,

150

and listened. He was surprised by how "normal" the conversations were. People went through all manner of small talk and then, slowly, he heard them drift to happy memories of pre-plague times. It struck him now what the conversations *weren't*. There was no talk of security, of dangers, of food, or getting supplies. These were the things that had dominated most conversations he'd overheard since the plague broke out. The difference was staggering.

Dranko looked up from his conversation with Angela, eyed Cooper from across the table for a minute, reading his thoughts. "People's environment affects them a lot."

He smiled at his friend. "Put a coffee mug in hand and civilization returns, eh?"

Dranko smirked. "It's not *that* simple. But, almost."

Angela, catching up with them, asked Cooper with a smile, "What do you think of the weather lately?"

"Fair to middlin' I'd say," he answered, grinning back at her. Within a few minutes, he was lost in jovial conversation with the others. When Jake returned a short while later, he joined in seamlessly. Of everyone at their table, he was biggest chatterbox of them all—likely a combination of his youth and the rush of receiving his first jolt of a caffeinated drink.

Once everyone had drained their cups of the last drop, Dranko stood up. "Don't despair friends, I'm gonna get us a bag o' beans to take back home!"

"Paul for President," Calvin shouted and the others applauded loudly.

Slowly, in the reluctant way people leave a good party, the group stood up and filed out onto the street and then toward their vehicles.

"Wow, that was *amazing,*" Angela exclaimed.

"Yes, it was," Calvin agreed.

She looked at Cooper. "Thank you. We all needed that. It was a genius idea to stop."

He laughed. "Genius? That's probably overkill. But, yeah, just remember that next time you disagree with a decision I make!"

"Fair enough."

When Dranko returned, he held up the very small bag of coffee like a barbarian returning victorious with the severed head of the slain king. This earned him a round of raucous cheers.

*

* *

The welcomed normalcy of the neighborhood disappeared after just a few blocks farther west. The pedestrian and bicycle traffic faded and then disappeared altogether. Some buildings were still occupied and functioning.

Many were not. Soon, the appearance of burned out buildings and houses appeared and increased until they dominated the area. The cars had been vandalized or burned to charred hulks of twisted metal and melted glass.

Cooper hurried a worn handkerchief to his face as the stench of rotting corpses assailed him. Thankfully, he could not see any and guessed they were from the houses or out of view down the side streets. Desperate pleas for help and futile threats were scattered on the walls of the buildings and residences that they passed. "Sadie, we went to Seaside," proclaimed one. "Looters will be shot," warned another from a clearly looted convenience store. "God Help Us," and variations on that theme dotted several houses and businesses. Cooper grimaced when he spied another: "Up with Cooper and the Truth," and then across the street another answered back: "Cooper is a traitor!"

They continued on in silence, awestruck by what they were seeing. Cooper exchanged a worried look with Jake, patted him on the head in a weak offer of comfort, and continued navigating the maze of debris in the road and broken down cars. Most had been pulled off to the side of the road and they never reached a fully blocked path, but it did require constant attention and detours.

Up ahead, they saw a large cross that had been erected next to the road and a man gesticulating wildly upon a small platform that had been set up next to the cross. As they approached, it appeared that the man had two or three supporters yelling and clapping at the right moments. A solitary man, with dark skin and rumpled gray hair, wearing raggedy clothes stood in front of the speaker and appeared to be listening. Cooper relaxed when he saw no weapons at the ready or pointed at them. When they drove past, he heard snippets of the man's speech. It was focused on God's judgment as evidenced in the plague and the desperate need for Man to repent. The preacher's eyes, a vibrant green, locked onto Cooper's as they drove past and followed him for a few intense moments before Cooper looked ahead once again and contact was broken. *The man has charisma; I'll give him that.*

They kept driving. They passed another area where things seemed to be functional, at least—a few open businesses, people out and about running various errands, and no immediate threat of death or violence. Then, the rapid transition that they had witnessed before repeated itself. However, this time, two bodies, crucified atop two telephone poles about twenty yards apart, greeted them. Cooper's stomach turned—and not because the bodies were badly decomposed and had a wretched stink. It was because he was looking at a woman and what appeared to be a pre-teen girl. Their dresses were faded from the sun and stained with dried blood and bits of gore. Faded black ink on the two cardboard signs was barely legible now, but they declared to the world "I Crossed Big Jack!" On the girl's sign, someone had scrawled in a small hand and in fresher ink, "Jack Rapes!"

152

"Damn bastard," Cooper grunted through gritted teeth.

Jake nodded vigorously and mimicked his father's look of abhorrence.

"I guess we are back to having news spread through signs, rather than Facebook or the latest..." Dranko commented, trying to lighten the mood.

Cooper looked at him, furious, and Dranko fell silent.

CHAPTER ELEVEN

They had arrived at the staging location, an abandoned office building about a half-mile from the radio station. Once a health insurance company's office building, Jeff's Portland connections had confirmed it had been empty since a few days after the outbreak.

"It's ironic isn't it," Dranko said as they began unloading their gear through the rear door into the building.

"How's that?" Angela queried.

"All those premiums these people paid and when it's needed most, their insurance is meaningless."

She grinned. "Yeah, I guess."

"The bigger problem is that the entire healthcare system collapsed and hasn't even begun to recover," Cooper added. "The bills coming due would be anyone's last concern."

"True enough," Dranko responded.

The conversation ended as they took up their positions in the building. After a brief scouting to ensure there were no squatters or signs of recent occupation, they bivouacked in the copy room and a conference room. Both rooms were near the rear and middle of the building, which kept them away from the windows and left them an exit route in the event of any problems coming from the rear or the front of it.

"This place is depressing," Calvin remarked.

"How do you mean, mate?" Jeff responded.

"You see the workers' pictures in their cubicles and offices. Who knows how many of those people are dead now? And, did you see those notes that had been put up?"

Cooper rubbed his chin. "Yeah, the ones pleading for help or those people trying to get word to one of their friends here?"

Calvin nodded. "Yes, they were heart rending. And, who knows if who wrote them are even still alive."

Dranko grunted. "It does feel like a morgue."

"What?" Angela asked, irritated.

"You all can be bleeding hearts. The one that struck me was the note someone left telling Cheryl that his wife was dead now and how he couldn't wait to see Cheryl again," Dranko finished, holding up a torn envelope and a letter.

"Let me see that," Angela demanded. She grabbed it from his hand and read it quickly.

Looking up with her face wrenched with chagrin. "Wow, you're right. That's pretty foul. All this guy could think about, with everyone dying, was how he could get together with his mistress?"

154

Jeff's grin was mischievous. "Like they say, in every crisis is an opportunity."

The others laughed, while Angela quickly wadded up the letter and threw it at him. "You're horrible."

"That's not what my lady friends say," he said, unfazed.

Angela started to shout a retort to him, but paused, and then her own wry grin spread across her face. "You *do* know women can lie convincingly, right?" This caused a round of catcalls aimed at Jeff.

He looked at the ground, smiling, and collected his thoughts. A moment later he returned her gaze. "True enough. I just know the women who *lie* with me have insufficient mental faculty afterward to *lie* to me or anyone for that matter."

Like a tennis match, the others then looked from him to Angela to see her response. It was fast in coming.

"Yes, Jeff. I can understand how the extreme shock of an incredibly disappointing experience could incapacitate a woman's reasoned thinking."

At this, the room fell out in raucous laughter.

Cooper stepped forward, and clapped Jeff on the shoulder. "You, my friend, just got owned."

Jeff dipped his head in a low bow directed at Angela. "Madam, I stand humbly in your dutiful service."

"Can anyone tell me what you all are talking about?" Jake asked sheepishly.

A softer round of chuckles circled the room. Cooper tussled his son's hair. "Son, it warms my heart you have to ask. We'll talk later."

Unsatisfied, Jake stomped out of the room. As the warm glow of humor left the room, the conversation soon turned to the guard schedule, assigning who was going to make dinner, and other mundane details as they prepared to bunker down for the night.

Later that evening, they reviewed their course of action once more. They planned their attack for seven in the morning, figuring that whoever still had access to a radio would listen in then, before they started their day's tasks. It was a simple plan, based on their information that the building had only two security guards in the lobby. They would send Angela in feigning as a damsel in distress to the front door and hoped to draw the security guards outside, or at least distract them. The group would assault the building from the rear and catch them by surprise, hoping to get the guards to surrender or take them out. Jake and one of Jeff's men would be posted in the building across the street, on the rear side of the radio station, to cover their escape route when the raid and occupation was complete.

*

* *

155

The night passed without incident and in the morning, the group set about the task of putting their gear on, checking their weapons, and mentally preparing themselves for what lay ahead. Angela dressed herself in some raggedy and dirty clothes she had brought on this mission. A pistol was holstered on a belt on her left side. It was concealed by a canvas trench coat that hung to her knees.

Looking at her, Cooper had an idea. "Hey, come here a second."

Angela paused for a moment, grinned awkwardly with a furrowed brow, but then walked over. "Something wrong?"

"No, I just have an idea. I think if you approach the building, staggering a bit, and with your hands on your left side, you can pretend that you are wounded in the side. This way, your hands can be much closer to the pistol." As he spoke, he mimicked the actions he wanted her to take.

She nodded enthusiastically. "I like it. Great idea."

He watched her as she walked away and tried out for herself how she would approach the building, walking wobbly. It distracted him for a moment before he returned to *his* normal pre-action routine of fidgeting with the safeties on his weapons and the magazines that fed them. A few minutes later, Jake walked up to him. The .22 rifle was slung on his shoulder and a pistol of the same caliber was on his hip. The tight smile he wore belied his nerves.

Cooper patted him on the head and motioned at his rifle with his other hand. "You know you're going to have to shoot at the neck and the head with that pea shooter, right?"

Jake nodded. "Yeah, Dranko already told me that." He paused, revealing the irritation that only adolescents can perfect. "Several. Times."

He ignored that display. "You stay out of trouble. It should be an observation role only. If it gets hot, you guys will need to skedaddle and..." He stopped when he saw the sudden blank look on his son's face.

"What's skedaddle mean?"

He burst out laughing. "Oh my Lord, you don't know?" He rubbed his chin in disbelief. "It means get out of there."

Now, it was Jake's turn to laugh. "Got you. Of course I know what it means—you say it *all* the time!" The dramatic roll of his eyes added to his sarcasm.

Cooper laughed again and then continued, undaunted. "After you *skedaddle* then, you meet us back at this rendezvous location. Got it?" Jake nodded.

"Let's rock and roll," Dranko shouted from nearby the cargo van.

"You be safe, son. I love you," Cooper said, locking his son into a bear hug. Jake hugged him back fiercely before jogging over to the SUV. Dranko's words were the catalyst for Cooper to realize his son was joining the fray. *And, I know it's not going to just be this one time either. This is the beginning of something new. His new life. In this new world.* He gritted his jaw and drove those thoughts from his mind.

*
* *

Even before the van's wheels stopped turning, Cooper yanked the door open and his boots bit into asphalt as he rocketed to a position behind a large electrical box. In truth, he was like a coiled up snake that shot out of the vehicle. He hated the long run up to action and vastly preferred to get into it—and out of it—as soon as he could. He had his rifle, the FAL, braced over the top of the green utility box and pointed toward the radio station. He had his radio positioned up near his shoulder so he could hear it well. The other men tumbled out of the van and took up various positions of cover around him. He looked at his watch. They had a few minutes to move up the two blocks that would bring them to the radio station building. He motioned the others forward.

They were in an industrial and commercial area. As they moved up the alleyway, the buildings on either side were of varying heights. Some were low slung and just a single story, whereas others rose up seven or eight stories high. A few derelict cars and overflowing dumpsters provided them ample cover as they leapfrogged their way forward. Most that they passed reeked from the smell of rotting food. Cooper was thankful he did not smell *anything else* in them.

"One minute out," Angela called to them on the radio's open channel.

Cooper motioned the others to pick up their pace of advance. There was no sign of anyone else, or even much recent human activity in the alleyway as they moved forward. They got into their positions just a moment before Angela went into action. Through the glass doors, Cooper had a clear view into the lobby area and then out in front of the building as well. *Perfect,* he thought.

"Help me, help!" Angela's forlorn and pain-filled voice came over the radio. Cooper assumed she must be in sight of the main entrance. Her breath was heavy over the radio. *She's getting an Oscar so far.*

She came into view a moment later, staggering up the sidewalk and toward the building's front doors. Cooper saw the guard stationed at the security desk grab his handheld radio and speak into it quickly. *He is radioing his partner.* The guard cautiously approached the front door and looked out, surveying Angela. It forced Cooper to duck behind the wall he was peering around when the guard quickly glanced over his shoulder to look at the rear entrance.

Angela continued her approach, wobbling a few paces to her right and then back toward her left. When she was in full view of the entrance and

157

must have seen the guard watching her, she held up her hands, which were covered in what looked like blood. It looked so real, and it had not been a part of their plan, which caused Cooper to do a double take in surprise. *I wonder where she got the red paint or dye?* This provoked the change she'd hoped for. The guard looked around once more, but apparently decided he no longer wanted to wait for his partner, and punched the bar on the door to open it. He then raced outside to reach her.

This galvanized Cooper's group into action. They raced forward, disregarding cover or caution at this critical phase of the attack.

"Only one guard out front, cover *all* entrances onto first floor," Cooper shouted to the others as they ran.

Jeff reached the outer door first, and held it open as the others passed. Calvin had done the same on the inner door as Cooper rocketed into the lobby. His rifle was up and at the ready, quickly scanning the area for targets. The only stairway entrance was behind the elevators.

"I got this, you keep going," he called to the others. Cooper dropped to a kneeling position and kept his weapon trained on the doorway leading onto the first floor. He was able to quickly glance to his right to see what was happening out front. He heard the others rush past him on their way to assist Angela. One of Jeff's men, Zachary, took up a similar position as Cooper, but was facing rearward to cover the area from which they had just come.

Out of the corner of his eye, Cooper saw the guard out front with his arms raised. Just then, the door flew open and another guard came running onto the first floor, panting and wheezing. Cooper had his rifle aimed directly at his center of mass. The man's mouth fell open when he saw Cooper.

"Hands up, now!" Cooper screamed at him as everything slowed down dramatically. The man, a young guy in his twenties, stumbled to a stop about fifteen yards from Cooper. He looked to be in a daze, but his hand was slowly moving toward his holster. Cooper's stomach turned, feeling like he knew what was coming. "Hands up now!" he shouted one more time, in an attempt to avert it. But the guard, still looking like he was in a trance, did not relent.

Looking down his sights, all Cooper could see was the fabric security badge on the man's white shirt. It was likely just over his heart, so Cooper had found it a convenient aiming spot. He let out half a breath and slowly squeezed the trigger, letting the violent explosion of discharge surprise him. His aim was dead on, the bullet blasting through the center of the badge. The man's eyes went blank and his limp body slowly fell backward and to the left. Cooper heard Zachary, who must have watched the entire sequence, vomiting onto the lobby's tiled floor, causing a loud splashing sound. Cooper gritted his teeth at the sound.

At that moment, the door clattered open as they brought in the other guard. They'd used a zip tie to secure his hands.

"Oooh, you got a mess in here, eh?" Angela was the one who asked first.

"Yeah, he just kept reaching for his pistol," Cooper replied.

The security guard's eyes flew open when he saw the other one laying on the floor. "Tony!" he called. He staggered over to his friend and fell to his knees in tears. The cries grew to a loud wailing and he put his head on the other man's chest. In a stupor, the others watched at the unfolding scene. Just as clarity began to descend onto the group, the security guard rose to his feet; his gaze fixed squarely on Cooper.

"You killed *him*," he shrieked in a bloodthirsty rage. He ran headlong at Cooper, with his arms raised above him. Cooper had only a moment to react; out of reflex, he raised his rifle to hip height and fired two rounds in rapid succession. He was so close it was nearly impossible to miss with these point shots. The first shot struck him in the left hip and the second in the middle of his torso. The man's momentum carried him forward, but Cooper was easily able to sidestep him and the man moved past him a few steps before collapsing on the ground. Cooper went to him, but his eyes only stared blankly up at him. Unable to talk, and with blood curling out of his mouth, Cooper watched the man take his last few breaths and then die. He reached down and closed them.

Calvin was at his side. "What was that about?"

"Brothers?"

He shook his head. "I doubt it. This guy has red hair and the other guy had black."

"Maybe they were good friends," Cooper said, cocking his eyebrow.

Calvin nodded in agreement. "That makes the most sense."

Jeff came up to him, talking excitedly. "Damn, that rifle packs a mean punch. He was going down once the first shot hit him!"

Cooper noted that the adrenaline not only made Jeff talk rapid fire, but it also eliminated his faux British manner of talking. He smiled to himself. He tapped the receiver on the FAL. "Yup, the power of .308, baby."

"I gotta get me some of that," Jeff said, looking down at his AR-15 with a bit of regret.

"Don't feel too bad—you got thirty rounds and he only has twenty," Angela offered.

"But one of my rounds will do what it takes three of his to do, so I still come out ahead," Cooper shot back, a wide grin on his face.

"Yeah, I suppose you want to get it done right the first time," she said, coyly.

"Isn't that always true," he said, playing along.

She winked at him and then turned to return to the main part of the lobby.

Cooper shook himself from the brief, post-combat revelry. "Move these bodies behind the desk and let's get ready for the main attack on the station upstairs," he barked. The others moved to get it done. While they did so, Cooper did a tactical reload—replacing the magazine that had fired three rounds with one that was full. When they were done, aside from the bloodstains, the lobby was clean and would pass a cursory inspection from someone outside looking in. *It's the best we can hope for right now.*

They assembled near the door that led to the stairway. They had briefly practiced how to get through doors and sweep a room as a unified fire team. Cooper had no illusions that they would function anywhere close to perfection, but he hoped to avoid acting like a group of Keystone cops.

"Everyone ready? Remember, call out your clear left and clear right. And, do it loud," he said, giving them their final instructions. The others nodded. Zachary, a few paces away, gave them a thumbs up. He was remaining behind to secure their exit. Jeff threw open the door that led into the stairway and the others moved through in the order they had practiced.

Once again, adrenaline raced through Cooper. Dranko was on point, with the shorter M4 better able to get around corners, but Cooper was right behind him. They were the two most experienced, so it made sense for them to lead the way. Angela and Calvin brought up the rear—the other place you needed experience. Neither had much, but it was the best they had.

The stairway was dimly lit; only the emergency lights functioned. Dranko's and Cooper's necks craned upward as they advanced. The radio station was located on the fourth floor and they had decided to bypass the other floors. They wanted to get to the radio station as quickly as possible and were working on the assumption that the other floors were unoccupied—or at least contained no security or armed people to cause them trouble. Cooper hoped they were right. When they came to the second floor landing, he glanced through the window slit on the door that led onto the floor. Nothing was visible, only darkened outlines of cubicles. He breathed a quick sigh of relief. When they reached the third floor, he was panting heavily. A look into the floor revealed the same as the second. Dranko was breathing heavily as well. The others fared as badly, save Angela who was flashed a confused look as Dranko paused so everyone could catch their breath. She quickly caught on, noticing the others. Cooper admired that she and Calvin immediately pivoted themselves facing rearward as they came to a stop.

"We'll move in twenty seconds," Dranko whispered to the group.

Cooper sucked in the air, welcoming the respite. But, stuck on the stairway, he felt incredibly exposed. He knew all it would take for the plan to go to shambles in seconds would be one person stepping into the stairway. He knew they needed to go onto the fourth floor at full speed and decided that Dranko had made the right call. He checked his magazine and ensured that the safety was off.

"Make sure your safety is off and your finger is off the trigger," he mouthed to those behind him. He had seen Dranko do the same already. He saw the others mimic what he had just done.

Dranko motioned them forward and stepped onto the next step. They advanced to the next floor rapidly. They paused briefly on the fourth floor landing to position themselves. Dranko and Cooper stepped to the right and Jeff, third in line, grabbed the door handle and yanked it open.

Dranko stepped through briskly, turning left. Cooper followed, turning to his right. The light was brighter on the floor, with all the overhead fluorescents turned on. Cooper squinted through it. He looked down an empty hallway and he neither heard nor saw anyone over the sea of cubicles that were laid out before him.

"Clear left," he heard Dranko call out loud enough for those around him to hear, but not to carry throughout the floor.

"Clear right," Cooper said, mimicking his volume.

Cooper advanced, calling out the cubicle lanes as he did so. He felt, but did not see, Angela and one of Jeff's men behind him. Jeff should have remained behind to cover the stairwell. Dranko, Calvin, and one of Jeff's men were a matched team going to the left. Their sounds faded as he advanced down the hallway. Cooper was moving in a crouched position, keeping his head below the height of the cubicles. Already, his thighs were beginning to cry out in protest.

The end of the building was about fifty yards in front of him; glassed offices loomed ahead. Suddenly, a man unaware and carrying a notepad turned around the cubicles and came into view at the end of the line.

"Hands up, don't move!" Cooper yelled at the man and his finger went into the trigger guard and found the trigger.

The man looked up, shock registering on his face as he came to a sudden stop. The pad of paper fell from his hands and then to the floor in slow motion. Cooper double-timed toward the man, his rifle trained on his midsection. A second later, the man recovered from his surprise and simultaneously began to dive to his left as his right hand shot toward his waistband.

Damn, Cooper thought as he squeezed the trigger. He got off another round as soon as his rifle recovered from the recoil. In rapid succession, the bullets hit the man in the stomach and the torso, a spray of blood cascading through the air. He collapsed to the floor like a deflated balloon.

Everything slowed down for Cooper. Despite not hearing his rifle's loud report, he heard the shell casings from his rifle bounce off the wall. He breathed deep and fought the temptation to rush toward the fallen man. Instead, he kept advancing methodically, checking the cubicle rows to his left. He did rise up to a standing position for a better view now that any notion of surprising anyone else was lost.

He saw a woman standing up in the next row of cubicles to his left. Her skirt was dark stained, where she had clearly urinated on herself. Tears were already running down her face.

"Hands up, don't move!" he screamed at her. Her eyes were wide in shock, but her hands tentatively rose above her head.

"Target left," Cooper shouted to Calvin and kept advancing. From the corner of his eye, he saw Calvin continue down the row toward her. He heard Jeff's man still coming up behind him.

He reached the dying man at the end of the hallway and quickly scanned to his left and right and saw no one. He knelt beside the man, feeling for a pulse. He had one, but it was weak. The man lay in a pool of blood. Cooper jerked him onto his back and the man offered a weak moan in response. He grabbed the pistol that was on the man's hip and flung it back down the hallway from where he'd come. Down the hall to his left, he heard a frantic voice shouting, apparently the man broadcasting.

"We are under attack… may God help us!"

Cooper leapt back to his feet and sprinted toward the voice. He could see through glass windows into the broadcast room. A portly, bald man was standing next to a large microphone. He looked like the poor man's version of Rush Limbaugh. His eyes went wide when he saw Cooper charging toward him. The man rushed toward the door to try and bar it, but Cooper got there first. He jammed his foot against the door to prevent him from closing it. The man rocketed back onto his heels. Cooper's rifle barrel was only a few feet from his chest.

"Hands up now!" he yelled at him.

The man kept backing up and he tripped on the chair next to the microphone, falling awkwardly to the floor. There, he thrust his hands above his head.

"Don't shoot, don't shoot," he plead in a panicked voice.

Cooper looked down at him. "Don't worry, we aren't here to kill you." He noticed the man had also pissed himself and the stench that hit him a second later told him his bowels had completely loosened in fear.

As Joe, Jeff's man, came into the room behind him, he ordered him, "Cuff him."

Joe knelt down and used a set of zip ties to tie him up. The radio broadcaster had devolved to whimpering and offered no protest. Cooper recognized him from billboards around town declaring him the "Voice of Common Sense for Portland," before the plague had hit. He couldn't remember his name though. He noticed that the bright red light above the microphone was still lit and assumed that they were still on the air.

"Get him out of here," Cooper barked. Joe quickly moved to drag the

162

man out. It took him a bit of time, given the bulk of the man and his inability to walk himself out.

Cooper looked back outside the room and saw Dranko and his crew coming toward him. He gave Dranko a thumbs up. When he saw it, Dranko looked pleased that they'd secured the broadcast booth, but equally and instantly looked ill at the prospect of broadcasting over the radio. He walked up to Cooper, placing his rifle on the desk in front of him, and fishing the scripted notes out of a pocket. He went to sit down, but Cooper caught his arm to keep him standing and levered the microphone up to face level. He took a deep breath, looked at his notes once more, and then began speaking.

"Greetings, fellow Oregonians. Yes, you've just overhead an attack on this radio station by Patriots who still believe in this country." He paused after his voice cracked due to nerves. Cooper patted his friend on the shoulder.

"Speak from your heart, brother," he whispered in his ear.

Dranko nodded once and then continued. "We cannot abide by the lies that our president and Governor Gibbs are spewing. Neither can we tolerate the incursions on our sovereign lands by troops and agents of a foreign government."

Cooper could hear him building momentum as his confidence grew. This time, he punched him lightly on the back for encouragement.

"We call upon the president to immediately come clean about what the government knew, and when it knew, about all details related to the outbreak of the Brushfire Plague. In the name of our forefathers, our flag, all those who have died in its defense, and for everyone who has lost a loved one in this plague—we make this demand."

From behind them, he heard one of Jeffrey's men call out. "You tell 'em, boy!" Dranko smiled.

"Furthermore, we call upon Governor Gibbs to immediately denounce the presence of Chinese military forces and police in the great state of Oregon. We believe firmly that they are here to enslave us—not to help us. Their behavior from the brutal massacre of longshoremen in California to depredations against innocent civilians in Oregon and Washington states make this clear to any honest American."

Just then, Cooper thought he heard the muted sounds of gunfire off in the distance. His stomach tightened with dread. Dranko continued as Cooper stepped back and pulled Jeffery in close. "Get on the walkie-talkie and see if our other positions are okay. I think I just heard gunfire."

Jeffery nodded with a worried face and stepped outside the room to get on it. Cooper turned his attention back toward Dranko.

"...and most importantly, we cannot forget the heroes who formed this country. It is now every patriotic American's duty to rise up and resist our corrupt president and governor. It is now time for us to come to arms unless they meet these reasonable requests to honor our country and everyone who lives in our great land. We must all use every means at our disposal to fight the Chinese invaders and any and all morally bankrupt politicians who kowtow on bended knee to them. We humbly ask that every red-blooded American join us in this call to arms to save our freedom and save our country from the abyss of foreign takeover and tyranny."

He finished by telling the audience of a needed "mass mobilization" in Salem to force the governor to heed the demands of the people or to step down. When he'd stopped talking, he looked around awkwardly for the switch to take them off the air. Several seconds of dead air followed until he found it and punched it. The red light above the microphone went out.

Cooper high-fived his friend. "Well done," he told him. "Perfect."

Dranko was smiling like the kid who aces the math test he never studied for. "Thanks."

Angela leapt into his arms and gave him a long and tight hug. Dranko's face turned red. "C'mon now. It wasn't *that* big a deal."

"Oh, yes it was! You nailed it," she exclaimed. She finished the display by kissing him on the cheek. He turned another shade darker.

Jeffrey pushed the door open and thrust his head into the room. "We got trouble—at least a squad of troops are in the street behind us. Jake and the other guy exchanged gunfire with them but then fell back, hoping to draw them away from us. He's not sure it worked."

"Is Jake okay?" Cooper asked frantically.

Jeffrey shook his head. "I don't know. Can't raise him on the walkie and they got separated.

Immediately, Cooper's head throbbed, bile filled his stomach, and another rush of adrenaline raced into his bloodstream. "Let's go!" he yelled and began to exit the room.

A firm grip stopped him. Dranko had his arm in hand like a vise.

"Calm down, brother. Rushing headlong won't do Jake a damn bit of good.

Cooper's free hand went to punch Dranko in the face, to free himself, but Calvin stepping in and crashing his forearm down across Cooper's blocked it. Rage flashed across his face and he shook himself free of Dranko's grasp. His hand began to raise his rifle up at them when Angela dashed in front of him and enveloped him in a bear hug. She pinned his arms to his sides.

"Cooper, stop. Just stop for a second," she beckoned. She looked desperately at him.

He was shocked into silence, but he shook himself out of her grip as well. "Alright, I'll give you a damned second. But, then we go after Jake," he fired back at them.

Dranko nodded quickly, "Alright, Joe, destroy all of this equipment. Angela, you remember the transmission room I pointed out on the way here?"

"Yes."

"Go smash it. We meet back up at the stairwell exit in one minute. Go!" he screamed at them. Already, Joe's rifle butt was smashing computers and electronic boards inside the studio. Angela raced from the room, back down the hallway that she had come up from.

As they exited the studio, Calvin motioned toward the radio host who was laying prostrate just outside it. "What about him?"

Walking by Calvin and without a word, Cooper raised his rifle and pointed it at the host. His zip tied arms went in front of his face, as if they would stop bullets. He shrieked, "Noooo!" Three rapid-fire shots from Cooper's rifle silenced him as his body jerked from the impact of the point blank rounds. The others looked on in horror, but they all continued walking toward the stairwell.

"What do we know?" Cooper shot at Jeffrey. Cooper's eyes blazed and he spat through clenched teeth, "What's next?"

Jeffrey shook his head, looked at the ground, then back up before beginning. "It looks like a damned random patrol. My guy said they were just driving through in two Humvees when someone spotted them. Our guys shot down at them. They think they hit two of them before they returned fire and our people fell back."

Cooper grabbed Jeffrey by the shirt collar and yanked him nearly off his feet. "How the hell did *your* guy lose track of *my* son?"

He looked back at Cooper with a helpless face. "I don't know, Cooper. I got what I could before he had to move on to his next shelter location. They were hot in pursuit of him."

Cooper yanked his walkie-talkie off of his combat webbing. "Jake, you there? Come in." Silence and static was the only response. Cooper looked at the walkie-talkie in disgust, but kept walking quickly to the stairwell.

Dranko used his walkie-talkie to raise Zachary downstairs. After a quick back and forth with him, he reported to the group. "He's clear downstairs. Two Humvees are parked right out back though, with machineguns on top and manned. He thinks they don't know we are in here yet. And, he hasn't been spotted yet." They'd reached the stairwell entrance. "That's good, we can exit the front," Dranko offered.

Cooper exploded, pushing his friend up against the wall, an arm across his throat. "What are you talking about? I gotta get Jake."

Dranko tried speaking, but Cooper had too much pressure across his windpipe. He was turning red. The others pulled Cooper off of him, despite a furious struggle from Cooper. Dranko pushed his arm away defiantly as soon as he was able.

"We don't stand a chance trying to go up against a squad that is dispersed amongst the buildings and alert. Hell, we might not even get past the machineguns. We need to get the hell out of here now! Then, we'll circle back and find Jake in a few hours."

Cooper shook his head vigorously. "I'm *not* leaving him behind."

Now it was Dranko's turn to throw Cooper up against the wall. "Cooper, you know damn well we have no choice. Anything else is a suicide march. You wanna see Jake alive again?"

Cooper looked back at him, wordless but incredulous.

"Then, do what the hell I tell you. My way is the best chance and you fucking know it!"

Angela came up just then. "All finished. This station is officially offline."

Dranko nodded. "Alright, let's go. Angela, you are with me on the descent. Cooper, you get in the middle and collect yourself."

Dazed, Cooper could only muster a solemn nod. They reached the bottom floor without incident. Zachary had positioned himself at the corner of the alcove that bore the elevators. He was occasionally taking quick looks around the corner, both to the front and rear of the building. The group assembled around him.

"What do we have?" Dranko asked.

"Same as I told you—the two Humvees out back have stayed put. They keep looking in here as they scan the area, but no one has made a move inside yet. The rest of the squad disappeared in the opposite direction."

"How many?" Cooper asked through clenched teeth.

"About a dozen, total. There is one wounded in the back of the rear Humvee.

"Let's take them out, now," Cooper said.

Dranko shook his head. "It only takes one of the fifties to open up into this building and we are all dead, brother. We'd be cut to ribbons. We gotta exit out the front and make our way back."

Cooper's face flushed red and he bristled as he grabbed Dranko by the shirt collar. "You're missing the damned point. Zachary just said they are scanning and not looking back here all the time. We *can* take them out by using the surprise that we have."

Dranko swept Cooper's hands away. "And, what then? We go bumbling around the adjacent buildings looking for Jake amidst a squad of soldiers where we *don't* have the element of surprise?"

Cooper sighed at his friend's words and fought his anger from coming to a head. "I told you I ain't leaving him. Either help me or not, but I'm doing this." Cooper pivoted hard on his heel, racked the bolt on his rifle to chamber a fresh round, and strode toward the corner that led to the building's rear exit. When he reached the edge of the wall, he knelt and carefully peeked around the corner. The men he observed were looking away from the building and Cooper quickly calculated how he could pull off two shots at two targets spread out over about fifteen yards between them.

"You taking the guy on the left or the right?" Dranko's voice interrupted his thinking, coming from directly behind him.

Cooper looked back, flashing his friend a smile. "I got left."

"You know you're one crazy bastard, right?"

Cooper nodded as he faced forward once more and readied himself.

"On three. One... two... three," he called out.

Cooper leaned out from behind the cover of the wall. The machine gunner on the Humvee had just started to turn back toward the building. Cooper quickly realized that he was now in a split second contest to fire and hit him before he spotted Cooper and opened fire on him. His rifle sights were lined up on the man's torso, but as he turned the machinegun, the gun shield went with it and offered growing protection to the soldier. He took a deep breath, released half of it, and slowly squeezed the trigger. His rifle fired and he was dimly aware that Dranko's rifle fired a half second after his.

He saw the soldier's body jerk and for a second he thought he had hit him. Then, as the man rapidly turned the machinegun to face him, he realized he had only been reacting to his shot. Adrenaline churned through Cooper as the soldier's hand pulled back the heavy bolt and he saw it rocket forward—making the heavy machinegun ready to rain metal down upon them. With the gun fully facing him now, Cooper did not have much to target—a thin gap between the gun shield and the man's helmet. He did the only thing he knew how to do, he snap aimed at the machine gunner and began rapidly firing—pulling the trigger again and again as soon as the rifle centered on target after the recoil of each shot. He got off two shots like this before the machine gun's barrel—which looked like a cannon facing him—exploded in a fireball. As he kept shooting at the target that he was intensely focused on, he was vaguely aware that the tile floor a half dozen yards in front of him was shooting up bits of dust and rock as the machinegun inched toward him, bullets smashing into the ground.

Time slowed even more, moving from slow motion to frame-by-frame speed. Cooper's rifle bucked against his shoulder. A glint of flame flashed off of the gun shield just a few inches from its top. He caught sight of the glittering empty shell casing floating up and away from his rifle before arcing precipitously toward the ground. Then, a floor tile disintegrated a few feet in front of him and he felt the sting on his cheek from the shattered tiles. Beyond that, glass was still crashing to the ground as the building's exterior glass panels disintegrated under the fury of incoming and outgoing bullets.

From behind him, he heard the reports *and* felt the air pressure changing as Dranko unleashed a bout of fire from the M4. He had no idea if he was still trying to dispatch his target or if he had shifted his aim to help him out. Cooper's finger squeezed again and the next thing he knew, the machine gunner's helmet rocked back and forth like a ship tossed on an angry sea. He could not see the man's eyes underneath his dark amber goggles, but he guessed they were wide open in shock. The man's hands flew back toward his head, and when they reached them, they cradled his helmet in both hands. He rocked back and forth, trying to shake what must have been a skull rattler of a hit.

Cooper wasted no time to celebrate. Instead, he took the moment to displace. He raced across the hallway to the opposite wall, being careful to stay low and avoid being shot in the back of the head by Dranko. When he got there, he crashed into the wall and fell into a kneeling position once again. By now, the soldier had recovered and Cooper once again saw flame spitting from the heavy machinegun's barrel. However, he had not seen Cooper's flight from his previous position and so he kept firing in that direction. Cooper knew this advantage would last for only one shot, and he also knew that he had no cover to protect himself in his new position. *One or done*, he mused to himself.

He carefully lined up his sights on the soldier and fired. This time, the man's body jerked and then a moment later, bright red spouts of blood shot out from his neck. In the morning light, the crimson spray might have been beautiful, if not for what it represented. The soldier looked from side to side in a confused manner and then abruptly slumped to his left.

"Let's go!" Cooper screamed at the top of his lungs. He leapt to his feet and charged forward. He dropped the nearly empty magazine and heard it rattle against the floor as he rammed a fresh one home and then racked the bolt. His boots crunched amid the litter of shattered glass that was strewn across the building's lobby.

Suddenly, to his right, the tile on the wall exploded and pelted him with debris. He craned his head to the right and saw a pistol pointed in his direction from the back of the second Humvee. He cursed himself for forgetting about the wounded man that Zachary had told him about. Before he could react, however, a flurry of bullets crashed into—and through—the Humvee's thin sides and window around the protruding pistol. Then, the pistol clattered to the ground and Cooper assumed the wounded man was no longer a threat. He looked over and saw Dranko lowering his rifle. The two men exchanged a knowing nod.

Now he was through the threshold of what was once the building's back doors and windows. He scanned to his left and right as his boots left the tiled lobby and crashed onto the cement outside. Nothing. He breathed a silent sigh of relief. He raced to the lead Humvee and looked inside. The vehicle was empty, save the dead body of the machine gunner he had shot. He looked to his left and saw Dranko and Zachary similarly clearing the second Humvee. Dranko gave him a thumbs up.

Cooper was already bounding across to the driver's side door. He reached in and punched the ignition switch. The powerful engine came to life and was quickly idling. "Spike that one and let's roll!" Cooper barked to Dranko. "Zachary, help me get this guy out of here," he called, indicating the dead soldier with an incline and dip of his head.

He and Zachary were in the middle of wrestling the man's body from the Humvee when he heard rapid fire as Dranko emptied a magazine of ammunition into the engine compartment of the other Humvee to ensure its inoperability.

When they got the soldier's body onto the ground—with Cooper taking the time to do so gently out of respect for him—the others were ambling up to the Humvee.

"Take his weapons and ammo," Cooper directed Zachary.

Dranko was at his side. "What now?"

"We find Jake," he said flatly, his jaw clenched.

"We are setting ourselves up for an ambush," he retorted.

Cooper shook his head. "That's where you're wrong. Let me ask: you are a Squad Leader. You just lost your vehicles—your primary means of speedy ingress and *egress*. What do you do?"

A devilish grin descended upon Dranko's face as he flashed recognition. "I pull my men back, regroup, and wait for extraction."

Now Cooper was smiling. "And why?"

"Because I assume I'm facing an overwhelming force—or at the very least a better trained one."

He tapped his friend's forehead with a pointed finger. "Exactly."

Dranko shook his head in admiration. "I gotta hand it to you. You *are* a smart bastard."

"You can say that later, when I can record it. Now, let's roll."

The group piled into the Humvee. Cooper took the machinegun, Dranko was at the wheel, and Angela was in the passenger seat. Calvin and Jeffrey were in the backseat, while the others slid uncomfortably into the cargo area.

Jeffrey called up to Cooper. "I can't get *either* of them on the radio now."

Like turning a shower faucet from hot to cold, an icy dread replaced the adrenaline that had been coursing through Cooper's veins. Images of his worst fears of Jake dead or dying raced through his mind. A vise gripped his throat. His mouth was instantly parched and his hands curled into tight balls of worry. Then, the headset that had previously rested on the dead soldier's head came to life. An unfamiliar voice called out for a recognition sign that Cooper did not recognize. An idea rescued him from the momentary paralysis. He grabbed the headset and slammed it up against his head.

He crushed the call button. "Yeah, your boy's dead. We got both your Humvees and we are coming for you."

A stressed out voice responded. "Who is this? This is a military channel and it's illegal for you—"

Cooper cut him off. "Didn't you hear me? We are *coming* for you because we are hungry." He paused for dramatic effect and then called out in a sing song voice, "Because we are hungry... ever so hungry!" He ended the act with the high-pitched cackle of the insane. Only static remained when he let out the call button. Cooper smiled to himself. When the idea seized him to convince them they were crazed cannibals out for bloodlust and food, he'd worried if he could pull it off. Now, he felt confident he had.

"Let's go. Take us around the next street over. Zachary, keep trying the walkie."

They left the disabled Humvee behind as they pulled away. It had been a long time since Cooper had handled an M2 heavy machinegun, so he quickly reacquainted himself with its controls and ensured one of the huge .50 caliber rounds was chambered. He kept his head on a swivel, continuously scanning in all directions for signs of movement.

He called back into the Humvee's main compartment. "Keep your eyes open and your weapons ready. Call out any sign of movement or hostiles, even if you aren't sure."

Dranko replied. "Yes, better safe than sorry, friends!"

He cranked the wheel to his left when they reached the end of the block. There was no sign of the enemy, just what had become the "normal" detritus of a ruined society: abandoned cars, piled up garbage, and empty buildings.

They took another left turn to survey the next street. It looked empty and they could see no sign of movement in the buildings that lined it.

"Anything on the walkie?" Cooper called down to Zachary.

"Still trying," he shouted back.

Dread was growing in Cooper's belly with each passing minute. *Why isn't Jake on the radio?* The nagging questions plagued him like no other. *Has he lost it? Is it broken? Or is it something much worse than that?* He gripped the machinegun tighter out of frustration. *I never should have let him go on this mission,* Cooper thought in bitter reproach. Toward the middle of the block, a wrecked car and dumpster combined to block their passage.

"Eyes up! Scan the buildings!" Cooper yelled, fearing a potential ambush site.

He carefully looked over the windows on the multi-story building to his left, but saw nothing. Thankfully, the building on the right was a low-slung structure that lacked windows on this side. Dranko brought the vehicle to a stop ten yards before the blockage. Calvin and Angela exited and ran toward the vehicle. They quickly ensured it was empty before turning their

170

attention to the dumpster. After a few moments of heavy pushing, they were able to create a gap big enough for. the Humvee to roll through. Cooper bridled with impatience. Then, the military handset came to life once again. Cooper grabbed it and brought it to his ear.

"Mr. Cooper Adams, we've got your son."

CHAPTER TWELVE

In the seconds that ticked by, Cooper remained speechless. He could not believe what he had heard. He could feel the blood drain from his face. His stomach threatened to unload on him. His knees weakened.

"What's wrong?" Dranko called up to him. Cooper numbly shook his head in response. Angela wormed her way through the opening that he occupied, her body pressed up against his. She took one look at him and grabbed the handset from him.

"Who is this?" she demanded.

"All you need to know is I'm with the National Guard. We have Mr. Adams' son in custody."

Angela looked from the handset to Cooper and back again in shock. "Is he safe?" she asked.

"He has a few bumps and scrapes from his apprehension, but otherwise he is unharmed."

"What do you want?"

"Ma'am, I'm just a grunt, but I know enough that the answer to that question is above my pay grade."

Cooper could hear everything through the loud handset speakers'. He still felt immobilized.

"Why'd you contact us, then?"

"Because I want you to withdraw from this area. We are in a well defensible location. You find us, and a lot of people are going to die. There's been enough of that today. Your other man is dead."

Cooper felt himself return to life, yanked the handset from Angela's hands, and yelled into the mic, "You hurt my boy and you're a dead man!"

"I assure you, sir, we will do him no harm. I know who you are and I recognize a valued asset when I see one. If you withdraw, I will take him to my superiors."

"Let me talk to him," Cooper said, trying to mask the anguish he was feeling.

There was a momentary pause. "Hello?"

Tears rushed into Cooper's eyes and his throat tightened, making it hard to breath. "Jake! You alright, son?"

"Yeah," his son sobbed back at him. "I'm sorry... I got caught."

Cooper waved his free hand in dismissal even though Jake could not see him. "Don't worry about that. I'm just glad you are alive."

"Save me, please!" Jake wailed, his voice showing every bit of a terrified child.

"I will," Cooper said, meaning every word of it.

"Okay. That's enough." The man came back on the handset. "Mr. Adams, you and your men withdraw from this area immediately. We will contact you on this channel. That's the best way to ensure your son's safety."

Cooper pounded the Humvee's roof in rage and frustration. He knew he had no choice, and that every other option led to likely harm. But, like a fox caught in a snare, he wished he could simply chew off his own leg to get out of this predicament. He punched the call button. "Okay, we will pull back."

"Roger that, good decision, Mr. Adams."

He flung the handset down into the main compartment. Angela's eyes met his with a wellspring of sympathy. Her hand caressed his cheek, but he brushed it away. He could barely move with her pressed into a crew area meant for one. He motioned for her to return to her seat and she wriggled back down.

He kneeled down so that he was in the main area as well. The others looked at him with a mix of concern and confusion. "They got Jake. We need to pull back."

Dranko looked at him, started to talk, saw the expression on Cooper's face, and then stopped. Instead, he put the Humvee in reverse. Cooper, not wanting to face the others, popped back into the cupola and looked vacantly over the heavy machinegun's sights. His mind swirled with a cavalcade of thoughts—most full of despair and fury.

The next thirty minutes were a blur as they made their way from the area and took a circuitous route back to where they had started the morning. Worried about surveillance from the air, they found a Jiffy Lube two blocks from the abandoned office building and parked the Humvee inside. As they walked back to the office building, Cooper stumbled behind everyone else in a daze.

*

* *

When they reached the office building, Cooper found a corner and slumped to the ground. He cradled his head in his shaking hands. Blood pounded in his temples. He cursed himself for letting Jake come along. He cursed the governor and he cursed the Brushfire Plague. His mind searched for an answer on how to get Jake back, but it kept returning to the one he dreaded: he'd have to turn himself in. He would do whatever he needed in order to save his son. He knew this meant that he could end up dead and that he'd never see Jake grow up. He was lost in the circle of despair and saw no way out of the maze. The others left him to himself for a while, but Dranko eventually approached.

Cooper looked up at the sound of footsteps and looked at him. "I'm going to have to turn myself in."

Dranko nodded. "I know. I don't see any way we can avoid that."

Hearing his friend's grim confirmation made it suddenly real. Tears welled up in his eyes. "Will you raise up Jake right?"

Dranko nodded somberly. "Of course. But I think there is still some hope."

Cooper looked at him with reproach. "Don't BS me."

"I'm not. I don't think a rescue plan is out of the question. We might be able to get the Washington National Guard involved."

Cooper shook his head. "I'll believe it when I see it."

Just then, Angela came racing into the room, carrying the handset. "They are asking for you."

Cooper was on his feet in an instant and took the handset from her. "Yes, this is Cooper here."

"Mr. Cooper, this is Major Cummings. I wish we were speaking under better circumstances."

"Me too."

"I'm sure you are anxious, so I will get right to it. You are to deliver yourself into our custody in one hour at Waterfront Park. We will release your son at that time."

"How do I know you will release my son?"

"You have Governor Gibbs' word on that, sir."

Cooper's unyielding commitment to the truth caused the governor's declaration of honor, which was so obviously false, shock him out of his stupor. Something clicked in Cooper's mind. *The governor does about his reputation, he has to.* That could provide the protection Cooper needed to get his son back. His heart leapt as he continued thinking about the possibilities. A moment later, he spoke. "That's not going to happen."

There was a momentary pause on the other end. *Is the Major thinking or consulting with someone else?*

"Excuse me, I thought I heard you refuse?"

"You did," Cooper answered, his voice as cold as a glacier.

Another pause. It was longer this time.

"Mr. Adams, if this does not occur, I can no longer guarantee your son's safety."

Cooper face turned to a scowl and his fist clenched at the threat. His voice was steel. "Oh, yes you can."

"How?"

"You tell the governor that I have the world's ear. You tell him that if a hair is harmed on my boy's head, he will have a revolution on his hands. You ask him if he thinks the good people of Oregon will stand it to hear that their governor hurt or killed a twelve-year-old boy."

There was another long pause. "Mr. Adams, for all the world knows, your son was killed in a vicious terrorist attack on a local radio station."

Cooper deliberately laughed into the mic before speaking. "Ask the governor if he wants to test my credibility versus his with the public."

He capitalized on the next pause by continuing, "And, if that is not enough, you tell the governor that I have a videotaped confession from a Mr. Jonathan Goodwin that he might want to have in *his* possession."

"Give me a minute, please."

Cooper welcomed the sound of worry in Major Cummings' voice. "Of course."

Dranko and Angela were looking at him with mouths agape.

"What are you doing?" Angela asked.

"Getting my boy back."

"You are taking a big risk, aren't you?" Dranko questioned him.

Cooper shook his head. "With their plan, I would be at their mercy if they'd even release Jake."

"And your way," Angela responded.

Cooper smiled confidently. "My father taught me about negotiations. We both have something the other wants. It just took me a minute to see my leverage in this situation."

They continued looking at him in disbelief until the handset crackled to life once again.

"What do you suggest, Mr. Adams?"

"You contact me on this channel in twenty-four hours and I will give you a location for the exchange. I've grown tired of all of this. The risk is obviously too great for my family and me. The terms of the exchange are simple. You give me my son and one million dollars in gold and silver and I will give the governor what he needs."

"You know I cannot commit to the money right now."

"I understand," he said firmly. "I'll need an answer in twenty-four hours."

"Understood. Out."

Cooper looked back at Angela and Dranko.

"You are one cold bastard, brother." Dranko was finally smiling.

Angela looked at him, confused. "I thought you couldn't lie, Cooper?"

The corner of his mouth turned up in a wry grin. "What are you talking about?"

"Well, are you really going to give him the videotape and disappear from all this?"

He shook his head, the grin growing. "I never said that."

"I thought you did?"

"Nope. I said I'd give the governor what he needs. Which, as far as I'm concerned, is a bullet in the head."

Dranko clapped his hands in a loud display of admiration. "Damn, you are good."

"We all have our strengths," Cooper demurred, grinning. He lazily handed the handset to Dranko. Now that the rush of the exchange was over and adrenaline fled his body as quickly as it had come, Cooper felt himself begin to crash. He yawned and rubbed his temple feverishly. He knew he was playing an "all in" brand of poker with the governor and he hoped that it was the right play. Despite how cool he had been in the negotiations, he *was* worried about the outcome. "I'm gonna lie down and take a nap. I'm exhausted," he said to them.

"Brother, you go from sixty to zero faster than anyone I've ever known," Dranko replied.

Cooper shrugged, grabbed his sleeping bag, and walked toward a quiet corner in the sprawling office space. "Wake me in two hours and can you bring everyone else up to speed?"

"Will do."

Laying down, he was asleep within minutes.

*
* *

"Cooper, wake up."

Angela was kneeling next to him, her hand on his shoulder. Her eyes were tender, looking deep into his. He returned her gaze as his hand found hers.

"Thank you," he said. She looked confused, so he continued. "Not for waking me up, I mean… for everything."

Her cheeks grew flush and she smiled as she squeezed his hand. "You're welcome, Cooper. It's been a pleasure." She lingered on the last word and she winked at him.

He squeezed her hand back as he sat up. His eyes remained locked on hers for several more moments. Then he let go of her hand and stood up. She stood up with him, but she could not conceal her disappointment.

"Where's Dranko? We have some planning to do."

She pointed to her left. "He's in the main room"

He did not know what else to say, so he strode off in that direction without another word. He entered the main room, where Dranko, Calvin, and Jeffrey were clustered around a pile of maps spread out on an office conference table.

"You're up," Dranko said, when he saw him.

Cooper nodded. "You guys figuring out a good exchange location?"

"Yeah, and I think we have one," Calvin answered.

"Only one road in and no way they can land a chopper within any sort of distance," Dranko said excitedly.

Cooper joined them at the table as they pointed out the location on the map. He looked at the surrounding terrain with pleasure. "How do we keep them from blockading the way out, though?"

"You will not be leaving by the road," Calvin said. Cooper cocked an eyebrow, so Calvin continued. "You will extract from this point. It is about a three mile hike through the forest, but mostly downhill."

He nodded. "Good plan. And, we will have men stationed so that the governor cannot infiltrate his men through the backside?"

"Exactly. You just need to tell him that if he puts men in the area that the exchange is off and that the recording goes public."

"Got it."

"There's only one problem, chap," Jeffrey chimed in.

He turned toward him. "What's that?"

"You must set the meeting three days out."

"What?" he said in disbelief.

"That's the quickest we can get our men assembled in Salem."

"I can't leave Jake in their hands that long. I gotta get my boy back!" he shouted.

Dranko held up his hands. "Relax, brother. This will give you more leverage. It will distract the governor's resources and if he was even considering a double-cross, he won't when there is an army on his front doorstep."

Cooper took a step back to consider what he had said. Inside, he was in turmoil. His heart wanted Jake back *now*, but, his mind churned over Dranko's words. He recalled his father's wisdom: *you want the boss to see the powder keg built up in front of their eyes, with the match alight.* He had said this once, when he was involved in organizing a big strike of workers, but it had stuck in Cooper's brain ever since. The war inside lasted the briefest of moments.

"Alright, I get it. We need the tinder built under a bonfire, ready to light."

Dranko's expression flashed from worried to relieved and he clapped Cooper on the back. "That's exactly right, brother."

Jeffrey stepped forward. "You ready to hear the whole plan?"

Cooper stepped to the table. "Yeah, lay it on me."

"We use the next three days to organize the bloody thing. We have strong groups of Cooperites in these towns that are near enough," Jeffrey said. He pointed at spots on the map: Portland, Salem, Stayton, and Silverton. "We barnstorm these places with meetings. Chap, we are going to use you to get them fired up. With that and some frothy hard work throughout our network, we can make the governor ready to piss down the leg of his knickers." He wore a broad smile by the time he had finished. With aplomb, he raked his driver's cap to the side for emphasis.

Cooper rubbed his chin. "I like it. But, we have to keep Jonathan and what he told us in reserve; that cannot be mentioned in the meetings."

Jeffrey's face fell. "Why not? He's the proof in the bloody pudding."

Their eyes met. "Leverage. Word is going to get back to the governor that I'm doing this. If I'm spilling the beans about Jonathan, it's like putting a match to the fire and we lose that leverage. We need him worrying about what happens *if* I release that video."

"But, we'd be taking one of our big cards off that table," Angela added.

He turned toward her. "Yes, but once you play a card, it's spent. I'm not going to risk *not* getting Jake back. This isn't negotiable."

After a moment of awkward silence and exchanged looks, the others slowly nodded in reluctant acquiescence.

Calvin broke the silence. "Are you really going to let the governor walk away from all of this when you get Jake back?"

Before Cooper could answer, Dranko jumped in. "You let me worry about that." Then, he turned to Cooper. "You just get me in on the exchange." Cooper looked at him, wondering what plan he had up his sleeve and decided to trust it in the end. Knowing his own penchant for the truth, he figured it was better he didn't know.

"I want in, too." Julianne had been standing, uninvolved, away from the table, so her words caught everyone by surprise.

"Why?" Cooper asked.

"I need to see him face to face, too, after what he and the others duped me into doing." Her voice dripped with emotion and her eyes glistened.

Cooper debated arguing with her, but declined to do so when he realized it probably did no harm to have her there. "Alright, fine by me," Cooper said and then turned back to the main group. "So, what's next?"

"We stay put today. Jeffrey already has the first meeting tonight in Portland, on the east side."

"Good enough. Are you able to get Jonathan down here for the exchange?"

"You think they will want him?" Jeffrey asked.

Cooper nodded. "I'd be shocked if they don't."

"Yeah, I can make that happen."

"Do we have any word from the Washington governor about moving more troops down this way?"

He shook his head. "Not yet, but we should have an answer by this afternoon."

"Okay, keep me posted."

The meeting ended at that. As the group dispersed, Cooper walked over to where Julianne was standing. "Walk with me," he said to her and she fell in step next to him. They wandered down a hallway, amidst the offices and cubicles. Once they were out of earshot, he turned to face her. "So, tell me what you really want to get out of seeing the governor face to face."

She wrung her hands nervously before she looked to respond to him.

"Honestly, I'm not sure. I'm looking for closure. I'm trying to make sense of it all, Cooper. I want to ask him some questions."

Cooper looked at her, still confused. Her face flushed and once again, tears welled up. "Just let me do this, please. I can't tell you it makes sense or if it will accomplish anything. I just *need* to confront the man. To get to the bottom of this damned thing," she said, her voice filled with emotion.

He slowly nodded at her. "Okay. Just make me one promise."

"What's that?"

"Can you keep quiet until we have Jake?"

She smiled, putting a hand on his chest. "Of course."

"Alright, I'll think on it," Cooper said, but he doubted he'd agree to it in the end. *Too risky,* was looping in his mind. "Good enough?" he asked. She nodded in resignation. He turned to walk back to the main group.

She clutched at his hand as he turned. He felt the same electricity he always did at her touch. Their eyes met and she took a step closer to him, her body nearly touching his. He had the urge to step toward her and pull her in tight, but he resisted. Instead, he took her hand and brought it to his lips. He inhaled her scent, which only enhanced the temptation. He kissed her hand lightly and then slowly moved it away. He gave her a longing look before firmly pivoting on his heels and walking away. She stood watching him as he disappeared down the hallway.

*

*   *

When he arrived back in the main area, he found a curious scene: six buckets of Crisco lay on a table. Angela and Dranko were cutting pieces of string next to them.

He gave them a quizzical look. "What are you doing?"

Dranko looked up at him and laughed. "Brother, didn't your mother teach you anything?"

"Well, she taught me not to take any BS, I can tell you that."

He laughed again. "Calvin found these stacked under one of the cubicle desks. Probably someone made a Costco run on break and never got these buckets home, I don't know. But, we are making candles."

"Candles?"

Dranko nodded. "Yeah, any prepper worth his salt knows that Crisco makes an awesome emergency candle that will last a month or more."

Cooper looked at him with amusement. "Really?"

"Yup. Just push a wick to the bottom and voila, you have a candle."

"And you just happen to carry wicks with you," Cooper said with a cocked eyebrow.

"Nope. But, that is where you improvise. I'm using the best string that I

179

could find and, luckily, Zachary was a hipster pre-plague and still had a can of wax for his mustache tucked away that he'd almost forgotten about."

"And?" Cooper asked, still confused.

"We just melted the wax, dipped the string in it, and let it cool down. Now, we are cutting the string to the right length. Just watch."

Cooper leaned back against the table. Dranko was using what looked like a rod used to open and close blinds to push the wick down into the Crisco buckets. It took some jiggering, but he managed to get the wick down to the bottom. He then took a wad of foil that he had cut a hole in and threaded the wick through that, before placing the foil disc on top of the Crisco, leaving an inch or so of the wick sticking through. Finally, he shook the bucket vigorously, forcing the Crisco to surround the wick as the rod had made a hole in the middle. Triumphantly, a lighter emerged in Dranko's hand and he lit the wick. Quickly, the wick burned down to where it met the Crisco.

"Like I said, voila!" Dranko pointed to the wick burning like any candle. He let it burn for a few seconds to prove his point and then blew it out.

Cooper looked on, impressed. "I'll hand it to you, that's pretty cool."

He bowed in dramatic fashion. "Why thank you, good sir."

*

* *

Cooper spent the rest of the day alternating between deep worry about Jake's condition and the risks associated with the bold plan to bring him home. He also had to prepare for what he would say at the meeting later in the evening. His father had taught him how meetings played a vital part in helping a group accomplish a mission or a goal. As Cooper sat fiddling with one of Dranko's improvised wicks between his fingers, his mind drifted.

Cooper heard his father come in the front door as he sat reading "The Hobbit" in the living room. Unlike when he was younger, he did not rush to his father to hug him when he came home from work. He assumed, as usual, his father would find him and greet him. He continued reading about the adventures of Bilbo and company, but moments later, he was distracted by a loud clang. It sounded like his father had thrown something in the sink with vigor. He set the book down and ambled toward the kitchen.

His father, an imposing man of stature to the ten-year-old child approaching him, was leaning over the sink. His arms were splayed out and his hands gripped the counter's edge. His head was turned to his left, gazing out the window over the sink into the distance and dark that the night afforded.

"What happened?" Cooper asked.

His father turned toward him, moving slowly, tired. He leaned back against the counter and pivoted his hands so that they once again gripped it tightly. "Just a tough

180

night," his father replied.

Undeterred, Cooper pressed on. "What happened?"

His father paused, then exhaled loudly, and closed with a warm smile. "Alright," he said, motioning his son to sit down at the kitchen table. Cooper swiftly took up a seat there. When his father sat down, he retrieved a metal cooking tray that held the remainder of some brownies. Cooper went to grab a piece, but he had his hand slapped away.

"Not right now," his father said.

He settled back into his seat, folded his hands, and looked deeply at Cooper. "So, we had a meeting tonight and it didn't go well." Cooper mustered a look of measured concern, one he'd seen his father make a thousand times, and simply waited for his father to continue. From past experience, he knew he would. "I won't bore you with the details... they don't matter anyway," he said. He thumbed a piece of brownie off the pan and looked at it intently. He saw Cooper's expectant eyes and flipped his fingers, indicating that it was okay for him to grab a piece of the leftovers.

Suddenly, his father's eyes went alight. "You see this!" He held the brownie on his palm, out toward Cooper.

"Yeah, it's a brownie," Cooper said in an incredulous voice.

"Ah, it's more than that. Tell me what you see. Look closely."

Cooper looked at his father as if he might be crazy, but decided to play along. "I see a brownie. I see chocolate and some walnuts. Not enough walnuts though." He paused, uncertain.

"What else do you see?"

"I don't know. Well, it's burned on the side."

His father leapt from the table. "Yes, that's it!"

"What?"

"My meeting tonight was the burned part. Tasteless, charred, ruined. But, a meeting can be the sweet delicious middle, too!"

Cooper was completely confused and watched his father pace a few circles around the kitchen. He was animated and thinking deeply while gesticulating wildly with his hands. Then he came to an abrupt stop. He walked to where Cooper sat and cupped his face in his hands. "I've got some re-baking to do son! But, don't you ever forget it. The burnt brownie. A meeting, or life, can be burnt or sweet."

At that, he rushed off and disappeared into a spare bedroom on the first floor of their house that often doubled as his office. Within seconds, he heard his father's animated voice on the phone.

Cooper didn't fully understand what his father meant that night. However, over time, he would describe every meeting as a "burnt brownie" and that would then provoke a question from Cooper: did you all eat the burned or the sweet part? His father's answer then would tell him whether it had been a good or bad meeting. Their inside joke culminated in tragic fashion.

One day, while his father was in prison on trumped up charges, Cooper had brought his father a cookbook of brownie recipes. He had hoped it would serve as a good reminder to stay focused on the good. Instead, his father had collapsed in a heap of tears when his *son proudly presented the book to him. In that moment, Cooper knew then that prison was sucking something irreplaceable out of his father.*

*
* *

"You ready to go?" Dranko asked him, rousing him from his memories. Cooper rose up, grabbing his rifle. "Yes, sir."

"You know what you're gonna say?"

He looked at his friend sideways and winked. "Yeah. The truth."

Dranko laughed and then turned to leave the building. Cooper followed him. When they got outside, he realized that they were going in a Jeep Wrangler. Jeffrey was in the driver's seat and Zachary was next to him. It looked like Cooper and Dranko would share the back seats. Zachary carried a pump shotgun and Cooper grinned at the accurate filling of the vehicle's "shotgun" seat.

"We traveling light?" he asked, turning to Dranko.

He nodded. "Yeah, we think just one vehicle can get us in and out a lot faster than a convoy. Onsite, we'll have plenty of backup from our supporters."

Cooper grunted his assent and climbed into the rear seat behind the driver. He noticed a belt had been set up attached to the roll bar. It was an improvised seatbelt, with either end lashed and secured to it. He didn't have to ask; it was clear that it was intended for someone to "tie themselves" in and be able to fire their weapon from a standing position in all directions over the Wrangler's roof.

He pointed his rifle toward it. "Your idea?" he asked Dranko.

He shook his head. "Actually, no, it was Calvin. Said he saw it on some TV show. You can cinch it down tight, so I think it will work. Mostly." He finished with a grin.

"We get into a situation where we need that, you should take it. Your weapon is more handy than mine," he replied.

Dranko nodded as he climbed into the Wrangler. Jeffery fired up the motor and they pulled out of the parking lot. Cooper reflexively checked and double-checked his rifle's safety and ensured the magazine was seated properly with a round chambered. This time, however, he had another thing to obsess over: his upcoming speech. He drew a piece of paper out of his pocket and began reviewing it, pouring through the notes he had scrawled earlier. He knew, in his gut, what he wanted to say to his fellow Oregonians, but the notes helped ease his mind as he focused on them. He fought to do so as the Wrangler jostled him whenever Jeffrey made a sharp turn to get around some blockage in the road.

He leaned over so that Dranko could hear him. "Where are we going?"

182

"East side. Near Powell Butte. Biggest concentration of your supporters is out that way and in Troutdale."

Cooper still wasn't used to hearing someone say "your supporters" or the "Cooperites." He couldn't grasp how he had become a political figure. *All I did was tell the truth. Hell, if more leaders and politicians had told the truth in the past, we wouldn't be in this damned mess.* He brushed off his discomfort and instead replied to his friend. "Good enough. You know how many people we are expecting?"

"Jeffrey said at least one hundred, but they don't really know. It's all rumor and word of mouth right now. We're meeting inside some Granger Hall."

Cooper nodded again. They had successfully crossed the bridge over the Multnomah River and were heading east. He ruminated that they would be passing within a mile of his former home on Lincoln Street. *So close, and yet so very far,* he thought to himself. They were on high alert as they proceeded. Most of Powell was abandoned or worse. Unlike the north end of town that they had passed through the other day, there were no functioning businesses here. Cooper almost wept when he saw that the iconic Powell Pancake House had burned down to a pile of rubble. He, Elena, and friends had ended many a late night or early morning there after being out on the town. A few times, they had taken Jake there for a regular breakfast. Thick pancakes and thicker slabs of bacon had been the place's calling card.

Unfortunately, many businesses along Powell had met a similar fate. Some buildings looked simply vacant, but most had been visibly looted or had been burned out. As they proceeded up the road, Cooper spotted a union hall where his father had once spoken. It was half a block off Powell, across from a park and a burger joint. He wondered if that was the same union the woman at the coffee shop had mentioned. He looked around again but saw no one outside at all. They kept going. He was alert for possible snipers or ambushes. Rolling up such a vacant and possibly dangerous street in an open-topped vehicle had them all on edge. Cooper stood and strapped himself into the belts tied to the roll bar. He wanted the full range of view that the position afforded him. He figured that with the long streets that ran off Powell, it was better for him to be in the position with the longer range and power of the .308 round.

They had made it through a wide section of Portland and were now approaching the I-205 highway that cut north and south and divided inner Portland from its outer section. He guessed the distinction was as much a convenience for the city's realtors as it was any real divide. He saw movement up ahead and off to the right. There was a derelict SUV parked up on the right shoulder, hanging in a shadow under the freeway's overpass. *Good location for someone to ambush from,* he thought as he noted the difficulty in seeing what was in the SUV. Cooper was pretty sure that he had seen the tailgate drift open farther than it had been. He tapped Jeffrey with his boot and pointed at the SUV with his rifle. Jeffrey responded by jerking the Wrangler into erratic slower and faster speeds. Cooper hoped that would make them a tougher target if someone were about to shoot at them. He clearly knew it would make it harder for him to return fire as he bucked and bounced against the roll bar.

Cooper heard the clang of metal hitting metal on the Wrangler. He saw no flash nor heard any gunshot, but he knew they were under fire. He had already kept his weapon sighted on the SUV and quickly fired two rounds in succession. One punched through the glass on the tailgate while the other went wild as Jeffrey bucked the Wrangler to his left just as he'd fired. Seeing this, Cooper fired two more rounds. Luckily, this time, the vehicle was stable and both hammered in through the Wrangler's thin sheet metal into the back passenger area of the SUV. They were about one hundred yards from the SUV now. Before he realized it, both Zachary and Dranko had dismounted from the Wrangler and were moving quickly forward in a leapfrogging motion toward the SUV.

Jeffrey kept the Wrangler motionless as they advanced. Cooper used the advantage to keep his rifle sighted squarely on the SUV. "Keep an eye on the other vehicles, including those up top on the freeway," Cooper barked at Jeffrey. He knew if it was an ambush, it was likely that other positions were set up to create an effective crossfire on anyone approaching.

"Right-o," he shouted back.

After the tension of what seemed like forever, Dranko and Zachary reached the SUV. Dranko had his weapon trained on the door as Zachary tentatively stepped to the rear driver side door and then yanked the door open. Cooper saw a man's body, small in stature, fall halfway out the door. Zachary staggered back, a hand swiftly going to cover his mouth. Dranko paused for a split second before methodically ducking inside the vehicle, weapon at the ready, to check the rest of it out. He re-emerged a few seconds later and lazily waved them forward.

As Jeffrey maneuvered the Wrangler, he stopped when Dranko came out about ten yards from the vehicle and waved at them. Beyond him, Zachary was squatting down, leaning his back against the SUV and breathing deeply. Once the Wrangler was nearly stopped, Cooper jumped out and began heading for the SUV. Dranko sidestepped a few steps to intercept him.

"You don't want to go there, brother," he said sorrowfully.

Cooper's stomach churned. Up until now, he had not thought anything was amiss. Dranko's words had the opposite of their intended effect: Cooper could not *not* see what lay inside now. He barreled past Dranko, pushing him aside with a firm down sweep of his hand. Dranko turned and watched his friend pass by. He sank into a crouching position and covered

184

his mouth with a free hand. He knew what was about to come.

From the moment of Dranko's words, dread descended upon Cooper like a fast moving storm cloud. His blood had turned to ice in his veins. His stomach had drifted to the ground. His mouth was as dry as desert sand. His head pounded. His hands and feet felt numb. He stumbled the last few steps to the SUV. He knew before he lifted the body that hung limply halfway out of the doorway. He'd killed a young boy.

Vacant eyes looked back at him when he lifted him up. His tongue lolled out of the side of his mouth. Cooper's nose was assaulted by the stench of loosened bowels and blood's acrid copper scent. The seat beneath the boy was soaked in it. He saw an entry wound in the back and a messy exist wound out of the front of the boy's torso. He looked to be thirteen or fourteen years old. His face had drained to an eerie shade of ghostly white. Cooper wanted, desperately so, to pull back and flee from this scene of horror that had been caused by him and the rifle he wielded. But, just before he could do so, he spied the outline of another shape inside the vehicle. This one was back inside the cargo area.

Like a man possessed, he unsentimentally pushed the boy's body to the side. He knelt on the bloody seat so that he could get at the cargo area. His eyes slowly adapted to the darker interior in the back. What emerged made him scream.

A girl, probably one year younger than the boy, was on her backside. She was sprawled across the cargo area. Her head had been reduced to pulp by a round from the .308. Cooper knew immediately what had happened: she had been the movement near the tailgate that he had seen! There were no weapons in view. Instead, his eyes were drawn to a forlorn blue object in her hands. He thrust himself farther into the back of the SUV so that he could reach it. He grabbed her still warm hand and delicately uncurled the fingers. They released a blue-hatted clown Pez dispenser and it fell into his hand.

He looked at it blankly. His eyes refused to focus. He wanted to drop it, but was unable to. His mind drifted back to that long-dead boy when they had travelled to Estacada. Yet again, a toy linked with a messy death jarred him to his core. *What are the odds?* He fumed as he cursed the world around him. He felt hands on his shoulders. Dranko was pulling him back and out of the vehicle. He didn't resist. His numb body was pulled from the SUV and Dranko pushed him up against it. His legs were unsteady and he slowly collapsed to the ground, leaning back against it. He clutched the Pez dispenser in his hand, unable to look away. He shook his head back and forth, trying to clear it. He started to speak, but couldn't. He felt a rebellion grow in his stomach and a second later he was leaning over and vomiting. It splashed across the rear driver-side tire. Absently, he wiped his mouth with his sleeve. Still, the clown stared back at him from his hand.

185

Finally, he found his voice, albeit weakly. "What the hell happened?"

Dranko was kneeling in front of him, his hands on Cooper's shoulders. "A tragic mistake, that's what happened."

Cooper nodded dumbly. "But why?"

"There is no *why*. There just *is*, brother."

Cooper shook his head vigorously. "No. I mean, why did I shoot?"

Dranko gently slapped him on the cheek and held his head so he couldn't avoid looking at him. "Hey! You listen to me. You shot because you *had* to. Ninety-nine times out of a hundred, hesitating there would have meant one of *us* would be dead."

Cooper laughed maniacally. "I guess this is my lucky day then. One out of a hundred. I win! You hear that, Mr. Clown?"

He looked intently at the clown and his fist clenched until his knuckles were white. He crushed the Pez dispenser in his hand and then slowly unfurled his fingers until tiny pieces of blue broken plastic fell to the ground. He wiped his hand on his leg and the last few pieces that had stuck to his hand fell onto the ground. He looked up at Dranko. Tears flowed. He grabbed Dranko by the shoulders and pulled him into a bear hug of an embrace.

"I'm just sick down through my heart," he sobbed.

Dranko returned the embrace. "I know, brother. You couldn't have known. You know that right?"

Cooper was silent, except for the sound of his sobs. This went on for several minutes. Slowly, Cooper's breathing returned to normal. His grip on Dranko lessened until the embrace ended. He leaned back, away from Dranko and wiped his eyes. He noticed that Zachary and Jeffrey were there. They had discreetly kept themselves facing away from them, both out of politeness as well as the need to keep a guarded eye in both directions.

Cooper knew there was only one thing to do. Any man in combat who has done or seen something horrific knows the same. He needed to put this away, like he had to do once in Iraq. Bury it down deep in a place that he could go back to at a time of *his* choosing, if ever. It needed to be so deep there would be no worry that it might involuntarily resurface. Slowly, deliberately, he turned the sorrow into an unidentified rage. When that was worked up, he let out a ferocious scream that startled the others. Then, he took the transformed grief and regret and wadded it into a tight ball. Finally, he found a cavernous recess deep inside to bury it.

When he'd finished, he slowly rose up. Then, he stomped his feet to return the feeling to them. The other men were looking at him; deep lines of concern marked their faces.

"What is done is done. We won't ever speak of this again. Understood?" Cooper walked briskly back to the Wrangler and climbed in. When he sat down and looked over, the others had remained flatfooted where they were.

He banged the roll bar with his hand loudly. "Let's go!" he shouted. This sparked the others into action and they were soon on their way. Dranko threw him a look of concern as they drove. Cooper gazed back at him. "Don't."

That single word erased the look from Dranko and they drove on in silence.

*
*   *

They arrived early, about an hour before the meeting was to begin. Already, scores of people had arrived. Cooper remembered his father's words. *A meeting will have great turnout if some people are there early.* He would have known, as Cooper's father had organized thousands of meetings during his time. The parking lot looked like an armed camp. Every man and woman was equipped, and most had a rifle in hand or slung across their back. Of the handful of children there, he noted that some of them were also armed. Seeing one boy, about ten years old, with a .22 caliber rifle in his hands was a painful reminder of Jake. Cooper saw that some had already assumed a guard role and had deployed themselves on the street corners in all directions. The guards eyed them warily as they pulled up.

Cooper exited the vehicle and stretched. Jeffrey and Zachary moved into the crowd and began talking to people.

Dranko stood by his side. "You gonna be ready for this?"

Cooper snorted. "As ready as I can be."

"You'll do fine, brother. You might not know much else, but you do know how to move a crowd," he chided his friend.

"That and I know how to put up with your nonsense," Cooper chuckled.

The two friends remained in silence. Cooper was lost in his thoughts. He was thinking about what he would say and fished out his notes once again. The other secret his father had shared on public speaking was simple: *speak from the heart.*

He watched Jeffrey and Zachary moving through the crowd, talking to people in small clusters. He saw them point in his direction and watched people's eyes widen in surprise. It wasn't long before someone approached him.

A man in his forties, dressed in wool pants and a ragged camouflage jacket, was the first. "Mr. Adams?" His green eyes were alight.

"Yes, sir."

The man extended his hand. "I'm Alan Moore, very pleased to meet you."

Cooper shook his hand. "Likewise."

"I thought you'd be taller."

He grinned back at him. "Why's that?"

"I just thought a man with cajones as big as yours would be taller!" Cooper laughed heartily. "To be serious, I want to thank you for what you've done."

"Anyone would have done it."

The man guffawed. "Have you been to D.C. in the last forty years?" He paused, his laughter subsiding. "I don't think so. Too many are afraid to tell the truth. Especially when it places them in harm's way."

"Well, I felt like I had to do it. My wife used to say that I had a fatal disease called truth-telling." His eyes misted over when he mentioned Elena.

Alan looked at him, concerned. "You lose her in the plague?"

Cooper nodded. "Yes."

"I'm sorry for your loss."

"Thank you."

A couple had walked up and stood discreetly off to the side, making it clear they wanted to talk to Cooper, but waiting their turn. Alan noticed them.

"Well, I didn't want to take too much of your time. I know there are others who want to chat with you. But, thank you for what you did, Mr. Adams. You did a good thing for our country."

Cooper felt awkward as he said, "You're welcome."

Alan lingered for a moment, started to turn to walk away, but then stopped himself.

"What I wanted to say," he paused, choking with emotion. "What you did gave me peace. I lost my daughters in all this. Now, at least I know why and who the hell to blame." His eyes were swollen with tears now.

Cooper put a hand on his shoulder. "I'm sorry, friend. Our job is now to hold the bastards who did all this to account."

The man gave him a weak smile, patted his hand, and then walked off. The couple stepped into the void he had left. The man, in his early twenties, reached out first. They shook hands and then Cooper shook the woman's hand. The man started to speak, but stopped himself. The woman took a step forward. "We're here because of our baby daughter. Those men killed her." She paused and looked at her husband, but he motioned for her to continue. "We wept for days when we heard what you had said. We didn't want to believe it." Her voice picked up speed. "We *hated* you. We didn't want to face the truth. To think of your dear baby Kimberly dead so a few men could make a buck!" Now, her voice was shaking. "My dear, how we cursed your name and agreed with every name we heard you called by the president and everyone else." She paused and took a deep breath, "But we finally looked at everything. We faced the truth. And, we wanted to thank you and apologize to you."

Cooper looked at each of them deeply. "Thank you. That means a lot to me."

The couple looked at each other once again, shook hands with Cooper, and then walked away.

An old man was the next to step up to talk to Cooper. He spent the next half hour hearing a similar story over and over again: of deep loss and stoked rage at those who had caused it. After the first few conversations, Cooper knew exactly how he was going to address the crowd that night.

CHAPTER THIRTEEN

When he went inside to collect his thoughts, the parking lot was already full, and almost two hundred people were milling about. Some had already gone inside to claim seats. The hall had that funky musk of old meeting places. Decades of sweat and beer had seeped into the walls and left their familiar smell.

Tagging along with his father from a young age, Cooper knew this odor well. Like many things, it made him think of his dad. He walked through the hall, shaking a few hands along the way.

Cooper and Dranko found a room off to the side of the stage area and went in. From the way he carried himself, it was not lost on Cooper that Dranko was acting as his bodyguard. "You worried about something?"

Dranko laughed. "I think you know, brother, I'm never worried. I'm just always wary."

He smiled. "Forgive me. What are you *wary* about?"

"I haven't seen anything particular. But, this meeting was obviously broadcast to *a lot* of people. It wouldn't be a shocker if the governor's people had heard about it. And, if they did, they could have sent someone to hit you here."

Cooper leaned back against the desk in the room and rubbed his chin. "You know, I hadn't even thought of that."

"That's why I'm here. To hold your hand, wipe your ass, and think of stuff you are too dumb to think of on your own."

"Well, I'm glad for it." He made a display of turning his backside to Dranko and motioning to drop his pants. "Would you mind getting a spot back there? I missed it this morning."

Dranko laughed and kicked his buttocks lightly. "I'm on break. This one, you'll have to do it yourself."

There was a quick knock at the door and Jeffrey popped his head in. His face was flush with excitement. "Lads, we are twenty minutes out and we are going to have a full house. More than that!" Cooper nodded. "You should feel good. You've done some great work." Cooper dipped his head to acknowledge the compliment. "We have someone running back home to bring an amp, some speakers, and a battery. We think we'll need to be able to broadcast your speech into the parking lot!"

"Wow, that's amazing." Dranko replied and paused only briefly before continuing. "How's security?"

Jeffrey turned serious. "I think it's good. We have teams circulating outside, looking for anyone suspicious. I'll have men on either side of you while you speak, the doors will be guarded, and I'll have people in the back corners and down the sides, too. Absent a suicide bomber, I think it will be

190

nigh bloody impossible for anyone to pull a weapon and get a shot off before we can deal with it." Cooper burst out laughing. "What?"

"Am I the only one who wasn't worried about me getting whacked at this thing?"

Dranko and Jeffrey exchanged a look.

"It appears to indeed be true, mate," Jeffrey said first, grinning. Then, he ducked back out to attend to his other tasks.

*

* *

Cooper stayed in the side room as the minutes ticked by. Dranko had positioned himself just outside the door to give Cooper his privacy and keep anyone from interrupting him. Jeffrey left after their security briefing and had gone off to deal with other preparations. Cooper could hear the buzz in the room as it filled to capacity. The excitement was palpable. He kept himself focused on what he would say. Before he knew it, Jeffrey knocked on the door, poked his head in, and said simply, "It's time."

Cooper nodded and followed him into the main room. Jeffrey wasted no time in mounting the stage. He held up his hands to call for silence and the hubbub of conversation slowly ebbed to something close to that.

"We all know what we are here for, so I'm not going to waste any more time talking to you. I'm proud to introduce Mr. Cooper Adams!"

The room erupted into applause as Cooper took the stage. He put his notes on the podium quickly and looked out at the crowd. It was an assemblage of faces that ranged from concern to expectant to delight. Like he had seen outside, they carried a plethora of arms. The room contained a mix of ages and men and women. It was a mostly white crowd, which was not a surprise given Portland's general population.

He cleared his throat. "Let me start by telling you that I have no polished speech for you. I'm not a politician."

"That's a damn good thing, Mr. Adams!" someone from the back of the room shouted. That earned him a smattering of applause. Cooper smiled in return.

"I'm here to do one thing. To tell you the truth, no matter how uncomfortable or painful that might be. For those who know me, telling the truth is the only thing I know how to do."

"Preach it," a black woman in the front row called out to him.

"I think you're here because you know what I know about how the Brushfire Plague started. What I wanted to tell you today is how gut wrenching it was when I found out. I bet it's a story that many of you share."

He stopped for a moment, sipped some water from a mug that Jeffrey had left for him on the podium. His voice choked with emotion as he spoke. "When I found out that my wife, Elena, had died not from some random act of nature turning on us, but from a deliberate act, I was devastated. When I had to confront that she had been torn away from me and my son, Jake, far too soon by a handful of wealthy and elitist bastards who wanted a few more dollars in their damned bank accounts in the Cayman Islands, I wanted to curl up and die myself."

In the first few rows, he could see many people wiping their eyes, shuffling their feet uncomfortably, or looking off in the distance.

"But, I knew I could not do that. I had to stand up, no matter the consequences, to tell our country the truth. That is what America is about and I knew I had to do that. I also knew it was the only way to bring justice to those who kept their heinous deeds in the shadows. I trusted the American people to hold them accountable." He took a few steps forward to the edge of the stage. "I only have one question: will you hold them to account?"

The crowd rose to its feet, nearly unanimously, in raucous applause. Shouts of "Yes we will" and "Damn right" resounded off the walls. Cooper waited to allow the crescendo to happen and then recede.

"Verrry good," he said, adding mischievousness to his voice. The group loved it and laughed in return. "Now, I must tell you that things have gotten worse. National Guardsmen, working at the behest of the governor, seized my son this morning and are holding him hostage."

The crowd was again on their feet. Chairs were pushed to the side in the frenzy. A few tipped over and clanged against the floor. Expressions of disbelief and concern were shouted at him.

He held up his hands to quiet them. "Oh, I'm gonna get my boy back. Don't you worry about that. But, I need your help. We are going to march on the capitol. Who's with me?"

The crowd was at a fever pitch now. Nearly every person in the room was on their feet. Cooper could feel the energy reverberating off the walls. Throughout the room, he saw several people hug or high-five one another spontaneously. Bright smiles were everywhere.

Cooper's voice boomed. "Thank you. Let's do this! Let's stand up for what is right!" He pumped his fist, riding the crowd's wave of energy.

When it finally subsided, he finished. "Jeffrey is going to tell you the details. But, thank you for coming and see you soon!"

He left the stage and went into the side room to gather himself. He could hear Jeffrey explaining the details of the pending march. In response, he heard more shouts of approval. He found the desk and sat down hard. He was still riding the adrenaline high from the speech. He was hot, and sweat trickled down his back. His heart was racing, so he took a few deep breaths to calm himself down. He heard the door open behind him and looked to see Dranko slip into the room.

Dranko pulled him into a bear hug. "You killed it, brother!"

Cooper had never seen Dranko with such a big smile on his face. He embraced his friend back. "Thank you! I think it went well."

Dranko pulled away. "Well? Even for a cynical bastard like me, *I* was fired up!" He was breathless as he finished.

Cooper was smiling now. "Thanks. You're right, it was good."

Dranko punched him in the shoulder. "Good? Say it was great. Say it was amazing!"

"Alright, I was damn amazing," Cooper said, laughing at it all.

"Good, that's more like it. You do know as soon as he's done out there, you are going to have to mix and mingle and be a rock star for a little bit, right?"

Cooper cocked an eyebrow. "Sure, I guess."

Dranko's face turned serious as he put a hand on his friend's shoulder. "You do know, too, that Elena would have been proud of you?"

He nodded solemnly in return. "Yeah, I think she *will* be once I get Jake back."

"Fair enough," he said

The crowd was cheering loudly again and the door opened. Jeffrey stepped halfway in. "Can you do us the honor, mate, and come on out?"

Cooper nodded and followed him back into the main room. Everyone was still on their feet. When they saw Cooper, the room exploded in loud applause and shouts. Cooper waved to them, not knowing what else to do. After a long minute, the din quieted. People milled about as the meeting came to an end. The noise began to rise as people engaged in numerous side conversations with one another. Cooper could feel the energy rising again and heard the excitement in their voices.

Within seconds, some people approached to shake his hand and to thank him for what he had done. Like before, their stories were eerily similar: of lost loved ones and rage when they had learned the truth, but ultimately a feeling of hope as they were involved in a plan to bring justice to those responsible. The details were different, and often heartbreaking, but the pattern repeated itself scores of times before the last person finally left the building. Cooper lost track of time, but it felt like he had been talking for hours.

Jeffrey and Dranko stepped in from the discreet distance where they had been standing. Cooper realized that he was exhausted. He felt spent down to his bones.

"That went splendidly," Jeffrey exclaimed. "We have over four hundred commitments to march on Salem!"

"That's very good," Cooper said, smiling. "My father always said to expect to see half of who says they are going to show up. But, I have to say, I don't think he often saw the excitement we saw today."

"Nor would I bet he dealt with people motivated by such loss and pain and thirst for justice," Jeffrey added.

Cooper nodded. "I agree. I think we are off to an amazing start."

"Don't start calling me an optimist, but most of the side conversations I overheard were people talking about who else they could get to go. So our numbers might be even better than we think," Dranko said.

Cooper turned in amazement toward him. "I think I'm going to have to start calling you Optimus Drankos from now on."

"Screw off," he fired back, smiling.

Cooper then pivoted to face Jeffrey. "What's the plan for tonight?"

"I don't believe it would be prudent to try to head back, as it's dark outside now. I shan't recommend it in any event."

He nodded. "Agreed. What's the plan, then?"

"We can bed down with the Sheffields tonight. They have a well-fortified place just a mile from here. They have also organized a tight neighborhood perimeter."

"Sheffield? Are they from England?"

He smiled. "Just a happy circumstance, I'm afraid. But, I'm sure the blood of the mighty empire builders of yore courses through their veins!"

Cooper put his head in his hands. "Oh my lord, I'm sorry I asked."

"I'm pretty hungry, so I'd suggest we get moving," Dranko interjected.

Outside the hall, they met with the Sheffields. The couple looked to be in their early fifties. Clarence resembled a towering version of Albert Einstein, standing well over six feet tall. His hair was stark white, unkempt, and flailing in all directions. He was skinny as a rail. Ruth, his wife, was a short woman of average weight. They both greeted Cooper and Dranko warmly. Cooper decided to ride with them to their house. Along the way, he learned that Clarence had been a high school biology teacher before the plague and, fortunately, had a robust gardening and aquaponics operation already in place when chaos erupted. Ruth had worked at the local supermarket and ashamedly confessed that she had used her insider knowledge to "liberate" key supplies from it before it had been overrun by looters. Cooper had to stop himself from laughing as her tone turned to scorn when she talked about looters. The irony was delicious, as Ruth had done the same thing just hours before the "horde of damned thugs" had turned to looting. Cooper recalled how his father had often remarked on people's ability to rationalize their own ill behavior whilst they damned others for the same. Ruth Sheffield, while an affable older woman, struck him as Exhibit A of this phenomenon.

They spent an enjoyable evening together. Within the city, they had an unusual lot that was just shy of an acre. As they gave Cooper a quick tour in the fading light, he was impressed by how they had made use of every available square inch to produce food in one form or another. They showed him how they grew potatoes in vertical boxes that produced an enormous amount in a tiny area. He had never seen this before and made some notes for his own future use. All the trees on their property were fruit or nut producing; berry patches were scattered about to strategically take advantage of the sun and soil conditions, and, of course, they had a wide range of vegetables produced in several enormous gardening areas. They even had some areas devoted to corn and wheat production, which was another surprise.

However, the aquaponics operation was the most surprising and astounding to Cooper. He was mesmerized as they told him how they grew fish in a self-contained system by mixing the right amount of water, fish, and water-borne plants. Their system essentially self-cleaned itself and was ecologically balanced. They explained how they could use fertilizer ingredients from the fish's excrement in their garden. When he learned that they were able to "grow" hundreds of pounds of fish for consumption per year, in such a small area, he was hooked. Dranko joined him in asking many questions and taking copious notes. It became so detailed that Clarence and Ruth finally looked at one another, laughed, and then Clarence retrieved a book from their house and gave it to Cooper.

"Here, just take this. We've been doing this long enough, we don't need it anymore." Cooper looked at the cover. *Aquaponic Gardening* by Sylvia Bernstein stared back at him. "We consider this one the bible of Aquaponics."

"Thank you very much. This is such an amazing operation you have!"

"I will say it will be tougher to get this up and running now. You might have a harder time finding the equipment you need. But let us know if we can help. We have a few spares on certain things. And, if you need help in starter fish, we can certainly assist with that."

Cooper was touched by their generosity and reached out to shake both their hands. "Much appreciated. Of course, I first have to get to a place I'm gonna stay awhile!" He chuckled to ease the tension of the predicament and conflict that faced him. "But I'm hoping we can get that figured out soon."

After the tour, and while enjoying some of the Sheffield's home-brewed beer, they reviewed the neighborhood security measures that had been taken. Cooper hadn't had a beer in a long time and he savored the bitter taste.

Dranko and Cooper were able to return the favor by offering them several valuable suggestions on how to improve the neighborhood's security. One glaring oversight they both noticed was that their preparations lacked defenses sufficient to prevent determined, or armored, vehicles from crashing their barricades and getting into the heart of their neighborhood.

Cooper explained to them, "The difference between now and when all this started is you have to be prepared for well-organized gangs or other groups that will be determined to get in after your resources," Cooper said pointing to likely ingress locations on the map. "Things will begin shifting from the loners or small groups trying to come in to these kind of groups. And, as time goes on, your neighborhood is going to make a juicier and juicer target—as resources elsewhere dry up."

Clarence and Ruth nodded seriously. Cooper went on to describe ways to better secure the neighborhood against this threat. "My biggest recommendation would be to put up heavy blockades on all sides and reduce yourself to only one way in or out of the neighborhood. Then, in that location you can put mobile blockage devices."

Dranko went on to describe several options on how to stop vehicles from being able to "crash" their neighborhood. Cooper noted the tension in Clarence's and Ruth's faces as they talked. *It's never easy to find out you are exposed when you thought you were secure.* He was glad that they reacted by listening intently, taking notes, and discussing how they would go about making the improvements, rather than being defensive or denying the reality of it all.

As the Sheffield's generously produced a second round of beer, the discussion moved to more mundane conversation—talking about the smaller details of life, children, and what the future might hold. Cooper appreciated that the conversation stayed light. Even the talk about the future was kept, somehow, at an optimistic place. For the briefest of moments, the night felt like a return to pre-plague days when friends or new acquaintances would gather over drinks and while away the night in meandering, but pleasant, conversation and humor. When he finally went to bed that night, he was plagued by worries about Jake and what was happening with him. His teeth gritted as he thought about it. Finally, a measure of peace came to him. As he dozed off, he couldn't tell if it was the beer or the return to a night of normal company and conversation that brought it, but in the end decided it didn't really matter. He ended up having one of the most restful nights he had in a long while.

*
* *

He awoke to a rooster greeting the dawn. Surprised, he looked out the window and realized it wasn't yet first light. He recalled someone once saying that roosters often did not wait for sunrise, contrary to the myth, and guessed maybe it was true. As soon as his eyes popped open, his mind returned to Jake and what was happening with him. No matter how hard he tried, it was impossible to fully push the worrisome thoughts from his mind. He doubted they would do any serious harm to him, but he could not be entirely confident of that. Nor could he know whether harms of another kind—psychological or less serious physical varieties—were being levied against his boy. It gnawed at him like a termite devouring soft pine.

He stretched, dressed, and wandered into the main living area of the Sheffield's home. He took care to be as quiet as he could, but was surprised when he smelled the deeply welcoming aroma of freshly brewed coffee when he stepped into the hallway. He found Clarence in the kitchen. His hair was slightly crazier than it had been the day before, but not by much. He was dressed in an adult sized one-piece pajama, the kind that children typically wore. They were complete with the padded feet and a pattern of small jet airplanes. *If you had any doubt you were in "keep Portland weird" land, consider such doubt removed,* he thought with amusement to himself.

"Good morning," he said to Clarence, whose back was turned. He noted a holstered pistol resting on the counter and realized he had, probably for the first time in a long while, left the bedroom without a weapon on him.

Clarence turned, a freshly washed mug in his hand. "Mornin'. You want some?" he asked, motioning toward the coffee pot.

"Absolutely," Cooper responded.

Clarence poured the hot, black gold into the mug and handed it to him. "I could go milk one of our goats if you'd like cream." His tone was such that Cooper didn't know if he was joking or being serious.

"I like it black, so I'm good. Thank you very much," he said as he took the warm mug into his hands. "How do you still have coffee on hand?

"I thought you said that you lived in Portland? Surely you know that we'll all starve to death before we run out of coffee," he joked.

Cooper laughed. "You know it's true. This city will probably be burned to the ground when the coffee runs dry!"

Clarence chuckled. "There's probably the last bunker oil-fueled tanker running right now at breakneck speed to South America to trade Oregon wheat or hops or hazelnuts for some green Columbian coffee beans," he replied.

Cooper smiled and nodded enthusiastically. "Damn, we missed an easy play there. That should have been our plan to topple that low down Gibbs! Anyone coming back with a tanker full of coffee would be swept into office!"

Clarence almost spit out his coffee, he laughed so hard. After he recovered, he asked, "What's your plan for today?"

"In a couple hours, we have a radio conference with the governor's people. To arrange the exchange with my son. After that, we head down to another town... Stayton I believe, to rally the troops. Like we did here yesterday."

"Well, you have the gift of gab so you're the right man for the job," he said.

"I just tell people the truth as I know it. It's all anyone can do," Cooper replied.

197

"You should give yourself more credit, Cooper. Most folks who are called leaders either won't or are too afraid to tell people the truth. And, the few that try often mangle the poor thing in the trying."

Cooper took another sip of coffee and nodded slowly. "Thank you. I guess you could say that I've just had a lot of practice with telling the truth. Since I was pretty young," he paused, losing himself in thought for a moment. "After what happened to my father, I've driven everyone crazy with telling the truth."

"What happened to him?"

Cooper couldn't stop his mouth from turning down in a disgusted frown when he replied. "He was put in prison based on some damned lies. It broke him and he died not too long after. I reacted by committing myself to never telling a lie in my life, no matter the personal cost."

Clarence gave the news a respectful moment of silence. "I'm sorry you had to go through that."

Cooper didn't want to continue down a morose path. "It was a long time ago. What I can tell you is that my wife probably would have preferred I'd tell the occasional white lie."

He smiled back. "Yeah, I'm not sure how any marriage can survive without a little bit of that."

"It wasn't easy," he laughed. "Let's just say I've had all manner of small objects thrown my way. Thankfully, it was never anything too hard."

"What was the most comical one?"

"Without a doubt, a half-eaten peanut butter sandwich." He chuckled at the retelling of that memory.

"What caused that one?"

Cooper shook his head. "I don't remember. I just recall the look in her eye. If a knife or a rock had been at hand, I don't think I'd be sitting across from you today, though!"

"Well, you're not the only one who's been there, I'm sure. At least your situation was based on telling an unpleasant truth rather than being caught in some lie."

"True enough."

"What's all this squawking about out here?" Dranko asked, walking into the room and rubbing his eyes.

Cooper turned to face him. "We are just arguing about your positive qualities."

Cooper yawned. "Having a hard time keeping track of them all, I assume"

"Nah, we were having a helluva time just coming up with even one," Cooper deadpanned. Clarence chuckled and Dranko let out an exaggerated groan.

"If it wasn't that I don't want to wake up Ruth, I'd kick your ass seven

198

ways to Sunday right now," he retorted.

Cooper didn't miss a beat. "Clarence, should we wake Dranko up? He's obviously dreaming while sleepwalking."

Dranko playfully punched him in the shoulder as he arrived at the table. While they bantered, Clarence fetched him a mug of coffee and offered it to him as he sat back down. Dranko took a drink and looked euphoric.

"Clarence just saved your life, you do know that, right?"

Cooper nodded. "I do."

"It's been a long while since I woke up to freshly brewed coffee."

"Well, we don't drink this every day. We save it for special occasions, so don't be too jealous."

"Well, we thank you for your generosity," Cooper replied.

They sat in silence for several minutes, each man lost in his own thoughts, but enjoying the pleasant aroma and taste of the coffee. When their mugs were empty, Clarence rose from the table.

"I'm going to heat up some water, mostly to cook some oatmeal for breakfast, but you can use a bit to wash up if you'd like."

"That'd be great," Cooper said.

*

* *

Cooper paced nervously. The Sheffield's ham radio loomed in front of him like an edifice. The planned call with the governor's people was just minutes away. He had played out in his head the myriad ways the conversation might go and how he would respond to each scenario. While he did his best to avoid the thought, he could not escape that his son's safety and life hung in the balance. Lost in his thoughts, he startled when Dranko put his hand on his shoulder.

"You alright?" he asked.

Cooper grinned. "Except for being as spun up as addict three days without their junk, yeah, I'm great."

He gripped his shoulder tighter. "You'll be fine."

"I hope so."

"I'm going to get us on the channel so that we are on time and ready to go."

Cooper patted him on the shoulder. "Thanks."

Dranko sat down in front of the radio and began working the switches and dials. Cooper continued pacing. Before he knew it, Dranko called him over to the radio.

"The governor's man is on," he whispered to him as they exchanged places on the seat.

"This is Cooper," he said immediately. "I want to speak to my son."

There was a long pause on the other end. "You can talk to him when the details have all been agreed to."

Even over the radio, the man's smug tone was evident. It grated on Cooper's nerves. "Let me be clear. If we agree to the details and you don't let me talk to my son or I learn he's been mistreated, then the deal is off."

"Agreed."

The next several minutes were spent laying out the location, time, and other details of the exchange. It went remarkably well for Cooper. He was surprised by how easily they agreed to the terms that offered the best protection for Cooper and Jake. As they neared conclusion, he exhaled a sigh of relief. It was short-lived.

"There are just a few questions that I have for you, Mr. Adams, before we conclude."

Is that a hint of self-satisfaction that I hear in his voice? "Sure thing."

"We know you are a man bound by his word, Mr. Adams. Is that still true?"

Cooper paused as a chill ran down his spine and his stomach dropped, fearing where this was going to go. "Yes."

"Is that still true today?"

"Yes."

"Fantastic. Will you attempt to kill, harm, or kidnap the governor at this exchange?"

Cooper gritted his teeth. He knew they had him trapped. He spat the word through a clenched jaw, "No."

"Splendid. Are any of your accomplices planning to kill, harm, or kidnap the governor?"

Cooper rubbed his temples. "No."

"Excellent. Will you allow any of your accomplices to do any of that?"

The vise that was growing tighter with each question felt like it was crushing his skull. "No."

"If you learn of any such plan, will you communicate that to us?"

"Yes."

"Will you comply with all the agreements you have made in arranging the exchange?"

"Yes."

"Thank you, Mr. Adams. You've been most cooperative. We know you are bound by your word and, as such, feel the governor's safety is guaranteed. You do know that if you violate any of the terms of this agreement, your boy dies?"

Cooper exploded. "Now, you hear *me*. You hurt a damned hair on his head and the governor will go down and I will spend my living moments going after *his* family, you sonofabitch!"

"You have no reason to fear that, Mr. Adams." The man replied so calmly, it triggered another fit of rage in Cooper. "Now, do you want to talk to Jake?"

Those words were like a tonic and Cooper's anger melted. "Yes, I do."

A short pause on the other end ensued. Then, the sweet sound of his son's voice came over the radio, "Dad?"

"Yes, son! How are you?"

His voice was shaky and Cooper's heart turned over hearing the fear in his voice. "I'm scared. I want to be back with you. I miss you." His son choked on the last words. Cooper clenched his fist and pounded the desk in heartbreak and impotency.

"Have you eaten rutabaga or chili since you've been there?"

There was pause. Cooper guessed his use of code words had jolted Jake. He hoped he remembered their code words from before. The former meant he was fine, the latter that there was a problem. While Cooper figured the governor's people would decipher the code quickly, he hoped it would give Jake enough time to answer before they caught on.

"Rutabaga."

Cooper's heart soared, but he played it cool to try his best to protect the meaning of the code. "I understand, son. In two days, we'll be back together and we'll leave all of this behind. For good."

He could hear Jake crying now. "I hope so."

"Be strong, son, this will be all over soon. You have my word on it."

"They are saying I have to say goodbye. I'll see you soon. I love you."

Cooper's voice broke. "I love you, too."

The man's voice came back on. "Good day, Mr. Adams. We will see you soon."

"Yes, we will," he concluded.

As the channel went dead, Dranko stepped in to quickly turn off the ham radio. Cooper paused for a moment, his head in his hands. Then, he slammed the headset down on the desk, grabbed the glass of water from the desk, and threw it against the opposite wall. It exploded in a shatter of glass and shards.

"The bastards! They roped me in good and tight!" His face was bright red and his voice shook with fury.

"At least you'll get Jake back," Dranko offered in a conciliatory tone.

Possessed, Cooper turned on him. He grabbed him by the lapels on his shirt and shook him. "Don't you understand? I can't exact revenge on that scumbag governor for what he's done!" His face was so close that he showered Dranko in spittle as he screamed.

Dranko just stared back at him and their eyes remained locked for several long moments. Cooper's were consumed with wrath. Dranko softened his as best he could. Then, Cooper loosened his grip and staggered back into the chair. His head and shoulders drooped and he cradled his head in his hands. Dranko looked on helplessly. Clarence and Ruth had poked their heads into the room when the glass shattered, but quickly retreated to give them space.

Cooper's head hurt. His mind whirred, trying to find a way out of the trap they had set. His clenched palms turned sweaty. His entire body felt like it was on fire. "Damn them. There is no way out," he finally lamented.

Dranko leaned against a side table, a safe distance away. "You could always decide that this was the *one* time in your life that it was okay to lie."

Cooper slowly looked at him like he was crazy. "No, I can't. Do you know what that would mean to me?"

"I know it would enable you to avenge your wife's death," Dranko returned firmly.

Cooper rose up and crossed the floor so quickly that Dranko flinched, expecting a blow. Instead, Cooper stood inches away from him once more, but did not put his hands on him.

"I thought you knew who I was," Cooper said, incredulous.

Dranko held his gaze, unblinking. "I do, brother. From what you told me about your father, he'd *want* you to put that bastard in the ground. *That's how you honor his life.*"

Cooper shook his head, disbelieving the words. "I can't."

Now Dranko grabbed Cooper by the lapels. "It's a new world we live in, brother. The old moral code doesn't apply anymore. Your god-awful fanaticism truth-telling is going to get you—or Jake—killed!"

Like an alcoholic confronted about his drinking, Cooper shook his head more vigorously, denying the words he was hearing. "It's impossible." He freed himself from Dranko's grasp and stormed away.

"Think about what is more just—you honoring your word to a liar and a man who has killed millions upon millions for money?" Dranko shouted after him as he was leaving the room.

Cooper waved his hand dismissively in response, but Dranko's words lingered with him as he fled from the room, chased by thoughts that were too damning to consider.

*

* *

They spent the day traveling to the next meeting. Despite that it was in a smaller town, the crowd was double the size of the one in Portland. They were meeting at a church, and this time, they had prepared to broadcast into the parking lot where they met. Still, the amplification was inadequate for those farthest from the speakers. The electricity was similarly magnified by the crowd's size.

Before the meeting, Dranko was as nervous as a cat on a hot tin roof.

While waiting for the meeting to start, he said to Cooper, "No way a crowd gets this big without the governor knowing exactly where you are." He insisted that Cooper greet the crowd inside, where it was easier to protect him. "You can't go outside; it's far too chaotic out there."

Cooper obliged him. He had never seen Dranko this stressed. His face was covered in a sheen of sweat and he paced constantly. His eyes darted about, detecting the scantest movement. Twice, he pulled his pistol and, embarrassingly, had to put it away when there was no danger.

Cooper's speech was the same as it had been the night before, but the crowd's response was greater still. As he ended, Cooper looked into the audience and saw raw emotion bordering on fanaticism. For a moment, it frightened him. He had never seen anything like this in his life. It was then that he knew he had the power to turn this crowd into a mob that would do whatever he asked of it. That fact sent a chill down his spine and he recoiled from it. *No man should have this kind of sway over others,* he thought. If the governor had been in the room, he would have been torn to pieces by bare hands.

When he finished his speech, the crowd bum rushed him and he was quickly pinned back up against the podium. Without its support, he would have been knocked down. Around him and pressed up against him, were rapturous faces. He couldn't make out what the individuals were saying, but it was a din of gratitude and praise. Hands were clapping him on the back, as others pulled him into a tight embrace. He spied Dranko off to his right. His face was panicked. He manhandled people out of his way, desperately trying to make his way to Cooper. He couldn't hear what Dranko was saying, but he was screaming at people. When he finally reached him, he enveloped Cooper in a bear hug, turned him around and began pushing him through the crowd, seeking an exit. Cooper did his best to keep his balance, but the people reluctantly parted as he made his way through. Jeffrey soon joined them to assist with their efforts.

When they had successfully retreated to a side room, Dranko locked the door and collapsed onto a couch as he let out a long exhale. He took a moment's respite, gathered his breath, and then exploded at Jeffrey. "What the hell was that?"

Jeffrey face turned crimson. "Bollocks! Chap, was I supposed to be ready for that?"

"You are damn right! He could have been killed seven ways to Sunday just now!" Dranko screamed. He vaulted to his feet and the men stood just inches apart. He had emphasized his last few words by jabbing Jeffrey in the chest with a closed fist. Jeffrey pushed it away.

Cooper stepped in, using his arms to separate the men who were about to come to blows. "Back off, both of you. Let's take a deep breath. Nothing happened. Let's just learn from this and make a better plan for tomorrow night.

Dranko spun to face Cooper and looked at him as if he had lost his mind. "What are you talking about? No way we do this again tomorrow night!"

Now, it was Jeffrey's turn to look incredulous. "We *have* to do tomorrow night. We have that bastard bloke right where we want 'im. We'll have a bloody large army now to march on Salem!"

Dranko shook his head firmly. "No way. Not happening. There is way too much risk."

Jeffrey started to react, but Cooper motioned with his hand for him to remain silent. He turned to Dranko. "Brother, I appreciate your deep concern for my safety, but we are moving forward. We need the pressure of the people marching on Salem to distract the governor's resources, and if he is thinking about killing me or Jake, that will be our best deterrent."

Dranko plunged his head into his hands. "You're impossible." He continued to shake his head slowly from side to side. "You do what you want. But, you get hurt or killed, it's not on my head and I won't be the one to tell Jake." His eyes were wet, something very rare for him.

He went to turn and storm off, but Cooper's hand grabbed him by the shoulder, belaying his retreat. Cooper looked him squarely in the eye. "Paul, that's exactly right. Something happens, it ain't on you. It's on me. You get that?"

Dranko's gaze and his pull to leave softened a bit. "I get it." He dipped his head in a reluctant nod and then shook himself free from Cooper and left. He had to push the door open and squeeze out, as there were still people crowding the door. Through the door, he heard him yell, "He ain't coming out, you can go home now!"

Cooper smiled. He turned to Jeffrey. "Shall we talk about security for tomorrow night?"

The other man returned a sly smile and said, "At your service, your majesty." The two men shared a laugh to ease the lingering stress. When they finished, the plan was to double the number of bodyguards and then form a bastion of men between Cooper and the crowd as he neared the end of his speech. Cooper was satisfied with the results and agreed to take on the task of briefing the sure-to-be-still angry Dranko.

*

* *

The final of his three speeches had the largest turnout, by far. Cooper tried counting, but lost his way around six or seven hundred. A few minutes before Cooper was going on stage, Dranko tried one last time to talk him out of speaking.

"I just don't have a good feeling about this."

Cooper looked at him, tired of the nagging he had experienced all day from Dranko on this issue. "Just give it a rest."

"You do know that Jeffrey had to go beyond his trusted inner circle to get as many bodyguards as we have now? That's a recipe for disaster."

"Yeah, you told me that about five times already." Cooper turned to directly face him, his irritation reaching a boiling point. "You know what a recipe for a disaster is? A leader who's too afraid to lead. My father told me that a million times."

Dranko started to respond, but Cooper held up a single finger and he demurred. At that time, Jeffrey opened the door and told Cooper it was time to go on.

Cooper stepped confidently to the stage. *The third time is the charm,* he thought. He was optimistic that this would be the best one yet. The crowd did not disappoint, with their boisterous welcome as he took the stage. He had expanded his remarks from the first speech. He felt awkward admitting it to himself, but he felt like a natural. *Maybe it's in the genes,* he thought bemusedly to himself. He felt like a conductor as he moved the crowd up, then down, and up again. He felt a rush as he both fed off the energy from the crowd and stoked it up just the same. He wondered if this was what rock stars on an arena stage experienced.

He had just concluded a rousing finish when it happened. People started leaping to their feet. Like the night before, there was a surge toward the stage in a pell mell rush. The sound of chairs being knocked over was deafening, as was the roar of the crowd. The bodyguards pushed mightily back against the crowd. Cooper turned to exit the room and, hopefully, relieve the pressure and pushing from the people. As he returned, something unusual caught his eye and it forced him to stop and turn.

A bodyguard had not joined the line of resistance, like the rest. He was kneeling on one knee. Cooper first wondered if the man was ill. When he saw the pistol in the man's hand coming to bear on him, he knew otherwise. Time slowed. Cooper watched the pistol come up. The man's face was contorted in rage as one eye closed so the other could be used to aim. Cooper had scant time to react, but instinctively tried to jump to his left, hoping to get some cover from the podium that was between them. He also screamed out "Gun!" in the hopes that someone would hear it over all the other noise.

Cooper was mid-leap when he saw flame jump from the barrel pointed in his direction. His shoulder flinched and burned when he was hit. As he landed on the stage floor hard, it knocked the air out of him and he winced when another round hit him in the side. He saw Dranko, who had been behind the stage, step forward with his pistol drawn. The pistol jerked multiple times and spat fire and smoke. Cooper turned his head, but could not see the other man, who was now blocked by the podium. He rolled onto his back, suddenly feeling spent and weak. He marveled at the feeling of blood puddling on his body before dripping off the side. He could feel every drop spilling. He shut his eyes and wondered if this was what it felt like to die. *Will I see Elena in the afterlife?* His heart ached so for her. *Who will take care of Jake? Surely Dranko will.*

Then, someone was slapping his face. Hard. His eyes fluttered open. Dranko stood over him. An unknown person was kneeling to his right, frantically bandaging his wounds. "Stay with us, Cooper," his friend barked at him.

"Jus' tir...ed," he mumbled.

"Think of Jake, Cooper. You can't leave him."

Cooper blinked hard, trying to rouse himself. "Yeah... know."

Someone propped his legs up. He didn't know why and his mind struggled to understand what was going on. The word "shock" looped through the fog, but he didn't fully understand the meaning of it.

Dranko kept moving his head about, whenever his eyes closed. "Jake. Stay focused on Jake, Cooper," Dranko repeated. After a few minutes, it struck Cooper as funny and he chuckled, but it hurt him to do so. "You stay strong, brother. We are gonna do a transfusion. We have several people here with your blood type. Just waiting on the equipment to arrive."

"Aw... right," he slurred, like a drunk.

Then, everything went black. And, nothing anyone could do would rouse him.

CHAPTER FOURTEEN

Cooper's eyes fluttered open. He had no idea how long he had been out. He was in someone's bedroom. Angela was asleep in a chair next to the bed. Her breath fell in easy swells. Early morning light floated in through the window and lit her up, beatifying her in its warm cascade. For a moment, he was stunned at her beauty that he had never noticed before. Her face, even in sleep, radiated peace and contentment. Clarity. He knew his choice was between the warm and placid comfort of a tropical sea or the tumult and energy of a frothing river.

Panic gripped him as he remembered the meeting to get Jake back. Ice filled his veins. His hand shot out and grabbed Angela's wrist. He jerked her toward him, harder than he had wanted. She nearly fell out of the chair as her eyes flew open.

"What?" she gasped, fear in her voice.

"Sorry," he said calmly, before spitting rapid fire. "What day is it? How long was I out? Did I miss the governor's meeting?"

She yawned as she shook her head and stretched her arms out. "You are fine. The meeting is later today."

He breathed a deep sigh of relief and then focused his attention on the rest of his body. His midsection hurt badly, but the rest of him felt alright.

"So, what happened, anyway?"

Her eyes fell to where his hand still held her wrist. He had forgotten that he held on. He awkwardly let go and gave her a wan smile. She grinned back at him.

"Well, the good news is that you didn't need a transfusion after all. You did lose a good amount of blood, but it wasn't life threatening. You got hit twice, but both exited clean. You are going to be sore for a while and you won't be able to move well, but you aren't dying."

"That's good to hear. So, who the hell tried to kill me?"

She shrugged her shoulders. "We don't know. Dranko shot the man up pretty good and the crowd finished what he'd started."

Cooper's brows furrowed. "What do you mean?"

She looked away. "It was pretty gruesome. They tore the man apart. Almost literally."

He gritted his teeth. "Damn, so we had no chance to question him?"

She shook her head at his rhetorical question. "Do you guys think it was the governor?"

She shook her head once again. "Your guess is as good as mine. On the one hand, if it was the governor, why send in one man? On the other, he's no friend of yours."

"Did anyone know who the guy was?"

"Yeah, when the dust cleared, he was identified by several people from this town."

"And?"

"He did lose his wife and daughter to the plague. No one could recall talking to him about you or the information you'd put out. So it's hard to say."

"Does Dranko think we go forward with the governor meeting?"

"I think he said it's your call, but he knows you are going to still go through with it." She winked at him as she talked.

He smiled back at her. "Yeah, that's pretty much right. That boy does know me, don't he?"

"Better than I do, that's for sure," she said as she stood up and turned away from him. *Was that hurt I heard in her voice?* He was pretty sure that it was. "I'll go get him," she continued without looking back and then exited the room.

He lay alone, waiting for Dranko. He mind rolled back to the decision that lay before him. Angela or Julianne? Although, with a relationship growing between Angela and Dranko, he wasn't as sure as he had been that it was completely his decision any longer. Nonetheless, he knew he had to decide. The longstanding debate continued slowly, and like the sun burning through early morning fog, he reached startling clarity. He was so lost in his own thoughts that it took Dranko standing next to him and shaking him for Cooper to notice his presence.

"I coulda slit your throat, y'know," Dranko said bemusedly.

Cooper looked up at him, smiling. "Yeah, but then you'd have not a single friend in this here world."

He shrugged. "Given how much of a pain in the ass you are, I'm not sure it'd be a big loss."

"Where the hell am I, anyway?"

"My friend, we are in the good Doctor Edward Shakes' house. He was onsite when it all went down. He's been checking on you like a proper nursemaid. You are quite his hero. It's kind of fun to watch."

"So, are we still on for the governor?"

He nodded. "I assumed that nothing was going to keep you from that meeting. We are going to have to move in about two hours, though."

"So, should I do it?"

"Do what?" Dranko asked.

"Kill the governor?"

Dranko drew back and stepped away from the bed and waved his hands about him and his voice was agitated. "I'm not getting into that anymore. I can't think about the consequences of it all."

"Alright, just calm down, then," Cooper shot back, irritated. "I'll figure it out myself. You do have some way for me to go into that meeting with

208

protection though, right?"

When Cooper said "protection," Dranko looked at him askance. "Yeah, I have a Doubletap for you."

"What the hell is that?"

Dranko stepped back toward him and drew a very small pistol from his front pocket. "It's a modern derringer. Two shots of forty-five. Thin as a cracker. You'll put this in your boot and it won't be noticed in a pat down. In fact, I have two of them, so you'll have one in each boot." Cooper took the pistol from him and examined it. He admired the sleek design and how tiny it was. "You just pull the trigger once and it'll fire and pull it again and then the second round fires. There are two extra rounds in the grip, should you somehow get a chance to reload it." Dranko showed him how to access the spare rounds as he talked.

"Neat little package. Perfect for up and close and personal work."

"You mean protection, right?"

Cooper grinned. "Sure, that's exactly what I mean."

"Let's get you up and ready to roll then," Dranko said dismissively.

*

* *

Cooper had managed to gingerly walk to the dining room table. Doctor Shakes turned out to be an elderly man, in his early seventies. Bald as a cue ball, he had a white beard that reached his chest.

"Yeah, I know I'm like Patrick Stewart meeting ZZ Top," the doctor joked upon meeting Cooper.

"I want to thank you for all you've done," Cooper responded.

Shakes walked over to him and grasped his hand in both of his. "No, son. Thank *you* for what you did. I can't tell you how many people I tended to and watched die when Brushfire Plague hit. Including my darling wife." He paused to make a sign of the cross. "Of course, I hated you when it all first came out. Didn't want to believe you. But, any sane man reading the facts had to understand it was all real."

"You are welcome, but I didn't have a choice. I had to tell the truth."

"Well, son, I know a million men who would have chosen the easy route," he said as he walked back into the kitchen.

Cooper noted the delicious smells of meat and pancakes. He started salivating as the aroma of bacon, eggs, maple syrup, and coffee sank deep inside him with each breath.

"Where'd you get all this stuff?" he asked.

Shakes looked back over his shoulder at him. "I think there's an old Russian saying that explains it."

"What's that?" he answered, chuckling.

209

"The doctor is the last man to starve in the village."

"Sounds like a Russian saying."

"Or, my grandmother, who was Irish just never wanted to admit that her people went hungry and so blamed it on the Russians!" Shakes laugh was deep and comforting. "Here we go," he called as he escorted a plate piled high and a mug of coffee into the dining room.

"Thank you," Cooper said as he fell to eating. He was suddenly ravenous. He was thankful that the doctor left him alone to eat, without the obligation to make small talk. After so long with bland food that only served to get enough calories on board, he caught himself eating far too fast. He paused and breathed deeply before continuing. Every bite was heaven on his tongue. Each aroma was a delight. Remarkably, just as he finished the first plate, Shakes was delivering a second piled just as high as the first. Cooper managed a knowing, and thankful, grin at him but kept on eating without stopping.

*

*   *

Dranko and Cooper drove on in silence as they made their way to the rendezvous location with the others. Cooper was mulling over the choices that lay in front of him, and Dranko had no inclination to wade into that conflict. They made it to the vacant gas station just off of Interstate 5 without incident and found the group waiting for them. He was able to lose himself in the camaraderie after their brief separation and he welcomed the relief of it all. Soon, after some hugs and handshakes, he found Calvin.

"Can I talk to you for a minute?" Cooper asked him. "I'd like your advice."

Calvin nodded solemnly as the pair walked away from the group to get some privacy. When they'd reached the far corner of the parking lot, they paced in a tight circle as they talked.

"What can I do for you?" he asked Cooper in a deep baritone.

"I'd like your advice on this dilemma I'm facing," Cooper said and then paused to think before continuing.

Calvin flashed him a broad grin. "Angela. Passion fades, brother. That is, if she'll have you still. You know she and Dranko…"

Cooper shook his head before interrupting him. "No, that's not what I was asking you about!"

Now, it was Calvin's turn to look bewildered. "What? You weren't asking me about choosing between Angela and Julianne?"

He shook his head vigorously. "No! That one I have figured out. I was going to ask you about—"

Now, Calvin interrupted him, holding up his hands. "Wait. Back it up.

210

First, tell me who you have chosen."

Cooper grimaced in irritated impatience. "Okay, fine. I'm going to see if I can move things forward with Angela."

Calvin stepped back, the corners of his mouth downturned in surprise. "Really?"

Cooper chuckled. "Why do you look so shocked? You just said yourself that she was the right choice."

His mouth turned to a broad smile. "I did. But, it is not often that a man chooses wisely when it comes to women; especially when a woman like Julianne is involved."

Cooper's eyes darted to the side and came to the rest on the ground. "There's no denying that. And, we have a connection that I don't even understand. But, there is no way I could have a future with her *and* Jake. He's not getting over his hatred of her anytime soon. I don't know why I hadn't seen this before."

Calvin grinned and pointed at his groin.

Cooper frowned. "No, it was more than that. A lot more than that." Then, as if shaking off a bad memory, he shrugged his shoulders. "I don't fully understand it all, but I know what I need to do. Please don't say anything, I'm planning to talk to Angela after this thing is done today to see if that's even a choice anymore."

"Sure thing. You may have lost her already to Dranko. You know that, right?"

"Yeah, I do. If that's where it lands, that will be fine. I'll be happy for him, honestly."

"So, what did you *actually* want to talk to me about?"

Cooper burst out laughing. "Oh yeah, *that.*" He shuffled his feet, eyes cast downward. "Well, the governor made me promise not to kill him today. So, do I become a liar so I can take him down or do I preserve my honor and let him be?" By the time he'd finished, he peered intensely at Calvin.

"I think it comes down to a question of what is the greater good…"

"Oh, don't hand me that crap. I *hate* situational ethics. You either have a principle or you don't."

Calvin looked right back at him, anger flushing his face. "I thought you wanted my advice?"

Cooper took a deep breath. "I do. Sorry about that."

"As I was trying to say, the principle here is what is the greater good? Why did you start telling the truth all the time without exception?"

"Because I saw the damage that lies had done to my father's life."

"And yours?"

"Yes, and mine," he responded, irritated at being pressed on a matter so personal.

211

"And, did you commit yourself to truth telling for yourself or for society?"

Cooper was bewildered now, not sure where Calvin was going and even less sure he would like it when he arrived there. "Well, both. I did it for me, but I also wanted to be an example for others. To show that telling the truth—always—was important."

"So, you hoped that society would get better as a result of your actions?"

"Yes," he said curtly.

"Now you need to tell me what was *most* important in your decision: yourself or society."

Cooper shook his head. "Yeah, I see what you're trying to do."

"Do you?"

"Yes, you are going to say that I chose to always tell the truth for society's sake and that's how I should make *this* decision. On what is best for society."

"Was that what *I* was going to say?" Calvin asked him flatly.

"Wasn't it?"

"I was just asking you questions to help you clarify your thinking. I have no agenda here, Cooper."

"You don't *understand.* You have no idea how badly I want to put a bullet between that man's eyes. But to do so, I have to swear off one of my life's core principles that I've *lived* for years and years!" Anguish consumed him.

Calvin put a hand on his shoulder. " You are right, I have no idea. What I was trying to do, how I was trying to help you get clear on what is most important to you, Cooper."

"Yeah, I know. And, I appreciate it. I think this is just one of those decisions that I have to figure out myself."

"Probably."

He exhaled loudly. "Thank you, anyway."

"Anytime. You ready to get back to the others?"

He nodded and the two men walked back to join the main group.

*

* *

The plan was very straightforward. They had chosen a location in the woods west of Salem that had only one road in. Cooper and Jonathan would be waiting about two miles into the forest from that crossroads. One vehicle from each side would meet at that crossroads and Governor Gibbs, one bodyguard, and Jake would walk in to meet u with Cooper, Dranko, and Jonathan. There, the exchange would take place. It was agreed the governor and Jonathan would then walk back out and leave. Cooper and Jake were to follow.

However, fearing treachery from the governor, Dranko and Cooper had agreed to two changes. First, they were going to pre-position Angela deep in the woods, but with a clear line of sight to the exchange location. She would be armed with the closest thing they had to a sniper rifle. Second, Cooper and Jake were going to take a detour and hike through the woods in the opposite direction of the crossroads to be picked up later. While no meet up like this was without risk, Cooper felt it gave them the best chance of success. He tried to ignore the numerous "what ifs" that could spell deep trouble. He had to take solace in that they had come up with the best plan given the circumstances and the resources they had available to them. Finally, he knew the gathering of thousands of armed men at the capitol building at the same time as the exchange would give the governor pause for thought if he was planning a double cross. Cooper smiled to himself about their "ace in the hole." He knew it was the most likely thing to keep them safe today.

Cooper had been replaying the plan in his head in a constant loop as they drove to the location. He admired the green rolling hills west of Salem. This was one of his favorite places in all of Oregon for a drive. He cursed much about the changed, more death-filled, world they now lived in. However, he liked that now—with the possibility of death always looming—made you appreciate the small beauties and wonders that surrounded you. This was one of those moments for Cooper. He cracked the window and breathed deeply in the scent of damp ground and the sweet aroma of spring.

"You alright, chief?" Dranko asked.

"Yep, couldn't be better," Cooper replied.

"You just looked to be daydreaming."

He nodded. "I was. But, a good kind. I feel really good about everything."

"That's good to hear."

"I think today is going to go well," Cooper said, his voice trailing off. Dranko allowed him to renew his wistful gazing out the windows.

*

* *

Cooper was out of the vehicle before it had fully come to a stop. His side hurt badly, despite the painkillers he'd taken earlier. He wanted to get his feet onto the ground in this place that would prove so pivotal in the next few hours. He watched as the others fanned out into the surrounding woods, looking for any signs that the governor had put men out there—in the way that they planned with Angela. He scanned the surrounding woods. They were thick, with no lines of sight extending more than fifty or seventy-five yards in any direction.

"You could hide a damned division out here," Dranko lamented.

"It is what it is, brother," Cooper responded.

He watched as Dranko disappeared into the woods, joining those who had fanned out to reconnoiter the area. Cooper used the time to remove his FAL rifle from the van and hide it behind a log within a few yards of the clearing he would stand in for the exchange. He left his backpack—filled with water, food, and other supplies for their trek out—next to it. A bandoleer that held eight magazines for the rifle was the last item to join the small cache. He had a handheld radio tucked into a jacket pocket and a pair of binoculars slung across his chest.

He pulled them up to his eyes and began scanning the surrounding area. The emerald green foliage and trees all appeared undisturbed. Again, he found himself struck by the beauty of the ferns mixed with the trees and the decay littering the forest floor. He continued surveying the area, but saw nothing that aroused his suspicion. He spotted the best place to position Angela and her rifle, about sixty yards from the clearing that provided excellent cover where a "V" was formed by two trees growing from nearly the same place.

Jeffrey was the first of the scouters to return. He sidled up next to Cooper and pulled a silver cigarette holder from his pocket and removed one.

Cooper chuckled. "Of course you have a fancy case for your smokes!"

He smiled back at him. "Mate, if you are going to do something, then you bloody well do it right."

He nodded at his remark. "Could I have one?"

Jeffrey looked surprised. "I didn't know you smoked?"

"I don't."

He handed him a cigarette and held out the lighter—what looked to be a fancier version of a Zippo and undoubtedly from England—for him. Cooper fumbled the cigarette into his mouth with unpracticed hands, lined up the end with the flame, and breathed in. He coughed on the first two puffs and those coughs hurt his sides, but then he settled in. Jeffrey looked at him with amusement. Cooper was immediately hit by the rush of nicotine and welcomed the feeling of light-headedness that descended upon him.

"How do you fancy it?"

"Not bad, but I doubt it's a habit I can pick up now."

"Likely not."

"How the heck do you still have cigarettes on hand?"

"I know this might surprise you, mate, but these are English. I order them in bulk, so I had quite the sizeable lot on hand when this glamorous affair kicked off." He gestured with his cigarette as he talked. "Dunhill," he added between puffs.

"Ah, well thanks."

The two men finished their cigarettes in silence.

"Here you go," Jeffrey said, handing him another cigarette and a Bic lighter he had fished out of a different pocket.

"What's this for?"

"You'll be out here bored for an hour or so," he returned.

Cooper cocked an eyebrow, but accepted the gift. "Thank you."

The rest of the group started to return.

"We went out a few hundred yards and it looks clear," Dranko reported.

Cooper nodded and then turned to Angela. "I think you should post up"

Angela cut him off, pointing. "Just over there, by the V-necked trees. Right?"

He nodded sheepishly.

"So, are we all set then?" Calvin asked.

"I think so," he answered.

"Alright, everyone, mount up," he shouted to the group.

The others loaded up into the van and drove off, leaving Cooper, Angela, Dranko and Jonathan alone in the quiet forest. Jonathan was sullen and angry. His hands were tied behind his back.

*

*   *

They waited expectantly. The hour dragged on. Cooper wished he could talk to Angela alone, but knew that trying to do so with Dranko present would have been awkward, to say the least. They made small talk of no consequence. Each passing minute brought growing tension as the planned exchange neared. Dranko looked nervously at his watch more than once. He checked in with the group at the crossroads more frequently than he needed to. Cooper fiddled with his rifle, while Angela just stared off into the surrounding terrain.

"I'm going to do another perimeter check," Dranko suddenly declared. He jerked Jonathan to his feet. "If I find any surprises out there, I'll want you on hand." He then wandered off into the forest, clutching his M4 like a life raft and prodding Jonathan in front of him with the rifle's muzzle.

Cooper knew this was his chance, and immediately his mouth went dry. *Just like a teenager about to make that first call to the girl I like,* he thought. Angela stood up, as if she was about to move out to her position.

"Am I too late?" he nearly croaked, coughing to clear his throat.

She turned to him, a half-knowing smile on her face. "What did you say?"

"I asked if I'm too late?"

215

Her smile grew wider now. "Too late for what?"

He could tell by her tone that she knew exactly what he meant, but she wanted him to say it. "For us," he replied.

She let loose a loud laugh, while a hand descended to touch his arm. "Cooper, you sure know how to woo a woman, I'll tell you that!"

He felt his face flush a darker shade of pink. "You like this, don't you?"

Her face turned serious. "Honestly, no." Her voice was filled with emotion now. "To be honest, Cooper, I don't know."

"You don't know what?"

"If it's too late or not." Her words made his stomach plunge to the forest floor.

"You must know Dranko and I have begun traveling down a road." He nodded and looked down. "I need you to answer one question. Why?" She pulled his chin up so their eyes met on her last word.

He didn't flinch, but stared straight into her eyes. "You're the right one."

Her brows furrowed. "What does that mean?"

"We fit. You fit my life with Jake."

She released her grasp on his chin, pivoted on her heel, and walked away in a wide arc. "I fit? Wow, that's a ringing endorsement."

"That's not what I meant," he called after her and took a few rapid steps to grab her and turn her around to face him. "I mean you are *right*. I know it and I *feel* it." His eyes burned into hers.

She returned the intensity. "And why not *her*?"

He knew he had to tell her the truth, but knew it would be horribly received. "Jake. Ain't no way we end up making a family."

She shook free of his grasp. "So, if you were alone then you would have chosen her?"

He shook his head. "I don't know. I *can't* know that." His eyes pleaded for understanding.

"Tell me what you think, Cooper."

He shook his head again. "I won't do that. You're not being fair. Damn it, I *chose* you!"

Her hands swung up above her head. "Oh, gee, *thank you* for *choosing* me, oh great one!"

His face flushed to red now, but it was anger driving it. "Look, you aren't being fair. Every relationship has a lot of things affecting it. Be pissed if you want that Jake figured big in my decision… that's your call."

That caught her flat-footed and she calmed down some. After staring at him as the seconds dragged by, she finally spoke again. "I'm just not sure I want to be second banana."

"I don't see it that way," he replied.

"Of course you don't." He was shocked as she nearly spat her words at him. Then, she breathed in deeply and exhaled loudly. "Let's just talk later," she said as she grabbed her rifle and bag and marched off in the direction of her sniper hideout. Before she turned her head, he saw that her eyes were clouded with tears.

Confused, he shook his head as he watched her go. *Perfect time for that Dunhill,* he thought as he fished the cigarette from the front pocket and the Bic from his pants pocket. He flicked the flame to life and inhaled deeply, hoping the cigarette smoke would push out the tense and empty feeling he felt in his chest. It was only partially a success, but he kept smoking anyway as he replayed the events that had just occurred over and over in his mind, trying to figure out where he had gone wrong.

CHAPTER FIFTEEN

His walkie-talkie sparked to life. "Package is inbound to you." It was Calvin's voice announcing the governor's pending arrival.

He jammed the mic button. "Is Jake alright?"

"Yes, he looks fine," Calvin replied, joy evident in his voice.

Cooper felt a wave of relief wash over him. He turned to Dranko. "About two miles. Probably a thirty to forty minute walk for those guys?"

He nodded back at his friend. "Closer to forty, I'd guess."

"You wanna go tell Angela?"

"Sure," Dranko said before ambling off in her direction. He returned about ten minutes later and they resumed the interminable waiting.

*

* *

The bend in the road was about a hundred yards from where they stood. They could hear the governor's men before they could see them. They were talking, not trying to hide their voices, but not overly loud either.

They must have been keeping Jake in front of them because that is who Cooper saw first. His heart leapt into this throat, and he involuntarily fell into a crouch, and his hand flew to his mouth. He was paralyzed with joy. Jake saw him and looked to take off toward him like a jackrabbit before a sharp rebuke from the governor's bodyguard belayed him. Cooper recovered as quickly as he could and stood up straight once again.

"Easy, brother," Dranko whispered from his side.

He felt like a penned up bull before a rodeo run as he waited for them to close those last hundred yards. He watched the men closely. The bodyguard did not have any visible weapons on him and they should have patted him down at the crossroads. He was a short man, but with an athletic build. The governor walked easily next to him, long strides closing the gap—still too slowly for Cooper. Seeing the governor, Mr. A.C. Gibbs, stirred a slurry of emotions in him—mostly a swirling hot rage. He was shorter than Cooper had anticipated and lacked the paunch he'd been expecting as well. He had TV anchor quality dark hair. His skin revealed the last remnants of what had to be tanning salon tan. He had a broad grin and smiled at Cooper the entire walk in. The man's cocksure attitude further grated on Cooper.

About twenty-five yards away, before they made the clearing, they stopped.

"Alright, you come toward us now," the governor called.

"Why's that?" Cooper asked loudly.

"For all I know, you could have three snipers sighted in on the clearing.

So, I want you to come to me."

Cooper cursed inwardly but knew there wasn't much he could do without blowing up the whole exchange. Instead, he nodded and then he and Dranko walked toward them with Jonathan firmly in tow.

When they stood just yards apart, Cooper was like a taut, vibrating bowstring that cannot be released, as he was so close to Jake but unable to embrace him. The bodyguard had a hand firmly wrapped around Jake's collar. Similarly, Dranko held Jonathan by the scruff of his collar.

"So, here we are," the governor said. His voice carried the tone of surety and from one who is used to being obeyed.

"So, we are, Gibbs." Cooper replied, letting every ounce of ice drip into his voice as he could. He noticed a flash of irritation cross his face when he hadn't used his proper title.

"Are we ready to transact our business and be on with our day?"

"I have to ask you one question, first."

"Let me guess... why did I do this?" Cooper nodded firmly back at the man.

"Well, Mr. Adams, the world is divided between two kinds of men: those who can see reality and those who cannot. I'm the former."

"That's your answer?"

"It most certainly is."

"That's all you have to say?"

Cooper noticed his left eye twitched and the narrowest of shades of pink flashed across his face. Though he tried, he failed to conceal his irritation.

"Oh, Mr. Adams, this can all be so tiresome. But, I'll indulge you. It's all very simple, really. China is clearly an ascending power and some of us decided to speed up that process and make a few dollars in the process."

"And kill a billion people." Cooper's voice was incredulous at the man's nonchalant tone. He couldn't believe the his arrogance.

Gibbs put his hands in front of him, as if to pluck a splinter from a finger. "People die every day, Mr. Adams."

That's when Cooper knew. He was as sure as when the last piece of a puzzle is added and the picture has been completed. He allowed that feeling of certainty to settle into his bones. It felt so good, like a Mack truck had been lifted off of his shoulders. When he spoke, his words were as certain as his feelings, "My wife would not have died." The raw pain and icy sound in his voice made the governor and the bodyguard reflexively take a step back.

The governor held up his hands in front of him, palms up. "Now, Mr. Adams. Let's stay calm and remember why we are here today. To get your son back, remember?"

He feigned returning to calm. "Yes, I know. I'm just so damn excited..."

What happened next was a blur. He had started to deliberately appear as if one of his legs had suddenly given out, and fell into a crouching position. At precisely that moment, a bullet whistled by where his head had just been. Next to him, Dranko was pulling a pistol he had concealed and spinning to his right—where the shot had come from. Time slowed, like it always did when your life was on the line. *Bastard had a sniper hidden away!*

Cooper screamed at Jake. "Get down!" He tore at his boot to free the Doubletap.

The bodyguard yanked a pistol from his back as well. Jake raised his foot and slammed it down on the bodyguard's right foot. At the same time, he brought his head forward and slammed it back toward the man. His wounded foot had caused him to pitch forward, so that Jake's head mashed the man's nose and face in a vicious blow.

The governor turned to run; rank fear plastered across his face. *Something looks good on paper, but it's a different world to live through it, Mr. Governor, isn't it,* Cooper thought to himself as the Doubletap yanked free.

Cooper lunged forward, grabbed the governor, and yanked him around. He *wanted* to see his face when he killed him. The man's face was filled with horrid panic. His mouth contorted to scream. "Nooooo...!" Cooper relished the fact that all of this was happening in slow motion. He jammed the .45 up against Gibbs' chest. He had a moment's pause as he felt a bullet-proof vest on him. This forced him to raise the weapon and point it directly at his face.

"This is for Elena," he spat into his face before it disappeared into a crimson mess as he pulled the trigger once and then a second time. At point blank range, the .45 did an obscene amount of damage and Cooper was covered in the governor's blood and gore.

He turned quickly toward Jake. He swung one arm to push him out of the way and used the other to reach down to pull the second Doubletap from his other boot. Time slowed even more as he realized that, despite Jake's best efforts, the bodyguard was going to bring his pistol to bear before he could do anything about it. His brain screamed out in agonized impotence, but his throat lacked the ability to get the words out. The bodyguard, blood oozing down his face, leveled the pistol at him and he stared straight down the muzzle. The .45 was now in his hand and coming up, but despair overwhelmed him as he realized it would be far, far too late to protect him. He couldn't bear to look and shut his eyes.

Then the world exploded.

It took him a full second to realize that he had *not* been shot and it was safe to open his eyes. The bodyguard was slumped to the ground. A neat round hole, leaking red, had appeared at his chest. That's when it hit him. *Angela. She must have repositioned herself just in time to get a clear shot.* He swung his head to the right to see if he could find her. She was in a crouching position. A broad smile was on her face. He raised his hand to wave back at her, a grin arching across his face.

Then, two sledgehammer blows striking him from his left side rocked him. He toppled to the ground like a leaden sack. His breath had been knocked from his lungs. He was lying there for several seconds, before he realized he had been shot. Twice.

He gasped for breath. Jake's face appeared over his. His mouth was agape and his eyes were wide. It broke Cooper's heart to see the anguish and panic on his boy's face. He heard more gunshots, but they seemed very far away.

"Dad!" Jake shrieked. He felt his son's hands frantically searching his body for the wounds. He weakly grabbed them with his right hand—his left wasn't working anymore. He brought Jake's hand to his lips. Though his mind called out to protest, he knew deep down that everything was fading away. Tears filled his eyes and emotion choked his voice.

"Son, it's alright."

"What can I do? What can I do?" Jake wailed.

Cooper shook his head. "Just be with me."

Jake began to claw at his chest like a drowning man grasping for the life preserver deep out at sea. "No. No. No, Dad. You *can't* go."

He wanted to soothe his son's agony, but did not know how. He grabbed his son's hand more forcefully and pulled him in closer, locking eyes. "You listen to me, okay?" Jake nodded frantically. "I love you son, more than anything. Always remember that," he paused. "I did…" Sobs choked out his words and he had to catch a quick breath to continue, "I did my best, son."

Jake looked at him with deep eyes and nodded emphatically. "I know. I love you too. Just don't go, please."

Cooper's brows drew together in deep regret. "I'm afraid I can't stop it, son."

Jake buried his head in his father's chest and sobbing racked his body. He cupped Jake's head with his hand and pulled him tighter against his chest. They embraced like this as precious seconds ticked by. His feet and hands were growing cold. His mind drifted. *Did I do the right thing? Was the world better for it? Was it all worth having to leave Jake an orphan?* He still thought so, but as he climbed the steps to death's door, he was less sure. *Will I see Elena again? Will Jake be alright?* His heart rendered at that question. *Poor Jake.* Cooper knew the deep wounds inflicted by losing one's parent too young. Jake was losing both, within months of one another.

Finally, he spoke again. "You must promise me one thing."

Jake rose up now, to look at his father. "What?"

"Don't let this world steal your humanity, son. Hang on to it. Treat it as your legacy to your mother and I. Can you do that?"

221

Jake's eyes narrowed and his jaw clenched. "Yes, I will."

He heard branches snapping and heavy footfalls. In rapid succession, Dranko and Angela were at his side. They began to survey his wounds, hands searching his body. His right hand weakly waved them off. "Don't bother." Something about his tone made them obey him. Or maybe it was the look in his eyes. Or the extent of his injuries. Dranko propped up his legs and he momentarily felt a surge of strength, but it abated in short order. Angela raised his head and rested it in lap. Her hands began stroking his head in comforting gestures.

Dranko's face was twisted in grief. "What can we do?"

"Promise me you'll take…" Again, his voice trailed off in agony. He had to look away to continue. "Take care of Jake for me."

Dranko nodded vigorously. "Of course." He swung an arm around Jake, as if to emphasize the point.

"Both of you," Cooper continued.

Angela leaned over him so she could look directly at him. "Yes, Cooper. It'd be an honor."

He nodded gratefully. He closed his eyes for a second to gather his strength. He knew he was fading fast now. Chills ran throughout him. Frantic hands grabbed him and they all called out his name. He flung his eyes open to assuage them.

He found Dranko. "You expose the governor and all the rest of the bastards, will ya?"

"You're damn right I will."

"If Jeffrey can swing it, I hope the rally becomes a revolution."

Dranko nodded. "Me, too."

"Hey, tell Julianne I forgive her, will you?"

Dranko nodded gravely.

Then silence. Cooper drank deeply of breath that was becoming harder to come by. The others looked on in impotence.

"You know I love you like a brother," Dranko said as he grabbed his hand and clenched it.

Cooper smiled wanly at him. "Me too, brother." Tears filled Dranko's eyes and he abruptly maneuvered a pack under Cooper's legs, stood up, and walked away.

Angela leaned in to whisper in his ear. "I would have chosen you." As she raised her head, he searched her eyes for truth. All he found was deep sadness and tears. In the end, he wasn't sure if she meant it or was simply moved by the emotion of the moment. He knew it no longer mattered.

He lifted Jake's head up from his chest once more. He cupped his son's cheek in his hand. "Be a good man, son. The world needs that more than ever."

Jake looked at him with a face contorted by sorrow. "I'll do my best,

Dad."

Cooper coughed and tasted blood in his mouth. "I love you more than life, Jake." He choked out the final words. He saw Jake's mouth move and form words, but he could not hear them. The world was going dark, starting at the edge of his vision, but quickly moving to the center. He clenched Jake's cheek hard with his last bit of strength. Then, darkness found him and he was consumed by peace.

*

* *

Paul Dranko stood over Cooper Adams' body. He was overwhelmed by grief and anger and impotence. Jake was still hugging his father's lifeless body and wailed without restraint. Angela cradled Cooper's head, tears running down her face, and reached out to try and console Jake by rubbing his head.

Jonathan kneeled nearby, his hands still tied behind his back. He looked at Dranko. "I'm sorry about all this."

Something snapped inside Dranko. All of his raging emotions became focused on Jonathan. He closed the gap between them with a few long strides. He raised his foot up high and brought it crashing down on him, slamming the man in the small of the back. He cried out in agony and sprawled into the dirt. Dranko glared down at him and saw desperate eyes looking back. He wanted to stomp the man into the ground, but reason prevailed. *I need him to fulfill Cooper's legacy,* he thought to himself. He strode away, walking off his rage before returning to where Cooper lay.

Angela and Jake had not changed their position in the intervening minutes. Jake's sobs had grown quieter and had become soft whimpering. Dranko knelt down beside the boy and put a comforting hand on his back. The three stayed there as the minutes passed.

*

* *

Jake transitioned from shattered heartache to the numbness of shock. He kept telling himself that his father wasn't dead. That it wasn't possible. He was too strong to be taken down. *You took my mother, so how can you take my father, too?* He thought to himself. *It isn't fair.* Pain consumed him like ravenous piranha as reality reared its ugly head. He felt the warmth draining from his father's body and he stood up abruptly. *I want to remember him as he was, full of life. Not some cold corpse.* Dranko stood up with him. Angela carefully laid his head back onto the forest floor and then scrambled to her feet. He removed the light jacket he was wearing and draped it over Cooper's

223

head. The three of them embraced as a group. Dranko and Angela both told Jake how they loved him and would take care of him. Jake heard the words, but was cold to their emotion. He was numb. He could feel himself shutting down.

There was a roar of an engine approaching them. Dranko tensed, but then the radio crackled to life. It was Jeffrey announcing their approach. They watched the bend in the road and a few minutes later, they came into view. They pulled their vehicle up next to them and Calvin, Jeffrey and those with him clambered out.

"Cooper?" Calvin sheepishly asked, indicating the body on the ground.

Dranko nodded. Calvin stepped forward and embraced Jake. "I am so sorry, son."

Jake said nothing, and buried his face into Calvin's chest before letting out an agonized wail that slowly turned into a whimper.

*
* *

Wanting to leave Calvin and Jake some privacy, Dranko stepped to the side, motioning Jeffrey to join him.

"So, what happened?"

Jeffrey scratched his chin. "Well, everything was splendid for a while. But, then they tried to bushwhack us. Julianne saved us, really."

Dranko looked around and noticed she wasn't there. "Where is she?"

He shook his head, casting his eyes at the ground. "She didn't make it."

"What happened?"

"Mate, she was the one who noticed the ambush seconds before they sprung it. Those seconds saved us all. Then, she fought like a crazed badger in the firefight. Reckless, honestly."

"Wow," was all that Dranko muttered in response. After pausing for several moments and shaking his head, he continued. "Given the double cross, what are you planning to do with your men in Salem?"

Jeffrey shook his head. "Honestly? I don't know. It's not like I know how to make a revolution! I do believe we shall start with arresting the top officials in the government and see if we can separate out those who will help us spread the truth versus those who are neck deep in the lies."

"I will help with that." Calvin's deep voice announced his arrival in the conversation.

Jeffrey nodded. "That would be great."

"I think Angela and I will need to take Jake someplace quiet for a while," Dranko added. The others nodded.

Calvin allowed a pause, but then broke the quiet. "I hate to say this, but I think we should use Cooper's funeral as a rallying point. Do it in Salem and all of that."

Dranko looked at him aghast. "His body isn't even cold. How could you even suggest that?"

Calvin held up his hands. "Because, it is the smart thing to do."

His look of disgust grew deeper. "I'm at a loss for..."

"Calvin's right." Jake's soft words brought Dranko's to a screeching halt. All heads turned toward Jake. "It's what my father would want. In fact, Paul, you promised him that you'd continue the fight to bring the truth to the world. The public funeral is a very good idea." Jake's words were so collected and the tone so calm that it unnerved Dranko.

"Alright then," Dranko muttered.

"One other thing. I will *not* be retreating somewhere."

"I just think that," Dranko began, but a solitary finger from Jake stopped him. Dranko did a double take as he recalled Cooper doing that to him the same way, a thousand times before.

"I will speak at the funeral and after that we can go off somewhere. But, it won't be for nothing. I want you to train me. Teach me everything you know. How to fight and how to survive. I will need that in this new world. Will you do that?" He looked desperately at Dranko.

"Of course," he replied.

With that, Jake walked away and returned to his father's body, kneeling to rearrange the jacket over his face.

The others looked at one another with amazement and spoke in hushed, reverent, tones.

Angela spoke first, "I guess he is a bit like his father, isn't he?"

"I am worried about how cold he sounded, though," Calvin observed.

"He's been through a lot. It'll be up to all of us to help him adjust," Dranko said to the others' agreement.

"Cooper would have wanted us to help him hold onto his humanity," Angela said, reaching out to grab Dranko's hand.

He looked at her tenderly. "Yes, he would have wanted that."

Calvin nodded. "And, it is the least we can do for him."

The minutes passed as everyone looked at the ground, lost in their thoughts, as grief saturated the air like a London fog.

Calvin finally spoke, "Well, it is time for us to get to work. There is a lot ahead of us." Their eyes met in turn and resolve flowed between them. Then, they moved as one toward Jake.

Made in the USA
Charleston, SC
21 September 2016